One blackout, a man, woman and their deepest desires!

AND SEDUCTION

Three sensual romances from
Samantha Hunter, Tawny Weber and
Heather MacAllister

Sunsets
AND SEDUCTION

SAMANTHA HUNTER

TAWNY WEBER

HEATHER W MacALLISTER

All the characters in this book have no existence outside the imagination of the author, and have no relation whatsoever to anyone bearing the same name or names. They are not even distantly inspired by any individual known or unknown to the author, and all the incidents are pure invention.

All Rights Reserved including the right of reproduction in whole or in part in any form. This edition is published by arrangement with Harlequin Enterprises II B.V./S.à.r.l. The text of this publication or any part thereof may not be reproduced or transmitted in any form or by any means, electronic or mechanical, including photocopying, recording, storage in an information retrieval system, or otherwise, without the written permission of the publisher.

This book is sold subject to the condition that it shall not, by way of trade or otherwise, be lent, resold, hired out or otherwise circulated without the prior consent of the publisher in any form of binding or cover other than that in which it is published and without a similar condition including this condition being imposed on the subsequent purchaser.

® and ™ are trademarks owned and used by the trademark owner and/or its licensee. Trademarks marked with ® are registered with the United Kingdom Patent Office and/or the Office for Harmonisation in the Internal Market and in other countries.

Mills & Boon, an imprint of Harlequin (UK) Limited, Eton House, 18-24 Paradise Road, Richmond, Surrey TW9 1SR

SUNSETS & SEDUCTION
© Harlequin Enterprises II B.V./S.à.r.l. 2012

Mine Until Morning © Samantha Hunter 2011
Just for the Night © Tawny Weber 2011
Kept in the Dark © Heather W. MacAllister 2011

ISBN: 978 0 263 89796 8

025-0712

Harlequin (UK) policy is to use papers that are natural, renewable and recyclable products and made from wood grown in sustainable forests. The logging and manufacturing processes conform to the legal environmental regulations of the country of origin.

Printed and bound in Spain
by Blackprint CPI, Barcelona

Mine Until Morning

SAMANTHA HUNTER

Samantha Hunter lives in Syracuse, New York, where she writes full-time. When she's not plotting her next story, Sam likes to work in her garden, quilt, cook, read and spend time with her husband and their dogs. Most days you can find Sam chatting on the Blaze® boards at eHarlequin. com, or you can check out what's new, enter contests or drop her a note at her website, www. samanthahunter.com.

Dear Reader,

Summer is here, my favourite season, and I am thrilled to be part of this collection with Tawny Weber and Heather McAllister. In *Mine Until Morning*, Jonas and Tessa spend a stormy night in a Philadelphia blackout. Blackouts have a way of bringing people closer, and Jonas and Tessa become *very* close during their adventure.

Jonas is also suffering his own personal blackout due to his recent blindness, but being in a blackout levels the playing field as he helps Tessa cross the city of Philadelphia in order to help a friend. Jonas also has three gorgeous brothers—all of whom will have their own stories, so keep an eye out for my BERRINGER BODYGUARD books.

Animals are a huge part of my life and often appear in my books, and *Mine Until Morning* is no exception. I hope you enjoy meeting Irish, the feline partner at the Berringer Bodyguard Agency! To find out more about him, be sure to check out Blazeauthors.com, and learn all about our new Pet Project!

Happy summer,

Samantha Hunter

Thanks to Julie Dutt, for help in understanding scent, soap-making, how to set up Tessa's soap shop, and for the great soaps she makes to go with my books. Check her out on Twitter: @latherati.

Many thanks to Diana Holquist and Madeline Walsh for help with Philadelphia specifics. Particularly thanks to Diana for info about the Fletcher St. Urban Riding Club that matches inner city youth with rescue horses, inspiring the appearance of one of Philly's Urban Cowboys in the book.

Many thanks to Eileen at SEPTA Customer Service in Philadelphia, for quick, friendly responses about SEPTA Blackout/Emergency policies and city route information.

And to Mike, much love and thanks for everything, as always.

1

1:00 p.m.
Philadelphia, Pennsylvania

JONAS BERRINGER FLIPPED the Closed sign on the door of the soap shop, Au Naturel. For the ten hours that the shop was open, all he could think about was being alone with the owner, Tessa Rose.

It was a swelteringly hot Philadelphia evening, which was the norm lately. Though it was cool in the storefront, the air-conditioning making it cool where he stood. Plain wood shelves were artfully stacked with every color and scent of soap and lotion he could imagine. Small baskets of samples, lip balms and various other trinkets and testers were placed strategically where customers would find them.

It was classy, elegant and yet still somehow warm and inviting, much like Tessa herself. Aromas of what he now recognized as jasmine, sandalwood, orange and vanilla, among others, filtered through his senses.

The back room wasn't air-conditioned, and a blast

of heat hit him as he walked into the small foundry, the workroom where Tessa made her products.

It was a little bigger than the actual store and twice as pungent. He'd gotten used to it though, and it didn't seem overwhelming anymore.

Several tubs and two stoves took up almost all of one wall, and there were shelves of wood soap molds and various containers, amber vials and tools there, as well. On the other side of the room, shelves of curing soaps lined a wall next to a refrigerated unit where more perishable supplies were kept. There was a table for cutting and wrapping next to the desk where Tessa did her accounting.

"Jonas," she said, her pretty blue-grey eyes warming as she looked up before he announced his presence. He knew that she'd been waiting for him, too. They'd been dancing around this, around each other, for several weeks. Now, it was finally going to happen.

He closed the distance between them, oblivious to the slippery coating of lotions and oils slathered on her hands; she'd been working. He didn't care about the mess as he pulled her up against him.

"Jonas!" she exclaimed with a laugh before he covered her mouth with his in a hot kiss that left no guessing as to how hungry he was for her. He walked her back until she was pinned between him and the table behind her. She moaned, pressing tight against him, returning his passion kiss for kiss.

Jonas buried his face in her neck. "You like driving me crazy, don't you?" he accused playfully, nipping her earlobe.

Tessa had always been hands off. The boss's daughter. A woman way out of his league. But being around her 24/7 for the past weeks had pushed his control to the limit, and now all bets were off.

She sighed against his cheek as he nibbled at the soft lines of her throat, and then pulled away.

"I've been trying my hardest. I thought you'd never give in," she said with a sexy smile. "You and that iron control of yours."

"You have too many clothes on," he said gruffly.

Continuing to smile at him in that minxlike way she had, she wiped her hands on a nearby cloth and slid the smock from her shoulders that she always wore while making her soaps and lotions.

Underneath, there was a simple yellow sundress with a halter top tied around her very graceful neck. When she reached up to hang the smock on a hook by the worktable, he could see her delectable shape outlined underneath.

He wanted to touch and kiss every inch of her.

"I'll be right back. I need to lock up," she said, sliding him a glance, still playing. Tempting him. Making him wait.

"I already did. We're alone. Come here," he said.

"You're so demanding," she murmured, returning to his arms.

"Desperate for you is more like it," he whispered against her lips.

"I like the sound of that," she purred. "And I feel the same way."

"I can't get you out of my head," he confessed, his arms sliding around her.

His hands shook with the effort to slow down, reminding himself that Tessa was a woman to be cherished. A woman *he* cherished.

He gasped when she nipped at his lower lip with her teeth, apparently rejecting his gentle approach.

"Don't hold back, Jonas," she said in clear invitation, linking her arms around his neck.

He swallowed hard, sliding his hands up over her slim arms and shoulders, tugging at the halter tie. Her eyes became smoky, her nipples hardening under the thin fabric.

"I'll give you whatever you want," he promised, and he meant it. "Whatever you need."

"Just you," she said, sending his pulse racing.

He pushed the dress down until her pretty breasts were bared to his view. His eyes moved over her as if unable to completely absorb how gorgeous she was. Taking a peach-toned nipple between his fingers, he pinched gently, then soothed and pinched again, watching her head fall back, cherry lips parting, the pulse in her throat pounding.

She tugged both his hands up to her breasts and covered them with her own, squeezing. She was so openly sexual, it mesmerized him.

"*More,* Jonas," she said, making his cock jerk in response.

Gentleness was forgotten in the wake of desire that took him over. Her apartment was right upstairs, her bed just seconds away, but that was too far, too long to wait. He'd take her here, as he had been fantasizing about for days.

Tugging the rest of her dress away, he pulled her up against him for a deep, hard kiss that made them both breathless, his hands everywhere. Over her shoulder, he perused the shelf of oils and ingredients, breaking the kiss to reach back for a bottle of sweet almond oil.

Dropping a light kiss to her neck as he poured

the rich-smelling oil in his hands, and smoothed the slippery-soft substance over her skin. He started with her slim shoulders, strong from the work she did, but still so delicately shaped. Then he worked his hands down over the slope of her back and hips. She leaned back into him with a sigh when he slid around to her front, where he spent long minutes massaging her breasts until her head dropped forward and a small moan delivered from her throat.

She was like a piece of sensual art, a perfectly sculpted woman come to life under his hands.

"Jonas, this all feels good, but I need more," she said, pulling away as she turned to face him. She stood before him in nothing but slight, yellow satin panties, her skin gleaming where he'd worked the oil over her. "You have no idea how much I want you," she said, looping her thumbs into the scrap of material and sliding it off until there was nothing between them.

"I think I have some idea," he whispered, taking off his own jeans and shirt. She walked into his arms and they were skin to skin, finally. The satisfaction of it was mind-boggling.

He ran his hands reverently over her thighs, the rounded globes of her ass, the curve of her hips. His erection jutted against her, eager and needy.

"I want you, Tessa," he said, his breath catching as he kissed her.

"Then take me," she invited with a sultry gaze.

He reached for an open jar of honey she had forgotten to put away and dripped golden dollops on her breasts then licked them off. As he finished, she was shuddering and straining toward him, her nails digging into his arms.

His hand slid under her knee to pull her leg up around

his hip, his cock brushing against the silky, wet flesh he wanted to bury himself in.

"Jonas, please," she begged. "Now."

"Not yet...let's make it last," he said. As much as he wanted her, something bothered him. There was something about the light in the room that didn't seem right. He looked around, making sure they were alone.

A lingering sense of dread held him off for a few more seconds.

What was wrong?

Nothing.

Tessa moved against him, oblivious to any problem.

But it was his job to protect her. That was why he was there in the first place, her hired bodyguard. There had been some threats against Senator Rose and his family, and Jonas had been more than willing to keep an eye on Tessa. In fact, he'd found it difficut to take his eyes off of her.

He glanced around the foundry once more. Nothing was out of place. He was imagining things, and turned his attention back to the woman in his arms.

Words evaporated for long, steamy moments as Jonas gripped her hips, lifting her up completely against him so that he could plunder her mouth as he thrust forward, planting himself deep inside her welcoming body. She was hot, tight, and they fit perfectly, as he knew they would.

She pulled back, watching him as he thrust into her. He could tell when she bit her lip, her eyelids fluttering shut, long lashes brushing her cheeks, that she was close.

He found a steady rhythm and tried to focus on every nuance of her as he held her. Small sounds came from her throat that were sexier than hell, her mouth forming a perfect O as she trembled and started to careen over the edge.

He bent to suckle a breast, flicking his tongue against her hardened nipple. That small touch pushed her over. A soft scream fell from her lips, her body tensing and pulsing around him as she came.

Jonas wanted to join her, but he needed more, thrusting faster, harder, focusing on the heat of her body, how soft her skin was under his hands. Her inner muscles fisted around him tightening and releasing again as she writhed in his arms, and he moved faster.

The satisfaction he'd craved was so close it was almost torture, but he couldn't quite get there. His body burned as he drove himself into her, precariously hanging on the edge of the orgasm of his life.

Tessa leaned back in his arms, watching him curiously, her expression serene, happy and satisfied, but somehow distant.

"My father is not going to be very happy about this," she said, sliding her hands up over her ripe breasts, smiling at him. The room around her became hazy and unreal in a way that made him squint.

Then she became transparent, too, the tight heat of her body fading.

"No, wait, please," he cried out, reaching for her.

The golden light around her was fading. The acute emptiness, the ache of satisfaction denied made him gasp in agony, chilled now, shivering.

He was alone. Only darkness remained.

JONAS SHUDDERED WITH cold as his eyes opened, unseeing, but awake nonetheless. He was sweating and the AC was blasting directly on him. As he rolled to the side, he swore as his foot tangled in a sheet and nearly sent him sprawling on the floor.

He was still hard from the dream, and even the cold blast from the AC didn't seem to diminish the ache between his legs. His body jerked as he remembered Tessa's imaginary touch. The emptiness that always followed the dream was an ache in his chest.

Providing his own release wasn't an attractive option. It wasn't an orgasm he craved; it was Tessa.

He had to get her out of his mind or he was going to go crazy. He supposed it was his punishment, a special little kind of hell, for letting himself get distracted from his job. He'd been assigned to protect her, not have sex with her.

He should have turned around and walked out the first time he entered the shop. When he saw her, it was like being set on fire. Jonas had had plenty of women in his life, but none that made him want at first sight. Not like Tessa.

Senator Rose was responsible for sending Berringer Security several contracts, particularly after Jonas's younger brother had successfully prevented a kidnapping attempt on the senator a few years earlier.

James Rose had even become a friend of sorts. When he'd asked them to guard his daughter after receiving threats concerning a bill he was authoring, they couldn't refuse. The senator had trusted Jonas to keep his daughter safe, and he'd done a rotten job of it. Not one of Jonas's better moments.

Jonas did the usual background checks, and he knew about Tessa's reputation going in. The senator's "wild child," Tessa was a free spirit, nonconformist. She was also heart-stoppingly beautiful and completely off-limits.

Father and daughter had a tumultuous relationship, to say the least. From what Jonas had seen at a distance, Tessa looked like one more spoiled rich girl who liked to rub her father's nose in her exploits. He'd known plenty of that particular type over the years.

Tessa had made several questionable choices in relationships, among other things, that seemed more about thwarting her father's control than anything else.

However, Jonas discovered that the view up close was somewhat different. For one thing, Tessa wasn't a girl anymore, but a mature woman who ran a successful business. As he got to know her, he couldn't help but see her in a different light, though he knew her relationship with her father was still troubled.

Getting in between the senator and his daughter was dangerous. Jonas had to pick one side or the other, and he chose the side that paid the bills. Besides, he knew too well how that kind of slip could come back and bite you in the ass.

Guarding Tessa had been a little more intense than his usual assignments. They'd been around each other 24/7 for several weeks, almost constantly together. He didn't let her out of his sight, day or night, as per the senator's orders. It made it harder to control the heat that had flared between them.

Tessa wasn't big on control, and she tempted his from every angle she could. One night, when they'd returned from a party, he'd given in, right in the parking lot behind the store.

He'd watched her all evening, dancing with friends in a dress that had been molded to her, what there was of it, anyway. A few of the friends she'd danced with had been male, and it made Jonas want to claim her as his in a very basic way.

Ridiculous, but true.

Her sharing even an innocent dance with another man had driven him crazy, and by the time they'd returned home, he couldn't hold back any longer.

He was so distracted that he hadn't noticed someone watching them from a dark corner of the lot.

The guy had approached from behind while he had her in his arms. A hard slam to the head had knocked him out. Tessa had fought back and, admirably, had taken out the intruder with a bat she kept in the back seat of her car.

Jonas had awakened at the hospital later, completely blind.

The senator's aide, Howie, was the first voice he heard after the doctors told him about his condition; apparently Rose wasn't available.

From what Howie said, it was clear Tessa had told them that Jonas had screwed up big time. He was off the job. Worse, she'd made it sound as if *he* had been pursuing *her,* and that he had seduced her that evening, instead of keeping his eye on the target.

She'd clearly used him to piss her father off for sending a bodyguard in the first place. He'd known she wasn't happy about the idea—the senator had warned him—and she hung him out to dry. He should have seen it coming. That he'd fallen for her added insult to injury.

Jonas had never liked Howie Stanton, but Howie was a Washington insider and had been with the senator for years. Jonas had noticed on more than one occasion when the senator had come to Tessa's shop how Howie's eyes followed Tessa. His expensive suit and high-profile position didn't make him any less of a lowlife.

But Howie had made the senator's wishes clear to

Jonas: stay away from Tessa, or there would be consequences. Jonas could hear in his tone that the aide relished delivering the news.

Jonas did as the senator requested.

He hadn't seen or talked to Tessa for a month since the attack, and he didn't plan to. He'd played the fool once, and it wasn't worth the risk to Berringer Security's reputation. The senator could do them a lot of damage if he wanted to.

Feeling for the edge of his bed stand, from which he knew it was about seven steps to the window, Jonas found the AC unit. After a brief struggle with the curtain and the controls, he managed to turn it down to low.

After getting a cup of cold water from the kitchen, he found his way back to the bed. Traffic was busy down on the street, people going about their normal lives. The apartments on his floor were quiet, everyone gone to work.

He picked up the basic clock that one of his brothers had bought him and removed the glass cover so that he could feel the hand positions.

One o'clock in the afternoon. He'd always been an early riser, but now he slept whenever he could and woke at odd hours.

His brothers, Garrett, Ely and Chance, were running the business without him until his sight came back. Doctors said his sight *would* return, but it hadn't.

What if it didn't? What if they were wrong? The chill that ran over him had nothing to do with the AC.

The hard hit to the back of his head had left him with a concussion and severe bruising to his optic nerve, causing temporary but complete blindness. The duration of "temporary" was unknown. Doctors had no idea when his vision would return. He'd seen four specialists, all offering the same fuzzy explanations of the mysteries of the brain.

Be patient, they'd said.

He shook his head, running a hand through hair that he'd let grow too long. It bugged him, especially in the heat, but he didn't feel like hearing the questions and sympathetic comments from his barber or anyone else. So he'd holed up here, mostly, waiting for life to return to normal.

Jonas reached to the left, groping to find his cell phone, and he held it in his hand. Thankfully, his was an older model with a hard keyboard that he could still use, though he sometimes hit the wrong button.

He still had the number for Tessa's shop on speed dial, number two, second only to the office, and he ran his thumb over the button, as if tempting himself. He should erase it, but couldn't quite do it.

Cursing, he put the phone down and found his way to the shower. As much as he wanted Tessa, he'd get over it eventually. His blindness made things worse, blowing his attraction to her all out of proportion. He was frustrated and bored. When he had his sight back, he'd be able to move on, get his own life back.

Maybe the hit on the head had kept him from making an even bigger mistake. At least the attack had happened before they were both naked, out in the open for anyone to see.

No sooner had he turned on the water when he heard a knock on the front door—soft, but he could still hear it. He'd always had sharp senses, even before he was blind. You didn't survive in his line of work without them.

Still, there was a noticeable uptick in his perception

that would have been kind of cool if it weren't at the expense of his vision.

"Keep your pants on, I'm getting there," he said as the knock sounded again, harder this time. He wrapped a towel around his waist and shut the water off. It had to be one of his brothers, come by to pull him out of bed, no doubt. He had another doctor's appointment that afternoon. It galled him not being able to go anywhere on his own and that he required help for everything.

It had to be Garrett, who had been fussing around him like a mother hen since the attack. Jonas made his way to the door, opening it and turning to walk back into the room.

"I know, I slept late, but the appointment isn't for another hour. Give me a chance to clean up, then we can go," he said.

"Jonas?"

He stopped in his tracks, frozen. He wasn't dreaming now. He didn't think so, at least.

"Tessa?" he said, his voice choked and not sounding like his at all. He turned toward her voice, knowing this was real as the familiar scents of honey and almond filled the room. His heart slammed in his chest.

"What the hell are you doing here?"

"Well, that kind of greeting sure makes a girl feel welcome," Tessa Rose countered with no small bit of sarcasm, hoping to cover her nerves.

She took a deep breath, in part for courage, and in part because seeing Jonas for the first time since the night of the attack had knocked the breath right out of her.

He'd lost some weight, his dark hair grown out from military short to longish, brushing the tops of his shoulders. He was clad only in a very small white towel, slung low on his hips and slipping lower. She found herself licking her lips, and tried to push back the lust that always erupted when she looked into those dark eyes.

Something was off, though.

He'd looked right at her when he'd opened the door and then turned away, talking to her as if he had expected someone else. That told her the worst of it.

"You're blind," she whispered, her voice stolen by her surprise.

"Yeah."

She saw the change in his body language, the way he tensed as he turned his face away from her, his jaw tight. He was wounded and embarrassed about it. Ashamed to be caught this way, exposed and vulnerable.

"I didn't know."

"Your dad didn't tell you? Oh, right, I guess you pissed him off royally, so he's probably not confiding in you these days."

She drew back at the bitterness in his tone.

Tessa had resisted the notion of having a bodyguard at first. It was reflex for her to resist her father. He was a great politician, she knew, but a total control freak, and he liked to control her life more than he should. It was an understatement to say they hadn't gotten along, and they still had their problems, though things had changed a bit since her mother had passed away two years before.

The senator manipulated everything to the benefit of his image, a necessity of his political career, he always claimed. Tessa had grown up resisting his control, and she'd be the first to admit that she hadn't always done that in positive or productive ways. But then again, her father hadn't always played fair, either.

As she got older, they had hammered out a truce of sorts, but mostly because she lived in Philadelphia where she ran her business—and her life—the way she wanted to, and he stayed in D.C. They got together on holidays, and it was enough.

When he said he was sending a bodyguard to her shop, they'd argued, but she'd relented when she sensed he was really concerned. He seemed to think this particular threat was very serious—and it had ended up that way.

She'd expected some stiff in a suit, but then Jonas had walked in the store, over six feet of muscle, brooding eyes and sensuality all wrapped in well-worn jeans and a bomber jacket.

Every bad-girl instinct she had surged to the fore.

The feeling she had when she was with him was like that zing of perfect chemistry that she always experienced when she made a new scent.

Scent was the most primal of the senses. Complementary scents attracted or enhanced a relationship, and the wrong scent repelled. It was the most basic principle of natural chemistry, the basis of most elements of survival. She and Jonas were a perfect combination, she could tell from the moment they locked eyes on each other.

Jonas obviously hadn't agreed. He kept his distance, his treatment of her businesslike to the nth degree, but she saw the desire in his eyes when he thought she wasn't looking.

That only upped the challenge. Tessa didn't give up when she saw something she wanted. To that extent, she was very much like the senator. She wanted to make her bodyguard lose that rigid control. It proved to be more of a challenge than she thought, until that night in the parking lot.

She'd met her friends for a birthday celebration—not hers—and she'd worn the sexiest dress she owned. Jonas didn't think she should go, but she told him that she was going, and if he wanted, he could tag along. In truth, she'd dressed for him. Danced for him. Tempted him in every way she knew how. And she'd almost given up—the man seemed to be oblivious—until they arrived home. He didn't say a word the entire drive back, but then hauled her against him as she'd stepped out of the car and kissed her until she couldn't breathe.

When she'd felt the hardness of his chest pressed against hers, she didn't back away. He didn't, either.

His wonderful hands had been sliding up underneath the sheer fabric of her gown, holding her backside against his hardness, his masculine scent surrounding and seducing her like a drug, when it had all gone wrong.

"We shouldn't be doing this," he'd whispered against her neck as she'd let her hands explore him the way she'd been dying to for weeks. He was a big man, in more ways than one, and her body craved him.

"Maybe that's why it feels so good," she'd replied, and she would remember the lust that had burned in his eyes until her dying day.

They were completely wrapped up in each other when the attacker hit Jonas from behind. He'd dropped from her arms to the pavement, leaving her to face her attacker, a political extremist who clearly was willing to cross the line to protest her father's work. Tessa still could feel the icy fear of that moment, thinking Jonas had been killed and that she was next.

She'd gotten very, very lucky, remembering the bat she had in the back of her car from summer softball games with her friends. Adrenaline served her well in fighting the man off.

She figured at first, when there was no word from or about Jonas, that he was just laying low. Staying out of the limelight, since the story had been all over the news, at least insofar as her and her father were mentioned. The Berringers might not have existed, which is what she supposed made them effective.

From her experience, some protective details, she knew, were all about the flash. They wore Armani and soaked up the media attention that guarding famous or powerful people granted them.

Berringer wasn't like that. They were serious security who put the client first. When she tried to find out about Jonas on the web, she'd found next to nothing; there were a few news articles from when he was on the police force, and the agency web page, which offered a minimum of information.

The Berringer brothers in the background, keeping their clients quietly safe.

It soon became clear that Jonas wasn't just laying low. He didn't want anything to do with her.

Her father was caught up in business on the Hill when the attack happened, and Tessa kept her distance from Howie, who was holding court in her father's absence. Tessa didn't ask Howie anything about Jonas, since she didn't want to encourage her father's aide. Howie had come on to her a few times, and she'd made it clear that she wasn't interested, but the guy didn't seem to understand the word *no*.

Jonas's brothers wouldn't tell her anything, either. She assumed that they all blamed her for distracting him and almost getting him killed. Rightfully so. She'd tracked him down now, intent on apologizing, but she hadn't expected this.

"I'm so sorry, Jonas," she said on a raw whisper as she dragged her attention back to the present.

He looked fierce as he closed the space between them. He might be blind, but Jonas honed in on her with no hesitation, his hands clamping hard over her shoulders.

"Stop it, Tessa. Sympathy is the last thing I want from you, or anyone."

"What do you want, then?" she asked, her mind trying to grasp the new discovery.

"What I'd really like is for you to go, and don't come back," he said harshly.

She lifted hands to frame his face, and he flinched, but she didn't draw back. No way was she leaving.

"What happened between us that night, Jonas, it—"

"Meant nothing," he interrupted. "Why are you here? Haven't you done enough?"

"What do you mean?" she asked, shocked by his tone. "I came here to apologize—"

"Come on, Tessa. Your father made it clear that you didn't want a bodyguard in the first place. He said you could be...difficult. So, what? Was getting me into bed the easiest way to piss the senator off and get me pulled off the job? Or was it just for fun? Were you bored?"

"None of that is true," she said, appalled.

"What happened that night shouldn't have. I take full responsibility for that, but I won't make the same mistake twice. You should go."

His obviously low opinion of her hurt more than she

imagined it would have. Did he hate himself that much for giving in to her? For wanting her?

"The way I remember it, you wanted me as much as I did you, Jonas."

He paused a second too long before nodding shortly. "It was a momentary lapse. It happens sometimes when mostly naked women throw themselves at you," he said unkindly.

"I see," she said, stepping in and tracing her finger down his chest, feeling his heart slam under the hard wall of muscle, and her own heart thudding even harder. She was angry, hurt and intent on not being so easily dismissed.

He was perfect. His skin was deep brown from the summer sun, taut and warm with a sprinkling of dark hair that provided softness over the hard cords of muscle that flexed under her touch. There wasn't an ounce of fat on him. Her fingers played over the sculpted muscles she had only fantasized about.

His hands grabbed at the air, seeking and then finding her wrists, holding her away. A pulse throbbed in the base of his throat. He wasn't unaffected by her at all.

"Stop, Tessa. No more games."

"No, Jonas," she said softly, not fighting his hold, but leaning in as she lifted her mouth to take his unsuspecting lips in a warm kiss. "No more games."

He resisted, standing rigid, his mouth firm and unmoving, until she sighed against him and licked at his lower lip. She inhaled deeply, loving the manly scent of sandalwood, soap and sweat. "You make me crazy. You know it's true."

He cursed against her lips. His hands tightened on her wrists, but then let go and his arms banded around her and pulled her in, his mouth opening to hers, taking control, plundering and ravishing her in a hard, punishing kiss.

Tessa gave herself up to him, let him take his fill as she took hers. They parted a few moments later, both breathless.

"Is this what you want, Tessa?" he asked when he pulled back, and she paused before responding.

He was hard, his arousal clear under the towel he wore. Not immune to her, not completely.

Or was it how he said, that any man would respond this way?

"Not like this," she said, seeing none of the warmth or desire in his face that had been there before.

He shook his head in disgust. "You know the thing that really ticks me off? That you would come here, intent on getting whatever it is you want, with no regard for the consequences to others. You don't care who gets hurt, do you, as long as you can stick it to your old man."

"I never did that. My father respects you, or he wouldn't have sent you to guard me. And he and I don't have that kind of relationship anymore."

"Right. As if you couldn't wait to rub what happened that night in his face. I'm the hired muscle, after all, not the guy he'd want you to end up with. That he sent me must have been icing on the cake."

"He has no say in the matter, but I didn't—"

"If you came here for more, forget it. I'd rather you don't use me as a way to make that point to him."

"What's between us has nothing to do with my father," she said, frustrated.

"There is no us."

"There could be."

"Not gonna happen," he insisted stubbornly.

Tessa stepped back, stinging at his rejection, but refusing to accept that there wasn't anything between them.

"Well, in case you decide to change your mind, you know where I am. But I wouldn't wait forever, Jonas."

She walked out, and he didn't say another word.

2

3:00 p.m.

THE NURSE IN his ophthalmologist's office had bumped against Jonas four times while showing him down the hall to the office, and then again in the office itself. She sounded cute and smelled nice, like jasmine and vanilla. She was also stacked, from what he could tell when she leaned past him as she'd opened the door.

As the door opened and the doctor came in, she leaned close and pushed a piece of paper into his hand, whispering, "Call me. Let's have a drink sometime. I can show you some tips for getting around without your sight."

"I'll bet you can," he'd said with a chuckle, but in truth it left him completely cold. All he could think of was Tessa, and cursed her again for her earlier visit.

He didn't even know how she'd gotten his address, but he supposed a senator's daughter had good resources. It paid to know people in powerful places—until you pissed them off.

"Hey, Doc," he said to Dr. Matt Sanders, his eye

specialist, whom he'd known in the Philadelphia business community and their basketball league for some time, though never as a patient.

"Jonas," Matt acknowledged from somewhere to the right and stepped in closer. "I hope you don't intend on answering my nurse's invitation," he said lightly, lifting one of Jonas's eyelids to look.

Jonas didn't pull back anymore, having gotten used to the closeness, as well as the poking and prodding around his eyes.

"Do you see anything? Flickers, shadows, flashes?" Doc Sanders asked.

"Nope, nothing," Jonas said, trying to keep his voice level. "Why shouldn't I call her?"

Matt chuckled lightly. "She's trying to make me jealous. That's why she waited until I was in here to slip you that note. Probably nothing written on it."

"I see. You two are—"

"Jury is still out," Matt said.

"So how does it look?"

"I'll probably ask her out, see how work mixes with pleasure. I don't want to lose her as my nurse. She's very good."

"I meant my eyes," Jonas said dryly. "No worries, Matt. About your nurse, I mean. I'm not interested in getting involved with anyone right now," he said. "She's all yours."

"Gee, thanks," the doctor replied, poking at Jonas some more, going back and forth between shuffling papers and checking his eyes.

"Any headaches? Nausea?"

"Nothing notable."

"Okay, well, it's looking much better. The swelling is almost completely gone, but it's the bruising that's probably causing the ongoing problem. That can take some time. If there's no progress in a few weeks, we'll run more tests, see what's up."

Jonas sat perfectly still, but his hands turned cold. Matt's voice was so neutral, that particular doctor tone that tried not to upset patients, but just made you all the more paranoid. Not that it took much these days.

"Do you mean this could be permanent?"

"No. Really, Jon, if I thought there was a serious possibility of that, I'd tell you straight up," Matt reassured, and Jonas breathed again when the doctor put a reassuring hand on his shoulder.

Jonas wasn't a particularly touchy-feely sort of guy. He and his brothers all had their ways of sharing physical contact—including fighting—and his family was probably more or less as affectionate as most. But since losing his sight, touch had taken on a completely new meaning. He welcomed it, and at some particularly dark moments, even craved it.

Matt continued, "The nervous system is delicate and unpredictable, and everyone takes their own time to heal. Your brain will let you know when it's ready to let your eyes work again. Give it a few more weeks, and if you aren't back to at least partial vision—and it's very likely you will be—then we'll figure it out, okay? Be patient. That guy nearly cracked your skull open. This could have been much, much worse."

Jonas nodded, grabbing on to the "very likely" bit with both hands. He'd always considered himself a patient guy until recently. First Tessa and now his eyesight had proven differently.

"All right, Doc," he said, standing and running his hand along the wall to the door. "I'll wait and see."

"You take care, Jonas. Let me know right away if

there are any changes. Make another appointment for a check in two weeks on the way out."

"Will do." He found the knob and opened the door. "Doc?"

"Yes?"

"Your nurse. She's getting impatient."

"What makes you think that?"

He rubbed his fingers over the paper in his pocket. "There is writing on the paper. I can make out at least three numbers," he said, handing the doctor the note and leaving Matt to think about that as he made his way out to where his brother Garrett waited for him in the lobby.

"What's the verdict?" Garrett asked. Jonas could hear the worry riding under his casual tone as they made their way out to the car after Jonas made his follow-up appointment.

"Same. Everything looks fine. It just takes time. Hopefully things will start working again within a few weeks, or they'll do more tests to see why not."

"Damn. Well, we have to stay positive. Things could change at any moment."

"Yeah, no reason to think otherwise, for now." It was easier to say it than to believe it.

"Smart man."

"Smarter than you," Jonas joked, delivering a solid, friendly punch to his brother's upper arm, nodding in satisfaction as he felt the solid muscle of Garrett's tricep under his fist.

"Pretty good aim for a blind guy," Garrett joked.

"Watch it or I'll aim higher," Jonas returned.

It was good to laugh about something. What other choice was there? Their family had seen their share of hard times, growing up on the lower end of lower working class, even though his parents had worked like dogs to provide their four boys with everything they needed. There were various crises along the way, always handled together with humor and love.

This was no different. His lack of vision made Jonas feel like an outsider, different, even with his own clan. People treated him differently, and he didn't like it.

"So she just walked in?" Garrett asked out of the blue.

Garrett had shown up as Tessa was leaving, bumping into her as she left the building. Jonas had been raw and completely unable to discuss the visit at the time, so Garrett had let it go, let him calm down. He still didn't want to discuss it as his brother led the way out to the car, but he knew Garrett wouldn't let the matter drop.

"Let's get some food. I missed breakfast and lunch." Jonas said, and then blew out a breath before answering the question. "Yeah. She just walked in."

"I knew I liked her," Garrett said, and Jonas could hear the smile in his voice. It was a new experience, hearing smiles. "I know *you* liked her, too," Garrett added, pulling away from the curb.

Jonas didn't answer. His brother was a romantic.

Lust had very little to do with liking someone, in his view, but he had to admit, he had seen a lot to like about Tessa while he had worked with her for those few weeks. More than he had expected to. More than he was comfortable with.

She was dedicated to her business, much as he was to his. Her obvious caring for her customers and her friends was clear, and she did seem to truly love her father, in spite of their differences. She was extroverted, sexy and gregarious, but not the reckless, selfish woman he had envisioned. At least, that was what he'd thought until she'd proven him wrong.

There were a lot of reasons to keep a principal—the term they used for the person receiving their protection—at arm's distance. Women in particular, even married women, had a tendency to fall for their bodyguards—a kind of transference, like falling for their doctors or therapists. Jonas never took the bait. Not before Tessa.

"You know what she did, Gar. She didn't have to tell anyone what happened between us. It was my bad for falling for it in the first place."

Garrett couldn't argue that. Losing a client like the senator was a major blow.

"I think you should give her the benefit of the doubt. She came by the office a few times, looking for you, and I don't know, Jon. She just didn't hit me that way. There might be more going on."

"How else to explain her father warning me off her?"

"I guess you have a point. But you were different when you were around her for those few weeks. I can't put my finger on it, but I thought she might be good for you."

"Frankly, after what you've been through, I'm surprised you have a romantic bone left in your body, Gar."

Jonas heard his brother's silence louder than any reply, and cursed under his breath at his blunder. "Sorry. I shouldn't have gone there."

"It's okay. You're right. Lainey and I had some wonderful years, and I lost her too soon. But what we had was great. You deserve that with someone. You're too much on your own all the time."

Rain was coming down a little harder than when they left, and Jonas remembered that some strong storms had been forcasted for later in the evening.

Jonas didn't respond, but his brother's words hit home.

They were different men, even if they were brothers. Garrett had lost his wife in a car accident while he was gone on a job, and it had nearly wrecked him. He'd bounced back, and from what Jonas could see, would be able to find happiness again someday. Jonas hoped he would. Garrett was made for family, being a husband, a father.

Jonas didn't see that in his future, but he still put family first. The senator's aide had made Rose's threat clear—if he went near Tessa, there could be serious repercussions to the agency, to Jonas's brothers and everything they had worked for. No way would Jonas risk that.

"You should come in the office today, listen up on some of the recent cases," his brother offered, changing the subject.

"Maybe," Jonas replied.

He'd like nothing better than to get to work, but he worried about being at the office too often. He figured it was better to keep his condition as hidden as possible. If clients discovered he had messed up or been seriously wounded on the job, it could compromise people's confidence in the agency, in their ability to do their jobs.

The car stopped, and Jonas detected the rich aroma of cheese steak and onions from their favorite shop just west of Center City.

"This way," Garrett directed, walking at his side. Jonas negotiated his way along with the cane, hating every minute of it, but he needed it to find his way through more obstacle-ridden environments like streets and crowded public places. As soon as they reached their table, he stashed it away.

"It's just a cane, Jonas. A tool. People don't even notice. Most blind people these days live very normal, active lives."

"I'm not a blind person. This is temporary," Jonas bit out, and then regretted his tone.

Garrett was right, but Jonas was edgy—an understatement of the emotional mess Tessa had left him in.

It had taken everything he had inside not to take her to bed right there and then. He was that hungry for her, and that fact generated even more self-disgust. How could he be so attracted to a woman who was obviously so manipulative? But if she hadn't said no, he knew it would have happened.

It was just pent-up lust and frustration, or so he told himself.

His lack of vision certainly hadn't seemed to put Tessa off any, he thought, remembering how passion and need had practically vibrated off her. Her scent was still on his skin. He didn't know if she was faking that or not. The senator was out of the country, and maybe she'd decided to finish what they'd started when her father was out of play—something like eating cake and having it, too.

"Well, if not with Tessa, you still need to get out more," Garrett continued. "You're blind, not under quarantine. When was the last time you were even on a date?"

"Now, there's the pot calling the kettle black," Jonas accused.

"I've gone on a few dates, but my situation is different."

Jonas frowned. "I don't *date*. I have plenty of women I know who are available when I want one."

"Classy."

"Drop it, Garrett. Can we talk about cases, the weather, anything but this? You're beginning to make me wish I'd gone deaf, too."

Garrett laughed and acquiesced as their sandwiches arrived and they dug in. They were delicious as always, though Jonas was getting a little tired of sandwiches, in general. They'd been standard fare since he lost his sight, as he didn't have to worry about using utensils to find the food on his plate, or embarrassing himself in front of others.

When his sight returned, he was heading for the first Italian restaurant he could get to for some pasta. Ideally, he would meet one of the women he called now and then to join him and kill two birds with one stone. If he could get back to his normal life, he knew his obsession with Tessa would fade.

"We're supposed to be getting some wicked storms today. It's already turning gray out there. The news said there were tornadoes down south, and it's all moving this way," Garrett commented.

"We could use the rain. Get rid of some of this heat," Jonas said. He loved summer storms, the power and energy of them. "What are Ely and Chance up to?"

"They're both in the field. Ely's finishing up the bank job down in Norfolk, and Chance will be caught up in New York for a while. Ely should be back tonight, depending on how the storm affects his travel. I've just been minding the store."

They always tried to have three in the field, with one

in the office. They alternated home duty. They didn't want a secretary, and Garrett did the books. The fewer additional people in the agency, the tighter the security, and that was what it was about.

Ely was the most serious of the bunch, the second youngest, a Marine and just returned from a lengthy tour in Afghanistan. He'd almost re-upped, but after recovering from a near-fatal injury caused by an IED, he'd decided to come back home.

Jonas had held his breath with the rest of his family for pretty much the entire time Ely was gone, and was never as relieved as when his little brother came home for good and joined their family venture.

Chance, aptly named, was their baby brother—and hated being called that with a vengeance. He was also the risk-taker of the family. If it could launch him over a cliff, speed him around a track or take him thousands of feet over the earth, Chance was up for it.

He was also a crack shot and a martial arts expert. Jonas always told him he was overcompensating for being youngest and two inches shorter, though at a solid six feet, it hardly made a difference. In so many ways, easygoing Chance was more deadly than all of them put together because he seemed to have no fear of anything.

"Another couple of jobs well done," Jonas murmured, proud of his brothers and wishing he could have felt as happy about his own work recently.

The Norfolk job, in particular, was one that James Rose had recommended them for. A high-profile case at a federal bank, it was a nice feather in their cap.

Not only had Jonas crossed a line almost sleeping with Tessa, but if anything had happened to her, he'd never have been able to forgive himself.

He was quite sure the senator would never forgive him, and Jonas only hoped that in time, they could still do business together.

He and Garrett made their way back out on the street. The air was even thicker than before, the humidity near smothering, though a warm wind blew around them. He could hear thunder in the distance rolling closer as wet drops splashed on his face.

"So what now?" Jonas said.

"I have some paperwork stacked up at the office," Garrett said, walking along.

Jonas was faced with the paralyzing anxiety he'd had every day since coming home from the hospital. When he couldn't work, he didn't know what to do with himself. He used weights, listened to books, listened to TV, which was maddening. There wasn't much he could do at the office.

He didn't like being at loose ends, useless to those around him. His thoughts and emotions tangled in the darkness that was his life at the moment as they got in the car and drove slowly down the city street. Heavy raindrops hit hard on the outside of his brother's car as a heavy gust of wind shook them.

Garrett started to say something when a crack of thunder and lightning boomed around them, and Garrett hit the brakes hard.

"What happened?" Jonas asked as they stopped cold.

"Tree down," Garrett said, sounding apprehensive. "Just split and blocked the street right in front of us. This is getting bad fast. The office is closer than your apartment, so let's head that way and hunker down there."

Jonas murmured agreement, his thoughts still on Tessa, though they shouldn't be. The humid air made her scent rise from his skin, and he swore he could still taste her from the kiss they'd shared that morning. The electric energy in the air from a nearby lightning strike seemed to exacerbate the memory.

He turned on the radio, listening to the storm warnings, trying to forget her, though he suspected it was going to take a very long time for that to happen.

"I SWEAR, LYDIA, I had no idea. It was such a shock. How could they not tell me that he's blind?" Tessa asked for the fourth time, pacing the hard tile floor of the foundry, her voice breaking with misery. "And it's because of *me*. My father had to know. He could have told me."

It was starting to rain harder, the drops falling more heavily from a blackening sky; even though it was only midday, it looked like evening. The weather approximated her mood.

Lydia Hamilton, who owned the tattoo shop Body, Inc. next door to Au Naturel, looked on in sympathy as Tessa paced.

"Your dad has been traveling, and you know how he is. It's not your fault, Tessa. These guys take risks every day," Lydia said in her usual frank fashion. "It's part of the work they do. It is a shame though. He was hot."

"He still is. He's blind, not maimed or dead," Tessa said, thanking the universe for that, at least.

It was part of why she always resisted the protection her father pushed on her. She could never stand to think someone died trying to protect her. What made her so special?

"Jonas was so…angry. He has some idea that I was using him to get back at my father."

"Well, that was your M.O. once," Lydia said, sliding her a knowing look.

"Yeah, back in my twenties. Not for a long time. Believe me, it didn't take long to figure out the jerks I dated to annoy my father didn't make me happy, either. I can't figure out why Jonas would think that. We got to know each other quite a lot in those few weeks. I thought he was starting to like me." More than like.

"Well, he's lost his sight. It's a trauma. People have strange reactions to things like that. Maybe he just had to strike out at someone, and you were there."

"I guess. But he was pretty specific about why he was angry with me."

Never had Tessa imagined the degree of Jonas's injury from that night. She remembered feeling reassured when she'd heard his voice as he talked to the EMTs when they had loaded him into the ambulance. She'd wanted to go with him, but the police wanted to talk to her about the attack, and then her father had sent Howie to check in on her, and everything was chaos for the rest of the night, with the press and trying to get rid of Howie.

"Are you sure he's angry with you? Maybe he's just upset in general?"

"*Furious* might be a better word."

"Well, maybe wait it out, see what happens. He might come around."

"I guess I shouldn't have pushed the issue by throwing myself at him. If he had a bad opinion of me to start with, that didn't help. I was just so hurt. By how he kept saying there was nothing between us."

"So you wanted to prove that there was."

"Yeah."

"I don't know. From what I saw, the way he used

to look at you, a fool could tell he was crazy for you," Lydia said, picking up a lotion sample and rubbing it into her hands, then smiling as she sniffed.

"I like this," she interjected. "Is it new?"

"Yes. I meant to tell you about it—it's a combination of gardenia extracts and spices."

"Nice."

"Well, I put the ball in his court. I told him if he wants me, he knows where I am. I'll be damned if I'll beg or humiliate myself any further."

"Under the right conditions, I might consider begging if a guy like Jonas was interested in me," Lydia said mischievously.

"You're a bad influence, you know that?" Tessa said, smiling at her friend.

Lydia smiled sympathetically, which accentuated the small crescent moon tattooed at the corner of her lips. "So I've heard. If he's smart, he'll show up at that door and apologize. If he doesn't, it's his loss. You have to be able to move on."

"I know." Tessa sighed. "I just never really felt with any other man what I felt with him."

"Then you haven't been with enough men, my friend."

"Again, the bad-influence thing."

"I have to get back to the store," Lydia said, looking upward as thunder crashed louder outside, offering Tessa a warm smile before she walked to the door. "I do love storms. I know you don't. If you need company, just text me. I'm closing down early."

"Okay," replied Tessa as two other people walked into the store.

She didn't expect any business in weather like this,

and the two women struggled to get their umbrellas folded and left their raincoats on hooks by the door.

"Welcome to Au Naturel, ladies. You are a couple of determined shoppers, to be out in this weather," Tessa said with a professional smile, helping them set their soaked umbrellas by the front window to dry.

"We had no idea the weather was going to be this bad, but we had to stop here before heading home," one explained, pushing a handful of thick, auburn curls away from her face, smiling.

"I'm getting married this weekend, and I need to buy some items for my honeymoon. You know, maybe some scents that will drive him a little crazy? A friend of mine was raving about your honey dust?"

Tessa smiled. Her organic honey dust—a body powder made of honey that made women's skin very soft and that was also very delicious to lick off—was one of her top-selling products.

"I have several new varieties," she said. "I'm sure I can find something that will work for both of you," she promised.

She had been working on a line of scents that were specifically for erotic stimulation, but many scents had arousing side effects.

Sage for boosting libido and quelling anxiety. Lavender to create a sense of comfort and safety, perhaps for lovers who were having rough times. Orange for joy and heightened sensitivity, and sandalwood, her favorite, to incite an air of earthy creativity, encouraging lovers to experiment and enjoy each other.

She was so excited about the new idea. Sex and scent were so closely aligned, more so than people imagined, but there were a lot of myths about scents, as well.

For instance, according to some studies, a woman's

sensitivity to musk scents was almost one thousand times more sensitive than a man's, being that much more arousing for women than for men, as previously thought. Hence, musk colognes for women didn't make much sense, depending on your sexual orientation.

Stopping for a moment, she closed her eyes, inhaling and remembering Jonas's scent. He didn't wear cologne, but he used a sandalwood soap that she had given him, and he had grudgingly admitted to liking it. She liked it, too. A lot.

She'd worn some scents including cinnamon and lavender around Jonas, the first known to arouse men and increase erections, the second providing comfort and an inviting aura.

People thought that sex happened in the brain, but the brain only processed all the things brought to it by other reaches of the body, like the nose or the mouth. Or the hands, the lips… and all the other parts she would like to share with Jonas.

Jonas had a very strong nose, and a firm, sensual mouth. She loved his hands. How he had closed his long fingers around her wrists earlier, even though he had been trying to stop her, still made a delicious shiver run down her spine.

"Miss?"

Tessa blinked, her cheeks warming as she realized she had completely lost track of the moment, and the two women were standing, gazing at her curiously.

"Oh, so sorry. I was thinking about which scents would be best for a bride on her honeymoon. Tell me a little more about your husband-to-be, his likes and dislikes, and your relationship. We can go from there," Tessa said, pushing thoughts and worries about Jonas to the back of her mind as she listened and focused on her work.

There was no point in torturing herself with thoughts of him—that was clear from how he'd walked away earlier, rebuffing her concern.

An hour passed, and before she knew it, she was hustling the two women back out the door to the cab she had called for them. It was normally still light outside, but the storm had made it like night. The winds were picking up, the rain coming down harder.

She flipped the sign to Closed and stared out at the wind-whipped rain, wrapping her arms around herself and holding on as a roll of thunder made a ripping sound that had her hugging tight.

She hated storms because when she was a kid, lightning had hit their house outside her bedroom and had started a small fire. It wasn't a major incident, the fire was put out before it became serious, but all she could remember was being shaken from a sound sleep by the crash of noise and blinding light, being hustled from her bed and then the sirens. Although lightning had started the fire, it was the thunder that always bothered her more.

She wished it was Jonas's arms she had around her, but that didn't look as if it was going to happen. When he was around, she hadn't feared anything. He made her feel safe. But he wasn't here, and he wouldn't be. She would be riding this one out alone.

The best solution was work, to keep busy. It was her usual solution to disappointment and heartache.

Maybe she could make some new scents—rosewood, jasmine and lavender for healing a broken heart. Though right now, as her mind rolled over all that had happened, she knew it would take a lot more than aromatherapy to make her feel better.

But it was a beginning.

3

5:00 p.m.

JONAS FOCUSED AS he ran his fingers along the edge of the window frame where he used duct tape to attach plastic sheeting to the edge. His entire right side was soaked from the rain coming in while he worked, and the wind kept pushing the plastic around, but he managed, proving to himself that he wasn't entirely useless.

A few minutes after they had gotten back to their offices, Garrett went to help a friend whose house was having some serious flooding in her basement.

Jonas smiled to himself. Melissa, the friend in question, was a particularly pretty friend who had been making no bones about her interest in Garrett. Jonas wondered how serious the flooding problem was, or if Garrett was going to have a little fun during the storm.

Good for him, if so. His brother deserved some of that particular variety of fun.

Ever the responsible one, Garrett had insisted Jonas

come along with him, but Jonas had made a point of wanting to stay at the office, telling Garrett to go. He said he wanted to listen to some of the most recent recordings of case files, and that he would call a taxi to get home. Garrett seemed happy about Jonas's apparent interest in work, and had grudgingly agreed but said he would keep his cell phone on.

Jonas didn't plan to interrupt him.

Jonas also wasn't exactly alone in the big old Victorian in West Philly that housed their offices, as well as a few other businesses, along with one apartment on the top floor. He'd heard sounds on the other side of the wall and assumed the insurance office that resided there was open if he needed anyone. He also had Irish to keep him company, though the big old tomcat who had adopted them the year before wasn't being much help. Irish was about six, they figured, and had some nicks and scars from his battles before he'd found his home. In that respect, he fit perfectly with the Berringers, who all had their own set of scars and histories.

Jonas knew Irish was really a lover more than a fighter, though. The big male cat had been caught soothing a sick kitten that lived next door, and wooing the pretty calico upstairs.

Right now, Jonas glanced down when he heard the cat's inquiring noise.

"I'm fine, Irish. Just getting this window taped up, bud."

As Jonas sat reviewing cases, a window at the back busted when a small branch had broken off a tree and fell through it.

Right now, Jonas was struggling to adjust the plastic sheeting to keep the rain out. He had asked Rhonda, the insurance company's secretary, for help finding tape and plastic down in the basement all three businesses shared. She'd been on her way out, but offered to help, in the neighborly spirit of most Philadelphians.

Jonas had heard her saying something about "the kids being all right" on the phone when he had walked into the office, and told her to go, he was fine. Which he was. Mostly.

He'd cut himself once, a minor injury, and had a few bruises from getting up and down on a chair to reach the top of the window, but he'd gotten the job done. He took an odd amount of satisfaction from that fact. It was good to do something, to be competent in spite of his blindness.

When his phone rang, he frowned. He hated not being able to see the caller ID for who was calling, but just answered, since it was his personal line.

"Jonas."

"Jonas, I was hoping you'd be there," Senator Rose's voice boomed across the line.

For the second time that day, Jonas was surprised by one of the Rose family. Not in a good way. He hadn't talked to the senator since his accident, and had no idea why he'd be calling now.

"Hello, sir. Are you back in the U.S.?" he asked, trying to sound neutral. The guy had a lot of nerve, threatening Jonas's family business, and then calling out of the blue, sounding as if nothing was wrong.

"No, no. In Italy, now, but I'm heading home early and I'll be back tomorrow. Has your sight returned yet?"

Jonas paused, wondering at the question. The senator was calling to check on his health? This was getting stranger by the second.

"No, not yet I'm afraid."

"Sorry to hear that. I need your help with something, Jon," he said.

Jonas experienced a surge of excitement—had the senator decided to forgive and forget?

"I don't know how much help I can be with anything right now, sir. But I can refer one of my brothers—"

"It has to be you. I need you to keep an eye on Tessa for me until I get back."

Jonas paused, quite sure he hadn't heard right.

"I'm sorry?"

"Tessa. There's a problem in my office. I can't say what it is yet. It doesn't have anything to do with Tessa directly, but I'd feel better knowing she wasn't alone for a day or so. Oh, and this needs to stay between us."

"You don't want her knowing she's under protection?" He'd done undercover guard duty before, but this time he wasn't sure that would work, or that he even wanted to do it.

"That would be best. You know how she hates my interference in her life. It's only until I get back. Then things will be straightened out."

"Sir, not to put too fine a point on it, but I'm blind. I can't see how—"

"Jonas, it's true I was less than happy to find out that you were messing around with my daughter. It could have cost both of you your lives," Rose said. "I know she can be a handful, and she likes nothing more than to take a shot at her old man now and then. But you two fooling around plays in our favor now. If anyone has a chance of staying close to her and not raising her suspicions, it's you. Blind or not, you're probably twice as effective as anyone else. Just don't let her get to you this time."

In other words, keep it in your pants, son. Jonas heard the clear subtext.

"But, sir—"

"I need you to do this for me. Don't let me down, Jon."

The line went dead.

Muttering a string of curses, Jonas shook his head at the strange call. Tessa was not exactly his biggest fan right now. How could he insert himself into her life without her being suspicious after he'd thrown her out that morning?

The sound of something crashing outside the window made him spin back, and he teetered, falling to the floor, his foot still caught in the chair. The wind knocked out of him, Jonas lay there for a moment, getting his bearings. He grunted as Irish landed on his chest and began licking his face, obviously concerned for him.

Standing, he winced at the twinge in his ankle. Great. Just what he needed.

He made his way to the bathroom and rifled through everything seeking the first-aid kit he knew was there, and found the package of Ace bandages he sought, stripping his sock and shoe off. He could feel some minor swelling, but it wasn't bad.

Trying, unsuccessfully, to wrap his ankle, he gave up and sought out the familiar feel of the jar of painkillers they kept on hand in the cabinet. It was barely a sprain, more of a twist, and probably didn't even need wrapping, anyway.

However, it was clear he wasn't up to doing chores around the office, and he reached for his phone to call for a taxi so he could get home.

And then he paused, thinking about the call from James.

Like it or not—and he didn't—the request to babysit the boss's daughter for the next few days was his second chance, his way to make amends for his screwup the first time. If nothing else, he owed it to his brothers to try to make amends for nearly losing their biggest benefactor.

But it was more than that for him, and Jonas knew it. His mind went back to that night with Tessa, to kissing her, as it had almost every day since it had happened.

He could still remember every detail of holding her. Kissing her. Her taste. Her scent.

The wind hit the side of the house hard, the thunder deafening.

Tessa hated thunder.

Maybe she needed him. If James thought she was in trouble, or even that she just needed someone close by, he couldn't turn his back on that. But the senator was right—she'd never allow him to guard her. She had issued an invitation—one he hadn't intended to respond to, but now things had changed. It gave him an in—cold, sure—but he had a job to do, and this time he would do it right. She'd hate him afterward, but that might be better, anyway.

Before he could think about it too much, he hit the second number on his speed dial.

"Tessa?"

She was so quiet at first, he thought they might have dropped the connection.

"Jonas?"

"Yeah, I'm sorry to bother you, but…um, I…I need your help."

A SHORT WHILE LATER, Tessa was banging at the front door. "Jonas, are you there? Let me in, I'm getting soaked out here!"

Through the glass, she saw him limping slightly on his way to the door, which he opened. She hurried in, soaked to the skin. Rain dripped off her coat, puddling on the polished wood floors.

"The rain is coming down sideways out there," she said, glad to have an excuse to cover her nerves about showing up.

When she'd seen his number on her caller ID, she thought maybe he'd had a change of heart—that he wanted to take her up on her invitation from earlier.

When he'd said he needed her help, she'd been worried sick, imagining every terrible thing possible between her store and the office, but from what she could tell, he looked in one piece, more or less.

"I'm sorry to drag you out in this, but you were the only person I could reach," he said.

His last resort, she thought, her hopes dipping. This wasn't exactly what she'd counted on. "What happened?"

"I turned suddenly, and I think I sprained my ankle. I tried to take care of it myself, but couldn't. If you could help me out with that, and getting me home, I'd appreciate it."

"What's been going on here?"

"A tree limb broke the window. I managed to get it covered."

She walked to the edge of the room on her left, seeing leftover bits of broken glass.

"You're going to trip yourself up again."

"Why do you say that?"

"You're standing here with one bare foot and an Ace

bandage twisted around it and trailing behind you." She couldn't help but smile as she watched a big cat turn into a kitten as he followed the edge of the strap, chasing it. "Your cat seems to think it's great fun, though."

"Oh. Yeah, he would."

"How could your brothers leave you alone in this storm? You shouldn't have been climbing up on a chair—you could have hit your head."

"I'm not completely helpless, you know. I shouldn't have called you," he said stiffly.

Tessa took a breath, and swallowed her disappointment. He obviously hadn't wanted to ask for help, and in particular, he didn't like asking *her* for help. But he had, and she'd do what she had to do.

Still, she wished it was because he had actually wanted to see her. Her pride kept her from saying as much.

"I don't mind helping. Let me find someone to take care of the mess and fix up your ankle. Then I can make sure you get home safely."

She led him back to the bathroom and while she worked on his foot, he talked to Ken, their handyman. It gave her a chance to concentrate. Apparently the handyman lived close by and assured Jonas he would come over to take care of the window and everything else.

"This doesn't look too bad," she said, trying not to feel ridiculous that the sight of Jonas's naked foot was enough to make her pulse jump, but it was a very nice foot, by all estimations.

"Do you have any liniment?" she asked.

"Probably," he responded tightly. "I left the first-aid kit out on the desk." She pulled her hands back, and he seemed to relax a little. Did he not want her touching him even that much?

She got up and went to look, coming back a few minutes later. The cat purred around her feet and blinked up at her, clearly flirting.

"What's your cat's name?"

"Irish."

"Interesting."

"Fighting Irish, given his battle scars."

"Ah, that makes sense," she said, taking a break to scratch the cat behind the ears. At least one of the Berringer men liked her attentions, she thought.

"You're pretty good at this," he said.

"I dated an EMT once. I used to ride the ambulance with him when things were slow. I even thought about getting my certification," she said absently, focusing on the task as a way of resisting the urge to slide her hand up his muscled calf.

"Isn't that against the law?"

She snorted. "We weren't too worried about that back then. I wish I had known what happened. I have an organic eucalyptus oil that works wonders, and smells a lot better than this stuff." She hated the stench of the ointment she was applying. Running her hand over the back of his strong calf to steady his leg, a desire shot through her.

She was supposed to be attending an injury to a blind man, and even that had erotic overtones for her. How pathetic was that?

"You can probably manage your sock and shoe alone," she commented, "though I'm not sure the shoe will fit unless you unlace it."

"I have a pair of work boots over in the mudroom. Could you grab them for me?" he asked.

"Sure."

She made her way through the classic rooms of the

old Victorian, admiring the way they had remodeled and updated it without erasing its original character. The last time she'd been here had been to try to get someone to tell her what was happening with Jonas, how he was. Where he was.

The brothers had such a strong bond, seemed so loyal to each other that she found it surprising they would have left Jonas here all alone, dealing with the storm. Still, as she'd recalled earlier, he wasn't a guy who liked accepting help. She was just amazed he had called her instead of hobbling home on his own.

"Thanks," he said grudgingly as she handed him the boots.

"You're welcome," she responded in the same tone. "Let me see if I can just reinforce that plastic around the window to keep the rain out, and I'll call a cab."

"You don't have to do that. Ken will be here soon."

"It will only take a few minutes, and it will keep your floors from being ruined."

He nodded reluctantly, and resumed trying to get his boots on. So much for him wanting her around—he seemed happy to have any excuse to ignore her.

Tessa busied herself adding more tape to the plastic around the broken window. When the job was done, she phoned for a cab. It took three calls to find a company who had someone available.

"Our ride will be here in a bit. Things are getting rough out there," she said, jumping a little as a crack of thunder sounded as if it was splitting the world in two.

"You shouldn't have gone out in this," he said, sounding as if he regretted calling her. "I know you hate storms."

"Emergency Services has enough on their plate right

now, and I didn't mind. Don't worry, you'll be away from me soon enough," she couldn't stop herself from adding, hurt and disappointed that he was so obviously displeased by her presence.

She knew he believed the worst of her, but she didn't deserve it. She also knew from a lifetime of being a politician's daughter that once people's minds were made up about you, they rarely changed their views. When she had been bandaging Jonas's foot, it seemed as if he could barely stand her touch.

"Listen," he said, running a hand through his already wild hair. "I'm...grateful you came."

She didn't say anything, and the silence stretched between them.

"You're welcome," she said eventually, and was relieved to hear the honk of a cab outside. She didn't say anything else, either. What was there to say? She thought that she cared for Jonas; they definitely had chemistry, or so she thought. But she wasn't going to beg him to be with her. Still, it hurt.

"What about Irish?"

"He'll be okay. He doesn't do well being transported, and his food, water and bed are here."

"Okay. If you're sure he's okay."

"He has a cat door in the back if he needs to get out, but he usually just hunkers down at night."

"Let's go, then," she said, and he pulled back when she took his hand.

"Cripes, Jonas, relax. I'm just helping you out to the cab, not trying to come on to you," she said, gritting her teeth.

He blew out a breath, seeming as tense as she was. "It's not you, Tessa. I hate this, my situation and being led around like a poodle all the time," he admitted.

Her own aggravation softened. He was a protector, a man who wasn't used to being vulnerable. He stood in front of others who were. She put her own feelings aside, realizing how difficult this was for him. He let her lead him out through the maelstrom to the shelter of the cab.

"Hardly a poodle. More like a rottweiler with a nasty temper," she muttered under her breath as they climbed inside the cab, and thought she might have seen him smile, just a little.

TESSA ALMOST BOLTED from the cab by the time they reached her store. The silent tension between her and Jonas was intolerable.

"No more fares," the cabbie said, looking back at them as she started to get out, but Jonas didn't.

"My friend needs you to take him home," she said to the driver, who shook his head vehemently.

"No more fares," he repeated, shifting his light to Out of Service, and staring at Jonas, not that Jonas could notice.

"He says you have to get out here," she spoke to Jonas.

"Yeah, I got that." His tone was clipped and short. He was obviously not happy about that option, and she couldn't help feeling insulted.

It infuriated her, but she held her temper. "You can come into the store and wait for another taxi," she offered.

She'd call one herself, and make sure she told them to hurry, she thought testily, helping him from the taxi. He insisted on paying the fare, and she let him.

"Careful stepping up," she cautioned as they ascended to the shop, and he pulled his hand out of her grasp, taking the railing.

"I'm fine. I have this whole property memorized. It was part of my job," he said.

She made some faint response, noting that he did seem to move easily up her stairs and inside the door, as if he could see.

Why did it make her heart constrict in an uncomfortable way to think he knew her space so well? That he had committed something about her to memory? It didn't mean anything, she reminded herself. He'd said as much.

It was just a side effect of his job.

"I'll call another taxi," she said.

"Thanks."

Tessa was on her phone for several minutes, watching Jonas stalk around her shop like a caged tiger. She called one company, and then another, but no one could send a ride for at least an hour, if then.

The city was paralyzed by the storm. The taxis were starting to return to the garage for the night.

As she redialed, she watched Jonas lift one scented bar to his nose and turned his attention to her.

"This is new," he said, and she blinked in amazement.

He paid that much attention to her products? Most of the time he had acted as if he couldn't care less.

"Yes," she answered, while seeking another taxi service.

She didn't tell him what he had picked up was one of the soaps in her new Erotic Enhancements collection. That particular scent could intensify orgasm. Standing and watching him lift the soap to his nose, inhaling, made her skin warm. Her heart fluttered. From her brief experience in Jonas's arms, he wouldn't need any help giving intense orgasms.

"Tessa?" he interrupted her train of thought.

"Oh, what? Sorry," she responded, shaking her attention away from Jonas and sex. Even when he was being unpleasant, she couldn't stop picturing him naked.

"Any luck?"

"No, I'm sorry. We can keep trying, but the city is—"

She stopped as everything went dark around her. The store was suddenly pitch-black, no light outside or in.

"Oh no."

"What?" he asked sharply.

"Blackout. Everything just went dark. Really dark."

"Are you okay?" he asked.

"Um, yeah, but it looks like you might be stuck here for a while."

He was quiet, and she bit her lip. He certainly couldn't think she'd orchestrated *this*.

She stepped down from the register where the phone was, and started to make her way across the store, but couldn't find anything to focus on, and gasped in pain as she knocked into the corner of a display.

"Where are you? Are you okay?"

"Yeah, just having a lot harder time than you making my way around in the dark," she said grumpily. It seemed the tables had turned.

"You stay put, but keep talking. I'll find my way to you," he said, and she thought she heard a slight smile in his tone.

"This isn't funny."

"I know."

"I don't know what to talk about," she groused.

"Then sing something," he offered, sounding closer.

"I don't sing outside the shower," she said, and then, a second later, felt his hand on her arm.

"There you are," he said.

His strong fingers closing around her forearm reminded her of that morning, and memories swamped her.

She had been so frightened by his call, and then so relieved to find him with only a minor injury, that it had been easy to set desire aside. Well, mostly.

Not so now. Here, in the familiar setting of her store, where they had spent so much time together, it was harder to ignore her attraction to him, stupid as it might be. He obviously didn't feel the same way about her.

His breath warm and close to her cheek in the dark. She had a feeling it wouldn't take much to turn her face to his and lean in for a kiss.

"I guess we could go upstairs and wait it out. This can't last for too long. I could get us something to drink," she suggested.

"Thanks. I—" he started, and then stopped. Then started again. "I know this is awkward."

"It is. Here, I can use my cell phone to light the way," she said.

"Don't use your phone as a light. It'll kill the battery. I can get us there."

"Okay."

He grabbed her hand this time, his grip firm and warm, and she stayed close as he navigated perfectly to the stairs.

"You didn't change any of the displays," he commented as they climbed.

"I don't, typically. I want people to find things easily when they come back for a second or third visit," she said. "I have an area for new items, and they know where to find those, too."

"Makes sense."

She did use her phone as a light for a quick minute to insert her key into the lock and let them in, finding her apartment as well in total darkness. It felt comfortable talking about the store, something neutral.

"We're both pretty soaked from the rain," she said.

It had been coming down so hard even the short walks to and from the cab had been drenching. "My brother left some things here after his last visit. They should fit you well enough, if you'd like to change."

In spite of being soaking wet, the heat and humidity made the apartment muggy, and she felt a fine sheen of perspiration on her brow. Or maybe it was repressed arousal.

"I'd appreciate that," he said simply.

"Wait here. I'll get the clothes and some towels." She carefully walked into the guest bedroom and found the Levi's and a silky black T-shirt in a drawer where Tim had left them behind.

Her brother, a criminal defense lawyer in Chicago, wasn't quite as broad in the shoulders as Jonas, but they were about the same height and weight, she figured.

She shivered in anticipation, in spite of herself. The storm didn't seem to be letting up. Jonas might be here for the night.

Maybe... No.

There was no way she could sleep with him. He'd just think she was using him again, to get back at her father or for some blue-collar thrill, whatever. He'd memorized her home, her store, but didn't he get to know her better in those weeks when he'd been guarding her?

Apparently not.

Could she have been imagining the chemistry between them?

She thought back to their encounter in his apartment, earlier in the day. It felt ages ago. He wanted her—he just didn't *want* to want her.

Though in all honesty, she was partly to blame for what had happened to him. She wasn't guilty of the things he accused her of, but she did bear some responsibilty. She'd set her sights on him, flirting, tempting, and did whatever she could to break his control.

That had backfired big-time. She also hadn't believed in the threat that he was guarding her from, and he had ended up paying the price for that.

So maybe he had good reason to be angry with her. And maybe this was her chance to make amends.

"Well, I have the clothes, but as to skivvies, I don't have anything like that on hand, unless you would like to try on something of mine," she teased lightly as she entered the living room.

He did chuckle then, a gravelly, masculine sound that warmed her blood.

"Not necessary," he said, and that turned her tease into a groan as she thought about Jonas and nothing between her and him but the thin denim.

Her mouth went dry as she put the clothes in his hands, and then the towels.

She licked her lips, impossibly turned on by him being here, so close and about to take his clothes off.

"You can use the bathroom," she said quickly, turning back to her bedroom to change her own clothes, and promptly slamming her shin into the table leg.

"Are you okay?"

"Yeah. Though I feel stupid for not being able to

find my way around my own apartment in the dark," she admitted.

"It gets easier with practice. Maybe you should use your phone for light before you really hurt yourself."

She frowned, but did light her way back to her room as he disappeared into the bathroom with no trouble whatsoever.

Stripping out of her wet clothes, she dried off and applied some smoothing sage and lavender lotion to her skin, enjoying the calming scents. Her phone dimmed a bit, and she knew she was losing the charge, so tried to finish her ministrations in the dark.

Peering out the window as she was slipping on a pair of light capris and a tank, she couldn't see a thing. Rain hit the glass so hard that the entire view was obscured, and everything was pitch-black, including the streetlights.

She wasn't sure how she was going to make it through this night. She wanted Jonas, but he clearly had no such intentions toward her. They were stuck together, and she'd make the best of it, but she ached inside and wished things could be different.

Making her way back out to the main room, she did as he instructed and walked slowly forward, until she caught the edge of the flip-flop she wore on the throw rug, pitching forward and landing with a thud on the hardwood floor.

A lamp fell from the table beside her and she cursed loudly. That was her favorite lamp, a one-of-a-kind that she had handmade by a glassblower in New York.

"Are you okay? Where are you?" Jonas called, emerging from the bathroom.

"Yeah, I just stumbled over the rug, and I think I broke a lamp."

"Don't move, you could cut yourself on broken glass."

The next thing she knew, he was there, his hands finding her in the dark.

The scent of sweet-smelling lavender and sage lotion on her skin rose between them as he helped her up and over to the sofa. As he sat down with her, he didn't let go.

She'd dabbed some patchouli oil on her pulse points earlier in the day. The sweet, earthy scent was traditionally one used in erotic ceremony, and connected historically to sensual practice. Right now, combined with the humidity in the room and Jonas's manly scent, it was a heady mix.

Or maybe it was the way one of his hands lingered on her back, and the other on her wrist. The storm raged outside, but Tessa hardly noticed.

"I shouldn't be here," he said.

"And yet here you are."

She saw the green light in the tense posture of his body, as if he was using every muscle he had to hold himself back.

Time stopped. The world outside the window was invisible, everything was swallowed by the storm. It was only the two of them, here, alone, and suddenly nothing else mattered.

"Jonas," she whispered, but it was all he allowed her to say before his mouth was on hers, and they fell back to the soft cushions of the sofa, forgetting everything else.

4

7:00 p.m.

JONAS KNEW HE was playing a dangerous game, but when he had Tessa in his arms, her scent intoxicating him, he couldn't stay away.

He didn't ask for this. If James hadn't called, he wouldn't even be here. But he was, and being this close to Tessa without touching her was proving impossible. It had been a mistake of grand proportions to accept this job from James, but it was too late now.

He wanted her more than he wanted his next breath, and in one move, he slipped off the thin tank she'd put on, and pressed her bare flesh to his. They both groaned as she twined her arms around his neck.

"You're not dressed," she said, rubbing her mouth against his collarbone.

"Not completely, no," he said, absorbing the sensation of her soft skin and pebbled nipples pressing against his chest, almost making him think he was dreaming again. "I was interrupted by you wrecking your apartment."

"Good timing on my part, then," she said, offering

her mouth to him. His hands drifted up and wove themselves into her hair, but alarms went off in his head.

What did she mean? Did she fall on purpose? Was Tessa playing games again?

He deepened the kiss, realizing he didn't care.

"You feel good," he said, though it was a radical understatement.

"You, too," she whispered.

The kiss went on and on, and he pressed his erection against her belly with a groan. He ran his hands and lips over her everywhere, committing every curve and shallow of her form to memory. Rolling her nipples between his fingers, he liked when she cried out, gasping in pleasure, and he did it again.

Her responses to him, at least, were real, and that's all that mattered to him right then.

Jonas gently pushed her breasts together and sucked in both tender nubs at once, feeling her entire body tremble under his. He'd always been one to enjoy sex with the lights on, but his blindness made everything more intense, and this was no exception.

She ran her hands down his chest, unzipping his jeans. He sucked in a sharp breath when her hand closed around him, stroking lightly, running her thumb over the broad crown of his cock.

"You're killing me, Tessa," he managed to choke out.

"I haven't even started. There are so many things I've thought about doing to you," she said on a whisper, sliding downward so that she could taste him, taking his length into her mouth. Jonas took a deep breath then released it, letting her do whatever she wanted.

He set his hand gently on the back of her head, holding her there for a long moment as she drew on him.

Not sure he'd last much longer, he pulled her back up against him and, quickly, silently, slid the bottoms she wore off, and then the slight, silky panties, as well. He lay over her, his shoulders nudging at the insides of her knees.

Oh, yeah, his body hummed.

Tracing a line down from her navel to the slick, hot flesh of her sex, he spread her wider, and only wished he could see. She arched, wanting more, quivering.

He flicked his tongue lightly against her clit. He relished the hot, womanly taste and abandoned the light touch to go deeper, rolling his tongue around her, parting her folds and seeking the ways to make her cry out. He had no idea how long he stayed there, the intimate kiss pleasing and arousing him as much as it seemed to please and arouse her.

She bucked her hips against him, but he held her in place, one climax triggering another until she was left spent and panting beneath him.

"Jonas," she said his name on a breath, the satisfaction evident in her voice.

Masculine pride suffused him, inciting the urge to take her and please her even more deeply. For the first time in weeks, he didn't feel at a disadvantage. He moved up, he planted his hands on either side of her shoulders, holding back.

"I don't have protection, sweetheart," he said. "Do you have anything here?"

She paused and then moaned one of frustration.

"No, and I don't take birth control. I'm healthy, but I don't want to risk other consequences."

He agreed, and backed away, though his body tensed in objection. So close. Like his dream coming true, much to his frustration, except that she'd stayed with him this time.

Tessa pushed up, her arm linking around his neck, pulling him in for a kiss.

"There's a twenty-four-hour drugstore two blocks down. I'll go. It will just take five minutes," she said, already scrambling up to grab her clothes.

"Careful where you step," he warned, remembering the broken glass. "You can't go out in this storm," he added, and she chuckled, a low, sexy sound he liked. A lot.

"Jonas, I would walk through fire to make this happen. A little rain is nothing."

As much as he agreed, he couldn't let her do it. He was here to keep her safe.

"It's dark out. There are fallen wires, looters, it's a blackout," he elaborated.

"I'm sure it will be—"

Her cell phone rang then, and then again.

"Are you going to answer that?" he asked.

He heard her grab the phone.

"Hello, Kate?" Tessa said, and there was clear concern in her tone as she turned away to talk.

The wind rattled the windows a bit. Jonas sat back, trying to breathe evenly, letting his body relax, if that was possible. He was hard and aching. It seemed he was doomed to never have Tessa.

Served him right, he supposed. He never should have taken this job in the first place, and since he did, he really had to try harder not to cave so easily to his desire. But when he was with Tessa, it was hard to think of anything else, especially when the world was so dark, and they were here all alone.

She came back to where he sat, done with her call.

He could sense the change in her mood, and his own heat waned.

"Everything all right?"

"Remember my friend Kate? The pharmacy has canceled deliveries tonight and she's almost out of insulin. She doesn't have anyone else. She's also blind, so can't go herself, and can't reach her neighbor. I have to go get the meds and take them to her. I shouldn't be too long. Maybe an hour. I can get our other…supplies, too."

"It's too risky, Tessa. There has to be some other way," he said. "Call 911."

"They won't consider it an emergency. She's fine now, she just needs another shot by bedtime. And you're not my bodyguard anymore, Jonas," she said, obviously bristling at his bossy tone. "You can't really tell me to stay or go."

Of course, she had no idea he was actually there to keep close, to keep an eye on her. Which meant he only had one choice.

"I don't think—" he started to object.

"Listen, I'm going. She needs me. If you want, you can come with me."

"How? There are no taxis."

"We'll take the trains."

"They may have shut down several routes in the power outage," he argued.

"I'm sure it will be fine. Even back in 2003, in the big East Coast blackout, only a few train routes were affected. It's probably our best chance."

He sighed. Tessa had her mind made up. "Where does Kate live?"

"Lena Street, in Germantown."

"Okay, we can take the subway north, and figure out how to go from there."

"That's how I've gone before," she agreed.

He didn't see that he had any other choice, though Jonas had a bad feeling about it. This was not a night to be out in the city.

Still, he admired her concern about the elderly woman. Jonas had promised James Rose that he would stick close by Tessa, and he planned to keep that promise. He wasn't sure how much help he could be to her, a blind man traversing in a city during a blackout, but he guessed he was about to find out.

Norfolk, Virginia

ELY BERRINGER CLICKED his phone off, shoving it in his pocket as he finished his beer in two deep swallows. He pushed his glass forward for a refill. The wind howled outside, but it didn't seem to bother the bar patrons, most of them from the nearby naval shipyards. They paid the flickering lights little mind as they watched a game on the big screen in the corner, probably having been through far worse out at sea.

Ely had finished his assignment, guarding a bank executive who had been receiving death threats for the last few weeks. The FBI had arrested the perpetrators, a group of thieves who had had significant success getting inside vaults by threatening the lives and families of the employees who had access.

Ely admired the single-mom bank exec who'd had enough spine to finally step up and contact law enforcement. Several others before her had caved to the threats, and one of those had been killed during the resulting heist. Berringer had been brought in on protective detail in collaboration with the feds. It was a first for their small company, and a big step forward.

Now it was over, but he was stuck in Norfolk for tonight, riding out the storm. The bar was a place he used to visit often. He didn't recognize anyone here now, but there was someone he was looking out for.

She was late tonight. Maybe the storm had her hunkered down elsewhere, but he hoped not. Human beings were tied to their rituals, and Chloe Roberts's had always been to come to this particular bar on a Thursday night for a drink before heading home.

He hadn't seen or spoken with her in three years, since she'd interviewed him upon his return from Afghanistan and his award of the Navy Cross. The interview had been a chore—Ely didn't care for publicizing his accomplishments—but the brass had insisted, said it would be good for recruitment.

The night following the interview, however, had been much more satisfying.

He'd hung out with Chloe for a few weeks, while he was in Norfolk, but realized too late that he'd read her all wrong. She came off as a modern, career-focused woman, the kind of woman you could spend a few nights or a few weeks with, but who had no expectations of more.

In truth, she came from a large family herself, he discovered, and she wanted the whole package: a husband, kids, the white-picket fence. He didn't realize that she had set her sights on him for the prize.

Ely hadn't made any promises, and they'd parted ways more or less amicably. More on his side, less on hers.

He straightened as he saw her come in, her trench coat soaked, her umbrella bent all to hell. She struggled with it for a few minutes before throwing it into the corner in frustration.

Looking up, her normally well-styled red hair was wild from the wind, and she froze as her eyes met his. He nodded in acknowledgment, indicating the open seat by his. She didn't move for a moment, looking unsure. A couple folks called out greetings, and she broke the stare, returning the hellos.

The removal of the traditional trench coat she always wore revealed the same bombshell body he'd enjoyed three years before. She hung her coat on the rack by the door and strolled over, her composure taking the place of her surprise at seeing him.

"Ely," she said with something that almost approached affection, leaning in to kiss his cheek before taking a seat. "What brings you here?" she asked.

She didn't need to order, the bartender delivered bourbon on the rocks for her without being asked. Ely knew it was top-of-the-line whiskey, and that on a normal evening she would nurse that one glass for two hours while poring over her notes.

It was the same way she made love, he remembered all too clearly. Slow, thorough and with the utmost attention to detail.

Some things really didn't change, much like the rise in his blood pressure, and below his beltline, at the sight of her generous breasts underneath the dark blue silk blouse she wore.

Maybe this was ill-advised, but he hadn't felt like spending tonight with a stranger, even if all they did was have a drink.

He was hoping for more.

"Just finished a job, and any port in a storm," he said, then winced at his poor choice of words. She didn't seem to take offense.

"It's a bad one out there, but not the worst I've seen,"

she said, holding her glass to full lips that needed no coloring. He'd always loved that she didn't wear lipstick. He hated the stuff. "So you're working with your brothers now?"

"Yeah, personal security. How'd you know?"

She smiled at him, her eyes sparkling. Stupid question. She was one of the best news reporters in Hampton Roads, and she knew a lot about everything, and everyone, between here and the District.

"I'd hoped you'd be here tonight," he said bluntly, meeting her bright blue eyes, and also appreciating the way her damp curls clung to her cheeks.

"Really?" she said, looking away. "Why's that?"

He smiled and took another sip from his beer, shaking his head. "Just finished a job that reminded me about how crazy stuff can be out there. I don't know. I guess I wanted to spend some time with a friend," he replied somewhat truthfully.

"Friends? Is that what we were?" Her tone was somehow humorous, skeptical and suspicious all at the same time.

"I hope so," he responded, and decided to cut to the heart of it. "When jobs are done, the intense ones, sometimes it's like..."

"Hitting a wall? Like go-go-go then full stop?" she supplied.

"Yeah," he said. He knew she'd understand. "You're on a constant adrenaline trip for weeks, not unlike combat in some ways. Then it just ends, and while that's good, I—"

"Have energy left to burn?" she asked.

"Something like that."

"And you thought you might burn some off with me?" she asked, her voice hardening, and she shook her head. "No, thanks, Ely. I'm not interested in being another one of your pit stops."

She stood, ignoring her drink on the bar, turning to leave.

Ely reached out, grabbing her arm gently, but firmly enough to stop her from walking away.

"Hey. It's not like that."

"That's not how I remember it."

"I know. I wasn't ready then. I was just back from Afghanistan, I hadn't even seen my family in more than two years and when I was in the hospital, I wasn't sure if I was going to see them again, period. I didn't know how to get back to normal, whatever that was. You helped. I'm sorry I left like I did. I never meant to hurt you. I just didn't know what I wanted."

"And I wanted too much," she added.

"Yeah."

Her stance softened a bit, and she looked back over her shoulder at him, but didn't pull her arm away.

"Looking for a second chance, Ely?"

Was he?

He'd been back in civilian life for three years. When he was in Kandahar, he hadn't had a chance to think about the future. When he'd gotten back, he couldn't stop thinking about the past. It had taken him a while to put it all behind him and accept that he even had a future, especially after he'd come close to being blown to bits.

Eventually, he'd looked around him, around his life, at his own family, and realized he wanted more.

Did he want more with Chloe? Is that really why he came here tonight? Hadn't he been thinking about it for days? Maybe longer? A second chance to find out seemed right.

"Yeah. Maybe, if you think we might have something worth taking a chance on," he said, letting his hand slide down her arm to find her hand.

She stood still for a minute, as if weighing her decision, and squeezed his hand, nodding.

"Let's get out of here," she said.

They walked out into the storm together, making their way to her car. When she opened the backseat door instead of the front, he paused, surprised, but then joined her, the storm surging around them as neither had any interest in waiting.

He hadn't planned on this, either, but he wasn't about to turn her down. Hunger took over, and he buried his face in the soft volume of her breasts. It all came rushing back, how sweet, how responsive she was.

She gasped as he pushed her blouse and bra aside, holding his head to her as he sucked a velvety nipple into his mouth, drawing on it as he laid her back on the seat, pulling the top off altogether. No one would see them at the back of the lot, through the fury of the storm.

She pulled at his clothes, too, obviously not interested in anything slow this time, and within seconds, they were both naked.

He covered himself without wasting any time and met her where she sought him, thrusting deep, feeling her clamp down around him, the two of them coming together within a few short, hot minutes.

"Oh, no," he panted, embarrassed and unable to believe he'd been so quick. "Sorry."

"For what?" she asked with a slow smile that had him hardening again.

Pulling her up with him, he sat so that she straddled his lap, still planted deeply over him. She ground her hips against him in a circular motion that had her dropping her head back, those marvelous breasts positioned where he could lick, nibble and suck his way to ecstasy as she rode him.

The rhythm picked up, and they were both mindless, as if having waited for each other all this time and not able to devour each other fast enough.

She looked down, framed his face with her hands, and kissed him so deeply that neither of them could breathe. His body bucked beneath her as she cried out, too. He bowed beneath her, jacking his hips upward in hard thrusts as he came with a fierceness that left him trembling.

They were both breathing heavily, held close against each other, wordless as everything calmed around them.

"You should know you're the first guy I've ever done in a backseat," she said with a smile. "But I knew as soon as I saw you that this was going to happen."

"Really?" he said, kissing her lovely, full bottom lip.

"Yep."

"My hotel isn't all that great. Your place?" he asked, hoping this wasn't the end of their night together.

"I'll drive," she agreed as she pulled her clothes back on and they moved to the front.

Ely could have cared less about the storm, watching her every second of the drive, reviewing everything he was going to do right this time. He hadn't planned on a second chance, but now that he had one, he wasn't going to blow it.

"So how did you get to be such good friends with Kate anyway?" Jonas asked as they ran into the train station, finally under cover, soaked through yet again.

"She came into the shop when it first opened, and I made some special items for her. She was always very lively and friendly, and she invited me and Lydia to lunch a few times," Tessa explained, getting their tickets and leading him to the platform.

"Then her husband died, and I knew that they didn't have children, or other family close by. Her diabetes was affecting her sight, and just this year she was declared legally blind."

Tessa peeked up to see Jonas's expression, which remained stoic as he listened.

"So, I started helping out, visiting her more, and it just became part of my life. I never knew my grandparents, at least not on my mother's side, and my father's parents, well, let's just say they preferred my brother," she said, laughing shortly.

"So Kate was like a foster grandparent for you?"

"Something like that, I guess, though I really consider her a friend. I like spending time with her, listening to her stories about her and her husband, and she plays a mean hand of canasta."

Jonas laughed, and she pulled back to look at him in surprise as they boarded their train.

"What?"

"Somehow I have a hard time picturing you sitting with a bunch of octogenarians playing cards on a Friday night."

"Well, it was usually Sunday afternoon, and I rarely won. Those ladies take no prisoners."

As they made their way through the passel of people vying for spots, she heard him chuckling.

She tucked herself inside the corner of the car at the end and held on to the railing. Jonas was so handsome when he laughed, she thought. He was handsome anyway, but when he smiled, he became wickedly so.

Tessa wondered if he was ticklish, eyeing the way the muscles in his side stretched and gathered as he reached to hold on to the rail, as well.

"It's nice to have lights for a few minutes," she commented about the train, changing the subject, and then realized he couldn't know if the lights were on one way or the other. "I mean, shoot, I'm sorry, Jonas, that was thoughtless—"

"It's not a big deal, Tessa. You can talk about the lights being on, the sun in the sky, the things you see... it doesn't bother me. I'm not that fragile."

She pursed her lips. "Well, maybe not, but that doesn't mean it's okay to rub it in. I can't imagine what it would be like not to see."

"It's...not fun," he agreed. "But it's also temporary."

"What do your doctors say? Did they tell you when?"

She had such a hard time thinking about Jonas being disabled in any way. Standing here with her now, he still looked undefeatable to her. She felt safe with him, regardless.

"Any time...things appear to be healing, but I just have to be patient," he said in a tone that told her that patient wasn't his strong suit.

Jonas was a man who took control, who called the shots. She knew this had to be maddening for him.

"I hope it's soon for you," she said, leaning in closer to plant a soft kiss on his cheek.

He frowned, and she wondered why. Did he regret what happened back at the apartment? Was he thinking she was still just messing with him?

"I hope the drugstore stays open," she said, needing to refocus. "I should make sure they know I'm coming. Kate has to have her injections or we will be calling emergency."

He nodded grimly while she pulled out her phone to call the pharmacy.

"They are open for a few more hours, so that's good," she said in relief.

"We'll get there, and it will be okay," he reassured her.

"Thanks. And thanks for coming with me. I know none of this was part of your night."

"True. If I weren't here with you, I'd either be limping around the office with a bandage still stuck to my pants, or home sitting in the dark, not that I would even know it," he joked, and she was so surprised she burst out laughing. A smile tugged at the corners of his lips.

"Why, Jonas, I've never known you to tell a joke," she said.

"There's a lot you don't know about me, Tessa." He winked, and she thought her knees might have trembled slightly.

Was Jonas *flirting* with her?

The thought made her heart race. There was a lot she didn't know about Jonas, but she looked up into his face as he peered, unseeing, around the crowded train car.

She looked forward to having the chance to find out.

5

9:00 p.m.

JONAS WAS SURPRISED that the trains were packed. While some of the peripheral routes were closed down, the main lines were running. He supposed it made sense. The worst of the storm had hit around rush hour, and with the roads such a mess, the trains were many people's only option to get home.

He could feel the heat and proximity of all the bodies crowded around where he and Tessa were tucked into a corner of the packed subway car. They were soaked from their dash to the closest station, a few blocks away from the shop, even having used umbrellas. It didn't matter. Though he tried to make casual conversation, all he could think about was how close she was, and what had happened back at the apartment.

He shouldn't have given in, but when it came to Tessa, he seemed to have a difficult time saying no. This time, hopefully, their indiscretions would stay between them. Senator Rose had said there was no direct threat, that he just needed someone to stick close to Tessa for a few days.

Rose had also been fully aware that Tessa liked to yank his chain, and was clear on the fact that she'd used Jonas to do it. Luckily, it appeared he wasn't holding Jonas completely responsible for the last time, but Jonas reminded himself not to be so reckless this time, even though he was on fire for her.

She was also confusing the hell out of him. He had her tagged one way, self-indulgent, self-interested. He didn't trust her motivations, and he still didn't—not completely. But that didn't fit the profile of someone who had traveled across town in the rain to help him, and now was doing the same for an elderly friend. Was she just playing a role, being someone she thought would appeal to him?

The air in the train car was humid and moist, though the riders were good-natured and fairly loud, everyone sharing a storm story or visiting with the person they were crunched up against.

He was pressed up against Tessa from stem to stern, and acutely aware of every inch of her. They stood inside a corner area, where she was against the outside of the train. He used his body to shield her.

He was hard again from the close contact, and grateful that it was so crowded, so no one would notice. It had been difficult enough dreaming and thinking about her for weeks, but being this close—especially after being naked with her less than an hour ago—was undermining his promise to the senator.

Tessa's breath caressed his cheek. She'd edged in closer to him. He lifted a hand, finding her face and rubbing his thumb over her cheek, her skin dewy from the rain and humid air. The touch was to "see" her, to measure her expression, her level of tension, as much as it was to just have an excuse to touch her.

"You okay?"

"Yes, just a little anxious," she whispered against his ear. "And far too turned on, considering our current location," she added, shifting her hips against him so that she nestled his hardness in the soft crux of her thighs. He bit back a groan, not that it would have been heard in the busy din of the car.

He leaned in, telling himself he was just playing a part.

She had played him before, right? So turnaround was fair play, as long as he could walk away from the job at the end. Nuzzling her, he found the soft shell of her ear with his lips, and whispered, "Tease."

"Not a tease," she responded, turning her lips to his. "I'll make good later, I promise."

He swallowed hard, thinking that if he inadvertently rocked a few more times against her as the train took corners and bumps, he wasn't going to last until later. He was so ready to come he had to do mental exercises to avoid it.

"What are you thinking about?" she asked. "You look so focused."

"Baseball stats," he said flatly.

She paused, then laughed against his cheek.

"You mean, like getting to third base, or sliding into home?" she asked suggestively.

He felt the vibration of her chest against his as she chuckled, and he had to smile, too. It felt good—better than good—to be so turned on, to be laughing.

To be with Tessa.

"Yeah, something like that."

He was actually enjoying himself. In spite of his wet

clothes and achingly hard cock, he felt more alive than he had in weeks. Suddenly, Tessa froze, and a collective gasp and sounds of unhappy surprise filled the car as it ground to a standstill, breaks screeching as everyone in the car lurched with the momentum of the train.

"What? What happened?" he asked.

"Power's out. It's pitch-black in here except for a few emergency lights," she said as people started grumbling and shouting around them.

A baby cried from the far end of the car, and the mood changed markedly as tension rose. A tremble worked its way through Tessa's body. He slipped his arms around her, holding her tighter against him.

"Stay next to me. It will be okay," he said against her hair.

"I can't see *anything*," she said in a hushed whisper, pressing even more tightly against him.

This wasn't good. Even friendly, good-natured people could be dangerous in a crowded, panicked situation. He noticed that a guy behind him was breathing too hard, starting to push against everyone around him.

"I have to let go of you for a minute, okay? Hug the wall, right behind you," he said to Tessa, turning to face the man while still protecting Tessa.

Reaching out, he found the man's arm and grabbed it before the flailing man hurt someone. The guy was shaking, starting to mutter in panic.

Jonas kept his voice casual. "Hey, buddy, you okay? Let's try to calm down."

The man pushed at him, but Jonas held firm.

"Let go of me! Who are you? Don't touch me! I have to get outta here, let me outta here," the guy started to shout, pushing at everyone near him. Jonas heard a woman gasp in pain, the man's other fist making contact, Jonas assumed.

People started shouting, and Jonas knew he had to do something before a potentially deadly scenario was set into motion. Sliding his arm up to the man's neck, he looped it around and felt for the slamming pulse at the side of the guy's throat. Tightening his grip as he slid his arm around front and pulled his forearm back, Jonas trapped the man in an armlock, trying to hold him still as he struggled to get free.

"Jonas? Jonas, what are you doing?" He heard Tessa's breathless question.

"Stay put, Tessa," he said loudly, fighting the man's huge bulk as he applied pressure.

"Sorry, man, but you need to chill for a few minutes until they get us out of here," he said, and increased the pressure until the man stopped shouting, the heavy weight of his form going slack.

Everything around them was eerily quiet.

"Someone help get this guy into a seat," Jonas ordered, propping the man up the best he could, the slack weight almost pulling him down. "He passed out."

"Yeah, with a little help, I bet," another guy said approvingly, and Jonas felt the weight lifted as others took him off Jonas's hands.

"Good job," someone shouted, and Jonas felt a pat on his shoulder.

"Thank you so much," someone else whispered in relief.

Slowly, conversation resumed and the tension resolved.

He turned back to Tessa, finding her hand with his and touching her face again to make sure she was okay.

He found that she was smiling slightly, and he ran a finger over her lower lip.

"That was pretty cool," she said.

The driver's voice over the intercom told them they would be stopped for about twenty minutes, and to please stay calm as people were working on getting them on their way again.

"He was a big guy—couldn't have him freaking out in here. People could get hurt."

"I know. And no one else here could have done what you did," she said, pressing a kiss into his neck. "Way to think on your feet, Berringer."

Jonas's heart beat hard in his chest, aware of her again, the two of them pressed tight.

"How dark is it in here, anyway?"

"Almost pitch-black, except for a few safety lights around the edges. I can barely see you, as close as we are," she said.

Jonas realized that this was the first time since he'd lost his sight that he didn't feel alone. Maybe because everyone around him was also blind, in a way, or maybe because he was here with Tessa.

"I hope they get us out of here soon. I don't think people will stand being crammed in together for long." She sounded nervous.

"I won't let anything happen to you."

"I know," she said softly.

He drew her to him, pressing his arousal close to her again.

"*That* certainly takes my mind off things," she said with a husky laugh.

"That was the idea." He heard the anxiety in her tone dissolve into a gasp as his hand covered her breast, her nipple beading under his palm.

Leaning in, he found and nuzzled the throbbing pulse at the base of her neck, loving how it sped up every time he tweaked or rolled the sensitive nub between his fingers.

Her hand was pressed against the front of his pants, rubbing along the length of him. He shuddered at the touch, pressing in, biting the lobe of her ear a little more sharply before covering her lips in a hot kiss.

"Good thing no one can see," he whispered.

"Yeah," she agreed.

He maneuvered them more tightly into the corner, the people behind him caught up in their own conversations. Some guys had started singing, and others were laughing. More than enough noise to cover their own activities.

All he was aware of was Tessa's scent, the honey-sweet taste of her kiss, and her nimble, satiny fingers as they slid his zipper down and then wrapped around his shaft.

"Tessa, I don't think—"

"Yes, don't think. Thinking is way overrated," she murmured against his lips as she slid her tongue against his in a thrusting rhythm that matched the way she was stroking him.

Jonas was normally a highly private person, and he couldn't believe he was letting her do this in a crowded subway car, but he was also too far gone to care. Too needy, too close to the edge.

If the lights came on, if anyone noticed, he thought, trying to find some way to stay in control. But that offered another surprise—the idea of being discovered increased the urgency and turned him on even more.

Her hands and lips were so soft, her grip just right, and his mind spun with the need to let go even as he still tried to resist. Creature of habit. As much as he wanted her, wanted this, he didn't want to give in.

"Let go, Jonas," Tessa whispered in his ear, her other hand sliding up inside his shirt and playing with a nipple, making him shudder and rock slightly into her hand.

"Yeah, like that," she encouraged.

When she slipped her hand down to caress his sac as she continued to stroke, Jonas sucked in a sharp breath, coming hard and fast with an intensity that made him bite down to keep from shouting her name out loud.

Pressing her back against the wall, the release shook him from head to toe, and he all but collapsed against her as she withdrew her hand. He caught his breath as he sensed her fumbling in her purse for something as he zipped up.

It wasn't the way he wanted to come with her, but it had been pretty fantastic, he thought, trying to get his composure back.

They righted themselves in the nick of time, as luck would have it; seconds later a cheer went up as the train rolled forward.

"The lights are on?" he asked, his voice still rough.

"Yeah," she said softly. "Thanks for distracting me."

He smiled. "I think I should be thanking *you*."

Her kiss at the corner of his lips had the heat building again, and he knew he would do what he had to to keep Tessa safe. Whatever game she was playing, he was more than willing to join in. James Rose had put him in this situation, and Jonas didn't care if the senator spontaneously combusted from finding out what he and Tessa were doing. It would be worth it.

Let her have her fill, and tell anyone she wanted. He'd deal with that later. Jonas wanted nothing more than to get her home, where he planned to drive them both to distraction for the rest of the night.

TESSA'S HANDS WERE shaking, along with her knees and probably everything in between as the others exited the subway car. Anxiety wasn't the cause; she was still so aroused from sharing close quarters with Jonas, feeling his heat, his passion—his *need*—that she hadn't been able to think of anything else but him.

The way he'd leaned into her, giving himself over to her when she'd touched him in the car had been sexier than anything she'd experienced, ever. He was surprising her time and time again. And confusing her.

He didn't trust her, but he did want her. He was angry with her, but protective of her. Would the real Jonas Berringer please stand up?

She was so glad that she had him with her in the dark confines of the car—especially when things had gotten tense with the blackout. The way he had taken control of the situation and kept her, and everyone, safe, had triggered a well of emotion that touched her deeply. He was an extraordinary man, though she knew he didn't think of himself that way.

She suspected a large part of his annoyance with her was because he liked her father. She could see it when he'd mentioned the senator, and how much her father had helped their personal security business. She also knew her father wasn't pleased about how things had ended, but Tessa hadn't been seducing Jonas to tick off her father.

She'd prefer that he knew nothing about her sex life, with Jonas or anyone else, frankly, but the senator made her life his business far too often. It rankled her to think that Jonas blamed her for her father's negative reaction, but there was nothing she could do but just try to show him she wasn't like that. That she genuinely cared for him and was attracted to him.

This was her second chance, and she wasn't going to blow it. Her father was out of the country and couldn't interfere.

Hopefully, she and Jonas could get to know each other well enough that her father wouldn't be able to butt his nose in again. Still, she was taking a risk. Jonas was clearly willing to think the worst of her. She had no guarantee that he wasn't just scratching an itch and would disappear in the morning.

Jonas obviously desired her, and he had said he would keep her safe—but did that include her heart? Though the sex was incredible, no matter what happened this night, she knew it wouldn't be enough.

So many emotions were scrambling around inside, she hardly knew what to do with them, especially as reality returned. They stayed in the car with the man Jonas had in effect apprehended. She knew they couldn't leave him, and that there was an ambulance on its way, but they had less time to make it to Kate now, she thought, looking at her watch.

Thunder still rolled overhead, sounding far away outside the train station. The guy in the seat had come to and was groggy and apologizing. Jonas assured him he was fine, and the EMTs would check him out to make sure.

"Where are we?" he asked.

"They diverted us. We're at the Spring Garden station," she said, tension winding in her chest.

The trip had taken her in the opposite direction of where she wanted to go.

"We'll have to find aboveground transport. I heard them say they were shutting down the city train routes until the storm passed." Again, she thought of Kate, alone.

"They don't want to risk another stranding," he said, nodding grimly. "That could have been really bad."

"There's a crowd of people looking for taxis and a line at the buses, so that could take forever," she warned. "Maybe I should try the car rentals."

Just then, a tall, black-haired woman and another man stepped onto the train, and Tessa saw EMTs filing in not far behind them.

Tessa could tell from her posture and stride that the woman was someone in a position of authority. The badge on her belt, revealed as she put a hand on her hip, cleared that up quickly. Philadelphia P.D.

Her green eyes lit with pleasure on Jonas, and then with curiosity on Tessa.

"Jonas! You're the guy who prevented a riot on the train car? I should have known," she said with a wide grin.

"That would be me."

"Well, that just made my job a whole lot easier."

Jonas smiled widely, and a twinge of jealousy grabbed at Tessa. He had never smiled like that for her, so openly. How well did these two know each other?

"Rachel," he said warmly, and accepted the woman's brief hug as EMTs boarded and took the man out with them.

Tessa stood, too, holding out her hand, meeting the woman's eyes. "Hi, I'm Tessa Rose."

The green eyes narrowed as the woman's head tilted

slightly to the side. "Detective Rachel Pankewski. I know you. You're Senator Rose's daughter?" she asked.

"Yes, but more importantly, Jonas's...friend," Tessa said pleasantly, holding the woman's stare.

The detective smiled widely, looking at Jonas again, seeming even more amused.

"So what happened here?" she asked.

"He started to panic when the lights went out. He was big, and started hitting, pushing."

"Yeah, we have someone with a bruised eye where he clipped them."

"I got him in a choke hold and tried to talk him down, but he got really riled up," Jonas said. "I know it was risky, but it was getting bad in there."

Rachel nodded. "He'll be okay. He's still kind of groggy and doesn't know what happened exactly. We'll explain the situation to him, and as long as the EMTs clear him, there's no problem that I can see. He was a public danger to himself and others. We owe you one. We're all doing whatever we have to tonight. It's nuts. I had an assault close by, so I responded. I'll write it up and catch up with you over the next few days. Thanks for keeping this from turning into a real problem." Rachel smiled. "What are you two doing caught in this in the first place?"

"Tessa has an elderly friend in Germantown who needs some help, she's low on insulin. We were trying to get there, but with the stoppage on the tracks, they rerouted us here," he explained. "We're trying to figure out how to get the next leg."

"You'll be stuck here for a while, and the streets are a mess. I have to go, but first let me see what I can do." The detective quickly reached into her jacket for her phone.

Tessa noticed two other things: her gun in its holster and her wedding rings on a chain around her neck.

"Old flame?" she asked Jonas, her voice not as casual as she'd hoped it would be.

"Old friend. We were street cops together, not partners, but had the same shift and we made detective together. She's a good egg. And very, very married," he added with another twitch of his lips.

Tessa's cheeks burned. She knew she was making an idiot of herself over a man who didn't even necessarily like her very much, except for the explosive sexual chemistry they shared. She thought again about how he had rarely shared the easy humor or banter with her that he had with his *old friend,* and she realized it was something she wanted with him.

She craved the passion, and the explosive sex, but she was interested in the other stuff, too. The things that real relationships were made from. The shared intimacy of tiny details that all couples experienced in everyday life. Coffee in the morning, holding hands while watching television, finishing each other's sentences.

She had no idea if Jonas wanted more than sex with her, or with anyone, for that matter. It pinched at her to think that was all they had, and barely that, even.

The detective joined them again. "Well, there's no way for me to get a unit down here to take you…we're stretched beyond capacity, as you can imagine. There is one possibility for transport, if you are open to it," she said.

"Anything you can do would be wonderful," Tessa said appreciatively, trying to make up for her previous jealousy. "My friend needs her insulin within an hour or so."

"Well, we've recruited some help from mounted

details, and I have officers willing to take you where you need to go, if—"

"Horses?" Jonas said incredulously.

"Yep. Some of the local cowboys and a few of the state police are offering services to get where regular transport can't go. They can get you there with no stopping, unless the skies open up again."

"I love horses, no problem," said Tessa. "I learned to ride as a kid."

Jonas looked less sure.

"I don't know, Tessa, maybe you should go, and I can wait—"

"It will be fine, Jonas. Just trust in the universe. This could even be fun," she said.

"Fun. Right."

"Don't worry. The officer will ride, and all you have to do is hang on."

"Right," he said again, sounding less than convinced. "Well, let's go, then."

The detective led them out through a side exit, and Tessa smiled at the large, handsome quarter horse that stood with his rider under a roof that protected them from the rain, which had lightened considerably, she saw with relief.

The quarter horse belonged to the state cop, who stood next to a younger man, dressed in jeans and a T-shirt. Tessa recognized him as one of Philadelphia's native urban cowboys.

The city had developed a program to help inner-city youth avoid crime and learn to ride, caring for their horses and riding them around the city, as long as they stayed out of trouble and did well in school. The program had some ups and downs over the years, and had

had its share of controversies. Struggling to stay afloat in terms of funding, it still was active.

Tessa supported the program through her business, and knew her father did, as well—it was one of the few things they agreed on. It was a good idea, and she loved seeing the horses being ridden down a Philly side street in the evening, the cowboys appearing like some vision from the Old West. She also liked to think about the kids in the program getting a second chance.

"Ricardo? Officer Styles?" Rachel greeted them, and introduced herself, as well as Tessa and Jonas.

"You think you can deliver these two safely to Germantown? They have a friend in need," the detective explained. "Jonas is a former detective with the force. Tessa owns a store down on South."

Jonas spoke up upon hearing the younger man's voice. "Ricardo? Ricardo Nunez?" he asked.

"Detective Berringer," the young man said happily. "I remember you."

"Not a detective anymore, but I take it you're doing well?"

"Yes. Thanks to you," he said. "Detective Berringer introduced me to the stables when I was a kid. He got me out of a crack house during a raid when I was ten and got me into a good foster home," Ricardo explained to the rest.

"Ricardo is planning to go to the academy," Officer Styles interjected. "He wants to be in our Mounted Division."

Tessa saw the pleasure reflected in Jonas's expression.

"Ricardo, that's great," Jonas said. "I'm proud of you."

The young man crossed to Jonas, who held out his

hand for Ricardo to find, shaking it and pulling the young man in for a quick, manly chest bump.

Tessa's throat was a little tight with emotion as she looked on. There was so much about Jonas she didn't know, and she wanted to know it all.

A roll of thunder was dull in the distance, and they all glanced up at the night sky.

"We'd better go. We can get you there pretty quickly, but we have to keep the horses out of the worst of this," Styles added.

"Okay," Tessa said, looking at Jonas. "You ready?"

He blew out a breath, offering a sideways smile that made her heart skip. "Ready as I'll ever be."

"REMIND ME NEVER TO do that again," Jonas said, wincing as he stretched out his legs in front of the counter where Tessa was waiting for the pharmacist who was gathering Kate's supplies.

"Oh, it was fun!" she said, smiling and looking as if she really had enjoyed herself.

It had only been a twenty- or thirty-minute horse ride to the pharmacy, cutting cross-lots, but it had been a bit rough considering he didn't have anything but his jeans between him and the saddle.

He hadn't been too crazy about Tessa riding with the mounted officer, either. Officer Styles had been enjoying her company a little too much, from what he could tell of the way the guy flirted, encouraging her to "hold on."

At one point, they had galloped across the park, and he and Nunez had to catch up. Jonas wasn't sure, but he thought he overheard the guy asking Tessa out.

Regardless of his confused feelings about her, he didn't want anyone else touching her or flirting with her.

Jonas hadn't been jealous of anyone in a long time, and he'd almost forgotten what it was like to feel this possessive.

He also reminded himself that he had no ties to Tessa, and didn't want any. The sexual chemistry between them was combustible. They were willing adults sharing some mutual enjoyment, but that was it.

In the morning, they would have to accept that nothing had changed.

Liar, an inner voice accused.

"It was kind of exciting, don't you think?" Tessa asked, interrupting his thoughts and sounding more relaxed. Jonas knew she was relieved to be at the pharmacy, and they could walk the rest of the way to Kate's. Officer Styles was willing to take her as far as she wanted to go, as he'd made clear, but once Jonas was down off that steed, there was no way he was getting back up on it.

"Exciting. That's one word for it," Jonas said dryly, and felt her nudge him.

"You looked good up there. You should take up riding. I can toally see you in a cowboy hat and boots," she said, and he wasn't sure if she was teasing.

"Not likely." He shifted uncomfortably from one foot to the other, recalling the ride. "I do have a bike."

"A bicycle?"

"A motorcycle," he corrected. "An eighties Harley that I take out on the road when I'm off duty."

"Very sexy," she purred, sliding up close to him.

"So, did the Mountie ask you out?"

"Hold on," she said, kissing him lightly and avoiding the question. "They just called my number at the counter."

Jonas sighed in frustration. She wasn't making this

easier. He couldn't get a fix on her. She was sexy and alluring, flirtatious and open about it. He couldn't see what had gone on between her and the officer, but he knew that flirty laugh, and figured she'd had a good time. It confirmed his earlier suspicions about her.

She was also a concerned friend and a kind person. A passionate woman who didn't hide who she was.

If he was really honest, maybe he was as angry at himself as he was at her. No matter how much he could blame Tessa for getting him in a bind with her father, Jonas had been the one placed in a position of authority, sent to protect her. He was also the one who'd caved to temptation.

And still wanted to.

It wasn't the first time he'd made that mistake. His mind wandered back to his last year on the force. His unit had been working with the Bunko Squad to take down an underground gambling ring.

The bodies of several people associated with the ring had surfaced around town, and Homicide was called in, where Jonas had made detective two years before. When Bunko undercover officers had snagged an inside CI, a confidential informant, to serve as a witness, she'd been given to Homicide to watch while the undercover team closed in.

Jonas, the junior detective at the time, had been on protection detail at the safe house. He still remembered Irena Nadik. Young, lovely and lethal.

The lethal part he'd had no idea about. Jonas had believed she was a victim, and that was how she played it. Forced to comply with a ruthless crime boss's orders, she'd tearfully relayed a story about her father's murder by the men who held her now against her will, the constant threats to sell her into the sex trade when they were done with her.

Jonas had fallen for her, let her seduce him, and looked forward to when the case was closed and they could be together. He'd even thought of marriage. Maybe that was how he'd rationalized breaking the rules for love.

He'd had no idea she was playing him the whole time. Slept with him, got him to tell her things he shouldn't have.

On the night of the raid, she'd drugged him, and used his own phone to try to warn the ring. Luckily, his partner had shown up and caught her before she succeeded.

The ring was taken down, Irena was in jail for a good long time, but Jonas had messed up big-time. He was suspended during an investigation, but eventually cleared for duty with only a light reprimand on his record.

But Jonas knew the truth. He couldn't look the guys he worked with in the eye each day and expect them to trust him when he had messed up so seriously. For a woman.

He left the force the following year and joined the personal security business Garrett was launching. It had taken him a long time to trust his instincts again, and that's what bothered him the most. He didn't know what to think about Tessa.

It was easy to focus on the job.

The senator was out of the country, and he was given a light-duty assignment to keep her company, make sure she was okay. He had no idea what the senator's agenda was, or Tessa's, for that matter, but he could focus on the job. That he knew how to do.

"All set. Kate's house is about six blocks from here, though we had better hurry," Tessa said briskly, breaking into his brief foray into the past. "The storm is winding up again."

He didn't say anything, still caught up in dark thoughts, but let her take his hand.

"I picked up a few things for later," she said mischievously, putting a bag in his hand, where he felt the corner of what he assumed were several rather large boxes of condoms.

"You're overestimating my endurance," he said.

"I just thought we'd like some variety," she countered.

Feeling cornered, wanting what he couldn't, and shouldn't, have, but not knowing how to walk away, he just kept moving.

"Everything okay?" she asked, clearly picking up on his change in mood.

"Let's get to Kate's before the storm hits," he said shortly.

He couldn't let this go any further.

He had to walk away. He'd get her safely to her friend's, then back to her place, and try to finish this job without making things worse. The crunching sound of the bag of condoms he carried seemed to mock him.

The wind was picking up, and she linked her elbow in his, picking up the pace.

"Is this storm never going to stop?" Tessa said breathlessly as they hurried down the street.

She guided him flawlessly, alerting him to step down or up, holding him close with her elbow linked in his. "It's like some bad *Armageddon* movie out here," she joked.

The end of the world as we know it.

Jonas twisted his mouth sardonically at his own sense of melodrama.

"Tomorrow the sun will come out, and it will just be a memory," he said, unsure if he was talking completely about the storm.

She yipped as thunder cracked overhead, and jumped closer to him, moving faster.

Jonas stopped suddenly, wrenching her to a stop as well, the flash of light obliterating any of his previous thoughts.

The flash that he *saw*.

He pointed. "Was that lightning—over there, this direction," he asked while pointing, his voice urgent.

"I think so," Tessa said cautiously. "It's kind of all around us."

Then it happened again. A dim flash at the corner of his eye, and he whipped his head in that direction.

"There!"

Tessa sucked in a breath, realizing what he was saying.

"Oh, my God, Jonas, you saw it! You *saw* the lightning!"

She let out a whoop and flew into his arms as the thunder growled even more loudly above, following the lightning strike.

Jonas held her, but lifted his face into the rain, eager, urgently wanting to see another flash, needing more confirmation that he hadn't imagined it.

Tessa's arms were tight around his neck, and he wasn't sure if it was rain or tears he felt on her skin. In his excitement, he'd forgotten how afraid she was of the storm.

"I'm sorry. I just remembered you don't like

storms. I...can't believe I might have actually seen something."

"I don't care about the storm," she said. "I'm so happy for you."

Then she was kissing him as the rain came down harder and the wind picked up around them. He gathered her up close, returning the kiss with everything he had, jubilant in the moment.

Tessa's not Irena, he thought, and neither were his feelings for the two women at all similar.

Irena had been exotic, different and had appealed to him as a younger man who was easily fooled by beauty and charm.

Jonas wasn't as easy to fool anymore—was he?

He wasn't so sure he could walk away, in spite of his temporary resolve to do so. They parted, breathing heavily, as the rain came down harder.

Jonas wished more than anything that he could see her. Maybe if he could see her face, her expression, her eyes, he could know if she was being honest with him. If any of this was real.

Soon, he thought, another bright flash showing up in his field of vision.

"We have to go," he said.

They ran the rest of the way to the address where Kate lived, and Jonas was relieved to finally be under cover as the weather worsened. On the relative shelter of the porch, Tessa searched for her keys.

"Damn, I left Kate's keys at home," she blurted in frustration. "How could I have done that?"

Jonas's attention was split. His body felt electric, as if the storm was surging through him. He'd seen several more flashes on the way to the house, enough to cement his certainty that his vision had started to return.

One of the flashes had even been very bright, from a relatively close lightning strike that had scared the death out of Tessa, but thrilled him—both because he saw it and because it sent her into his arms.

He couldn't find any way around his dilemma. There was no way to counter the damage that Senator Rose could do to his family, but he would take every chance he had to taste, touch and experience Tessa while he could.

"Kate will love meeting you, but I warn you, she's a real pistol," Tessa said, pressing the doorbell.

"I'm looking forward to it," he said, nipping at her earlobe. "You're delicious, you know," he added.

"Behave," Tessa warned playfully as they stood outside Kate's door, and she pushed the buzzer one more time.

There was no answer.

"It's me, Kate. Tessa. I have your medicine," Tessa called through the door, knocking again as they saw someone pull back a curtain near the window.

"Who? I don't know you. Go away," the woman yelled through the door, sounding frightened.

"Kate, it's me, Tessa," Tessa said again. "I have your medicine." She tried to turn the doorknob, but it was no use.

"I don't take any medicine. You are here to rob me," the older woman claimed in a high-pitched voice.

"She must have miscalculated for her next dose," Tessa said worriedly. "Confusion and paranoia can be part of ketoacidosis. We have to get in there."

"Call 911," Jonas instructed. "Do you have anything small, like a bobby pin?"

"No—wait," Tessa said, clearly shaken. "I do, here,"

she said, shoving something into his hands, dialing her cell phone to call paramedics.

Jonas focused, finding the door lock. He hadn't done this in a number of years, and he'd never been great at it, but urgency fueled his movements.

He found that not being able to see actually increased his awareness of the mechanism of the lock. Not using his eyes, he could focus instead on the sense of movement or resistance offered by the pins, and almost as soon as Tessa hung up her call, he had the lock open.

"You are amazing," Tessa said, opening the door, only to find the chain and a chair propped up against it. Kate really did think they were there to rob her.

"Time for a little brute force, huh?" he guessed.

"I think so," she agreed, and they both put their shoulders to the door and shoved, breaking the chain and pushing the door inward.

"What do you think you're doing?" a voice bellowed behind them. "I have called 911!"

Tessa turned to see an older woman on the porch holding a broom up in the air as if to swat at them. She calmed as she squinted, focusing in.

"Tessa, is that you?"

"It is me, Betty. I'm so sorry to worry you, we have to get inside to help Kate—she's out of insulin."

"Oh, no," Betty said, dropping the broom and joining them, sizing up Jonas in the process.

"And you are...?" the older woman asked him.

"Friend of Tessa's."

"Do you have a name?"

"Jonas, ma'am."

"Do you knock doors in often?"

"Only for beautiful sounding women," he said with a smile, and Betty smiled back.

"Emergency is en route, but we have to keep her calm and give her an injection right away, if we can, the 911 operator instructed," Tessa said.

Jonas nodded. "I can try to hold her still if need be, while you do that."

"I'll help keep her calm. She might recognize me," Betty offered, and came in with them.

Kate was resistant but weak, and still very confused. Jonas felt terrible having to restrain her, even gently, but he spoke quietly in her ear, saying small, nonsensical things until Tessa had administered the shot of insulin. Kate seemed to relax against him moments later.

"She passed out," Tessa said, sounding panicked just as the sound of the EMT sirens could be heard out on the street.

"The EMTs will take good care of her," Jonas said just as patiently. "She'll be fine. You got here in time," he said to Tessa, putting his hand to her face and feeling hot tears.

He wanted to go to her, to hold her, but he was supporting the unconscious woman and couldn't move.

"You're very handsome, you know," Betty interjected, silencing him and making Tessa laugh as EMTs came in and took over for them.

"I hope she's going to be okay," Tessa said, holding Jonas's hand. "Will you excuse me for a moment? I need to use Kate's bathroom," she said to Jonas, and squeezed his hand before she walked away.

Jonas chatted with Betty and a few other neighbors who had come out to see what was going on while the EMTs prepped Kate for transport.

"Tessa is such a special girl," Betty said. "She's always so good to Kate, and even brought us homemade soup when my husband was sick last winter. She even cleaned house for me."

"Really?" Jonas asked.

"You're blind?" Betty asked curiously.

"Yep."

"Well, I can tell you that she's gorgeous, inside and out. I hope you appreciate that," Betty told him.

"I'm starting to," he said more to himself than to anyone else.

Jonas thought the older woman might ask about his intentions, next, but was glad when one of the other neighbors engaged Betty in conversation.

He knew Tessa was gorgeous. As for the rest, he was trying to match his earlier assumptions about her with everything else he was learning, and was coming up short. All he had to base his ideas of her on were media reports, her background check and her father's opinion.

But he had his own opinion, as well.

Could he have been wrong about her motives?

"Hey, what are you doing here, Jon?" Jonas heard a familiar voice ask.

"Brad?" he guessed, not sure he was identifying the voice right.

"Yeah, it's me, buddy. How are you?"

Brad was a firefighter/EMT that Berringer Security had helped out a while ago. Brad's sister had been bothered by an old boyfriend, and Chance had helped keep an eye on her and made it clear to the ex that he needed to go away for good.

"I heard you lost your eyesight. Tough break. Job go bad?"

Jonas decided to skip over that, and got to the heart

of it, hoping he could use this connection to their advantage.

"Yeah, something like that, but it's temporary. I think my vision will be back soon," he said. "Listen, we're kind of in a bad spot here. I was hoping we could ride along with you. My friend is this woman's caretaker, and is very concerned, but we don't have a vehicle."

"The blonde? She's your client?"

Jonas could hear the high five in Brad's tone.

"Yeah. She's mine," he said, maybe a little more possessively than he meant to. "I'd appreciate it, though I know it's not usually allowed."

"I can make it happen. It would be good for the patient to see someone she knows as she comes out of this, too," Brad said.

Jonas thanked him and returned to tell Tessa, who hugged him tight, much to the tittering approval of the older women looking on.

"Thank you, Jonas. Thank you so much for your help with Kate," she said, hugging him again. Her concern and her gratitude were so authentic, he felt like a total jerk for ever doubting her motives about anything, and doubly so for lying to her about why he was with her.

If Tessa knew that her father had ordered him to be with her right now, he had a feeling she wouldn't be as thrilled with him. But he was also under orders not to tell her. James was right, that if she knew, she would not only be upset, she would reject his protection, and he couldn't let that happen.

As they started following the EMTs out as they wheeled Kate along, Jonas heard his name called from behind. Betty, the woman who had thought he was handsome, met him as he turned around.

"Here, handsome, you forgot these," she said

conspiratorially, pushing the small bag he'd dropped out on the porch—the condoms—into his hand. "Being blind is no excuse for not being careful," she added.

He choked out a thanks, and felt his face turn hot as he turned back to Tessa, who was laughing. Hard.

"Jonas, if you could only see your face," she said, breathless with laughter.

He smiled, optimistic for the first time in a while. "Soon enough, I think. Soon enough."

6

11:00 p.m.

TESSA WAS EXHAUSTED, happy, relieved, hopeful and worried all at the same time as she walked out of Kate's hospital room. Everything was fine, and after being treated, her friend had returned to being her old self in no time.

In fact, Kate had shooed them out of the room after properly interrogating Jonas as to his intentions, and receiving only stuttering replies. Tessa hadn't minded at all, since she was a little curious about Jonas's intentions, as well.

He seemed to go in and out of high and low moods all night, as if he was waging some internal struggle he couldn't tell her about. She assumed it had to do with his sight more than anything to do with her, but she hoped that maybe he was seeing that she wasn't the conniving manipulator that he thought she was.

That was the worrying part. Jonas had politely excused himself so that she could have a moment alone with Kate before they left. Kate had held her hand tight, looking somewhat worried herself.

"You love him, Tessa?"

The words had hit her like a straight-on lightning strike, and her first impulse was to deny it.

"I care about him. It's too soon for anything else, Kate."

"Oh, that's ridiculous. I knew I loved my Hank within five minutes of seeing him and knew that I'd marry him within ten."

"Jonas and I have had a rockier start. I'm not sure he even likes me that much."

"How on earth could you think that? The man is out in a terrible storm, at your side," Kate said. "Men don't do that for women they don't *like*."

Tessa sighed, and related the earlier conversation, and how Jonas believed that she had only wanted to use him against her father.

"You were a child when you did those crazy things," Kate objected. "It has nothing to do with the woman you are now."

"I hope he realizes that. I think there's more going on, though I'm not sure what it is."

Kate squeezed her hand. "Well, I think he has more feelings for you than he realizes, but only time will tell. A woman has to protect her heart."

"Thanks, though it might be a little late for that," Tessa said, feeling tears burning hot behind her eyes, but not wanting to upset Kate after her ordeal. "But I'm a big girl."

"And you deserve a good man. I hope he's smart enough to figure that out," Kate said.

"I hope so, too. You be well. I'll be back tomorrow to help you home," Tessa said.

"You get some rest. Betty offered to do the same. You focus on your young man and making things work. I'll be fine."

"Thank you, Kate. I'm so glad you're okay. You really scared me." Tessa hugged her and still planned to be there the next day.

It was what happened between now and then that had her in knots.

Jonas had waited outside the room, quiet and pensive. He didn't say a word as they turned to the elevator, but then were waylaid by one of Kate's nurses.

"Hey, I have something for you," she said, thrusting a pile of blue scrubs at them. "Kate asked. You guys are leaving puddles wherever you walk," the nurse said with a grin, "and you're going to get sick. There's an empty room at the end of the hall, with a bathroom. Feel free to go down there and get clean and dry before you head out."

Tessa was sure she'd just died and gone to heaven— her skin was clammy, and her hair was dripping down her back. She felt like a drowned rat and was, selfishly, kind of glad that Jonas couldn't see her.

She knew she looked like hell. Surgical scrubs weren't exactly fashionable, but they were soft, clean and dry, and she took Jonas's hand and headed for the room.

"This is awesome," she said, giddy with relief as she walked in and shut the door.

"I have to admit, it would be great to get out of these soggy jeans, and to wash the horse smell off," he admitted, stripping off his jacket.

The shower in the bath was only big enough for a single person, so much to Tessa's disappointment, they cleaned up quickly using what shampoo and soap were available. They weren't as nice as the things at her shop, but she felt a million times better when she emerged. The scrubs fit just right, and were so comfortable. She sat back on the bed and waited for Jonas as he did the same.

Was this the end of their evening, or just the beginning? Had he changed his mind about wanting to be with her? A few minutes later, he emerged, dressed and smelling completely horse free. She had to admit, it was an improvement.

"You look like McDreamy," she said with a grin, and wondered if they dared commandeer the room any longer to make use of the bed.

Jonas smiled, but didn't go to her. Had he changed his mind?

"We'd better be on our way," he suggested, and she agreed, trying to hide her disappointment as they made their way to the main entrance.

Awkward tension settled between them as they stood beneath the fluorescent hospital lights.

"Crazy night," she said, hating small talk, but unsure what else to say.

"Trains, taxis, horses and ambulances," he agreed with a short chuckle. "What next?"

Their answer came as they stepped out to the main entrance, and looked for their cab.

"Not here yet," Tessa said, feeling increasingly tense. "Things are so overwhelming tonight for everyone."

"It might take some time."

Were they still talking about the storm? she wondered.

He seemed preoccupied and distant, and she wasn't sure what to do.

A stretch limo pulled up and parked in front of them.

Tessa watched the driver get out, an older man clad in a long raincoat and hat, who held two huge umbrellas as he made his way to the main entrance.

Looking at her and then Jonas, he approached them with a smile. Tessa figured he was seeking shelter himself or thought they were his clients.

No such luck.

"Tessa Rose?"

She paused in surprise. "Yes, that's me."

"I'm your driver, Collins. This way, please," the driver said, and held the two umbrellas out to them.

"Wait, there's some mistake," she sputtered, and then halted. "Did Senator Rose send you?" she asked cautiously.

The driver seemed surprised. "No. I received a call from Ms. Masters to come pick you up here. At your service, miss," the driver said again, guiding a shocked Tessa to the passenger door, and then helping to guide Jonas to the other side.

Kate sent them a limo?

Only then did she note the name of the transport company embossed on the inside of the rich leather door.

Masters's Luxury Transport.

"Kate owns the limo service?" Tessa said in shock, catching Collins's smile in the rearview mirror.

"Yes, ma'am. It's a small company with only five vehicles, but we do a steady business. Her husband started it many years ago, and left the majority of it to her when he died, with a small share going to me, as well, for my retirement, but I enjoy the work. Hank Masters hired me twenty-five years ago. He was a good man."

Tessa sat back in the luxurious seat, shocked. She never would have guessed. Kate lived so conservatively, and even took the bus and train to get around town, at least as far as Tessa knew.

Collins leaned in, his arm on the door. "Kate told me what you did for her tonight. She tried to contact me earlier in the evening, to pick up her medicine for her, but I was in Baltimore dropping off a couple to their wedding and couldn't get back in time. Thank you, ma'am and sir," Collins said expressively, obviously very fond of his employer.

"I would do anything for Kate," Tessa said truthfully, taking Jonas's hand. "And thank goodness Jonas could get that door open," she said. "I could never have done it by myself."

"You let me know if you need anything," Collins said. "I am at your disposal for as long as you need me."

Kate was obviously trying to help her and Jonas along a little, Tessa guessed. A compartment opened on the other side, sliding out to reveal a champagne bar, strawberries and pretty, foil-wrapped chocolates.

"Some privacy, perhaps?" Collins asked with a twinkle in his eye.

Tessa, still stunned, nodded.

"Enjoy," was all Collins said as he closed the door and slid into the driver's seat, which seemed yards away from where they sat. A solid, and probably soundproof, barrier rose between them. A minute later, the car pulled smoothly away from the hospital.

The vehicle seemed to cut through the wind and rain like butter, the dark windows lit only now and then by a flash of lightning.

"I can't get over this," she said. "In all the time I've known Kate, she never said a word about owning a business."

"It sounds like it was her husband's venture, and maybe Collins runs it now," Jonas agreed.

"I'm so relieved. I always worry about her being comfortable, or paying her bills."

"People of their generation don't make an issue out of wealth like some do," Jonas said. "It's good to have friends who care about you. Kate obviously values that," he said.

"I do, too," Tessa responded, hoping he knew how much she meant it.

A buzzer sounded. Tessa pressed the button that lit up on the console.

"Yes?"

"I have your addresses, ma'am, but Ms. Masters wondered if you would like a late meal, since you may have missed dinner while getting to her apartment. There's no hurry."

"Now that you mention it, I am hungry," Tessa said. "And please call me Tessa. But we're not really dressed for dinner," she said. They looked like a couple of surgeons coming home from work.

The idea triggered a fun idea for role play—she would love to play doctor with Jonas, she thought mischievously, but then returned her attention to Collins.

"If you have any preference, let me know. I'm sure your attire won't be an issue."

An idea sparked immediately, and Tessa put down the divider, climbing forward to whisper something in Collins's ear. She knew the perfect place.

Putting the divider back, she eyed the champagne. "Okay then. I guess we're riding in style," she said to Jonas as she poured two glasses of champagne and went back to sit by his side, handing him one.

"I'm so glad it wasn't my dad who sent this car," she said honestly.

"Why?" Jonas asked, and she wasn't sure if she detected a note of suspicion in his tone.

"I don't like owing him anything, or having him monitor my movements. He says he doesn't, or that he's just trying to keep me safe, but I know old habits are hard to break."

"He's just looking out for you. Dads are usually protective of their daughters."

"Protective is one thing. Dad takes it to a whole other level."

"How so?" Jonas asked.

"When I was young, we were close," Tessa said, remembering.

Her father had been the sun, moon and stars back then. He'd taught her to ride a bike, played tea party with her and had sent her first flowers, delivered by a florist on her thirteenth birthday.

"But he confuses protection with control. I don't like to be controlled," she said, remembering less pleasant teenage years when her father had made her life miserable more than once. "As I got older, I realized he wanted me to be who he wanted, not who I am."

"Isn't that typical with teenagers and parents? My brothers and I gave my parents a few tough moments, as well. All teenagers rebel."

"It was more than that. I couldn't have a normal social life, even more so than what happens with other politicians' kids. He wanted to approve my friends, my activities, my boyfriends. It seemed like I only mattered so far as I was a reflection on him."

"I'm sure he didn't think that," Jonas said. "Your

father has always seemed to genuinely care for you. He's proud of you."

Tessa snorted. "That's the image he shows to everyone else. He was furious when I dropped out of college."

"Seems like most parents would be."

"Yeah, probably, but I was only studying law because he wanted me to. I'd gotten into soap-making as a hobby, but I loved it. I was good at it. I was selling soaps online and to classmates out of my dorm room," she said with a laugh.

"You couldn't do both?"

"I didn't want to. Maybe if he had let me do something more creative, more…me, I would have stuck it out, but I hated what I was doing, and I knew I wanted to open a shop. He thought that it was frivolous, the shop, the soap-making. He forbade me to do it. He tried to stop me, at first."

"How?"

"He blocked the business loans I applied for, and did anything else he could to thwart me," she said, remembering how ugly that had gotten.

A woman who had been buying her products for a while, who also happened to work in credit services, told Tessa why her bank loans weren't getting approval.

She'd been furious and felt betrayed by her father in the most hurtful way.

"He really did that?" Jonas said, sitting up, his blind gaze focused on her as she spoke.

She knew he only saw the facade her father provided, the solid politician who cared about country and family. The man who put up with a wayward daughter who was selfish and ungrateful. It was what everyone saw.

James believed his own press, and she figured he really thought he did the things he did for her own good.

"Yeah, he really did that, and more."

"Like?"

"Well, the worst offense, other than the store, was paying off a guy I was crazy about in college. He was in the music program, wanted to be a guitar player. We were so in love... and suddenly he received a paid scholarship to Juilliard."

"That's a huge break," Jonas said, frowning.

"Yeah. One that my father funded, I found out later. He would have had a heart attack if I had married a rock guitarist."

"Oh," Jonas said, frowning deeper. "So what happened with the store?"

"I proved to him that I can play hardball just as well as he can. I knew a city reporter, a guy who was dating a friend of mine, and I told Dad if he didn't get his nose out of my business, I would leak the story to the press, about how a city councilman, which was his job then, was using his clout with local banks to block small-business loans. If I went on record, it would have been a nasty political blow," she said. "And I had the paperwork to prove it."

"That sounds...bad."

"It was. He backed off and let the loan go through. It didn't matter. If he hadn't, I would have just used my trust fund left to me by my grandfather. He couldn't touch that, but I didn't want to use it if I didn't have to."

She sighed. "We didn't speak to or see each other for two years after that. Then my mom got sick, and when we were trying to be there for her, and after she was gone, it brought us together again. He had to admit

I was doing well, and things got better. He even came to the shop, and we have lunch now and then. But I'm always wary of him."

"I had no idea," Jonas said quietly.

"No one does. My exploits, as you know, were fairly well noted in the media. I know I was wrong to act out like I did back then, but I couldn't help it. He was smothering. He says it's all out of love, and I think he believes that sometimes, but it's hard for him to let me be who I am."

"You're probably more like him than you think," Jonas said.

Tessa drew back. "Why would you say that?"

"I'm sorry. It didn't come out how I meant it. Just that…you'd have to be a strong personality not to let someone like him, with his own strong presence, completely obliterate you."

She took a deep breath, and released it, relieved. "Yeah. I never thought about it that way, but I suppose that's probably why we came at each other so hard over the years."

Jonas was quiet then, his face pensive, and she watched him closely.

"What are you thinking about?"

He blinked, as if not realizing he had mentally wandered off.

"Oh, sorry. I just can't imagine growing up with all that pressure."

"Different families have different dynamics."

"Yeah."

She noticed he hadn't taken even one sip of his champagne. "You don't like your drink?"

"Not thirsty."

"Me, neither," she agreed, and set the glasses down.

She quickly stripped off her scrubs and returned to the seat, straddling his lap. His arm grazed her bare skin, his hand finding its way down her arm to her waist, hip and leg, his pulse slamming in the base of his throat.

"You're naked."

"You noticed."

She leaned in to kiss him. "I hope Collins takes the long way," she said, bringing both his hands up to cover her breasts.

"Where are we going?"

The way his voice lowered and caught ever so slightly as he massaged her made her happy. She wanted him to be affected by her.

"It's a surprise," she said.

He didn't say anything, and seemed to be holding his breath, as if deciding something.

That internal war again, whatever it was, she knew.

So she decided for him, leaning forward and kissing him until she had his complete attention. If he still thought she was seducing him for her own purposes, he was right.

Maybe he had the intentions wrong, but this was definitely selfish. She wanted him, and she knew he wanted her. She was willing to deal with any backlash later to have him now.

But he seemed to come around to her way of thinking rather easily, taking her into his arms and easing her down to her back. She stretched out on the sumptuous leather, and he followed, covering her with his own body.

She pushed his shirt up over his head, and he kicked his pants off. Then they were skin to skin, head to toe, and she almost purred when the strong, muscular legs wedged in between her thighs in a very erotic way. He didn't rush to get inside her, but lay there, covering her, touching her and whispering sweet things she'd never forget.

Tessa closed her eyes in the bliss of Jonas's body against her. As they settled into each other, nestled in the soft leather of the seat, Tessa had a sense of rightness she hadn't ever felt before. She knew she was meant to be with this man. She had the rest of the night to convince him of that.

JONAS WAS A GONER as soon as he'd realized Tessa was naked.

Though their discussion had created more questions than answers for him, at the moment he had had five feet seven inches of delectable, delicious woman spread out beneath him.

He sighed softly against the skin just below her ear.

"This is nice," she said breathlessly.

"*Nice* is a weak word," he said lightly, nipping her earlobe, then sucking on it, swirling his tongue around the delicate inner shell. "Awesome. Fantastic. Mind-bending," he offered, punctuating each word with a kiss, then a bite, then another kiss to soothe the sting.

Jonas was so hungry for her he didn't know where to start. His hands explored lower, sliding down the smooth lines of her back to cup her firm ass and pull her up against him. He groaned as his erection rubbed against a soft patch of curls and slick flesh.

Being so close with Tessa shook him to his core. He took his time, moving his shaft slowly along her sex, driving them both crazy. He was gratified when her nails dug into his back and she pushed up against him, seeking him, a wordless sigh and whole-body tremor releasing yet another wash of heat from her body.

She made the prettiest sounds, her body cradling his perfectly. Drawing a lush, erect nipple in between his lips, he let the sensations of touch and taste roll over him.

"I wish I could see you," he said, rising to find her lips for a kiss. "I've only ever touched you in the dark."

"You're right," she said softly. "I hadn't realized that. It will come back, Jonas." She moved against him. "And when it does, I'll still be here, if you want me to be."

Her words made him ache. He was starting to want that more than just about anything, and that was dangerous, he knew. What she'd told him about her father had explained a lot. Jonas had made a hell of a leap based on partial information.

And he was keeping a secret that would tear her from his arms, he knew.

"I guess until then touching and tasting every inch of you will have to suffice," he teased, injecting lightness into his voice, though his heart was heavy.

"I can live with that," she said, sliding her hand down his chest to his lower stomach, finally caressing his cock and making him suck in a sharp breath.

As she left fluttering kisses all over his face, neck and shoulders, he moved to accommodate her as she worked her way lower and took him into her mouth.

He dived his hands into her hair, enjoying the multitude of sensations her mouth was creating as she licked and sucked, her warm mouth and soft lips nearly driving him over the edge. Pulling her around, he slid his hand between her legs and found her soaked, hot. He slid a finger inside, then two, and loved how her moans made her mouth vibrate around his cock.

"Condom. Now," he demanded raggedly.

The next thing he heard was the ripping of the packet. He held his breath, waiting, hoping…and hissed out a sigh as she deftly covered him, kissing and teasing while she did.

Jonas eased her back on the seat, sliding his hand down to her ankle and pulling it up to rest against his shoulder.

"I've dreamed of this," he confessed.

"Me, too."

Turning his mouth to find the soft skin of her inner leg, he moved his fingers down to the crux of her body, seeking the hard, pebbled nub of her clit and stroking in slow, rhythmic motions.

Tessa's whole body twisted toward him on the seat as she sought more, writhing under his touch, her gasps and moans increasingly urgent.

"Jonas, please, I want you inside me when I come," she panted.

He pushed her a little more, turned on by her restraint, how she held back even as her body trembled with the effort.

When Jonas was sure she was as close to the edge as he was, he guided himself into her welcoming body, the very act drawing the breath out of him. She closed around him like a fist as he filled her with one, deep, purposeful thrust that made them both groan in ecstasy.

He'd never felt anything quite so perfect, he was sure of it. He paused, fighting the impulse to move, soaking up the sensation of her hot, inner muscles pulsing around his cock.

"Please, Jonas," she begged, arching up under him.

He granted her request, withdrawing slowly and then thrusting forward again, his hand caressing her calf as he tried to create the image of what she must look like in his mind's eye.

He nipped and kissed the flesh beneath her knee, opening her farther to his thrusts as he moved faster, letting need set the pace. She drove him on with hot, raw descriptions as she joined in, touching herself, telling him what she was feeling, what she wanted him to do to her.

He wanted to do all of it, over and over again.

He was sure he'd died and gone to heaven when he felt her hand down between them, her fingers circling the root of him as he thrust inside her.

"So. Good. Jonas," she moaned, alternating touching him and herself.

Pulling her other leg up over his other shoulder, Jonas pumped into her without restraint, all the pent-up desire, need and anticipation he had for this woman driving him.

The orgasm was like nothing he had ever experienced. Release created a splash of color behind his eyelids as it shook his body. He kept thrusting, and amazingly, when normally the sensation would start to fade, it was instead followed by a second wave of pleasure that had him gasping as she clenched him tight, her nails scraping his chest as she cried out her own release.

Finally the urgency eased and he lowered her legs, withdrawing from her body reluctantly and pulling her up against him. Jonas had never been what he would call a snuggly kind of guy, but he needed the contact as if to reassure himself that this was real, that Tessa was really here with him.

Her skin was damp with perspiration, which intensified the scents of soap and sex. Her body was pliant and he stroked her wherever he could touch.

"Keep that up," she said on a sigh, "and we'll be reaching for the box again soon."

"Sounds good to me," he said.

He sought her lips for another kiss, the heat actually growing again between them, when a buzzer sounded somewhere close. Collins's voice followed on the intercom.

"We're close to our destination, unless you'd like me to drive around more. If so, hit the intercom button twice."

Jonas and Tessa laughed at their driver's discretion in not asking for a verbal response.

"He drove all the way from Baltimore already tonight. I think we can get dressed and give the guy a break," Tessa said, extricating herself from Jonas's embrace, though slowly.

"We can," he agreed, but didn't let her go before he pulled her in for another heart-stopping, promising kiss.

The next few moments were filled with the sounds of them righting themselves, dressing and hoping they were presentable before they gave the okay to Collins.

The car stopped, and a door opened on Tessa's side. While making love to Tessa, Jonas hadn't even noticed that the pounding rain on the outside of the car had lightened to a drizzle. The winds had calmed and he heard thunder rolling gently off in the distance.

As Collins opened his door, Jonas looked skyward, though he couldn't see anything. The reflex to look was automatic, especially now that he had some hope that his vision was returning.

"It appears the worst of the storm has passed, sir," Collins confirmed. "But the blackout is quite widespread and has not been rectified."

"Where are we?" he asked.

"It's a restaurant called Noir," Tessa said.

"I've heard of it," Jonas said. "They serve meals in complete darkness. The waitstaff is blind, as is the owner," he said, unsure how he felt about that. "But how can they be open during a blackout?"

"A lot of the businesses have back-up generators, especially restaurants, since they need to keep food cold," Tessa elaborated. "Though I imagine they might have a limited menu tonight."

"That makes sense."

He guessed Tessa was trying to make him feel more comfortable, which wasn't at all necessary. He'd be just as happy going back to her place and finding something to eat there—preferably naked.

She stepped up close to him, and he could still detect the scents of sex on her skin, his soap mixing with her flowery scent. It was so sensual, he didn't want anything to break the mood.

"I've heard such great things about it, I thought it would be…interesting," she said, sounding unsure. "One of the things about Noir is being able to understand what it's like to be blind. I want to understand how you're experiencing the world right now, Jonas, but if it bothers you, we can go somewhere else."

Taking his hand in hers, she absently rubbed her thumb over his knuckles, waiting for his answer.

"I've eaten all my meals in the dark for the last

month, but I'm still curious about the place," he said. "It'll be fun," he offered gamely.

They walked in and followed their server's instructions to follow the handrail along the wall of the dark hallway to the back dining room, where a private table had been reserved for them.

"You are two brave souls to venture out tonight. We had dozens of cancellations, understandably," the server said.

Jonas heard Tessa's surprised gasp, and felt her stop beside him.

"Tessa?"

"Sorry. There's not so much as a slant of light in here. It's so *black*...it feels like it swallows you," she said, and her fingers closed around his a little more tightly.

"We don't have to stay," he said.

"No, I'm fine. I was just thrown by how dark it is, stupid as that sounds, especially since we've spent all night in the dark."

"Not stupid at all," the server interrupted. "People often have that initial response to complete dark. Though you may turn off the lights at night, most places still have degrees of light twenty-four hours a day, whether from the moon, streetlights, night-lights, et cetera. So the experience of complete darkness can be quite startling," he explained kindly.

"You're right. I never thought about it that way," Tessa confessed, sounding more relaxed.

"But you learn to use your other senses, and you learn to trust the people around you. You'll see," he said, and led them to a table, seating them next to each other.

"Being in the dark can be a revelation. You start to know each other in a new way, to find out things even about people you thought you knew well."

As they settled into their seats, the waiter offered a short history of the restaurant.

"Dinners in total darkness started, as far as we know, as early as the nineteenth century. In the 1990s, Europeans began experimenting with dark dining, dark bars and similar events. The Paul Guinot Foundation, a French organization for the blind, came up with the idea of dinners in total darkness called Le gout du noir or 'Taste of darkness.'"

"That's fascinating," Tessa responded. "But how is the food prepared?"

Jonas admitted that he, too, had initially thought it was only a marketing angle, and had no idea of the history of the place.

"Our cooks are able to see, along with minimal other staff," the waiter assured them before asking if they had any questions. He also cautioned them to stay at their tables, to keep the area where he walked clear before he left.

"Are you sure you're okay?" Jonas asked, leaning in close to find her neck, nuzzling it.

He was concerned about how disoriented and fearful she'd sounded when they'd walked into the room, so he made sure he kept touching as they sat in the dark. Though it was not all for her benefit, he had to admit.

Now that he'd had her, he was even more needful to be with her again. Soon.

"I'm okay now. It's very…shocking. I walked into this room and it hit me how awful it must be to live in complete darkness all the time," she said.

He squeezed her hand. "Well, this has been a good reminder that I've spent a lot of time feeling sorry for myself when other people have spent every day without their sight and go on with their lives just fine."

"That wasn't my intention, not at all," she rushed to say, and he shushed her.

"I know it wasn't. But I think when I lost my sight, my first reaction was to feel like this was only happening to me. The waiter, and being here, reminded me otherwise," he said with a sigh, regretting his own attitude over the last month.

He, at least, had the return of his vision to look forward to. Others never would have that. It was humbling.

"I'm sure my brothers would confirm I've been a huge pain in the ass," he said with a smile, but then turned serious.

"I think you're being too hard on yourself," she chastised.

She leaned in, intending to kiss his cheek, but ended up kissing his shoulder instead, making them both laugh.

"Obviously my coordination in the dark needs some work," she said ruefully, finding his face with her hands and offering another kiss.

"You were doing just fine in the subway car," he said huskily as the door opened again, their waiter returning with drinks and appetizers.

"Maybe later we can find a blindfold," she said in a suggestive tone. "One thing is for sure, your other senses really do take over when you don't rely on your sight. Everything is so…intense."

Jonas agreed. If there was one word for what was happening between him and Tessa, it was *intense*.

7

1:00 a.m.

"OHHH...THAT'S WONDERFUL," Tessa said with a sigh as Jonas found her lips with his fingers, letting her nibble a piece of the rich cheese that the waiter had delivered to their table. This had very possibly been the best meal of her life.

Though at first it was awkward, the waiter's prediction had come true: as each course was served, they became more proficient at handling their food using their other senses, and even trusted each other's coordination enough to feed each other.

Tessa knew that she trusted Jonas with her life. She had, literally, on several occasions. She hoped their experiences together were helping him to trust her more, too. He seemed to have relaxed toward her since their conversation in the car, and since making love.

A shiver ran over her skin. She couldn't wait to get him alone again.

Tessa absorbed the experience of dark eating full-on. This was definitely something she wanted to do again.

After she let go of her sense of disorientation and fear of the complete dark, she found she could manage more easily.

She wondered if Jonas would want to come back here after his sight returned. She wasn't sure how she would feel about that in his shoes.

What she was finding entertaining and enlightening might be a bad reminder of what he went through. There was still a huge difference between spending a few hours in the dark and being blind. She knew she could walk out of the room and have her sight back. Jonas, and others who had lost their vision, didn't have that luxury.

Though another part of her wondered if people who relied on their vision weren't the ones who missed out. Being in the dark demanded such focus that it enriched as much as it denied.

"So tell me something that you could only tell me in the dark," he said.

She paused. "I can't think of anything."

"Really? A secret that you never told, a fantasy that you are too shy to share in the light of day? Isn't that what blackouts, airplanes and dark restaurants are for?" he joked, but she knew he was serious, too.

Her heart beat a little faster at the idea, and the seductive tone of his voice.

"Maybe," she said, unsure.

"Tell me."

Tessa couldn't believe she was so nervous. She wasn't shy, in fact, she was often the one who initiated sex with her partners. But there was one thing…she had never told anyone. She didn't know if Jonas would be okay with it. What if he thought she was demented?

"The problem with sharing secrets in the dark is that

we have to go out into the light at some point," she said, thinking twice.

"Tell me, Tessa," he said again, stroking her hand with his thumb.

Sparks lit along her skin and she almost expected to see them light up in the dark.

"Okay. There is one fantasy I've often had..."

"Mmm-hmm." His hand was on her thigh, rubbing lightly there now, and she had a hard time focusing.

"I'd like to have someone watch me have sex."

His hand stopped. "What do you mean exactly?"

"I'd like to perform for a lover. You know, just have you, for instance, sit back and watch. Maybe I could use a vibrator, my hand or some other toys, but I'd love to feel free enough with someone to do that, to know that they could enjoy just staying back and watching me pleasure myself," she said, her voice catching. She was getting turned on just talking about it, but also felt embarrassed admitting it.

"I can't imagine anyone saying no to that," he said, his own voice a little rough.

"Men don't want to think women can find pleasure without them. It's a dent to their egos, I guess," she said.

"Not mine. I could do that. If you want, I want to do that," he said, his hand rubbing her leg again, moving higher. "When I have my eyes back, I mean. Just say the word."

She was incredibly turned on by sharing that with him, and by the prospect of being able to do it. But as he buried his face in her neck, she pushed him back.

"Your turn."

He took a breath. "Right. I don't suppose I can get

away with the standard guy fantasy of two women, right?"

She laughed. "I know you can be more creative than that."

"I don't know. I have always been a pretty traditional kind of guy in bed. What you did to me on the train... that was about as kinky as I have ever gotten."

"Seriously?"

"Yeah."

"So is there anything you've ever thought you'd like to do? You know, the thing you can only share in the dark?"

She put her hand on his thigh now, mimicking his motion on hers earlier.

"You are evil," he said.

"Tell me."

"Okay. I've never done it, but I think I'd like to try..."

Tessa realized she was actually holding her breath.

"Maybe being tied up," he said. "and tying up my partner in return."

"Bondage?"

"Yeah," he said softly. "I've never trusted anyone enough to allow myself to be completely at their whim. To let them do whatever they wanted to me. For them to be completely in control. No pain or anything like that... or maybe just a little," he said in a tone that tantalized her. "And hopefully they could trust me in the same way."

Tessa took a deep breath to try to slow down her speeding heart.

"I could so do that," she said, enjoying the image of Jonas bound to her bed. "I mean, if you ever thought, you know, if you wanted me to—"

She stopped, realizing she had dug her nails into his thigh. When she pulled her hand away, her fingers brushed his cock, hard and testing the looseness of the scrubs.

"I'll go find our waiter to see if he can bring a check," she said quickly.

He got up, too, and as she turned on her heel, she bumped into the chair and stumbled forward.

Amazingly, Jonas was there, his strong hands closing on her upper arms, steadying her and then pulling her in to hold her close.

"Hey, careful."

"Good catch," she said, linking her arms around his neck.

"Mmm," he said, kissing her.

"We all go through life stumbling around in the dark, Jonas, looking for something to grab on to that makes sense. You and I, we seem to keep bumping into each other. We fit."

He pulled her against him, fitting her to him tightly as he deepened the kiss. She didn't resist, letting him take his fill, and getting hers in return. But for all the desire and passion between them, she couldn't help but think there was something else Jonas hadn't told her. Some other secret that stayed between them in the dark.

ELY SNUCK THE KEYS out of Chloe's pocket as he pressed her against the doorjamb, her arms locked around his neck, their kisses even hungrier after their backseat encounter.

She was gorgeous, he thought, sliding the key effortlessly into the lock and opening the door without missing a beat, getting them inside where they could dispose of soaking-wet clothes and he could take his time with her.

"You have great hand-eye coordination," she said against his mouth.

"I was very motivated to get that door open and get us inside," he responded as he deftly undid the buttons on her wet blouse.

"I wasn't talking about opening the door," she rejoined, nibbling at his bottom lip, making him laugh and groan at the same time.

She tried the light switch on the wall, but apparently the power was still out.

He felt...*light*. For the first time in recent memory.

"I'm glad you stuck to your old habits," he said, thankful he'd gone to the bar and that she had walked in.

"Me, too," she whispered, lifting a hand to his face, running her fingers over the stubble of his jaw. "Let me get out of these clothes—"

"My thinking exactly," he interrupted.

She laughed, and he liked how it infused her entire expression with warmth. Her laugh reverberated through her entire body, the cool, distant reporter erased, a vibrant, passionate woman revealed.

He'd known there was magic between them before, but he'd been too raw then, too fresh from his return to be good for anyone. He hadn't been ready for more then, but he was now.

"How about we get dry, have a glass of wine...take our time," she said, leaning in to kiss him again. "No need to rush."

He nodded, sighing. "You're right. There's time," he agreed.

It was a luxury he was still getting used to. Time had

seemed to stop in Afghanistan, and since then, it was punctuated by the start and stop of various jobs where he'd experienced things that often made him acutely aware of how time often ran out.

He didn't want to waste any more of his.

They walked into her bedroom, and he watched as she moved around the room, lighting several candles set on dressers and tables. The warm light revealed ultrafeminine decor that he only vaguely remembered, taking in the thick, old-fashioned quilt of cream and roses, the ornate, Victorian lamps and lacy curtains. It spoke to the old-fashioned, traditional woman who lived beneath the image of the hardened career woman.

The space was so feminine it made him feel too big and cumbersome, like if he moved, he'd break something. Classic bull in a china shop. At the same time, he liked it very much. She was different than the other women he knew in a way that spoke to him.

"You're quiet," she said, stripping down to the black bra and panties that took his attention away from the room altogether.

She had an amazing body, all legs, curves and delectable soft spots he loved to explore and hadn't gotten nearly enough of. The soft, flickering candlelight completed the fantasy.

He grinned, shucking his shirt, liking the way she looked at him when he did so. "Just taking in the room, and you," he said, wiggling his eyebrows at her and making her laugh.

"You're different now," she said, watching him closely.

He shrugged. "Not really."

"You were so closed off back then. I know that interview was torture for you," she said.

"I was still adjusting. It's disorienting, being in the desert one day and back here the next, surrounded by people who all want something from you."

"You never said much, even during our night together."

He didn't remember that. He remembered touching her and losing himself in what she'd offered him. But now he realized how selfish he'd been.

"I'm sorry. I wasn't myself then. I should have walked away when you asked me back to your place, but—"

He'd needed the comfort, but more than that, something about her had beckoned him. Something about Chloe had given him what he needed, which was way more than sex, even though he didn't recognize it at the time.

"I'm glad you didn't. I only wish you hadn't walked away after," she said. "Are you going to walk away again now? Am I going to wake up in the morning to find you gone again?"

"No," he said simply, the word his promise.

"Okay," she said, accepting it.

She put on her robe, and then grabbed another one from the closet, handing it to him.

He took the garment, staring at it for a moment. It was definitely a guy's, and that bothered him for a second. He looked up to see her staring at him, one eyebrow arched.

"What? Did you think that I didn't sleep with anyone for three years, just waiting for you to come back?" she asked, smiling, though there was no barb in the question.

He took a breath. "No, not that. Hell, I didn't even really know I was looking for you again until tonight… or maybe I knew it all along, since I got down here in

Norfolk. I was reading your articles...you're still an amazing journalist," he said, and saw pleasure bloom in her expression. "An amazing woman."

"I kept track of you, too," she admitted, turning to the dresser and fussing with something, opening a drawer where she put some items, and closed it again. "I often thought of contacting you, but I don't go begging. Though you were the first man who made me consider it," she said, walking up close and sliding her hands over his chest.

"I don't imagine you were a saint either."

He frowned. No, he hadn't been a saint. There had been some women, several, in fact, but none that really mattered. None he ever saw again or sought out.

"Let's not talk about the past. It's done," he said. "The present—and the future—are much more promising."

"I like the sound of that," she agreed.

She seemed smaller here, more fragile and feminine, her hair undone and curling from the rain, falling down over her shoulders. He slid his hands through it, feeling possessive and lucky—why did he wait so long?

Her mouth was like velvet, and he let his robe drop to the floor as he dived the other hand into her hair, kissing her until she was trembling with need. Possessing her.

His, he thought.

"Ely," she said his name on a breath when he released her lips. He was sure he couldn't hear it enough, wanted to make her scream it.

Falling to his knees, he undid her robe, slid his hands up her legs, parting her slim, silky thighs. Parting the soft folds of her sex with his fingers, he tasted her lightly at first, but as she heated up, becoming slick, he lost himself in kissing her, sucking the hard, aroused pearl of her clit between his lips.

Chloe knew how to take charge—one of the things he loved about her—and her hands held his head, directing him, pressing and urging until he gave her everything she wanted, which he was more than happy to do.

She did scream his name when she came, and he didn't let it end there, making her crest one more time. She sagged against him as he stood and took her in his arms.

Her cheeks were flushed with satisfaction, her pupils dilated, mouth soft as he kissed her fully. He wanted her again, but also wanted to wait. He needed her to know that he could be there for her, not always satisfying his own needs, oblivious to others as he had been before, when he left her.

They had time. He'd make it up to her.

"How about that glass of wine?" he asked. "Maybe something to eat to go with it?"

She nodded against his shoulder.

"I have to wait for my knees to feel solid again," she said, gazing at him with eyes he thought he might like to see staring at him every morning. Eyes he might like to see on smaller versions of both of them.

Whoa, Marine, he cautioned himself. *Slow down a little there.*

But Ely had always led the charge, committed to the mission, focused on the target. He didn't see the point in second thoughts or delaying action.

"I can help with that," he said huskily, bending down and scooping her up, smiling at her gasp of surprise as she linked her hands around his neck and held on.

"Ely, this is hardly necessary," she said, laughing as he carried her out to the living room.

"But it is fun," he said, kissing her nose as he deposited her on the sofa.

"Matches?" he asked, noting more candles on the fireplace mantel.

"Up by the picture of my father," she directed, pointing.

He saw the picture, and grabbed the box of stick matches, lighting one, taking in the portrait.

"Navy officer," he observed, sliding her a glance. Her father was a highly decorated submariner.

"Yes. Retired now."

"You never mentioned him."

"You never asked."

It was true, he hadn't. Besides the interview, where she had focused on his life, they hadn't talked much at all.

He lit the candles, and then walked to the kitchen, telling her to stay put. He had a lot of making up to do.

Coming back with a tray of cheese, fruit and crackers and a bottle of wine, he joined her on the sofa.

"Well, now I am feeling very spoiled," she said, taking a glass of wine from him. "I could get used to that."

"All part of my evil plan," he agreed, taking some cheese and crackers, and settling back with his own glass.

"So where are your parents? Norfolk?" he asked, intent on learning as much as he could about her.

"The house is in Annapolis, but they aren't there much. My dad has his sailboat there, and they live on the water for most of the year, sailing to vacation spots. They fly back from wherever they are for holidays, and seem to be enjoying life."

"Sounds like the perfect retirement."

"I don't know that I'd want to spend that much time

on the water, but my mother loves it. And for so many years they were apart when he was at sea."

"Squid are a species unto their own," he said, shaking his head. "The idea of spending that much time under water gives me the heebies," he admitted.

"Seriously? I thought big tough Marines weren't afraid of anything?"

"I didn't say I was *afraid*," he corrected, puffing out his chest. "Just that I'm not particularly fond of the idea of being under several hundred feet of water."

"Ah, okay, I see the distinction," she said.

"Thank you."

She grinned and threw a grape at him, which he caught in his mouth.

"So what about your brothers? I was sorry to read about Garrett losing his wife—how tragic," she said, more serious.

"It was beyond tragic. We weren't sure he was going to make it through for a while," Ely said, still feeling punched in the chest when he thought about his older brother's loss. He'd liked Lainey a lot, too. It had been a loss for all of them.

"And Jonas, Chance? They're well? Married?"

"Chance is Chance. I don't think he'll ever settle down, or find a woman who can put up with his need to jump off high things every other day," he said, laughing. "But Jonas has been in tough shape."

Ely related the story of Jonas's protection detail, and about the loss of his sight.

"That's terrible!" Chloe commiserated. "But he'll get it back?"

"So they say. No word yet."

"And you said he's involved with Tessa Rose, James

Rose's daughter?" she asked in a tone that alerted Ely's radar.

"Well, it seemed that way, until he backed off big-time after the accident. But she keeps coming around. That's like one determined lady," he admitted. "Why?"

He liked Tessa, actually, and thought it was high time his older brother found a steady woman, but Jonas was even more of a lone wolf than Ely had ever been.

Even with his own brothers, Jonas had always held himself separate to some degree. When they were kids, Jonas was the one who spent more time doing his own thing rather than playing in a group, who spent more time in his room, reading or studying, than out partying in college.

He'd become even more isolated after he left the police department, or so Garrett and Chance reported. Ely had been off to basic training back then, and had only heard of what happened to his brother.

Jonas didn't talk about what went down when he'd been caught in an undercover mess, but Ely knew it wasn't the way the papers had painted it. After being in a war, he knew exactly how the media could spin things.

Chloe shifted uncomfortably, taking another sip of her wine before she replied, and then he felt her reporter persona slip back in place, the distance reasserting itself.

He was willing to bet she knew something about James Rose that she didn't want to share.

"What are you thinking about?" he asked.

"There's a huge story breaking in a few hours," she said. "Rose's office is one of the ones that will be implicated."

"For what?"

"There's an embezzlement ring on the Hill. Several aides have been using their resources to siphon off funds from campaign coffers, using it for all manner of criminal business. I was clued in, and it's going to be a huge scandal," she said, her eyes lighting up.

"And Rose is in the middle of this?"

"Not him directly—but his aide, yes. You can't say anything about this, Ely, not until the story breaks. The arrests won't happen until morning, right before."

Ely smiled at how her color rose and her eyes brightened at the prospect of a hot story. She was passionate about her work. It was one of the things he loved about her.

"I won't say a word, I promise."

Still, his mind went to his brother and Tessa. They weren't together, but he hoped none of this would hurt the reputation of their agency.

"I can't say I'm surprised, and not even a little glad," he said. "That guy, the aide, Howie Stanton, is a slug. He came to the hospital the night Jonas was admitted and told him if he went near Tessa again, there would be bad consequences for the business."

"You're kidding. Well, the only bad consequences I see are ones coming down on him."

"I'll drink to that," Ely said, smiling.

Chloe was the kind of woman men dreamed about. Beautiful, smart and sexy, she knew how to do her job. It was one of the things he found sexiest about her.

Setting down her wine and reaching to take his glass, her eyes told him she didn't want to talk anymore. Loosening the tie of his robe, she trailed kisses down his chest, obviously intent on ending the conversation and returning the pleasure he'd provided her earlier.

Ely was determined to be a better man this time, to

not be as selfish and self-involved as he was when he'd first been with Chloe.

He also loved how she took control and pushed him back to the cushions, focused on her task.

She stroked his erection, looking at him with sheer pleasure and mischievous intent as her tongue darted out, tasting him, making him catch his breath.

"You stay put, Marine, and don't come until I tell you to. That's an order," she commanded with mock seriousness as she closed her mouth around him, sending his heart rate through the roof.

Ely gladly submitted. He was trained to take orders, and knew he wouldn't disobey this one if his life depended on it.

8

3:00 a.m.

TESSA WAS EXHAUSTED and had actually nodded off for a few minutes curled up on the seat, her head cradled on Jonas's shoulder as Collins took them back to the store. The intimacy of the night and the dark in the restaurant was giving way to morning, allowing her some light to study him.

He was dozing, too, the manly lines of his face softened in sleep. She stared at the fullness of his mouth, which she couldn't get enough of. He looked peaceful, which was rare for him, she thought. They'd turned a corner of sorts, leaving the restaurant with the connection between them stronger.

Still, she worried. She hadn't asked Jonas the question she was dying to: why he had thought so badly about her after the accident. What had Howie said to him? Was her father up to his old tricks, controlling her life, and her love life?

Jonas was clearly under the impression that she had used him to get back at her father, or that her father had not thought he was "suitable" enough for her. There were things going on beneath the surface, and Tessa planned to find out what they were.

One thing she knew for sure was that Howie was a snake. She'd never liked him. Her father had suggested once that Howie had an interest in her, and that they would make a "solid match." The thought made her gag. Her father occasionally pushed one of his plastic political harpies in her direction, even though she never showed any interest.

Jonas said she didn't care about the cost to others. What costs? Could her father have threatened his business? She wouldn't put it past him.

Jonas didn't deserve any negative flak for what happened that night they'd been attacked. He stepped up to protect others, but leaned on no one. There was a loneliness at his core that made her ache to change it, to make him see how much she cared for him.

How much she loved him.

She wasn't afraid of the word. She'd often wondered if she would find anyone that she'd truly fall in love with. Then Jonas had walked into her shop, and she knew she had found the other half of her perfect combination.

She leaned in, snuggling into his shoulder again and loving how his arm came back around her so naturally. Turning her face into his chest, she inhaled, enjoying his natural scent, how it mingled with hers. Their bodies loved each other, but how could she convince him it was more than that?

Tessa had been fighting for what she wanted in life since she could remember, against her father, mainly. But also against the world in general or at least it always felt that way. Everyone always assumed the worst of her, and so she had once decided to walk the talk.

Even friends had often thought that as the daughter of a wealthy politician, she would never have to work for anything in her life. That it all would be handed to her.

It could have gone that way, had she made other decisions. She'd taken a very different path, and was glad for it. She hoped Jonas was coming to see who she really was, too.

"I can see you thinking," Jonas said sleepily, and she looked up to find he was watching her. "What about?"

"Just about you. Us."

"How so?"

"When I said, back at the restaurant, that we fit...I don't know. It just seemed like you were holding back. I was wondering why. And what you aren't telling me."

"We do fit. In some ways. And in others—we don't."

"Like?"

"Like physically. Otherwise, we come from very different worlds. You wouldn't be happy in mine, not for long. And vice versa."

"You hardly know me, Jonas. How do you know what would make me happy?"

"I've been through this before. My job is dangerous."

"I know that."

"And it's not great for relationships, let me tell you. If you and I were together, I might have to go on a job where I would be protecting someone, another woman, and living at her side for weeks—how would you deal with that? If the tables were turned, I wouldn't like it one bit."

"I agree, that would be hard. But there are four of

you, and you can divide the jobs accordingly, right? But if you *had* to do that, well, I guess I would just have to trust you. That's what we're talking about, right? It's not about different worlds, or your job or mine—it's about the fact that down deep, for whatever reason, you don't trust me. I'd like to know why. Do you really think I am so superficial that I would use you or anyone just to get at my father?"

Silence loomed between them, and the hurt spread from her heart to encompass her entirely, the same way the dark restaurant had done.

"I guess that's my answer," she said, twisting away.

"Tess, stop. Listen. I want to trust you, but I don't understand why you did what you did."

"Which was?"

He took a deep breath, and let it out. "Why you told your father's aide about our...kiss that night. Why you made it sound like I had initiated it, but more than that, I wonder why you told them at all? That was private, between us. I could only assume that—"

"That I had seduced you, and then run to tell my father about it as fast as I could and blamed it on you as a way to get out of having a bodyguard, and to shove it back in my father's face."

"Well, yeah."

"Here's a news flash, Jonas," she said. "I'm all grown up now, and I don't play those games anymore. I'm not my father. What you see is what you get."

"Well, your father was pretty pissed. He took me off the job, and his aide suggested that there could be trouble for me and my brothers if I got anywhere near you."

Tessa's mind went still. So she was right in her intuition. Her father had found a way to come between her and a man she wanted. Or had she done that all on her own? She hadn't been entirely forthright with Jonas from the start—he may have made the first move that night, but only because she had been pushing him to.

"Listen, I remember showing them where we were standing when the attack happened. Howie was there. Where you had fallen back, and how I had grabbed the bat, but I didn't say anything about us kissing. I guess they could have assumed, but I swear, I didn't tell them what was going on," she said. "And if anyone is playing games here, it's the senator. I told you what he did before, with my college boyfriend. He may like you working for him, but—"

"He wouldn't think I was good enough for his daughter," Jonas finished flatly, and she nodded.

"It's possible. He sees everything as reflecting on him, his career. But I don't think that. I never thought that. I never would use you. Not like you thought I did."

She wrapped her arms around herself, suddenly feeling cold. Then Jonas was there, pulling her in, holding her tight.

"I'm sorry, too. I was such a mess at the time, but I should have told you about my sight. I should have asked you before I assumed what had happened. I believe you, Tessa," he said, kissing her cheek gently and taking her arms from around her middle, twining them around his back.

She held on tight, seeking a deeper kiss, as if trying to let him know with her whole body how much she cared, and how much she never would cause him any pain, not if she could help it.

Heat rose between them, but this wasn't the place to pursue their newfound intimacy.

"I want to talk to my father as soon as possible about what happened that night, and set it right. I absolutely will not let him blame you for something that was not your fault at all," she said vehemently.

"Well, I wasn't exactly blameless, Tessa. And I would rather you didn't talk to your father, if that's okay. I can handle it. Let's set it aside for now, okay?"

"Okay," she said reluctantly. She wasn't surprised that he would want to handle it on his own, but still felt that she should do something to make it right.

The car stopped, and she frowned, hearing the sound of music playing out in the neighborhood, resisting the urge to argue with him for the moment.

"The electricity is back on," she said, but saw no evidence of that except for the music. The streetlights were still out, though the dawn was bathing the street in soft, after-storm light.

"Thank you so much, Collins. It was so nice to meet you. Tell Kate I will be in later today to check on her and help her get home," Tessa said, offering the older man a hug, which surprised him, and which he seemed happy to accept.

Jonas shook Collins's hand, and they waited as the car left.

"Well, at least the rain has stopped," he observed. "Where is the music coming from?"

"Looks like Lydia's having a party," she said, noting the candles and flashlights visible through the window of the tattoo parlor, and the sign in the window that announced a Blackout Party.

"Hey, where have you been?" a voice behind them asked, and Tessa turned to find her friend and neighbor Scott, who owned the deli across the street, walking toward them carrying a huge cooler.

"My friend Kate had a medical emergency," Tessa explained as Scott put the cooler down on the sidewalk. She gave him a hug and watched as he shook hands with Jonas. "It's been quite the adventure getting to her."

"How did you end up in scrubs?"

"We were soaked, so a nurse took pity on us."

"Nice. So your friend is okay?"

"Yes, we made it just in time, and she's fine. What's happening here?"

"They aren't predicting the power'll be back on until sometime tomorrow, so I had to use these cold cuts and salads before they went bad. Lydia had the idea to throw a blackout party for people around the neighborhood."

"Clever," Tessa said.

"Good to see you, too, Jonas. Wondered where you had gotten to, and was sorry to hear about your eyesight. Rotten break, but it's supposed to come back, right?" Scott asked, and Tessa saw Jonas straighten uncomfortably, nodding.

"Yes, that's what they're saying," Jonas confirmed briefly.

Tessa frowned. She should have told her friend Lydia to keep their previous conversation about Jonas private, but it was too late now.

"Come on in and have a sandwich or something. It's turned into a pretty good time," Scott said, picking up his cooler again.

"We just came from dinner, so—" Tessa started, but then Lydia appeared in her doorway, clapping excitedly.

"You're back, and you're okay! I'm so relieved. I went over to get you for the party, and the place was all closed up. I wondered where you'd got to," she said, and then smiling, noticed Jonas. "But now I can see you had other things to do."

Tessa rolled her eyes at her friend's unrestrained glee at seeing her with Jonas.

"We're really beat, Lydia," Tessa tried to beg off, but Lydia wasn't hearing any of it, and linked her arm through Jonas's, standing up on tiptoe to kiss his cheek.

She looked at Tessa and made a silent mime that Tessa could not quite decipher. She probably wanted all the details about her night with Jonas, knowing Lydia. Tessa nodded, letting her friend know she would catch up with her later.

Even Jonas's surly demeanor cracked at Lydia's happy welcome, and he offered her a kiss back.

Tessa knew he'd always enjoyed Lydia's visits, the two of them quipping and harassing each other like siblings.

Lydia didn't have any family, and Jonas didn't have any sisters. Tessa figured her friend enjoyed the brotherly back-and-forth she had developed with Jonas, and it gave Tessa yet another perspective on him, playing the big brother. She wondered what he was like with his own brothers, and hoped she'd have a chance to see them all together someday soon. If Jonas was interested in seeing her.

"Come on, it'll be fun." Scott led the way. "You can take some food for later."

Tessa laughed at her friend's insistence on pushing off his extra food and followed. Inside, she was greeted by several other business owners in the neighborhood as well as a few of the residential neighbors as music blasted from a speaker in the corner where someone had set up an iPod and food was set out everywhere.

Never one to miss a business opportunity, Lydia was also offering Blackout Special henna tats until the lights came back on.

"I have an opening. How about you let me paint you?" Lydia said to Tessa, catching Tessa staring at the sale sign on one of the food tables.

"No, thank you," she said.

"Jonas, don't you think Tessa should get a tat? I could do something very personal, and very tasteful... something only special people could see," Lydia said mischievously, and Tessa felt her cheeks heat.

"Lydia—" she warned.

"I think it could be fun," he said, surprising both women. "You game?" he asked Tessa.

"It's only henna," Lydia cajoled.

Tessa took good care of her skin. It was an important part of her business to show how well her products worked, but also to care for her health. She didn't sit in the sun for long periods of time and with no disrespect to her friend, had no interest in permanent ink. Still, she was feeling daring, and a temporary henna tat would be fun.

"Okay, why not?" she said. "I'll pick out yours, and you can tell Lydia what you want for me. We don't get to see until it's done."

Jonas looked slightly apprehensive. "No fair. I'm blind. I could end up walking around with who knows what on my forehead."

Tessa leaned in, feeling mischievous and whispered in his ear, "It wasn't your forehead I was thinking about," she teased, and then added, "I guess you'll have to trust me."

"Okay. I can do that," he said, and she knew they were talking to each other about far more than a tattoo.

"Actually, I think I have the perfect idea for both of you," Lydia said, and led them to the corner where she proceeded to sit them both down before her in comfortable chairs, and then grabbed a scarf from the shelf.

"Hey, what are you doing?" Tessa objected at first, as Lydia started to tie it around her eyes.

"It's supposed to be a surprise, right?"

"Lydia…"

"Trust me, Tessa."

Tessa sighed. It seemed to be the theme of her life at the moment, and she did trust Lydia, who winked at her as she tied the scarf around her face.

"This won't take long. It's a simple scroll, but it will work very well."

They listened to the music and conversations behind them then as Lydia worked, and Tessa laughed a few times, her palm tickling as Lydia painted there, and then turned her hand over, continuing.

"Um. I thought this would be small."

"It comes off in four to six weeks, Tessa. But you're going to like it, I promise."

Then she left Tessa to work on Jonas who was so quiet she thought maybe he had fallen asleep.

"There. Done!" Lydia pronounced, and Tessa wasn't sure she wanted to open her eyes, but when she did, she caught her breath in pleasure at the delicate scarlet-and-black scrolling that weaved its way around her hand and fingers, to the center of her palm, where it ended in a starburst.

She looked over to see Jonas grimacing. "Tell me she didn't paint flowers or kittens on my arms, please," he said.

Lydia snickered.

Tessa took his arm, and knew immediately what

Lydia had done, and she glanced up, meeting her friend's eyes.

Lydia shrugged. "It seemed right. You two fit," she said, echoing what Tessa had told Jonas earlier.

His was similar, but heavier, more manly, and also worked around his fingers, wrist and palm.

"You, uh, need to hold hands to really see how it comes together. It's a concept I developed while I was designing. You are the first ones I've tried it on. I call this one Completion."

Jonas shrugged and held out his hand, obviously disappointed that he couldn't see his. Tessa took it, and caught her breath. As their fingers wove together, their palms merging, so did the design. The scrolls connected into an intricate weave that created an entirely new design.

"Lydia, that's amazing…" Tessa breathed, and tried to explain it to Jonas, though she felt as if she couldn't do it justice. She wished so much he could see it, and said as much.

"Well, like I said, they last several weeks. And you said you had some signs your vision was coming back?" she asked Jonas.

"Yes."

"And you figure you'll be around in a few weeks?" Lydia asked baldly, to Tessa's horror.

He smiled. "Yeah, I hope so."

That made Tessa's heart stop.

"So there you go then." Lydia cleared her throat as they stood there, holding hands. "Okay, I'm going to go check on the party, and you guys can show off your tats, if you would, so it could drum up some business for me. You know, before you head upstairs to—"

"Lydia!" Tessa cut her friend off, laughing, and Lydia laughed, as well.

Gone, Tessa didn't let go of Jonas's hand as she went into his arms.

"I think you'll like it. It's very badass. Promise."

"Yeah, sounds like it," he said doubtfully, but found her lips and didn't seem overly concerned about the tattoo.

"I probably have soap that would remove it sooner than normal, if you like."

He squeezed her hand, and kissed her lightly. "I'm good with it. You want to mingle for a few minutes and then go upstairs?"

"Yeah. I'd like that."

Tessa wasn't sure she'd ever been this happy. Jonas seemed to have accepted that she wasn't his enemy, and more than that, he'd said he planned to be around. His sight was coming back, and he wanted to be with her.

Her father had tried to separate them, but fate had a different idea. Tessa was supposed to be with Jonas, she thought, looking down at how the designs on their hands merged into a perfect image that they showed off to guests who were suitably impressed.

They were together now, and she wouldn't let anything hurt them, least of all her father, she thought as they finally left the party and went back to her apartment, where she could have Jonas all to herself.

9

Norfolk, 6:00 a.m.

ELY STRETCHED ON the bed, twisted in sheets and slowly waking up to note he was alone in the bed. Then the sound of the shower filtered through his consciousness. He smiled, feeling satisfied and well used in the way only a night of great sex could offer.

Though it was more than sex this time, he acknowledged. He may not have been ready for more back when he first knew Chloe, but he was now.

He wanted something meaningful, something right, and he was amazed that it had been there all the while. He'd always imagined that he'd like to have a marriage, a home, just as his parents had. He'd just never found the woman he could imagine it with.

Or he had, and he'd almost lost her.

Swinging his legs over the side of the bed, he thought about joining Chloe in the shower.

Maybe in a minute.

Checking the clock, he realized he should probably touch base with his brothers. They'd been expecting him home the night before, but he could catch a flight back this morning, and be there by noon. After he talked with Chloe.

Finding his jeans pockets empty, he frowned, then smiled at the memory of the night before. His cell must have fallen in her car when they'd been fooling around.

Her landline was on the desk, and before calling his brothers, Ely decided to make reservations at a nice place down the road that served brunch. That way they could talk and make some plans. For the future.

He whistled as he opened drawers searching for a phone directory, only to find a diamond winking up at him. There was a flat card with writing under it—he looked, his hands cold. Picking it up, he read the delicate scroll, and then let it fall from his hands.

It was a wedding invitation.

Chloe was getting married. In four weeks.

He slammed the drawer shut, cursing under his breath. Clenching his fists in anger, he fought to gain control as the shower shut off.

He was a fool.

Opening the drawer again, he took out the ring to examine it more closely. Definitely an engagement ring. He set it on the dresser, carefully. Some poor slob had spent several months' pay on that rock.

Chloe came out from the shower, a towel wrapped loosely around her luscious form, her cheeks rosy. She was gorgeous as sin, but she wasn't the woman he thought she was. Not by a long shot.

"Beautiful ring your fiancé bought you—is that what you were stashing last night when we came back here?"

The color drained from her face, and her eyes

darkened so quickly he thought she might pass out, but then he recognized it was anger. At being caught.

"You went through my things?" she accused, her hands gripping the towel more tightly around herself.

"Not intentionally. I was going to make breakfast reservations, and had to use your phone since I dropped mine in the car last night while we were...well, you know what we were doing," he confessed. "Somehow I don't think it's my ethics that are in question here."

"You don't understand," she said, approaching him. "It was always you, but you didn't want anything permanent, you walked away. And I met him, Lance...and he reminded me of you. He's also a Marine. A good man."

"Then he deserves better than this," Ely said angrily. "How could you do this? So you used him because you couldn't have me, but then you screw around with me behind his back?"

"You're right, I know, I just...I planned to break it off with him, Ely. From the minute I saw you last night. That's why I took the ring off. So we can be together. I know I should have told you, but—"

"If you had told me, I never would have laid a hand on you," he said, feeling dirty, ashamed that he had been a part of this.

"I know. I'm sorry. But can't we just go from here? What we have together is so good. We're right together," she said, looking up into his eyes. She put a hand on his chest, and he stepped back, breaking the contact.

Ely stared at her as if he'd never really seen her before, and admitted that he didn't know her. Not really. He had only imposed his own perfect image of the woman he wanted, not the real woman she was.

"No, Chloe, nothing about this is right. It was a

fantasy I had, but that's over now. Whatever you do, have a nice life." He strode to the door, shaking his head at himself that he had even considered a future with her or with anyone.

"Ely, no—" she called after him desperately, but he was dressed and already gone.

BACK IN HER APARTMENT, Tessa was joyfully preparing to experience a fantasy she'd been harboring about Jonas for weeks. She turned on the hot water and sprinkled something in the tub that immediately infused the air around them with a sultry, spicy scent.

"What is that?" he asked, kissing and nuzzling as he pulled her scrubs off as she undressed him, too.

"Gardenia musk bath oil. It's part of my new erotic collection."

"I can't say I'm one for scented baths, but I don't think I care so long as it's you and me in there," he said with a chuckle, letting his hands drift over every curve of her body.

"Here, let me help you in. Be careful," she said, stepping into the deep bath and helping him get in safely, as well.

Her tub was huge. He'd always teased her about it, why one small woman needed such a large tub, but it made sense for someone in her line of business, he supposed.

He had also secretly fantasized about sharing it with her.

He sank back into the hot water with a groan.

"Feels good?"

"Everything with you feels good."

They relaxed into the heat, and she wanted to keep hearing him talk, liking the sound of his voice.

"Tell me about your brothers," she said as she washed his shoulders.

"You met Garrett?"

"Definitely," she said, unable to repress a sigh.

Jonas laughed. "I take it he was a brick wall?"

"That's putting it mildly. I don't think he approves of me," she said, the dark and the tenor of the conversation drawing out a need to confess. "I feel awful that I distracted you, Jonas. I know you might not have lost your sight if it weren't for me."

"He doesn't think that. Hell, *I* don't think that. I was the one who lost focus. I can't blame you for that," he said.

"I still feel responsible, at least in part. I didn't take my father's concerns seriously enough. We put up with that kind of thing all the time growing up, and it never came to anything. I guess I never really thought anything would actually happen."

"That's why I was there. You weren't supposed to worry about it. I let you down, Tessa. You and your father," he said insistently.

She didn't comment. She never felt as if he'd let her down until that morning, when he told her he thought she'd used him.

"Gare does like you, actually," Jonas said, though she wasn't sure if he was just being polite. "But, in order, from youngest to oldest, it's Chance, Ely, me and then Garrett. Chance is the only one who inherited my mom's light coloring. The rest of us are dark, like Dad. Chance is the risk-taker. When we were kids, we thought we were picking on him by hiding his favorite stuff in the tree out in our backyard and making him climb up to get it, but he loved it. He was never afraid of anything," Jonas said with clear affection in his voice.

"And Ely?"

"He's the ex-Marine—though every time I say that, he'll say, 'There are no ex-Marines,'" Jonas mimicked. "Ely is the quiet one, the strategist. Garrett is the prototypical big brother. He thinks it's his job to watch over us all."

"And which are you? How do you place yourself in that lineup?"

"I've never really thought about it."

"Can I take a stab at it?"

"Sure."

"I think you're the loner. You may not be the oldest, but you're the one who takes the heaviest load on yourself, and you don't like to bother anyone to help you carry it."

"That's a romantic notion," he said, sounding uncomfortable.

"Not at all. I didn't say it was a good thing. Everyone needs help sometimes, dealing with life's burdens. But you think you can carry them alone," she said bluntly.

"Garrett was saying something similar. Maybe it's true, but it's who I am."

"Losing your sight must have been even more challenging in that respect, making you depend on others for a change. Like having to call me when you hurt your foot."

He was quiet for a few beats, and she wondered what he was thinking.

What Jonas was thinking was how he was in way too deep, and how he had really messed this up. He was falling for Tessa—hard—and his being here was a lie, at least to an extent.

He was a coward. He hadn't told her about her father's

call because he knew it would be the end for them. But he had to make things right.

He'd take this time with her, right now, and then he'd go, he knew, feeling her hands slip over him. He wasn't strong enough to leave now, but soon. And he'd make it right, he vowed to himself, one way or another.

"Sit up a bit," she said, and they maneuvered so that she was on her knees behind him.

"What are you doing?"

"I have some massage oil you're going to love," she told him, and the same scent that was in the bath was suddenly twice as pungent as her hands made their way expertly over his back and shoulders, massaging and working each muscle individually.

"Wow, you're good at that," he sighed, his heart aching while his body sang. "I don't care what scent it is, just don't stop."

"I love touching you," she said close to his ear.

He felt her breasts press into his back as her arms reached around and held him in a curiously tender gesture.

"I love you touching me," he said roughly.

A second later she was sitting in between his thighs, and she took his hand, putting some oil into his palm.

"Do me," she said sexily, and he groaned.

"With pleasure."

He did as she did, smoothing the oil everywhere, seeking out any tension, knots or spots that he could massage to tenderness, slipping around the front to do the same to her breasts. He ran his hands over her to memorize every inch of her, hoping that when all was said and done, this wouldn't be the last time he touched her.

"I don't think I can ever take a bath alone again," she said, leaning back against him.

"Time to get out?" he asked, kissing her neck.

"Absolutely," she purred in a vixen voice that turned him on even more.

She handed him a towel and helped him out. Somehow, having Tessa assist him didn't bother him as much now. He didn't feel needy or dependent, but connected. And any excuse to touch her was okay with him. They dried each other, touching and driving each other crazy in the process.

"Bedroom," Jonas growled as she licked a straight path down his chest in a straight line to his erection.

"Come with me."

They walked in hand in hand, and Jonas found his way to the bed, sliding up to sit on the pillows, wondering why she didn't join him.

"What are you doing?"

Then she was there, straddling him and rubbing her finger along his lips.

"Taste."

He did, licking his lip and then sucking her finger into his mouth.

"Mmm. Sweet."

"It's my signature honey dust...you like?"

"I like how you taste with or without it, but it's very nice, yes," he said, tired of talking.

He pulled her closer, his mouth tracing a trail of the dust from the pulse at her throat to the tip of her breast, where he tasted deeply, drawing on her nipple until she was whimpering.

"Oh, you are tasty," he murmured.

"It's for both of us," she said, her voice trembling

as she lifted, and the next thing Jonas felt was a light, tickling sensation that made his cock surge.

"What—"

"More honey dust—applied with the feather that comes with every jar. So I can taste you," she said.

His mind blanked as her tongue was the next thing he felt, licking and darting out to taste until he was strained to the limit and fighting for control.

"Please, Tessa," he said, unsure how much more he could take.

"Oh, I do like that," she said in a sultry tone, dragging her nails up and down his thighs. "So sexy, Jonas."

She took him whole then, making his entire body arch off the bed.

"That's enough, you vixen," he said, and she laughed as he pulled her up and over him.

He loved her laugh.

"I never imagined this side of you," he said, enjoying how she took control. "I like it."

"There's so much more, Jonas. I like to play," she said as she rolled the condom over his erection with warm, loving hands before settling herself over him.

"I need you," she said, meaning every word as she took him inside with a sigh.

Jonas couldn't speak, the perfection of it robbing him of words. If only he could see her, it would be perfect, but he could imagine her blond curls riotous, her cheeks flushed, lips red from sucking him. Her hands planted on his chest as she moved, and he could picture her breasts moving as she did.

"So good," she whispered, rocking gently until she started to make the soft crying sounds he loved.

He covered her breasts with his hands and then dived in to lick away the rest of the sweet dust, sucking at her tender skin until she rocked faster, her cries becoming louder. His breath came in short panting bursts, his body feeling like a bow strung too tight.

"Yeah, sweetheart," he crooned and pushed his hips up as she rocked over him. She planted her hands on his shoulders, finding the rhythm she needed, and he held her hips, jackhammering up to meet her as they both lost any sense of control, pushed over the edge of a hard, simultaneous orgasm that left them shaking and panting as she fell against his chest, their bodies still deeply joined.

"More," was all he said, easing her over to her stomach and lifting her hips, positioning her on all fours before him. He felt primal, possessive, taking her this way.

"Tessa, you are every man's fantasy come to life," he said, running his hands over her completely, teasing every inch of her.

"I only want to be yours."

Regret and need for her warred inside him, and he pressed his face against her back where he trailed kisses down her spine, making her shiver as his fingers did delightful things between her legs. She was slick from her first orgasm and his touch, and yet she needed more, too.

"Please, Jonas," she begged shamelessly, sighing in sheer happiness as he slid inside, burying himself deep in response to her request.

"You're perfect, Tessa," he said reverently, still touching her back, her thighs, until his hands rested on her hips as he thrust faster.

Jonas massaged her perfect ass as he moved inside her, then reached down to circle his fingers around the slick, hot nub in a way that would drive her crazy.

"Jonas, oh...yes," she managed to breathe, easing back against him for more, which he was happy to provide. His balls pulled tight, feeling full and heavy, his body hot.

"Come for me, Tess, again," he said raggedly, increasing the tempo until every muscle inside fisted around him, clenching and releasing as they both shouted out their mutual release.

They rode it out, not wanting to stop until they fell back to the bed.

Tessa burrowed into his chest as his arms came around her, hugging her in close. They nestled and nuzzled, lost in a cocoon of intimacy that closed out the rest of the world.

JONAS KNEW WHAT HE had to do, but it was the hardest thing he'd ever contemplated. Previously, he thought leaving the police force had been the hardest decision of his life, but it didn't even come close to leaving Tessa.

He wanted to do nothing more than go back to her, to lie in her arms and wake up with her, but he couldn't. Not until this mess was straightened out.

Jonas liked James, or thought he did. Listening to Tessa's stories about how he'd wrecked her relationships and tried to keep her from starting her business—what kind of parent did that?

Jonas's father and mother had encouraged all the boys to be who they were, regardless. Hard work, discipline, loyalty—these were the things that counted. How they dressed, who their friends were, what they wanted to do with their lives—Jonas's parents never put any obstacles in their way. They still lived in the family home in Fishtown, and Jonas saw them regularly, not only for holidays.

But more importantly, Jonas had to step away before he did further damage. He couldn't be Rose's weapon of choice anymore, and certainly not when it came to Tessa.

She probably wouldn't want anything to do with him when she found out, but that was how it was. He'd brought it on himself. All he could do was tell her the truth and let the chips fall where they may.

Feeling around on her kitchen counter, he knew she kept notepaper by the phone, and found that and a pen.

Swallowing hard, he wrote:

Tessa: I didn't mean to lie to you. Not really. It was part of the job. I never expected to fall for you—that wasn't part of the job, either. I know it was wrong for us to be together when I am still working for your father, but I want you to know, what happened between us last night was real. I hope you can forgive me someday,
Love,
Jonas

He scrawled out the message and left the paper on the table, and picked up the phone to call his brother.

As he dialed, Jonas gasped, the pain in his head nearly doubling him over. The room spun, and he gripped the edge of the counter, and to his amazement, he saw it—saw it all. The marble pattern of the counter, the ray of sunlight cutting across his hands, the note with his crooked scrawl on it.

Then darkness again as his stomach lurched, nausea and disorientation turning his hands cold.

His vision was returning? Like this? His hands shook

as he tried to grab at the phone, but missed. He needed to call Garrett, but the headache was debilitating.

Sliding to the floor, he never did make that call.

10

9:00 a.m.

TESSA WOKE UP alone, and lay still in bed, smiling. The night before had been like some kind of wild fantasy, traversing the city by all means available, and ending up here, with the man of her dreams in her arms.

Her body ached in a delicious way from their lovemaking, and she stretched, yawning and wishing he was here with her so she could curl around him and go back to sleep. Yeah, right. Sleep wasn't exactly what she wanted right at the moment.

Where was Jonas? Peeking at the clock, she saw it had only been about an hour, and she wondered what he was up to. She didn't hear the shower or anyone moving around. In fact, it was too quiet.

Concerned, she got up and grabbed a robe from her dresser, padding into the other room. Nothing there.

Then she heard a groan and walked quickly to the kitchen where she gasped in fright, finding Jonas sitting on the floor, holding his head.

"Oh, my God, Jonas," she said, rushing to his side as he slumped down to the floor, his face white.

"Call my brother," he said weakly, not sounding at all like himself. She could see he was in terrible pain.

Tessa called emergency first, and then his office, hoping to hell someone was there.

"Berringer Security," a man's voice answered.

"This is Tessa Rose—is this Garrett?"

"It is," Garrett said, sounding wary.

"I'm calling for your brother Jonas—"

"Is he okay? I just got into the office, and the place looks like a wrecking ball hit it. The first-aid kid is out, and I've been calling the hospitals, since he isn't answering his phone—"

"He's with me," she said, interrupting. "He's been with me all night, but I don't know if he's okay. I've called the paramedics. I found him here on my kitchen floor, and he's holding his head, and somewhat incoherent."

"Are they there yet?"

"I hear the sirens now."

"I'll meet you at St. Mark's Medical, and I'll call his doctor. You take care of him, Tessa."

"I will."

She didn't see the slip of paper on the counter until she hung up the phone, and scanned it quickly.

Her heart broke, and she forced away tears. Jonas had been leaving her? With a note?

And he had been lying to her?

Now was not the time for this. Pushing the pain and the anger aside, she kneeled by Jonas and took his hand. His skin was cold, clammy, and worry clashed with the other emotions that rocked her.

"It'll be okay, they're coming, and Garrett is meeting

us at the hospital," she reassured, even as she looked up at the counter again, seeing the note, as if to confirm she'd actually seen it, and not just imagined it.

He'd been working for her father? How? Why?

Dozens of questions erupted, none of which could have answers while she sat here with him.

Paramedics knocked hard at the downstairs door, and she raced to meet them. Just a few minutes later, they were taking Jonas to the hospital, and she was left standing in the kitchen in her robe, staring at the note.

Daylight glared through the window, but she barely noticed, numb to her core.

No doubt her exhaustion had something to do with magnifying her feelings, but her disappointment and hurt that Jonas had deceived her was cutting deep.

Right now she couldn't indulge that pain. She needed to go to the hospital and at least make sure he was okay. Then she'd come back here and nurse her own wounds.

It was a particular form of self-torture, but she reached for the note, staring at it.

She felt stupid, used and vulnerable. Was that how he had felt when he thought she had done the same to him? Was it really a job, or was this just revenge?

Putting aside the pity party, she padded into the shower, heart heavy, needing to wash his scent from her body, but at the same time, it was so incredibly painful to do so. She wanted him to come back. To hold her.

Jonas didn't want her. He was only doing a job.

She'd been so sure that they had something perfect, something incredible.

It was only sex, she thought morosely, pausing before she turned on the water, giving in to tears. The last eighteen hours or so seemed like a dream. One that had left her with a rude awakening.

She soaked herself beneath the spray as tears flowed. She'd allow herself a few minutes to cry over what she'd thought was something wonderful, but promised herself that after she left the shower, she wouldn't waste one more tear on him.

She squeezed a fragrant honey-almond liquid soap on her loofah, and washed as if intent on scrubbing his touch from her skin. That brought on more tears. It would be some time before she could forget how he'd touched her, and how she'd responded.

But she would, eventually.

Getting out of the shower, she wanted only to go to bed, to lose herself in sleep where she wouldn't have to think about any of it, but, she had to get dressed and go to the hospital. In spite of it all, she had to know if he was all right. As she dropped the towel, her phone rang.

News about Jonas? She looked at the caller ID and saw her father's number on the screen.

Her anger flared anew, and she answered.

"Hello, Dad," she said tersely.

"Hello, sweetheart. I was calling to make sure you're okay."

"Just drop the act, Senator." She knew he hated it when she called him that.

"What's going on, Tessa?"

He had the gall to act exasperated, as if she was being unreasonable.

"Why would you be worried? You hired Jonas to babysit me until you got back, right?"

Her father sighed heavily. "He told you?"

"Yes, though not everything. Don't ever do that to me again," she said, her voice breaking.

"Honey, what's wrong? What did he do?"

"He didn't do anything," she sobbed.

Just broke her heart in two—the both of them together had done that, her father and Jonas.

"He's at the hospital, St. Mark's. I think something is happening with his vision, but it didn't seem right. I found him barely conscious on my kitchen floor," she said, unable to stop tears from springing forth, and hating it.

"I'm on my way back there now. I'll be arriving in an hour or so. You stay where you are."

He cut the call before she could say goodbye, and hung up. She was dazed and tired down to her bones, but she had to get to the hospital. Dressing quickly, she heard more knocking at her front door, rushed to answer.

She found Lydia, looking frantic.

"I saw paramedics taking someone out—what's going on?"

"It's Jonas. I don't know, something was wrong with his head. I just found him here," she said, and burst into tears again.

Lydia hugged her, and dug out a wad of tissues from her purse. "Oh, honey, it will be okay. Let me get my car, I'll drive, and you tell me what's going on, okay?"

Tessa nodded, relieved to have one person she could count on in her life. Lydia had never let her down. Maybe she should have listened more closely to her friend, who was a classic commitmentphobe. Lydia had several lovers, and didn't believe in getting too attached to any of them. Tessa attributed that to her rather rough upbringing, mostly in foster homes, but she also knew that Lydia was into some kinky stuff, sexually speaking.

Way more than Tessa ever experienced.

None of that mattered. How her friend ran her sex life wasn't Tessa's concern. Lydia had always been there for her, and that's what mattered. In fact, Lydia was like the sister Tessa had never had.

As they made their way to the hospital, she told Lydia all of it, and her friend shook her head in disbelief.

"I can't believe he would do that. Why? It's clear he's crazy about you—why not just tell you the truth?"

"He was obviously more worried about upsetting my father than he was about being honest with me," Tessa said dully as they got into an elevator at the hospital. "I guess it's good to know where his loyalties lie."

"I think you all need to sit down and talk once this is over, and we know he's okay. It sounds to me like there's a lot of confusion in the air, and you can't make any assumptions until it's all out."

"It's pretty clear, Lydia. He left me a note—he was leaving."

"And you said he told you he cared, and that what happened between you was real. Hold on to the good things, Tessa, not just the bad."

Tessa grumbled something and yawned as the doors opened in front of the nurses' station.

They got the information for Jonas's room, and he was permitted visitors.

"I don't know. Maybe this isn't a good idea," Tessa said, stopping halfway down the hall.

Lydia took her hand. "You have to see him to make sure he's okay, at least. Then we can go, okay?"

Tessa nodded, her stomach in knots. She was worried sick about him on top of everything else, and Lydia was right. She had to make sure he was okay before she could let herself be angry with him.

They walked down to the room, where a nurse came out, her cheeks flushed, eyes bright. She smiled at Tessa and Lydia.

"Is this Jonas Berringer's room?"

"Oh, yes," the young nurse said, giggling, her cheeks flushed.

Lydia rolled her eyes at Tessa, but they soon found out what had the young woman so flustered.

Walking into the private room where Jonas was sitting up in bed, looking none too happy in a hospital gown, Tessa saw why the young woman was so worked up.

"Oh, my," Lydia said, seeming flustered herself.

Four big men filled the room, standing around Jonas's bedside. There was so much testosterone that Tessa could have bottled it and made soap. All the male gazes turned to look at them.

One she recognized as Garrett, and from Jonas's descriptions, could guess which ones were Ely and Chance, though she didn't know the fourth.

"Tessa," Jonas said, and she realized after a second that he had turned to see her.

He could *see* her.

She lifted a hand to her mouth, her eyes flooding.

"Jonas, you can see me?" she said, awed.

He nodded. "Mostly. Everything is still kind of fuzzy around the edges, and shapes are blurring together, but yeah, I can see you," he confirmed. "Or a blob that more or less looks like you."

"You sure know how to talk up the ladies, Jonas," one of his brothers, the one she assumed was Chance, teased.

They looked at each other for several long minutes, until someone cleared his throat.

"Jonas, there's no need for you to stay. The initial pain and dizziness you experienced was normal, if uncomfortable," the man Tessa didn't know explained.

His doctor, obviously.

Jonas said, grimacing, "You're telling me."

"The meds I gave you should take care of that. You just had too much blood surging to that area of your brain as the vessels opened up," he explained.

Another of his brothers made some sideways comment about that being surprising, as they thought it would have all been elsewhere.

Jonas threw his brothers a dirty look, and then nodded to the doctor. "Thanks, Matt."

He met Tessa's eyes again, and Garrett spoke up. "Okay, I guess we can maybe go get a cup of coffee while Tessa and Jon talk," he said, almost pushing his younger brothers out of the room.

They all smiled at Tessa and Lydia on their way out, and Tessa noticed Lydia's gaze had not wandered far from Ely.

"Mind if I join you? I don't think I'm needed here, either," she said, introducing herself to the men as they all exited the room, leaving Tessa and Jonas together.

Tessa inched farther into the room.

"Close the door?"

"Okay," she agreed.

When she turned back to him, she didn't know what to say. It was all too much to process.

"I can't believe you're here. That you came," he said.

"I had to know that you were all right. You scared the life out of me," she admitted.

Among other things.

"I'm sorry, Tessa."

"For what? For thinking I used you? For lying to me? For not telling me you were working with my father? For leaving me with a *note?*" she accused, pacing back and forth by the bed, the emotions flooding back. "God, Jonas…it's no wonder you didn't think we have any chance together. You were undermining us at every turn."

"I know," he said, and seemed to struggle to say anything else.

Silence loomed between them.

"I thought your brothers were out of town," she said, needing to say something.

"Ely was already on his way back, and I guess Garrett called Chance as soon as he was off the phone with you, and he was also on his way back from New York. Not necessary, but—"

"They're your brothers."

She realized then that his choices didn't just have to do with his loyalty to her father, but his loyalty to his family, as well.

No doubt he was worried about how her father's displeasure would affect their agency, and she couldn't completely blame him for that, but at the same time, she wondered where she fit in. He seemed as if he was willing to hurt her before any of the rest.

Not a glowing start for a relationship.

"Can you come closer, Tessa? It's still hard for me to make out faces at a distance. Or even up close for that matter," he added dryly.

She walked to the side of the bed, and her heart stuttered at the sight of the tattoo on his hand. The other half of hers.

"Was it all a lie? A game? Last night, did you really even fall and hurt yourself? Or was that just a way to get me to come to you?" She felt like a fool as it was.

He shook his head. "Both. I knew it wasn't a good idea to take your father up on his request, but I also couldn't say no."

"Why?"

"Because I owed him for messing up the first time, and because it would allow me to see you again. Because I was worried about you being alone if something was wrong. I was trying to convince myself that you had been using me, and this was just an opportunity to set things right with your father. But it was all an excuse to be with you."

"You were worried about your agency."

"That, too. Your father's aide made it clear that there would be repercussions if I saw you again."

"Howie?"

"Yeah. So I kept my distance. And then, there you were in my apartment yesterday, and…I wanted you. I hadn't been able to stop thinking about you for a minute after the night of the attack."

"So why didn't you tell me that?"

"I didn't trust your motives," he admitted, shaking his head. "I had been through it once before. Fell in love with someone back when I was on the force, and it went bad. Really bad. I found out she was using me just to get information. It nearly got people killed. It was why I left the force."

"So you saw me as doing the same thing?"

"Sort of. I had screwed up once in my past, and people suffered for my mistake. I didn't want that to happen again. I tried to talk myself into believing it was your fault, but I think that was because in the end, I really was afraid you'd never really be interested in me for the long run. That it was just a fling."

"What, some kind of bodyguard-fantasy thing?"

"It happens," he said flatly, and she assumed he had some experience in that area, too.

Jealousy flared in her chest. She didn't like to think about women he guarded coming on to him, and remembered their earlier conversation about his work.

Maybe she wouldn't handle that all as coolly as she imagined.

"Well, I don't know what to do, Jonas. I...care about you. A lot. But it hurt so much to find that note."

"I was trying to do the right thing. I assumed once you knew, you'd want me gone. I couldn't blame you for that."

"You didn't even give me a chance. Just like he does, you just made my decisions for me," she said, throwing her arms up and walking away, then back to the bed.

It was painful being this close to him and not being able to touch, even though her heart was bruised and her mind wary.

"You're right. I didn't. I don't know, Tessa. I've never felt this way about anyone, and I don't know how to deal with it."

Tessa was torn. Everything he said now helped her understand, but she didn't know if she could trust him again—what about the next time he felt he had to keep information from her, or he lied to her to "protect" her?

She was tired of being manipulated and controlled by the men in her life, and how they always seemed to think it was for her own good.

"I don't know either, Jonas. I...I thought I loved you, but now I don't know if I really knew you. Maybe it was only sex," she said, and jumped when his hand reached out to grab hers.

Tessa caught her breath, looking down at how the scrolls Lydia had painted on them entangled, completed each other.

She was so confused.

"No, it wasn't just that. I know I don't deserve another chance, Tessa, but I'd like a chance to do this right. To show you that I...I think I love you, too."

Tears welled and dropped down onto their hands where they were clasped together on the bed, and she couldn't find anything else to say.

She wanted to believe him more than anything, but she didn't know who she could trust anymore. For the moment, she just stayed there, quiet, and held his hand. She was afraid that if she let go, there'd be no going back.

IN THE HOSPITAL'S WAITING lounge, Ely sat with his brothers, waiting for Jonas to emerge from his room. It was taking some time. He was willing to wait, relieved that his brother was going to be okay. Garrett and Chance were in the corner talking about the job Chance had just returned from, and Ely was just...waiting.

He didn't have all the details, but Ely only needed to look at his older brother's face when Tessa had come in. Jonas had fallen, and fallen hard.

He'd also screwed up royally, by the looks of it. Not that Ely had anything to brag about in that area.

"It gives the phrase 'get a room' a whole new meaning," Tessa's friend, Lydia, said, from her seat beside him as she glanced back at the door.

Ely had to chuckle. Lydia was...different. Not his

type, not by a long shot, but she was nice enough. And funny.

"Yeah, I guess Jonas had some explaining to do."

"I hope they work it out. They really are perfect together, even though I don't buy into the whole soulmates thing. I have a feeling Tessa is just what your brother needs in his life," Lydia said. "Some people can make it work."

Ely watched the length of the tattoo that seemed to move as she lifted her hand, bringing coffee to lips that sported one piercing at the edge. His gaze landed on the tiny moon at the corner of her mouth.

She slanted her eyes up. "Yes?"

He broke the stare. "Sorry. Just admiring your tattoos."

Or wondering at them, he thought. He had one tat on his shoulder blade. It was something he did as a right of passage in the Marines, but Lydia's practically covered every inch of her skin. He wondered if that was literally true, tracing the inked patterns that dipped beneath her clothing, and realized he was staring again.

"Sorry, again," he said, meeting her quizzical gaze.

She grinned, apparently not offended at all. "No problem. I get that a lot."

He imagined that was true.

Her black hair hung to her shoulders like a satin sheet, her skin pale, but covered in ink. Her eyes, though… they sparkled with humor. And mischief.

"Did you do all that ink yourself?"

"Some of it. What I could reach anyway," she said with a wink.

Ely wasn't quite sure what else to say as Lydia grabbed his arm and directed his attention to the news on the TV in the corner. When she popped up and ran to turn up the volume, he couldn't help but notice what a sleek little body she had, though the black lace and leather she wore didn't hide a whole lot.

When she backed away from the television, Ely stiffened, feeling as if he had just been punched in the gut.

Chloe's face filled the screen.

She looked, as always, perfect. Makeup hid any shadows that might have cropped up under her eyes from the night before, and when she peered into the camera, she might as well have been looking directly at him.

"You know her," Lydia said. A statement, not a question. She was observant, and Ely knew he was not easy to read. That came with his training.

"Not well," he answered, and it was the truth.

They all turned their attention to the broadcast of the arrests being made in the Senate and House, a total of fifteen aides taken into custody in an embezzlement scam that was rocking the Hill.

The aides were all highly placed, and were privy to some of the most secret information handled by their official's offices. There was speculation about the selling of secrets as well as misdirecting funds.

Ely was rapt, watching as Chloe delivered the news. She didn't miss a beat. She was also wearing her ring. Maybe Lance would fare better than he had. He hoped so.

"Wow, that's huge. I can believe that slimeball Stanton was involved, though. He's come by the store a few times and he always gave me the creeps," Lydia said, shuddering. "He wanted me to schedule him for a tat, and I refused. There was always something about him."

"People are not always what they seem," Ely said,

feeling as if he'd been shaken out of a trance as Chloe's image disappeared from the screen.

When he looked up, he raised an eyebrow as he recognized the formidable figure of Senator Rose walking by the waiting room, heading toward Jonas's door.

Ely met Garrett's gaze across the room; he noticed, as well.

"Think we should go give Jonas some backup?" Ely asked.

Garrett shook his head. "Let them figure it all out."

Lydia had pulled her knees up to her chin on the chair, and he was again distracted by the ink that flowed down her slim legs, peeking out from under the edge of the tights she wore, that stretched only midthigh.

Everything about her was firm and lithe, and she turned her eyes to his to catch him staring, again.

She smiled, looking a lot like a cat who would like to lick the dish clean.

"I could use another cup of coffee. You want to walk down with me?" she asked.

"Sure. I could use another cup myself. It's been a long couple of days," he elaborated unnecessarily, but there was something about the small Goth woman that threw him.

It was unusual. Maybe he was losing his touch in civilian life—he'd been completely taken in by Chloe, and now Lydia was making him feel unsteady, as well.

He watched as she unfolded herself from the seat, though at full height, and even in the clunky, black platform shoes she wore, the top of her head was barely level with his chin.

They paused outside the waiting room and watched

as the senator knocked on Jonas's door and then disappeared inside the room.

"The suspense is killing me," Lydia said, nibbling at a nail that was painted black. Delicate, inked vines trailed down her slim fingers.

"C'mon, let's go get that coffee," Ely said, putting his hand to her shoulder, and he registered a shock of surprise at his response to the softness of her inked skin, and how small she felt, as well as strong.

Her eyes met his, and there was heat there.

He pulled his hand back. After what he went through with Chloe the night before, he wasn't getting involved with anyone again for a long time, let alone someone who was clearly so...odd.

He was sure his response was just some kind of backlash from his disappointment the night before—and that wasn't fair to Lydia, either, who seemed like a perfectly nice person.

She was also Tessa's friend, and with any luck, Tessa would be part of their family one day soon.

Ely pasted on a polite smile and made a promise to himself to stop staring at the strangely attractive woman who stepped inside the elevator with him. Unlike his brother, he learned his lessons the first time.

11

11:00 a.m.

"MAY I INTERRUPT?" a voice intruded from behind, and Tessa turned as they saw her father come inside.

"Dad," she said, and Jonas felt the sting of it as she wrenched her hand from his.

"Sir," he said as well, but more cautiously. Why was Rose here?

"They said you have some of your sight back, Jonas. That's good news," James said, walking up close to the bed and hugging his daughter. Tessa didn't hug him back.

Jonas couldn't make out faces well enough to see Tessa's reaction, but she didn't say anything.

"I'm fine, Senator. You didn't need to come."

James Rose sighed, sounding very tired. "Do you mind if I pull up a chair? It was a long flight, and unlike you young guns, this old man can't go twenty-four hours at a time."

He saw Tessa move then, pulling a chair up for her father, who sat.

"Truth is, I should have come the first time you were in the hospital, that night of the attack. Maybe that would have solved a lot of problems. This time, I needed to make sure I could help clarify what was going on for you two," he said, though Jonas didn't know what he was talking about.

"I think we're clear, Dad," Tessa said. "You threatened Jonas's business if he came near me again, accusing him of failing to protect me the first time. Then you used my attraction to him to have him watch me last night, too, but why? Why would you do such a thing to us?" she asked, her voice quavering.

"Ah, I'm so sorry, Tessie. I take it you haven't seen the news yet?"

They shook their heads, mystified. What did the news have to do with anything?

"It's a grand mess, and I only heard about it all yesterday morning," he started, and then filled them in on the embezzlement scam, and Howie's part in it. "It's why I had to cut my trip short and come back. This will take some sorting out."

"So you sent Jonas to stay with me? Why? It's not like I was involved," Tessa said, and Jonas couldn't figure out the connection, either.

"There's more than the news made known. I got some of my people on the job as soon as I was told, and they discovered something...disturbing. I have enough information to suggest that Howie orchestrated the attack on you the night Jonas lost his sight," the senator said with a sigh. "He paid off the guy who broke in. There's a money trail."

"But why?"

"It's my fault. It's *all* my fault, actually," James said, sounding tired and old in a way that surprised Jonas.

It must have surprised Tessa, too, as he saw her draw closer to her father.

"What do you mean?"

"You know I pushed Howie in your direction, Tessa. I thought he would be a good match, though it was obvious you didn't even like the man. He made it quite clear to me that he wanted to ask you out, however, and at the time, I thought he was a reliable, solid kind of guy. He'd been with my office for almost three years."

"So you think he attacked us because he was… jealous?"

"Well, I don't think he was in love with you, no offense, Tessie, but I think he wanted to get in as close to me as he could. He was like the lot of them, power hungry, and willing to do anything to get it. Steal, resort to criminal activity, even. I was fool enough not to see what was happening under my nose. I think he viewed Jonas as a threat to that—noticed the attraction you two had."

Jonas thought about what the aide had said to him at his bedside that night. Howie Stanton had obviously been the one manipulating the situation, not Tessa or her father.

Jonas was suddenly very angry at himself—if he had not jumped to conclusions and just believed what he was told, maybe he could have found that out sooner. But then he remembered James's phone call—it seemed to confirm his beliefs about what was going on.

His head started to ache slightly, and he took a deep breath.

"So how much of what he said to me that night was true?"

"Well, I wasn't happy to hear what happened, of course. Though Howie played me, too, and made it all sound much more salacious than it was—hopefully, anyway," he said, looking at Jonas.

Jonas couldn't see his expression clearly, but felt the weight of it. He was starting to speak, when Tessa interrupted.

"There was nothing salacious about what happened between me and Jonas," she said hotly. "And it was my fault, not Jonas's. I had been trying to get him to notice me. To respond to me. But he was so...businesslike. Then that night, things just...happened. But I didn't do it to lure him in, or to get back at you. I know you probably don't believe that, either of you, but it's true."

"You think I was angry at him because you two had...an attraction to each other? I don't care about that," her father claimed.

"Then why?" Jonas asked.

"I fired you because you didn't do your job, Jonas. You didn't protect her, and you could have been killed! Both of you," he added. "I wasn't thinking straight, and I knew if I went to the hospital, I'd say things I might regret. But I never told Howie to level any kind of threat, and I wasn't angry that you and Tessa were attracted to each other. I never forbade you to see her."

Jonas didn't detect anything but sincerity in the senator's voice.

"I let you down. I put her in danger, and you're right about that," admitted Jonas, understanding how the aide had manipulated things to his own ends. "I should have spoken to you directly, sir. I'm sorry about that, about assuming the worst about you, and about Tessa. I hope this hasn't damaged our friendship too severely."

"Well, the girl did have a history of liking to rub things in my face," the senator said. "But if you hurt her, I—"

Tessa huffed, inserting herself into the fray.

"Hello? I'm sitting right here? It's all very well and good how you two are making nice, but what about me? I don't care if you think you are protecting me, or whatever other rationalizations you have to tell yourselves. None of this was right. It doesn't excuse either of you lying to me," she said angrily.

"You're right, of course, Tessie. It's hard to change an old dog. I hope you believe it when I tell you, I was trying to do the right thing, but I just made things worse, apparently," James said.

"What do you mean?" Tessa asked suspiciously.

"I was worried about the story breaking, not that I thought you were in any direct danger. But I knew things had gone bad between you and Jonas, that you weren't speaking. At first, I thought that was because Jonas was irked about me firing him, and taking it out on you. But then I was put in the picture about this whole scandal possibly breaking, and it was a chance for me to try to make amends. It made sense that Jonas was the only one who you would let close, so I used that to get you two...together again."

Jonas and Tessa were shocked silent for a few minutes, until Tessa stuttered.

"Are you saying...you were...*matchmaking?*"

"Well, I don't know about that. But I was aware you were miserable when he wouldn't see you, and that was my fault. I didn't know how Howie had interjected the rest, until I learned about the scam. I thought, if I could get you together, just for a night, or a few hours, and if nature took its course...then maybe you would be all right."

"Nature taking its course?" Tessa squeaked, and

Jonas also settled back against the bed pillows, absorbing this new information.

"So you were never out to drive us apart? You were trying to...push us together?" Jonas asked, finding it hard to believe.

"That's the gist of it, yes. But when I spoke to Tessa earlier, before I landed, it was clear it hadn't gone well, because she found out I was involved. I knew that would anger her, and not put you in a good position, either," James said to Jonas.

Jonas shook his head, incredulous.

"I don't know what to say," he said honestly, seeing the senator stand.

"I do," Tessa said, standing and gathering her purse.

"I'm so tired of all this. Of the manipulation, the lying. It sounds like your intentions were good, mostly, Dad, but it doesn't change much. Jonas still thought the worst of me, and you did nothing to dissuade him."

She took a breath, continuing, "Then, when you deemed we should be together, you tried to put us together hoping nature would take its course?" she said, clearly seething.

"I can't trust either one of you because no one has been honest with me from the start. You clearly care more about what each other thinks, and you just move me back and forth like some...pawn."

"Tessie, that's simply not true. You need to—" James started, his voice stern.

"No. You need to back off, Dad. You need to stop manipulating my life and everyone else's."

Jonas's heart sank, though he couldn't blame her. She was right. He should have been honest with her from the start, at least as much as he could be, given James's manipulations.

"I do love you, Jonas," she said, making his heart race. "But I can't do this right now. Neither of you have treated me well, with honesty or respect. I can't be in a relationship that doesn't have either of those things, with either of you."

"Tessie—" James tried again, but Jonas stopped him.

"It's okay, James. She's right. If I could do this all again…I don't know. I would do it differently, I hope. But…I understand," he said to Tessa.

"I need some time. To process all this."

"Take as much as you need. I'll be waiting, if you want me," Jonas said, echoing the thing she had said to him when she came to his apartment the day before. He knew it was the right thing to do, to let her go, but he felt vulnerable and raw as she walked out, and wished the senator would leave, too.

"Don't worry, Jonas. I know my girl. She'll come around."

"I'm not sure you do know her, James. Not the way you should. Maybe that's something you should consider changing, if she gives you the chance," Jonas said. "I know I will. I'd like to get dressed and get the hell out of here. Could you leave, please?"

Jonas felt the senator's hand on his shoulder, and then watched him walk to the door.

He dressed and buzzed the nurse that he was ready to go.

It would have been one of the happiest days of his life, getting his sight back, if he knew he was ever going to see Tessa again. As it was, everything was still gray.

TESSA'S MIND WAS REELING, and when she walked out the room, she looked around for Lydia, feeling deflated when she couldn't find her. No one was there, and she assumed they had all flown the coop after leaving her and Jonas alone.

No matter, she could take a cab home. She just wanted to sleep, and to have some time to process everything in her head, and her heart.

Jonas said he loved her. She thought she loved him, but did that matter when things were so messed up?

Checking her watch, she saw it was close to noon, and wondered if Kate had been discharged yet. Making her way to her friend's floor, she found what felt like a party going on in Kate's room.

Kate was in a chair, dressed and obviously ready to leave, smiling and holding court with several other visitors. Tessa recognized Betty and several of the women from the neighborhood who came over for Sunday cards at Kate's. They all smiled when they saw her, and ushered her into the room, though she now had a few second thoughts too late.

"Tessa! I told you not to worry about me today," Kate admonished when Tessa walked in and said hello, giving Kate a hug and a kiss on the cheek. "You did more than enough last night, and you must be exhausted," she said with a mischievous wink.

"I'm fine, Kate. And I am so happy to see you're doing well. You gave us a real scare last night."

She said hello to Betty, and the other women, but suddenly, Tessa really wanted to go home. The thought that she had just walked away from Jonas, and the urge to run back to him, was confusing her.

"Where is your young man?" Betty asked. "He's a strapping fellow. Very handsome, like a movie star. I bet he's a tiger in the sack," she said, making Tessa cough in surprise.

"I trust you had a nice ride home last night?" Kate interjected with a chuckle. "The limo seats are *very* comfortable, don't you think?"

Tessa's cheeks warmed as she remembered just how comfortable they were.

"Yes, thank you so much, Kate. It was completely unnecessary, but it very considerate of you, and Collins is so sweet," she said, the memories of the night before coming back before she could finish.

Tessa put her hand to her mouth to hide the sudden, choking sensation of tears that clogged her throat. She turned away, feeling stupid, and also not wanting to upset Kate. Why was she losing it now? She should have gone straight home. Her nerves were raw after everything that had happened.

She wanted so much to be able to believe Jonas, and her father, too. She wanted the two most important men in her life to be part of it, but not in the way they had been doing.

"Oh, Tessa! What's wrong?" Kate asked with great concern, hearing her muffled sob, and suddenly Tessa was surrounded. The other women flanked her, making sure she was okay. She had to laugh and cry at the same time, and they all patted her back, urging her to sit down.

"I'm so s-sorry. I'm just tired. It's been a very long night."

"Hmm, I think there's more to it than that," Kate said. "What happened? What did *he* do? Did he break your heart? And here I thought he was such a nice young man."

Tessa waved her hand as if to wave off Kate's concern,

and grabbed a tissue with the other, trying to get hold of herself so she could stop feeling foolish. Something about sitting here with these wonderful, caring women kept the tears flowing. In so many ways, she was closer to them than she was to her own family, and that made her sad, too.

"I'm not sure we can be together," Tessa said, choking up again. "It's such an awful mess."

"There's an answer for everything. It probably just seems bad right now. Tell us what happened," Betty urged kindly.

"I think I should go," she said, standing. "I don't want to bother you all with this, and it looks like you have more than enough help to get home, so if you don't mind, Kate, I can just—"

"You're not going anywhere when you are so upset," Kate said adamantly, and the other women agreed, gently forcing Tessa back into the chair.

Betty went out into the hall, coming in a few seconds later with a cup of tea, handing it to her.

"This will help, even if it's a bit weak," she said, patting Tessa's hand. "If we were home, I would put something stronger in it, but for now this will have to do."

"So spill your guts, Tessa. We want to hear the whole story," Kate said. "Don't leave anything out."

Tessa sighed and sipped her tea. It was clear that she wasn't going to be able to leave until she told them what happened, although she definitely left out the sexier parts of her night. Somehow she just couldn't imagine telling her octogenarian friends about her sex life.

When she finished, they all stared at her in clear disbelief.

"Well, that's a better story than all the nighttime TV I watched this week," Betty said.

Kate reached for Tessa's hand. "Tessa, you are in a very difficult spot, being someone who is loved too much by the men in your life."

Tessa drew back. "I'm sorry. I'm not exactly getting that feeling."

"Your father obviously loves you very much," she said. "But in the wrong way, as men, and parents, so often do. It's a tough job, being a parent, and children sometimes need to be forgiving. But it's never too late to learn, and it sounds like he tried, at least, to do the right thing."

"But—" Tessa tried to interject.

"And your Jonas...well, we all know about *men,*" she said with a sigh, and the other women murmured agreement.

"I was reading an article in *Cosmo* that said men are like cats, not dogs," Betty said, and they all looked at her, wondering how she had made that connection.

"Well, it makes sense. Domestic dogs are not like wild dogs, wolves, et cetera—house dogs aren't in touch with their wild instincts. But cats, no matter the size, are all the same. The domestic house cat has the same behavior as the lion—cats are very primal."

Tessa listened politely, trying to follow.

"Men who are in love will rely very much on primal reflexes, their baser instincts. Just like cats. They are hunters. They possess, but they also protect what they see as theirs," Betty explained.

"I'm sorry, I don't understand," Tessa said, frowning and trying to digest Betty's rather convoluted point, but also that she read *Cosmo*.

"Men show love in several ways. One way is through

sex. Another is through providing for those they care about. Another protecting them, at any cost. It goes back to caveman times," Betty said. "But they have all that testosterone flying around in their brains, and sometimes, well, they just get carried away. They forget we're adult people who can make our own decisions."

"So what you're saying is that both of them think they are protecting me?"

She knew that, she was just sick and tired of their methods. Tessa didn't want to be protected. She wanted respect, honesty and love.

"Yes, in a nutshell, and they are being complete asses about it, but that's as old as time, too. No one is perfect. And you said they both had things in the past that colored their perspectives. As did you," said Kate.

"What do you mean?"

"You were wrong about your father's motives, too. He was trying to get you together with Jonas, albeit he didn't do a great job of it, but he wasn't trying to do what he did to you in college, driving the man you loved away. But your past experience made you see things a certain way, too."

"I saw a show the other day," Betty interjected. "The psychologist had a couple with similar problems, and he asked them if they wanted to be happy, or if they wanted to be right."

"I think there's room for both," Tessa said stubbornly, seeing their points, but a little surprised that her women friends didn't see her perspective more clearly.

Or maybe they saw it very clearly.

"Tessa, you said your father never wanted you to open your shop, but now he sees what a success it is. He was obviously able to see what a good match you are with your Jonas, too," Kate said.

"I suppose. But the problem with this theory is that it means neither one of them is considering me an adult who is able to make her own decisions. I don't think I like that," Tessa said.

"Oh, believe me, they know. But for fathers, their little girls never grow up, and for Jonas, well…love scrambles people's brains." Kate smiled patiently. "But they can't change if you walk away from them. And that won't make you too happy, either, will it?"

"I can't think straight at all, about any of this."

"That's why we get so confused when we try to think our way out of these things. You know the answer, in your heart. Strong men like Jonas, and your father, for that matter, are not attracted to weak women," Kate said. "They both let you walk away. The ball is in your court. Follow your heart."

Tessa absorbed the women's advice. If she were to truly follow her heart, she knew exactly what she needed to do. Could it really be that easy? Was she just letting her pride get in the way of being happy?

It seemed so stupid.

"Kate, it does seem like you have more than enough help here. Do you mind if I leave you for today? I have… something I have to do."

Kate's eyes sparkled with interest as she gestured Tessa forward for a hug and whispered in her ear.

"Don't let him get away this time."

12

1:00 p.m. (24 hours later)

JONAS TURNED AS the door to the back room of the office opened, and he saw Garrett approach where the brothers had congregated to catch up.

"Lunch," he said approvingly as the aroma of food permeated the space. His sense of smell was still serving him well, but he was hungry for everything he could see, which, granted, at this point, wasn't much. Mostly blurry blobs moving around, shadows and shapes, but he absorbed every nuance completely, eager for his full range of vision to return.

Matt said he should be back to his full eyesight within a week, but that he might need some glasses, depending on how well his vision recovered. Jonas was fine with that. Anything was better than the complete darkness he'd been living in.

"Chinese. I didn't get breakfast, and I'm starving."

Several minutes later, as they consumed the food with no small bit of teasing about Jonas missing his target as he tried to eat the noodles and chunks of meat in the lo mein he loved—he felt more renewed and ready to dig in again. Irish purred profusely on the floor next to where Jonas sat, content to have all of them there, and happy with whatever chunks of food were being offered.

"Irish really likes that pork lo mein," Ely observed.

"He has good taste."

"Anyone know where Ely took off to?" Jonas asked, reaching down to scratch the cat behind the ears, rewarded with even louder purring.

"Any egg rolls left?" he asked.

"Let me get that for you," Chance said matter-of-factly, putting an egg roll into his hand. "He took off with the tattooed chick, Tessa's friend."

"Lydia?" Jonas said, surprised.

"They were heading to the hospital cafeteria, but that was the last I saw of them. Maybe Ely got lucky," Chance said, and Jonas could almost see his younger brother's grin.

Jonas wasn't completely happy to hear that.

"Lydia's a friend," he said, sending his brother a look. "She doesn't deserve to be Ely's rebound lay," he muttered, hoping that wasn't what his brother was doing.

It didn't seem possible. Lydia and Ely were about as different as he could imagine.

"Rebound?" Chance asked. "What did I miss?"

Ely had told Garrett and Jonas in the hosptial about the encounter with Chloe. Jonas had wanted to talk about anything other than his own issues, and noticed right away that his younger brother was out of sorts.

"She was getting married?" Chance said, clearly outraged. "That sucks."

"Yeah."

"How about you, Gar? You never said how your night went last night," Jonas prompted.

"I helped Mel with her flooding, and then I went home. Nothing to tell," his older brother reported. "It seems like you guys were getting into enough hot water for all of us combined."

"That's too bad. I like Melissa. She's had a thing for you for a while."

"She's just a friend. And I'm not interested in going there," Garrett said in the older-brother voice he used when he was telling his brothers to back off.

"It's been three years now, Gar," Jonas said gently.

"I know how long it's been, Jon. Eat your lunch."

Jonas nodded. He wasn't in the habit of poking at his brother's wounds, but maybe his own feelings about Tessa had him wondering whether any of them would find happiness in love.

He ached, and set down the egg roll that Chance had given him, suddenly not hungry at all.

"You okay?" Garrett asked.

"Yeah. Tired."

"And you miss her."

"Yeah."

"You could call. Go to her," Garrett suggested.

Jonas shook his head. "No. It has to be on her terms, what she wants, even if it's to be left alone. I really screwed it up the first time, so I'm just going to have to wait."

He was hurting, missing her more than he had ever missed anything, including his vision. But he meant what he said. It had to be up to her.

It did feel good to talk about it with his brothers, though. One thing he had learned with Tessa, and from being blind, was that he didn't need to do it all on his own. Part of that was probably because he knew now that his sight was returning, but also because accepting help in general was suddenly not such a huge deal. It cemented his connections with others, and he'd never really thought about it that way before.

The defensiveness he'd felt for the last month seemed to go away, and it was a relief. He felt stronger for having shared his problems with his brothers—and for his time with Tessa—not weaker.

"Well, maybe you won't have to wait as long as you think," Garrett said while unwrapping a fortune cookie.

Jonas took a bite of his egg roll, and chewed thoughtfully. "I'll wait as long as it takes."

"I'm glad to hear that," someone said behind him, and he immediately knew it was Tessa's voice.

He heard his brother chuckle. Garrett had known she was there.

"Tessa?"

"Yes," she said.

He felt her hand on his shoulder, and he reached up, covering it with his own.

"How long have you been there?"

"Long enough," she said, and he could hear the tears in her voice. "Thank you," she whispered, leaning down to plant a kiss on his cheek.

It was all Jonas could do not to pull her down into his arms, and not let go. But he let her set the lead.

"For what?"

"For understanding," she said simply.

Jonas was silent with surprise. A part of him was sure she'd never come back, never forgive him. He tightened his grips on her hand, to make sure she was really there.

"Here, have a seat," Chance said at the same time Jonas heard Garrett offering his chair, too, and the guys scrambled around him as they all tried to make Tessa welcome and comfortable.

Jonas smiled, and heard Tessa chuckling and thanking them as she took a seat beside Jonas, her hand still wrapped in his.

"I'm sorry about this morning. The note, scaring you. I wish it had gone down differently," he said.

"No, that's the point, Jonas. I'm so tired of everyone trying to protect me from everything," she said, tilting her forehead against his. "I know it's your job, and your nature, to do that, but I don't want you, my father, or anyone protecting me when it means not being honest or letting me know what's going on in your head, or your heart."

Before he could say anything else, his brothers, as if coordinated ahead of time, rose and briskly left the room.

"There's one thing you're missing."

"What's that?" she asked.

"I did want to tell you, and I should have. About my blindness, the job—but I was afraid. It wasn't as much about protecting you as protecting myself," he said with no small amount of self-disgust.

"How so?"

"Howie's threats were an issue, but it was easier to use them as an excuse and to pretend it was all your fault than to face you and have you see me as…diminished, I suppose."

"You thought the loss of your vision would matter to me?" she said in surprise. "How could you think that?"

"Because I felt that way about myself, not just because

I was blind, but because I had let the attacker get the upper hand, had failed to protect you…I don't know, it all wrapped up together in some way in my head. And then, when your dad offered me a chance to be with you again, I took it, but the lie ate at me. I knew it was wrong, but I did it anyway, because I knew when you found out, you'd be gone."

"So instead, you decided to leave first?"

"I thought I could try to find a way to make things right."

"You're doing that right now. But I was part of this, too," she said. "I saw what I wanted to see, followed my own selfish desires—"

"I love your selfish desires," he said.

"You know what I mean. We have a lot of time to make up for…just getting to know each other. Really know each other. I want to know everything about you."

He definitely loved her, and leaned in, toward her scent.

"I can't believe you're here," he said, sliding a hand up into her hair, pulling her in for a kiss, feeling as if it had been days, weeks, instead of just a few hours.

Her hands framed his face in a tender gesture as she kissed him back, and the mood wasn't one so much of desire—though he certainly wanted her—as it was of… gratitude.

And something much, much deeper, he realized.

"I do love you, Tessa," Jonas confessed, the words so easy to say it almost surprised him.

She let out a shaky breath. "That's all I needed to hear. I love you, too. And we'll make this all work out, somehow."

"What about your father?" he said.

She laughed. "Jonas, he clearly likes the idea of you with me, so no worries there. I like that idea, too," she said. "But I'll talk with him, too. Maybe this can be a fresh start for me and him. His heart was in the right place, and maybe it always has been, but I was too defensive to see it."

"I know that feeling," he murmured against her throat, suddenly wishing they were alone, not here with his brothers nearby.

Where he had ever gotten the idea that she needed his protection in the first place now mystified him. She'd taken out the attacker in her apartment, and she'd taken on her father, and him. She'd been strong enough to tell them to leave, to stand on her own and still to come back, to forgive.

Her lips found his again, and it was long, rich moments before either of them spoke again. Jonas saw the shape of the window behind her, and lifted his hand to follow the shadowed contour of her head.

Soon, though hardly soon enough, he'd be able to see her again, fully and clearly, but until then, he was more than happy to use his hands, and all his senses, to compensate for what his eyes missed.

ELY OPENED HIS EYES, not quite sure what he was looking at as he stared upward at the brick red ceiling. He'd been in so many places over the last week, he'd lost track.

Red satin sheets rubbed against his naked skin, and then he remembered.

Lydia.

Pushing up on the bed, he heard voices sounding as if they were coming from the floor below, and it came back to him.

Going without any sleep for forty-eight hours had finally caught up with him, and he'd completely passed out—after discovering that Lydia did, indeed, have tattoos in places where only lovers could see.

They'd ended up going for a drink instead of for coffee. A couple of drinks, actually. Not smart when he was already tired, but he was sick of worrying about it. He'd been raw inside from seeing Chloe, and even told Lydia the whole sordid story.

She'd taken him by the hand, took him home. Undressed him.

Told him it was just for the moment.

He'd needed...something. Someone to wash away Chloe's touch, and Lydia had done a fine and thorough job of that. She was the complete opposite of Chloe in every way, and that was what he'd needed.

He rubbed his wrists, noting a few bruises.

Right. The handcuffs.

Sliding off the side of the bed, he looked around, noting how her bedroom reflected the woman. Leather clothing hung over a chair, and an assortment of S and M paraphernalia adorned the walls.

He pushed past the black lace curtain that surrounded the huge four-poster bed, and took in the classic French boudoir decor mixed with modern-day dungeon.

It was feminine, sexy and...more than a little kinky. Black and white nudes were framed on the walls, though the faces weren't visible, and he wondered if it was Lydia in the photos. He looked at them, finding them incredibly erotic, which was probably the point.

It was all new to him, and suddenly, for all of his experience, he felt completely vanilla, as if there were a whole lot of sexual horizons this Marine had never explored.

Lydia had helped him see that. Why did he want to get tied down—so to speak—with one person?

He was an idiot to think he wanted anything long term. He'd seen his brother Garrett suffer a terrible loss, and who knew how things would end up with Jonas. He'd almost lost his sight, and his life, over Tessa.

And Chloe had proved that his romantic notions were an illusion.

Lydia seemed to understand that, too. As she said, they only had the moment. It was how he was going to live his life from now on, he thought, hiking up his jeans and slipping his shirt on.

Walking out into the main room of the apartment, he found nothing like the bedroom. The walls were painted in strong colors, but there weren't any chains or shackles on the walls. In fact, the place could belong to a librarian, with all the books that lined the walls.

He heard voices coming from below, where she was probably working. She'd left some doughnuts out on the counter with a carton of orange juice, but he wasn't hungry. Checking the back, he was happy to find stairs leading down to a rear alley.

No need to disturb her while she was with a client.

Finding his way out, Ely put everything from the previous twenty-four hours or so behind him.

Epilogue

November, three months later

"ARE YOU sure you're okay?" Tessa asked again as Lydia helped her manage her dress.

"You're the bride—aren't I supposed to be asking you that?"

Tessa laughed, but she wasn't at all nervous. She'd been so excited to finally be marrying Jonas that she couldn't wait to walk down the aisle.

"I know something happened with you and Ely, Lydia. You two avoid each other like the plague. What did he do?"

Lydia smiled, but didn't meet Tessa's eyes.

"Nothing that I didn't want him to." The tone of her voice communicated that she wasn't going to say more. "You look perfect. I'm not such a fan of white, as you know, but this is one of the prettiest dresses I have ever seen."

They were doing everything very traditionally for the wedding—in deference to their parents' wishes—though it was a small ceremony. Jonas's parents were wonderful, and she had loved them immediately. Emily

Berringer had wasted no time taking Tessa under her wing and helping her make wedding plans, for which Tessa was so grateful. It was overwhelming, in a good way, but she loved the Berringers' hands-on way of doing everything.

There would be some media at the event, a few hand-selected reporters and one photographer from the paper that her father had approved. Tessa was okay with it—it was part of being the daughter of a politician.

The pretty Quaker church that was set among the hills of the Pennsylvania countryside was perfect, their guests few but special to her and Jonas.

Tessa looked in the mirror, studying the dress. The full-length silk felt wonderful against her skin. It was fitted, strapless, with hundreds of tiny pearls and rhinestones arranged in flowering patterns that caught the light as she moved. The design was in some ways plain, but stunning. She wore only gardenias in her hair, and her bouquet matched the special scent she had created just for the wedding—and the honeymoon.

She'd blended something special for Jonas, too, a more subtle, masculine scent that would promote stamina, she thought with a smile. He was going to need it. Not that she had any complaints.

If she thought the sex the night of the blackout had been intense, what they had shared since openly declaring their feelings for each other had been off the charts. She couldn't wait to see what new levels of pleasure marriage would bring. She knew that all the cynical comments people made about being lifetime partners with someone were wrong, at least for them.

Far from losing the heat of the initial meeting, everything just got more intense the closer they became, not less so.

She shifted in the dress, slightly, her nipples beading in anticipation.

"Geez, you're worse than me," Lydia said, laughing and meeting her eyes in the mirror. "You're already thinking about the honeymoon, aren't you?"

Tessa grinned. "Guilty as charged. I mean, I'm looking forward to this, to marrying Jonas, but the wedding is really for our parents, and everyone else. I just want him."

"You two are amazing. You almost make me believe it can happen," Lydia said. "Though it's not for me."

"It might be, when you meet the right man."

"You know my philosophy on that."

Tessa did, and it made her a little sad. She hated being one of those brides who went around wanting to see all her friends married, too, but she wanted Lydia to be as happy as she was, someday.

"Jonas is going to go blind again when he sees you, you're so gorgeous," Lydia, her only attendant, said, stepping back.

"Well, let's hope not," Tessa said with a smile. She had some treats planned for Jonas, and he very much needed to be able to see.

Uncharacteristically sentimental, the women hugged, and Tessa was determined not to cry, or she'd ruin her makeup again for the second time that morning.

It had been bad enough when Chance, Ely and Garrett had all come to see her and welcome her to the family, each presenting her with a small gift of their own.

She'd noticed, though, how when Ely came in, Lydia had gone, the two not even sharing a glance.

"Ready?" Lydia said.

"So very, very ready," Tessa replied, taking her

flowers and heading out to meet her father, who was giving her away.

As the music cued, and Tessa saw Jonas at the other end of the aisle, heart-stoppingly handsome in his tux, she swallowed hard.

Oh, these were the nerves everyone talked about, she thought, freezing for a second.

But then Jonas smiled, and her father took her arm in his, and everything was okay again.

Lydia led the way, and took her place on the left side of the judge—a prestigious friend of her father's—and Garrett stood on the right with his brother.

She knew this was hard for Gar, her heart breaking. The last wedding he had attended had been his own.

As she came closer to Jonas, she had eyes only for him, and felt her cheeks warm again as his eyes landed on her, and took her in.

His gaze consumed her, as it so often did. Even though he had had his vision for more than a month, she still caught him staring, as if he couldn't take in enough.

He took her hand, raised it to his lips, and the world came down to the two of them for the next few minutes.

Later, everyone congregated in the hall next to the church for drinks and some food, and Tessa looked around for where her new husband had disappeared to.

"Gar, do you know where Jonas went?" she asked her new brother-in-law.

"He's getting his gift for you."

She raised her eyebrows, wondering what he could be working on that would be so mysterious. Smiling, she invited Garrett to dance with her, which he was pleased to do.

She noted Ely dancing with the woman he'd invited as his date, and who was clearly one of his recent string of conquests. Tessa knew Jonas was worried about his younger brother, who was normally quite conservative.

Chance, who was the complete opposite, was dancing with three partners, never one to be outdone.

Lydia sat chatting with Tessa's father, and Tessa frowned, but turned her attention back to Garrett.

"So Jonas said that you're leaving, too, after the reception?" Tessa asked Garrett.

"Yep. It's slow right now, and a good friend on the West Coast is getting married, so I'm going to go out there to the wedding, and then take a month for vacation. I've never been to California," he said. "It should be fun."

"Sounds great. Thanks for being Jonas's best man," she said gently. "I know it must bring back memories."

"Just good ones," he said, smiling at her, but his eyes were still a little sad.

"You could have brought a date, too," she said, no subtle way to broach the topic. By now, Garrett probably qualified for a monastery.

"I'm fine, Tessa. Better than fine. I'm thrilled for you guys. I have to admit, weddings are not my favorite events, but it's been a while, and I'm a big boy."

"I know, it's just that…we want you to be happy."

"I was," he said, and then shook his head. "I mean, I am," he corrected. "Besides, there are only so many perfect women in the world, and Jonas just took one of the last ones."

Tessa reached up and planted a kiss on his cheek.

"Hey, I think your gift from Jonas is waiting," Garrett said, grinning as they were interrupted by a loud, growling noise.

"What is *that?*" she exclaimed, and saw everyone going to the double doors at the front of the hall.

"It's his other love," Garrett said laughingly. "Go on," Garrett urged. "It's about time you two meet."

She looked at him curiously and made her way forward, walked through as the small group parted down the center to allow her access. When she reached the door at the top of the steps, she stopped.

Surprise didn't cover what she saw.

Jonas. Dressed completely in black leather, sitting on a huge, black motorcycle, smiling up at her.

He looked...dangerous. A thrill ran down her spine.

He'd mentioned the bike, but hadn't ridden it since getting his sight back, and she'd wondered why.

The bike was decorated with Just Married decor, and he dropped the kickstand, taming the roaring noise as he hopped off and met her at the top at the door.

"Ready to leave on our honeymoon?" he said, taking her hands in his.

"On that?" she asked, looking at the bike apprehensively.

"You'll like it," he said, nuzzling her ear. "I promise."

She wasn't so sure.

"We're taking the Harley to the airport, and then we have a private charter to St. Thomas, a gift from both of our parents. From there we'll take a sailboat that will sail us to a private cottage on a beach in Anguilla, and down through several of the other islands."

Tessa was so moved, and so surprised, she turned to hug her new in-laws, and her father, who hugged her back, and, she suspected, was having just a teeny bit of a hard time letting go.

But he had been so good about everything. Their relationship had never been better.

She'd had to try to pack without really knowing where his parents were shipping their luggage off to, keeping it a surprise, but she wasn't prepared for this.

"I thought we could keep up our tradition of using as many modes of transportation as possible," Jonas said, hugging her close. "And discovering how we might take advantage of them."

She checked out the way the leather hugged his body and a tingle raced down her spine. She had no doubt they would find a lot of new erotic possibilities along the way.

"But I can't ride that…not in this," she said, looking down at her dress.

"That's where my gift comes in," Lydia said happily, appearing on the step and pushing a box into her hands. "Open it."

Tess opened the huge, heavy box and found a succulent leather jacket, skirt and boots inside, along with some very sexy lingerie. Jonas smiled broadly as she closed the box before others could see the naughty accoutrements.

"Go change," he whispered in her ear. "I can't wait to see you in this outfit, and to get you out of it."

Cheers went up as Jonas took her in his arms for a deep, consuming kiss that left Tessa more than willing to leave as soon as possible.

The wedding had been wonderful, but she wanted to get her new husband alone. They would be making more than one fantasy come true on their honeymoon, and she had a few surprises in store for him, as well.

Jonas wasn't sure he had ever known such a perfect moment as he did easing down the road on his Harley, Tessa pressed up tight against his back, the fall colors brilliant as they rode down the highway.

He pulled to the side of the road, into a tree-lined alcove, where he stopped the bike.

"Is something wrong?"

"No. I just need to be alone with my wife," he said, turning and lifting her hand to his mouth, loving the sight of his rings on her finger. "We have some time, and I thought you might like to experiment with some of the more creative things people can do on a motorcycle seat," he said, pulling her close and taking her lips in a hot kiss.

"I have to admit, the vibration has been quite… stimulating," she said, and smiled as he unzipped the tight leather and her bare breasts fell free. The cool air tightened her nipples invitingly, and he dipped in for a taste.

Jonas groaned, appreciating her choice to forgo any of the lingerie that Lydia had bought her. He had a feeling they might not make it all the way to the airport, and had been thankful to find the protected spot.

His hands slid up her thighs under the leather, and discovered that she wasn't wearing anything under the skirt, either. The wide seat of the motorcycle meant her legs were already open to him, and he drew a finger along her sex, finding her wet already. His cock pressed against his own leather, needing to be inside her.

He caressed her more deeply, watching her head fall back in the dappled sunlight as he made her come with just his touch. She was so responsive, he had a hard time keeping control.

But his wife had plans of her own. Reaching forward, she cleverly released the front of his leathers, his erection full and ready, straining toward her.

"Someone might see," she said, knowing how to make his pulse race.

"The trees are hiding us, but maybe we had better make this one quick, just in case," he agreed, pulling her up from straddling the seat to his lap, sinking her down over him until they were completely connected.

She wrapped her arms around him tightly as he turned the bike back on, letting it idle and purr beneath them in the most delicious way.

"Oh, my, that's very nice," she said breathlessly, and he had to admit to enjoying the subtle vibration before he gripped her hips and sought his climax more energetically.

He watched her again, fighting not to close his eyes through his own climax as she cried out, biting her lip and giving herself over to it. She was so beautiful, and she was his.

After a few moments, he set her gently aside, kissing her tenderly as he zipped her back up. "I love you, wife."

"I love you, husband. And just in case you think I forgot, I have a surprise for you when we get where we're going."

"What's that?"

"My gift for you is with our luggage, so it will have to wait until tomorrow, but let's just say I bought something to make both of our 'in the dark' fantasies come true," she said, adding, "You said you'd be more than willing to watch…and now that you can…"

Jonas was sure he had died and gone to heaven.

"I think we'll find a lot of new things to do on the boat, and maybe even on the plane," she teased, and his heart raced thinking about it.

"I already have a few ideas," he said, holding her tight for one more kiss.

She handed him his helmet, and slid from his lap to the seat. "Let's go. There are only so many hours in a day, and so many fantasies to explore."

"We'd best get started then," he agreed, looking forward to every single one.

* * * * *

Just for the Night

TAWNY WEBER

Tawny Weber is usually found dreaming up stories in her California home, surrounded by dogs, cats and kids. When she's not writing hot, spicy stories for Blaze®, she's shopping for the perfect pair of shoes or scrapbooking happy memories. Come by and visit her on the web at www.tawnyweber.com.

Dear Reader,

Who can forget their first love? Or their first heartbreak?

In *Just for the Night*, Larissa Zahn reunites with both when she sees Jason Cantrell again. And all she wants is to get away. Enter Fate, always a wily trickster, in the form of a huge power outage. Suddenly, she finds herself alone with Jason, trapped...for twenty-four hours!

This book was such fun to write because I got to spend a lot of time with two characters who are so perfect for each other, yet so challenging to each other. There's nothing like a little forced confinement (and a yummy jar of chocolate body paint) to stir up some sexy adventure!

If you're on the web, please drop by my website at www.TawnyWeber.com and let me know what you think of Jason and Larissa's story. While you're there, check out my blog, vote for the hunk of the month, or enter my current contest. I'd love to hear from you.

Tawny Weber

To Beth Andrews, my best friend and awesome critique partner. Thank you for always being there, always seeing the heart of my stories and always cheering me on. I couldn't do it without you!

1

"For a girl who isn't about to get laid, you're spending an awful lot of time obsessing over your underwear choices."

"These are important decisions," Larissa Zahn insisted as she sifted through the multitude of fabrics and patterns in the satin-lined box. "My entire future could be riding on this."

"On the choice between lace and satin?" Chloe Carpenter, Larissa's oldest friend and current roommate asked with a laugh. "C'mon, 'Risa. Put your panties away and let's go see a movie."

"I don't have time for a movie tonight. I need to make sure I have the perfect selection of merchandise for the test display tomorrow. I want to show Cartright's team that my concept for Isn't It Romantic will fit perfectly in their hotel's mall." Larissa waved a hand at the myriad of merchandise strewn all over the living room.

Boxes of romance, she'd been calling them over the last eight months as she collected possible items to stock when she opened her store. She stared, wild-eyed, at the mess. At the moment, it seemed a little more like an obsession gone overboard.

"Haven't you picked out your perfect selection already?"

Chloe lifted a red binder over her head and waved it around, tabbed pages of lists, photos and sketches fluttering like little tattletale flags. "Like, four times at least?"

Looking at the notebook, Larissa gave Chloe a weak smile. She knew her friend was right. Once upon a time, her dream had been easy. Since she was a teenager, she'd dreamed of buying the cozy independent bookstore she worked in, of getting married to her true love and starting a family. But two years ago, that dream had fallen apart. So she'd rebuilt her dream. This one depended on her and nobody else.

She'd started by asking herself what she believed in enough to devote her business, her time and all of her attention to. The answer? Romance.

Despite a heart-bruising breakup, Larissa still believed in romance. But romance with rules. The kind that kept a girl from getting so caught up in the fluff she got hurt by the reality. So just for fun—and, yes, as a way to clarify her own set of romance rules—Larissa had started a blog two years ago. Quickly gaining in popularity, it had swiftly grown into a monthly newsletter which had also become a huge hit. At first it had been about all of the wonderful romance novels she loved, pointing out the strength of the heroines. But over the last year it'd expanded to include songs and movies, romantic getaways and recipes for breakfast in bed. All things romantic. Six months ago, her fun little column, *Larissa's Rules of Romance,* had been picked up as a monthly feature in a nationally syndicated magazine. Now, in addition to her column, she also answered romance questions and offered tidbits of advice to the entire country.

It'd been the perfect foundation to use to open a store. All things romantic, based on her rules, advice and observations. She'd carry books, movies and music, of course. But she'd have more. Everything a woman could want to bring more romance into her life. The only thing Larissa needed was a location.

Only now that the most amazing location was right there, a fingertip away, she wasn't sure she was ready for her pitch. She knew the display she set up was crucial to selling her idea, so it had to be perfect. But did she go old-fashioned romance or modern-day romance? Did she focus on her favorites—books, movies and music—or should she make the gifts and romantic mementos the centerpiece of her presentation?

"You look like your head is about to explode," Chloe pointed out with a worried look. "Maybe you're right. We should stay in tonight."

Larissa shrugged that off. She knew she looked like hell. Her shoulder-length curls were knotted in a bandanna, black corkscrews spraying out the top of her head. Since it was her day off from her job as manager, clerk and stockwoman at the bookstore, she hadn't bothered with makeup and her small frame swam in baggy red shorts and a ratty purple tank top featuring a smart-ass bunny cartoon.

"I just want to make sure I bring the most up-to-date selections," she defended. "What do you think? Which one screams *buy me* louder? Bridal white or sweetheart pink?"

Larissa held up two separate gift bags, one flocked with roses and edged in white feathers, the other covered in foil hearts and sporting a lacy handle.

"Do you think guys care about the color of a girl's panties? All they're concerned with is how hot the contents are."

"Not my future customers," Larissa dismissed. She gave a disdainful little sniff. Then she ruined it by grinning when Chloe rolled her eyes.

"You're going to have to work on that snooty attitude

if you want to make it uptown," Chloe chided. "Cartright Hotels are known for bringing in the hoitiest of the toity and the richest of the bitches."

Chloe was right. Cartright Hotels were known worldwide for their themed resorts. They had a golf hotel, with its world-class eighteen-hole green in Palm Springs. They had a spa hotel in St. Tropez and a hunting lodge-styled resort in the Adirondacks. And now they were opening a romantic getaway here in South Carolina.

A romance hotel, right here in Larissa's backyard. It was totally meant to be.

"Are you sure this is what you want?" Chloe asked, not for the first time. For a woman who specialized in leaping with her eyes closed, Chloe was sure picky about doing height checks on Larissa's jumps.

"Romantic getaway, Chloe," Larissa cried out, waving the baby blue silk panties in her hand to punctuate the exclamation. "This location is totally made for me. It's my dream. I've put in the time. Eight years working in Mr. Murphy's bookstore. Four years perfecting my brand as a romance specialist and two more building the Romance Rules network."

Sure, she could settle for a small store somewhere else, but why? If she wanted great things to happen in her life, she had to *make* them happen. Nobody else was going to make her dreams come true. Romance Rule number one, *It's Every Princess for Herself.* This was her shot at her very own store in a fancy upscale place like Cartright Plaza. It was perfect for her.

She just had to convince the committee in charge of choosing the boutique vendors that she was the perfect choice for them. And convince herself that she wasn't jumping too high, given her lack of experience as a business owner.

"Have you told Mr. Murphy yet?" Chloe asked, referring to the man Larissa had worked for since high school.

"Not yet. But it won't be a big deal. I mean, he's retiring, so it's not like I'm leaving him in the lurch."

"But he's been hinting around that he'd like you to buy him out, hasn't he?"

Larissa's gleeful bubble of hope burst a little. She shrugged, tossing the blue silk panties into the case of lingerie.

"Sure, he'd sell me the business. But if I buy it, it's still his store, under new ownership, you know? I'd be keeping Mr. Murphy's dream alive, not living my own." Despite that, a part of her wanted to settle. She had enough money to make the down payment. When she'd first toyed with the idea of buying his store someday, she'd still been living with the wealthy aunt who'd raised her after Larissa's parents had died.

But then her aunt had died, leaving her home and all of her wealth to the Preservation of Feral Felines. And leaving Larissa homeless. Larissa had started saving money for her future, but working as a bookseller wasn't known as a road to riches.

She was sure Mr. Murphy would carry the rest of the loan for her. But she knew if she settled, she'd never take the leap. She'd always be reminded of her naive belief in happy-ever-after and thinking that some prince would sweep in and make her world perfect.

Nope. If she wanted her dreams, she had to make them happen herself. Now. She laid a hand on her queasy stomach.

"It's all for the best," she said, not sure if she was trying to convince herself or Chloe. "This way, I'm starting fresh. That's what I want. I mean, I think it's what I want..."

"You want it or you don't," Chloe pushed. "Decide. Then,

for crying out loud, quit second guessing yourself. You know what your problem is?"

"My choice in friends?"

"Don't be silly. You'd be miserable without me. You'd hole up with a stack of books and your dreams with the curtains closed while life flew by."

Larissa grinned, tilting her head in agreement. She couldn't argue with the truth. She loved nothing better than curling up with a romance novel, losing herself in the delights of happy-ever-after.

"Your problem is you think everything has to be perfect," Chloe said, tucking her feet under her as she lounged on the chair.

"What's wrong with perfect?"

"Nothing, as long as you realize that life isn't that tidy. If you're always holding out for some shiny image of perfection, you miss a lot of great living." Chloe gave her an arched look and shoved her hand through her long blond hair, purple nails glittering. The nails perfectly matched the zebra stripes in the magenta leggings she'd paired with her black tunic.

A freelance makeup artist, Chloe was the epitome of a free spirit. She went through life turning lemons into gourmet lemonade. The few times Larissa had tried to make the metaphorical drink, it'd damn near choked her. Given how badly she sucked at turning bad into good, she tried hard—really, really hard—to make sure her life was lemon-free.

"I live," Larissa defended.

"Sure you do. But it's like you've created this litmus test for life. There are some great things out there that aren't perfect, you know."

"Of course I know that. I live with you, don't I?"

Chloe snorted. "Good point. And okay, yes, Cartright

Plaza is a great fit for your dream store. It's almost as if Conner built it with you in mind."

"But he didn't," Larissa said quickly, trying to hide her grimace.

Conner Cartright and his brother, Daniel, ran the Cartright empire. When Larissa's parents had died in a car accident, she'd gone to live with her aunt, a wealthy, eccentric spinster. Conner was the poor little rich boy who'd lived up the street. He'd had a crush on her for a while, but he'd given it up after he realized she'd only ever see him as a buddy.

Their friendship had almost bit the dust two years ago, when a selfish *jerk,* incapable of understanding a mature relationship, had misconstrued their friendship, then used it to break Larissa's heart.

She ground her teeth together in frustration, as irritated at the memory as she was at the fact that it could still get her so worked up and angry. Seeing her expression, thankfully Chloe let the subject drop.

Instead, her friend dug into a box labeled Chloe's Fun that she'd hauled out of her closet when she'd seen Larissa's collection of boxes. She tossed a few items willy-nilly into Larissa's collection of merchandise already deemed worthy of displaying.

"What are you doing?" Larissa asked, grabbing one of the objects midflight.

"Sending you with a few of the Chloe Kits I made."

Larissa looked at the beautifully wrapped box in her hand. The silver paper glinted and the velvet bow added just the right touch of elegance above the label stating the box contained One Romantic Evening.

Knowing Chloe, that meant a tiny bottle of tequila, a handful of flavored condoms and an edible guy-size thong.

Larissa didn't bother to sigh. Instead she set the box on

the table and decided to go with the pink bag and lace undies she'd been considering earlier.

"What's the deal?" Chloe asked, her voice rising. "I thought you loved my kits? Are you really afraid your future customers won't be looking for a good time?"

"I'm selling the promise of a happy-ever-after, Chloe. I'm not going to dilute it with gratuitous sex."

"Sex doesn't dilute, it spices things up." With that, Chloe tossed a few of her kits into the keeper box. Larissa gave up, figuring it wasn't worth the argument she'd hear if she took them out. "And even you, the ambassador of pure romance, have to admit that lovin' is better spicy."

"I don't need sex to make my point," Larissa insisted half-heartedly. Through with the gift selection, she turned to one of the multitude of bookcases lining the living room wall to choose which of the hundreds of romance novels and self-help books she wanted to feature.

"You mean you don't want to use sex to prove your point," Chloe said, getting up to go into the kitchen and grab some chips to snack on. "But it is an important part of romance. You keep trying to gloss over it and you'll end up with some sterile, boring ode to platonic fantasies. I mean, yuck."

Larissa lowered two handfuls of books to stare, open-mouthed, as her roommate returned with a bag of crisp, cheesy potato goodness.

"Yuck?"

Who the hell yucked romance?

"Yes, yuck. Would you really want a sexless romance?" Her emerald-and-turquoise MAC shadowed lids glittering, Chloe's eye roll was a work of art.

"I'm not saying I want sexless romance. I'm just saying I don't think sex is the number-one priority."

"I'll bet your customers think sex is a priority," Chloe said, crunching away, then licking chip dust off her fingers.

It was like talking to a stubborn three-year-old. Larissa slapped her fists on her narrow hips and glared at her oldest friend.

"Quit, already," she insisted, starting to feel bruised from the constant poking. "It's not that I think sex doesn't count. But that's not what I'm selling. Isn't It Romantic is all about teaching men, and yes, women, to pay attention to the sweet little gestures and tender moments that make a relationship special."

"And I'm not saying that *those* things don't count," Chloe said in the long-suffering tone of patience she'd perfected in her teens. "I'm just saying that if you keep shuffling sex to the bottom of your priority list—or worse, trying to hide it in the closet—you're going to lose out. Both personally and professionally."

"Look, my store is going to be called Isn't It Romantic. Not Prudes R Us. Quit making it sound like I have something against sex."

"But…don't you?"

Larissa blinked a couple times. Then she bent over a box of cozy blankets, unfolding and testing out the different mohair and cashmere blends to see which one she wanted to bring. She finally decided on a lush, white angora blend that felt like a cloud of silk in her fingers, adding it to her display box.

"You make it sound like I'm some kind of nun. I'm not. Aren't all of my favorite romance novels hot and spicy? There's nothing more satisfying than reading about hot tension, the building intensity, then an explosive, um…" Even though the two women were alone in the apartment, she still lowered her voice to a whisper, "climax."

"See! You can't even say it."

"Oh, bull," she shot back in her normal tone. "I love sex."

At least, she loved the memory of sex. It'd been a while since she'd loved it firsthand. Not for lack of interest or out of any sexual prejudice. But a girl got busy, focusing on her career, and there just wasn't much time left over for the frills.

"When was the last time you got any?" Chloe challenged.

Larissa opened her mouth to shoot back a snappy retort, then clamped her lips together. Answering would only prove Chloe's point. Instead, she said, "When was the last time you had any that was good enough to be in a romance novel?"

Larissa didn't need an answer. She knew she'd won. Heck, she regularly listened to Chloe's complaints about lousy sex. Heck, she'd used it in at least a half dozen of her romance columns.

Of course, that's not all she talked about. After all, she'd had plenty of personal experience with mind-blowing, life-altering, headboard-banging sex. Her very own romance novel sex. But that'd been a lot of years ago and she'd learned the hard way that there had to be more. Trust, companionship, common goals. Those things might not make her scream in ecstasy, but they sure went a lot further to making the romance long term than a triple chocolate-dipped orgasm.

"Look, I'm just saying you have to consider a wider clientele than just you," Chloe said, giving Larissa's shoulder a quick squeeze. "Just because you've chosen to bury your sexual needs beneath eight layers of romantic fluff doesn't mean everyone will. Isn't the purpose of this business to succeed?"

"Of course I plan to succeed," Larissa said, ignoring both Chloe's point and the panic clutching at her own belly. "I know what I'm doing."

"I do, too. You're ignoring an automatic tie-in with your store's theme because you've got issues with sex."

Finished avoiding the topic, Larissa dropped onto the rocking chair, folded her arms over her chest and got her pout on.

"I don't have issues."

"How would you know? It's been so long since you had any, you can't even test that theory out."

Larissa's pout deepened. She dug her chin into her chest and stared at the perfection of her French pedicure. "Maybe I don't have a sex drive."

Chloe's snort bounced off the walls. "Right."

"Maybe we all peak at different times," she defended before her friend could explain the reasons behind her snort. Some things were better left unsaid. "Maybe I hit my peak and now I just have to accept that my sex drive is on the way down."

Chloe sighed, then uncurled her long body from the round chair and crossed the room to give Larissa a hug. She kneeled and offered a long, serious look at odds with her wild appearance.

"Or maybe you're giving Jason Cantrell too much credit. It's not like he has a magic dick, Larissa. It wasn't coated with orgasm glitter or anything."

Larissa wrinkled her nose. Not at the crude expression. She was so used to Chloe's vernacular, she barely noticed. Nope, her wince was over the mention of Jason's name.

"If you were a nurse, you'd be the kind who grinned over giving people shots in the ass, wouldn't you?" Larissa said with a narrowed look.

"Why?" Chloe challenged, her lips twitching at the accusation. "Because hearing Jason's name hurts you somehow?"

"I'm not hurting."

Chloe waited.

Larissa closed her eyes for a moment.

Sure, she might not trust men anymore. She might lie awake at night, wondering if she'd ever have the perfect storybook romance like those she read about. And maybe she was a little wary of being called out as a fraud for not having any real romance in her personal life. But that wasn't hurt.

It was more like a cute pink bandage over the top of a big ugly scab hiding a three-year-old boo-boo.

She winced. Okay, so maybe she wasn't completely over him. But she mostly was, and that's what counted.

"Maybe I'm a little cautious," she finally acknowledged. "But that only applies to my personal life. Not to my business."

"But you're letting your hurt and bad feelings over your breakup with Jason color your business choices, aren't you?"

Larissa pressed her lips together, wanting to deny it. But she was a lousy liar.

"Sometimes I feel like a fraud," Larissa confessed. "Who am I to claim to be an authority on romance when my one and only relationship failed."

"If you could do it over again, would you have done anything different?" Chloe asked. "Kicked him where it would hurt, maybe? Or defended yourself when he accused you of cheating?"

"Why should I have to defend myself?" she replied. "He should have trusted me. Without trust, there is no relationship."

"Hey, I'm not defending the guy," Chloe denied. "He broke your heart, he deserves to die. I'm just saying that maybe it's time to let it go."

Larissa stared down at her tangled fingers, remembering

the short—less than a week, short—time a diamond had sparkled there. A part of her had known when Jason had given her the ring that their engagement wouldn't last. There were just too many differences between them. But she'd hoped. Oh, how she'd hoped.

Chloe, obviously realizing she'd made her point—and was in danger of delving into tequila-healing territory when Larissa couldn't afford to do the presentation with a hangover—changed the subject.

"All I'm saying is that if there is a way to guarantee your store has a better chance of surviving the first year, you should do it. And widening your focus just a bit would increase those odds," Chloe persuaded.

"No." She crossed her arms over her chest and lifted her chin. She'd had this dream for too long. "I'm not going to ruin my dream with a compromise I'll hate."

"Bending, just a little, doesn't mean you're caving," Chloe said quietly. "Remember, Mr. Murphy offered to let you buy his store when he retires next month. If you're not willing to change your concept, maybe you should consider a lower rent venue. Because once you make this choice, there's no going back."

The safety of that was so appealing. Larissa loved the old Victorian that housed Mr. Murphy's bookstore. She'd nursed her love of romances there, built her skills as a communicator and a salesperson. She was safe there…as long as she did things his way, kept with the same old program. But if she changed things? Would people come? Would she lose the bulk of the tried and true customers who had expectations that she couldn't meet anymore because she was pursuing her own hopes and dreams?

Larissa looked at the mess she'd made of boxes, books and all of the accoutrements she deemed necessary for romance. Even though this time she was risking her career and her finances, it was still as difficult as it had been with her heart. But this time, she knew what she was doing. She wasn't falling in love without a clue, she was prepared.

"I can do this," she said decisively. And she'd consider the sex stuff, too. Maybe this was her chance. Time to change her business, and her personal life. She was through hiding behind the past, waiting for Prince Charming. She was putting "get a sex life" on her agenda, dammit. Right after she dealt with her career, of course.

Determined, she stood and put the lid on her box of merchandise. She was as ready as she was going to get. "But I need to decide what to wear. Want to help me pick out the perfect snooty outfit?"

Chloe rose, studying her carefully. Then she gave a slow nod. "Sure. I specialize in snoot."

See, Larissa thought as they headed for her bedroom and its overcrowded closet. She'd prove, to Chloe and to herself, that she didn't need a magic dick to make her dreams come true.

2

JASON CANTRELL HANDLED HIS BMW like he was on a racetrack. Fast, tight and controlled. He hit the freeway off-ramp doing eighty, Aerosmith's rhythm beating through the speakers like a war drum.

He spared a glance at the clock on the dash.

Late.

He gave a mental shrug. No point wasting energy on what he couldn't change.

His plane had been delayed, then he'd got caught up in customs where he'd had to explain the three-foot penis he'd brought back from the Papua New Guinea. Well, maybe not so much explain, since the kotekas, or penis-sheaths, were pretty self-explanatory. Still, his was special.

Aerosmith's walking instructions were interrupted when the Bluetooth in Jason's dash pounded out its own beat. He flicked a button on the steering wheel.

"Yo," he answered.

"Yo, yourself. How'd the meeting go?"

A quick glance noted there was no traffic. With a flick of his wrist Jason took a corner at twice the speed limit.

"I'm on my way, big brother," he said. "I called Daniel when I landed and told him I'd be late. He's missing this meet but said he'd pass the message on to the committee. Don't worry, the pitch practically sells itself. We've got it in the bag."

"I'm not worried about the pitch," Peter said. "You could sell snow to a polar bear. I'm just... Well... You know."

Ever the wordsmith, that was Peter Cantrell. Jason gave a rueful shake of his head.

"I know. It's going to work out. Quit stressing, okay."

It, being their business. A business the two brothers had started at twenty-two and twenty, respectively. They'd grown up traveling with their archaeologist parents and were on their second passport before they'd hit puberty. At first, the brothers had led a few buddies on trips as a way to make beer money in college. Mountain climbing, rafting, hiking. Soon they'd developed a rep for creating awesome adventures. They had inside knowledge of places they'd already visited and they made it a point to turn each trip into a special event. That beer money had quickly turned to seed money. They were doing so well that by the time Peter graduated, Jason had dropped out to take on Can-Do Adventures full-time.

But now they needed to make some changes. Because he wanted to settle down with his fiancée and play happy hubby, Peter had decided to take a step back from the regular trips. Only neither brother wanted to hire help. They couldn't control the quality of a trip halfway around the world unless one of them was leading it. Which meant cutting their income in half...unless they found a way to advertise to a higher-paying group of adventurers and woo in some bigger groups.

Hence, Cartright Hotels. If they snagged this store, they could easily tap into the promotional benefits of the hotel conglomerate, entice the wealthy clientele and support both brothers on the same number of trips led just by Jason. Cartright was offering a primo deal, advertising their newest businesses in their press packets for the first year. They were doing ads in airline and travel magazines, linking their loyalty points to the use of their own vendors—of which Can-Do would be one, if Jason played his cards right—and launching a huge media blitz.

In return, the Cantrells would add specialized/couple adventures, exclusive to Cartright guests, to their repertoire. Adventure honeymoons and wild getaways. All at vastly discounted rates, if booked while staying at one of Cartright's resorts.

An all-round win-win deal, if he did say so himself.

"You sure you want to do this?" Peter asked. "I mean, if they don't go for it, we can still salvage the business. I'll kick in part of my income to keep things afloat, and continue to handle the bookings after you find another partner."

Peter had just lined up a job with a local sports store, selling equipment, teaching rock climbing, basically catering to the weekend warriors. Jason knew his brother hated the idea, but he needed the income. It was yet another reason to make this deal with Cartright work—Peter could man the store instead of selling tennis shoes and ski equipment. It really sucked that his brother had been talked into becoming more "steady."

"I don't want another partner," Jason dismissed. He didn't dismiss the offer to supplement Can-Do's income, though. He knew damned well that between the business and family expenses, he couldn't carry it all on his own.

A few years back, their mother had a stroke that had not only physically debilitated her, but had also destroyed her marriage. Because neither brother was able to take care of her themselves, Jason and Peter had been forced to choose between the depressing rehab center her insurance would cover, or ponying up to put her in a nice, cheerful housing program.

Ever their father's son, Peter's first suggestion when he'd said he needed to step down at Can-Do was to move their mother to the less-expensive assisted living unit. That'd been one of the few times Jason had blown up at his brother.

So now it was up to him to make sure everything worked out.

"We'll make it happen," he vowed. "I know I can pull this off."

"Well, you'd never find a partner as good as me, so I don't blame you," Peter joked. His tone was still stressed, though. Like he wasn't sure if he should push his brother to go it alone or take him at his word.

"You're hard to beat," Jason agreed. "Of course, I'm still the best."

"You wish." Peter laughed, sounding relieved. "Are you sure you don't want me to meet you, help with the pitch?"

"Nah, I've got it. Between the pitch and showing them the koteka as an example of the kinds of things we'd display, I'm sure it's in the bag. Besides...you've got enough to do. I'll come by in the morning and let you know how it goes," he promised. "You get the coffee ready and I'll bring my penis."

"Mine's still bigger," Peter promised.

Jason's smile slipped as the phone turned off and Aerosmith's "Sweet Emotion" filled his ears. The endless competition was just one more thing he was going to miss if Peter didn't come to his senses before the dreaded I Do-Day.

And the chances of that were looking sadly slim. Not that Jason had anything against Meghan, the sweet little thing his brother was marrying. But they already lived together. Peter was getting all the goodies—why sign on for the long haul? Especially when that haul meant ruining Can-Do Adventures.

Jason was going to have to run the business alone if

this little brainstorm didn't play out the way he wanted. Because he'd be damned if he'd take on a new partner. He liked doing things his way, on his own terms. Besides, he knew damned well that relationships didn't last. So it was his job as a good brother to keep things going so Peter had something to do when the Meghan deal went belly-up.

Ready to pitch and win, Jason pulled into the almost-empty parking lot, tires squealing. He parked next to a little red Mini S convertible, bounded from his car and strode toward the building.

A quick glance told him the location was prime. The almost completed hotel to the right, the city's business district three blocks past the park on the left. The place would pull in travelers and upscale shoppers alike. And all of them were potential customers for a Can-Do Adventure. More importantly, Peter could manage the store until he came to his senses and got back to living life to the fullest.

And in the meantime? They needed to make enough money to keep Can-Do afloat and cover their mother's expenses. Which meant not only cutting their tours in half without Peter, but slashing their promotion budget.

And that was where Cartright Hotels came in. It wasn't the location alone that had Jason excited. It was the promotion package offered to the vendors. Co-op, inclusion in Cartright's worldwide advertising, massively discounted television ads. One year here would set Can-Do up for the decade. It was plenty of time for Peter to get his head together.

All Jason had to do was snag that last store space.

No problem. Daniel Cartwright was a good friend. He and Peter had been frat buddies. The Cantrells had lived up the street—on the poorer side—from the Cartrights growing up, too. They hadn't actually run in the same circles, but Dan was a good guy even if his younger brother, Conner, was a jerk. No matter who else he had on the hook for the storefront, Jason was sure Can-Do was the frontrunner.

And just in case? He gripped the padded crate under his arm and grinned. Daniel said the hotel, and its adjoining boutique mall, were an ode to coupledom. Not something Jason had much experience with since his one attempt had been a huge bust. But he figured the one thing couples all wanted was a good sex life, so he'd brought his secret weapon. The koteka was supposed to be magic. The promise was that it'd bring blessings and hot sex to the wearer. Jason figured that if the Powers That Be weren't bowled over with his pitch, he could offer the koteka as an incentive. After all, what guy could resist the promise of hot sex?

That, his charm and the brilliance of his idea were all he'd need to snag this space and settle his life back on the track he wanted. Can-Do Adventures would survive. Neither storms nor mechanical failures nor a commitment-seeking woman would stop the brothers from their appointed purpose. Which was to see as much, do as much and discover as much of the world as possible.

In other words, to live. Free and easy. The only way to be.

"THIS IS STUNNING," Larissa said breathlessly, laying her hand on Conner's arm. She stared, wide-eyed, taking in the glorious view. Lush plants decorated the long, posh concourse of the mall. The floors were glossy marble. The walls were papered in rich silk. The windows glinted like diamonds and the entire space shouted exclusivity.

And her store would be here. It was like fantasizing about being swept away by a pirate, then finding herself on a deserted island with Johnny Depp. A dream come true, multiplied by a hundred.

"La Perla, Armani, Godiva," she murmured, shivering

in delight as she read the gilt signs already above some of the stores. She squinted, imagining Isn't It Romantic tucked up there between such stellar names, and grinned.

The place was small by mall standards, only eighty thousand square feet, but it didn't feel that way. The wide concourse with its lush greenery and center benches gave the feel of an outdoor garden. Only five stores on either side lined the concourse, with two discreet hallways angling off to the restrooms and the employee maintenance area.

She turned to face the man who used to be one of her best friends, but whom she hadn't seen much of in the last two years. Not since the *big ugly fiasco,* as she mentally referred to the worst night of her life.

She was glad Conner seemed to be over the whole humiliating incident and was willing to not only see her again, but to give her such an incredible opportunity. Still, she didn't figure reminding him of the *big ugly fiasco* was a good idea.

So instead, she gave him a cautious smile. "Conner, this is all so fabulous. You and Daniel must be so proud of the hotel, and of this mall."

"I'm actually quite proud of what I'm about to pull off," he said. His smile was innocuous enough, but there was something in his tone that caught Larissa's attention. She narrowed her eyes, wondering what he was up to. But then he added, "Want to see the space that's available?"

"My store?" she queried, only half teasing. "Heck, yeah."

"Right this way."

Her wheeled cart carrying the boxes of sample merchandise squeaked behind her as she let Conner lead her to the only store with its arched, glass doors open wide. Her breath hitched. She blinked quickly to clear the sudden tears from her eyes.

It was perfect.

Large, bright and, oh man, so, so luxurious. The counters were granite. The walls were lined with gilt-framed mirrors. She could see a dressing room off to the back and a sign indicating a bathroom. Other than the checkout counters, the room was empty except for a deeply cushioned settee against one wall. She spun around to check the view as she imagined herself behind the counter thanking her customers.

Just perfect. Through the pristine front windows, she could see the lush plants surrounding a plush velvet bench and a statue of Aphrodite, just inside the hotel lobby.

Larissa's Romance Rule number one: Appearances count. And appearing here would count for so much. Thrilled, she hugged herself tight.

"So, is it what you were hoping for?" Conner asked. "Can you imagine writing your column from the Cartright Boutique? Romance à la Cartright, catchy, huh?"

Larissa's brow went up before she could stop it. He was kidding, right? But she managed to keep the question to herself. Old friend or not, pissing Conner off was a bad idea. Cartright's policy was to promote all the stores on their properties on their website, in their other venues and with little gifts and special mailings to their patrons. There was no way she could ever afford that level of marketing on her own. The only way to get it was to snag this store space.

"Is that my new byline? The Romance Authority, brought to you by Cartright Hotels?" Her joking tone faded as she saw that he was serious. She knew that promotion was a big deal for Cartright, and that by taking a space in the mall, she'd be included in the co-op.

But this? She wasn't sure how she felt about it. It felt wrong, somehow. Like she was selling out.

Conner must have sensed her hesitation, because he

laughed it off and gave her shoulder a quick pat before stepping away. "I'll give you time to set up your display, hmm? The committee is meeting in a half hour. Would you mind coming back to the boardroom then to give your presentation?"

A little confused and conflicted, Larissa silently nodded, then watched him leave. It wasn't until she heard the echo of the elevator door closing in the empty mall that she let out her breath and looked around again.

Then realizing that she only had thirty minutes to make the store scream Isn't It Romantic, she shoved her worry to the back of her mind and got to work. After all, seeing was believing. She was sure the committee would fall in love with her store as soon as they saw how well her lovely merchandise fit in their exclusive space.

FORTY MINUTES LATER, Conner nervously fiddled with his pen as he listened to Larissa's pitch. He shifted in his chair, then adjusted his tie. The third time he ran his hand over his hair, he elbowed his marketing VP, Ben Jackson, giving him the evil eye.

Time to chill. Conner forced himself to calm down and act like the responsible, clear-headed businessman he usually was. He had too much on the line—both with this hotel and mall, and with his own private scheme—to blow it now.

They were in one of his newly completed hotel boardrooms, just Larissa and the three-man committee who would decide the fate of her dream. Conner had hand chosen the two men on the committee. Both were golfing buddies and good friends. But more important, both had a decent level of acting skills, which were vital if his scheme was going to work.

"Gentlemen," Larissa said with a charming smile that

made Conner want to sigh. "Your focus on couples, honeymoon packages and romantic getaways ties in perfectly with my store. Isn't It Romantic will totally enhance your guests' stay. I'll stock romance books, both fiction and nonfiction. Romantic movies through the ages. All the necessary accoutrements to bringing the pleasure of romance into your—our—guests' visit, as well as providing them with mementos of their wonderful stay that they'll appreciate for years to come."

As she continued, Conner let himself get distracted by how she looked. The same as the last time he'd seen her, yet, not quite. Her hair, often a riot of wild curls, was a tame fall of ringlets framing her sharp face. She wore a black suit, its austere color softened by a ruffled jacket and a skirt that hugged her hips and legs to the knee, where it echoed the jacket's ruffle. The darkness of her clothing was offset by vivid red heels that sent a few fantasies skittering through Conner's head before he reminded himself that he didn't think of Larissa that way.

Drew Franklin, the guy on his left, kicked him under the table. Conner started, then remembered the game. His plan was to keep her off balance until the, well, the surprise he'd been calling it. She might refer to it as the big betrayal. Or the knife in her back. Maybe some other title that included ugly swear words.

No matter, he owed her. And a Cartright always paid his dues.

"Larissa, this sounds great. The committee has a few questions, though," Conner said. He kept his voice a little distant instead of encouraging.

He hated to see her smile dim, nerves clear in her eyes as she nodded and said, "Of course. I'd be happy to answer them."

"It's a nice idea, I agree. But why just romance?" Drew

Franklin asked, embracing his role as the doubtful hard-ass. "Why such a narrow focus?"

"My impression was that you were looking for boutiques, not department stores," Larissa said, sounding a little less like a polished businesswoman and a little more like the spunky girl Conner knew. Good, she was going to need that spunk today.

"Sure. Boutiques are the goal. But couldn't you diversify a bit? You know, maybe spice it up or something?" he prodded.

"Or something?"

"You know, something sexier." He said it like sexier was a euphemism for kink on a stick.

Larissa wrinkled her nose, looking like she wanted to ask if he was a member of the pervert-of-the-month club. Conner looked down at his blank notepad to hide his grin.

"I do understand the appeal of diversification," she said after a deep breath. "And if you consider it, you'll see that I have diversified in a big way. Isn't It Romantic is more than a bookstore, or a movie store, or one focusing only on candles and scents. It's got it all."

Apparently deciding it was time to wow them with her charts and diagrams, Larissa handed each man a folder containing sketches, swatches and photos of the array of items she planned to carry.

"This is great," Ben said, flipping through the contents enthusiastically. He gave Larissa a flirtatious look, making her smile dim. She shot Conner a baffled, do-you-only-employ-creeps look.

He resisted the urge to pump his fist in the air. His plan was working. The worse he made guys look in the next half hour, the better she'd respond to his surprise.

He hoped. If not, his brother Daniel was going to seriously kick his ass for scaring away not one, but two perfect candidates for the storefront.

"Ben's right," Conner agreed. "You've really nailed the concept here. I think your idea is unique and would fit in nicely with Cartright's message."

"I still think it's a little, well, boring," Drew said, starting to tap his pen on the unopened folder she'd given him. "If a couple is staying at this locale, they're already covered with that romance thing. They want spice. They want excitement. They want—"

"I don't think romance ends when a couple checks into the hotel unless he's paying her by the hour," Larissa said with an arched brow. Then she smiled. "But that isn't really romance, is it? Or the type of hotel you're opening?"

Conner tried to disguise his laugh as a cough. Ben wasn't quite as successful.

"But I can see where you're coming from," she said, obviously encouraged that two-thirds of the room seemed to be on her side. "And I guarantee that Isn't It Romantic would cover the gamut of tastes, from sweet to spicy."

"Ms. Zahn, I think I speak for all of us when I say you've made a strong impression. Your store would align nicely with the other business we've chosen to represent us at the Cartright," Ben told her.

Conner nodded while Drew had pasted on an over-the-top bored look.

"I'd love for you to see what I have in mind for the space," she offered quickly. She placed her hand on the large box she'd carried in. "I've brought a few of the items I'd stock with me and I've created a display in the store that will give you a better understanding of the atmosphere and aesthetic I'll bring to the South Carolina Cartright."

Ben nodded enthusiastically. Drew gave a sigh, though,

as if getting up and walking to the elevators was more work than he'd intended to do today.

Before Conner could add his own two cents, a message flashed on his cell phone. He read it and grinned. Perfect. He looked at his colleagues and gestured with the phone.

"I just received the message that our earlier appointment has finally arrived. This is great. We can wrap up the interviews now, before heading out for the weekend," Conner said. "Larissa, if you'd please wait in the antechamber, we'll head down to the mall to look at your display just as soon as we finish with this appointment."

He offered Larissa an innocent smile and said, "Our next interview won't be long. Would you mind making yourself comfortable?"

She frowned, then with a quick shrug, gathered her charts and diagrams and tucked them away in her briefcase. She gave him a couple of searching looks, like she was trying to see what he was up to—or was that just his guilty conscience?

He wanted to rush the table and wrap her in his arms, assuring her that he'd make everything right for her.

Larissa had always had that effect on him. She was so pretty, with her riotous black curls and huge, dark eyes. He'd had a crush on her ever since he was fourteen, when she'd moved in with her eccentric aunt up the street.

Unfortunately, he'd made the mistake of acting on that attraction, only to be rebuffed in the most painful way—with sweet pity. And he'd reacted poorly. Acting like a spoiled brat, he'd lashed out. Not at her, but at the fiancé she'd refused to leave for him, hinting to the other man that there was something more going on between him and Larissa. Conner had felt justified, since they broke up. For about a week. Then he'd felt like shit. His greedy obnoxiousness had hurt two people, one of whom he cared about deeply.

He was hoping to make it up to her now. By tomorrow, she'd either love him again—as a friend. Or hate him.

FOLLOWING THE DIRECTIONS Daniel Cartright had given him, Jason made his way through the empty hotel. He glanced at his cell phone to check his battery. It was heading for dead, but probably had enough juice for him to offer up a convincing slideshow during the presentation.

Looking forward to seeing Daniel, who, after rooming with Jason's brother for three years in college, was as much Jason's buddy as Peter's, Jason sauntered into the boardroom with a wide grin on his face. The grin faded as he stepped through the doorway.

Instead of finding Daniel sitting at the head of the shiny new boardroom table, Jason was greeted by his younger brother, Conner.

Jason barely noticed the other two guys flanking him. He was too focused on the sudden fury flashing through his brain.

Memories washed over him like a monsoon. Larissa. Damn, he'd fallen hard and intense for her. He'd been young enough, stupid enough, to think he'd been in love with her. Their affair had been hot, wild and intense. Until she'd cheated on him with Conner.

Bombarded by feelings he'd been sure were long gone, he clenched his teeth and resisted the urge to tear into the guy.

His shoulders clenched, his hands fisting at his sides. He was being ridiculous, he reminded himself. Conner had been in Europe, not aware that Jason and Larissa were a thing when he'd asked her out. And when he'd found out, he'd completely backed off. Conner wasn't to blame. Larissa was.

On the surface, Jason and Conner had made their peace

a couple years ago. The past was over. And if there was one thing Jason prided himself on, it was being the kind of guy who didn't dwell on stuff that was already put away. Especially not anything as useless as emotional baggage.

Especially not now, when he had a business to save.

"Hey, Conner," Jason greeted, his words only a little stiff. He forced himself to stride through the wide-open doors of the partially furnished boardroom. "This is a surprise. I thought I was meeting with Daniel."

Conner, looking like the successful tycoon he'd always been, rose with a smile to shake Jason's hand. For a brief, stomach-churning second, Jason could see why Larissa would go for the guy. He was just like one of those romance novel heroes.

Stop, Jason mentally snapped at himself. Focusing on the past was useless. Put it away and make today happen.

"Jason, good to see you. Unfortunately, Daniel was called away and couldn't be here. But we're glad you could make it. Since we're running behind, let me introduce you to the committee and we'll get started. Then we can catch up later, if you'd like."

"Sure thing." But before Conner could say anything else Jason made his way around the table, and with handshakes all around, introduced himself.

He dropped the case holding his trump card, so to speak, onto the polished table, barely noting the tufts of dust that rose as it hit the wood.

"Have a seat," one of the committee members suggested. "Conner's told us about your ideas and I'll admit, I'm loving the prospect of working with you. But we have another contender for the space and we are in a bit of a hurry. So if you don't mind, grab a seat and tell us about your plans."

Jason eyed Conner, wondering just what he'd told the committee. Daniel had taken a few trips with Can-Do. But

Conner wasn't really the roughing-it type, so he'd always passed. Sure, they were all cool now. But given that, at one time, Jason had threatened to toss Conner out a window, he wouldn't have been surprised if the dude still held a grudge.

Nice to know they were both too big for that kind of crap, Jason thought, giving Conner a friendly smile. Then, parking the past into the history books where it belonged, he focused on the here, now and more importantly, the future.

"I'll skip the sitting invite, if you don't mind," he told the partner. "I just flew in from the Galapagos by way of Zimbabwe, so my ass is pretty numb."

"Pace away, my friend," Conner said with a wave of his hand. "I'd love to hear about your latest trip, too. But Ben has a plane to catch, so why don't you give us your pitch before he goes."

Jason gave a friendly nod. "No problem. First off, I'd like to say thank you to all of you for considering Can-Do Adventures. Regardless of whether we end up working as a team here at the latest Cartright Hotel, I hope you'll all accept an invitation to take a trip as our gift. Any adventure, from the Andes to Tanzania, just give us a call and we'll set it up."

Jason reminded himself to let his brother know. Peter was the money-man, which meant he'd probably throw a fit at the thousands Jason had just tossed on the table. But it was worth the gamble. Besides, if they didn't get this space, Can-Do would be Used-To, so it wouldn't matter.

"What makes you think a travel agency would thrive in a hotel catering to couples?" the pudgy, less-friendly guy asked.

"Fair question. Ben, isn't it?" Jason stuffed his hands in his front pockets and rocked back on the worn heels of his hiking boots, waiting for the guy to nod.

"First off, Can-Do isn't a typical travel agency. We don't book cruises and family trips. We specialize in adventure. In thrills and excitement and pushing the limits. No two bookings are alike, since no two people want the same thing. We customize one-of-a-kind tours. And if we're aligned with the Cartright Hotels, we'll be offering very exclusive, very impressive tours for Cartright's patrons."

He emphasized that point, since it was one that was near and dear to his heart. It was also the first one that'd have to go if this deal didn't come through. He pictured himself leading his tenth hike of the month through the Daintree Rainforest, on a first-name basis with the tree-kangaroos, and shuddered. Gorgeous, yes. But with that kind of repetition, there was no excitement. Travel for the sake of seeing the same thing over and over was as bad as sitting on his ass in front of a television watching the nature channel.

Totally not his thing.

Not that he hadn't considered it, once. Giving up the wild trips, playing it safe. Or at least, safer. He'd almost left Peter in the same lurch his brother now had him in. That was why he couldn't be too pissed at the guy. Women—some very special women—could make a man go stupid.

Jason eyed Conner and wondered if he should've thanked the guy all those years ago instead of getting ugly. After all, if Conner hadn't swooped in with his rich boy charm and swept Larissa away, who knew what kind of craziness Jason might have gotten into?

But he'd learned his lesson. And his brother probably would, too. That was the reason Jason had to seal this deal— so they both had a career when Peter came to his senses. Or got bored playing house, whichever came first.

"Can-Do is the perfect pairing for the Cartright Hotel. Your clientele is used to the best, and we're it. They're used to being catered to, and we excel in catering. And by aligning with us in this location, we'll offer the same discounts and packages to the patrons in all of your venues. In addition, we'll create a deeply discounted Cartright Exclusive weekend adventure package."

He went on to explain how Can-Do would utilize the space, more like a small museum, which would be more appealing than the bland travel agency storefront many would expect. Showcasing artifacts, curios and specialty items from the many places they offered tours, the space would act as a Can-Do maintained attraction for the hotel guests.

Jason finished his pitch with the videos on his phone, then told them about the antique penis sheath he'd brought back from Papua New Guinea as an example of the quality of merchandise they'd show in the store.

"Jason, this is fabulous. You've given us a lot to think about." Conner glanced at the two men, one of whom was making a show of looking at his watch. "If you don't mind, we need to talk for a minute before Ben has to go. Would you be so good as to wait in the antechamber while we tie up some loose ends? Then we'll let you see the space for yourself."

"Sure thing," Jason said. He thanked the other two men, exchanged a few quips, then noticing Ben looked like he was about to explode, he graciously gathered his koteka under one arm and sauntered into the antechamber.

Still riding high with the success of his presentation, he caught a glimpse of movement across the room. The scent hit him before he turned. Soft roses, with an underlying layer of sexy heat. It made him think of making wild love in a garden under the full moon.

Crazy, he told himself as he stepped fully into the room and let the door swing shut behind him.

Then his brain sputtered. His heart raced as if he'd just

taken a long, deadly dive off a high cliff. His muscles tightened, his senses on full-alert. It took Jason's body a few extra seconds to filter the rush of energy flying through his system. Lust mixed with shock. Memories cascaded like a waterfall, pouring over forgotten hopes and hurts.

Sonofabitch.

Thickly lashed brown eyes, tilted like a startled cat's at the corners, stared back at him. He recognized the horror in her gaze, just as he recognized the flash of hot desire beneath it. Pale color rose, washing over her high cheekbones.

It'd been two years. And still, he could perfectly remember how those silky curls felt in his fingers. He knew exactly how that wide, mobile mouth would feel on his skin. He could see that lush little body stripped of its frilly black suit, naked and poised over the hard length of his.

He rocked back on his heels and grinned.

"Well, well," he murmured. "If it isn't the luscious Larissa. Who knew hell would freeze over this quickly?"

3

"JASON?"

Larissa stood, pressing her hand against the freshly painted wall trying to steady herself while the room spun wildly. She blinked. If she hadn't been afraid taking her hand from the wall would result in falling on her ass, she'd have rubbed her eyes.

She was hallucinating, right? This was a dream? A mirage brought on by her insistence that sex didn't matter. Payback for arguing against something she secretly lay awake at night fantasizing about?

Damn Chloe.

Slowly, reluctantly, Larissa slid her gaze over the illusion—or was that delusion—in the doorway. Six-foot-two of long, lean sexual magnetism. Unable to stop herself, she took in the sight. From the sun-kissed tips of his shaggy brown hair to the enigmatic look in his too-pretty-to-belong-to-a-guy blue eyes. Her fingers twitched with the need to comb them through those silken strands and push that one recalcitrant lock off his forehead.

She nearly sighed as she took in the view of his wide, muscled shoulders, wrapped in a soft cotton workshirt that perfectly matched those hypnotic eyes. His broad chest, with that light dusting of hair visible above the top button, was better than any pillow on earth. Her eyes dropped down to the well-worn denim lovingly covering his...

Oh, God. Larissa ripped her gaze from his crotch, where she was pretty sure she'd just visually licked him.

If she wasn't careful, she'd actually be climbing over his body and nibbling on all of his man parts before she knew it. He had that effect on her. He was danger, pure and simple.

It was all Larissa could do not to run from the room and yell for Conner.

Conner was safe.

Conner was her friend.

Conner was the reason she and Jason had so painfully split up two years ago.

No, she corrected herself. Jason himself was the reason behind their breakup. Him and his lack of trust.

She frowned, the wheels of her brain starting to turn again. Why was Jason here? Conner knew their history. Why would he—or any other sane person—bring the two of them together in the same room?

Conner was obviously an idiot, she decided.

"What are you doing here?" she asked after clearing the shock from her throat. "Shouldn't you be swinging from a vine in some jungle with a half-naked woman attached to your waist?"

He looked just as shocked as she was. And, from the heated glance in his eyes, he'd been sucked right into that same evil sexual vortex that had caused them both so many problems in the past.

"I left my loincloth with Jane," he responded in an absent tone. His attention was clearly more focused on his inspection of her body than on taking insult with her question. "You're looking good, though."

Larissa trembled, her thighs quivering a little at the sexy heat in Jason's eyes. God, that's all it took from him, a single look and she melted. He was like a fairy tale hero out of one of her favorite romance novels.

"So, obviously you and Conner are still tight," he said, crossing his arms over his chest.

Larissa's lusty reaction burst as if she'd been drenched in an ice bath. Her shoulders stiffened and she jutted out her chin. Romance hero, her ass.

"Obviously," she replied in a chilly tone.

If that's what he wanted to think, good. He was still a mistrusting idiot. He'd thrown away the best thing to ever happen to him and still wasn't smart enough to realize it yet. He'd known Conner for years, first through his brother and then later through those stupid trips the guys had taken together. Hell, Conner had even been the one to introduce Larissa and Jason.

Her thoughts, and the accompanying tension pounding through her spine, were so painfully familiar, Larissa wanted to cry.

Holy crap, it was like being sent back in a time machine. Larissa pressed two fingers to her temple, trying to stem the throbbing vein. Crazy. Anything she had with Jason was in the past. She'd be damned if she'd let him know how much seeing him still hurt. Or give him any idea how devastated she'd been when he'd left her.

Cool, calm and collected. Yep, that was her.

"So why are you here again?" she asked, silently reciting her new mantra.

"I'm here to see the Cartright brothers about a business deal." He raised a brow. "And you? Waiting for a date?"

"What?" She ignored the date dig. Jason was here about the storefront? That was impossible. "This is a joke, right? You can't be interested in the available retail space. You're too busy chasing your childhood, running all over the planet looking for new ways to risk your life."

"Aww, you know me so well," Jason replied as he made a show of slouching against the wall, while giving her a look so intense, she glanced down to make sure her jacket was buttoned and her boobs weren't hanging out. "But despite that deep insight into my character, it's actually true. I'm opening a store here at the Cartright."

"You mean *you'd like* to open a store. There's only one space available and I'm pretty sure Conner and company will be giving it to me," Larissa answered, trying to sound cocky. Then, seeing the fake affable look on his face slip a little, she shook her head quickly before he could make some snotty guy remark about how she'd convinced Conner to give her the space. "Why would you need a storefront, anyway? Don't you have mountains to climb?"

"Not getting much climbing satisfaction these days, huh?"

Larissa tilted her head to the side and gave him a long once-over. "Oh, believe me, I've never climbed mountains as satisfying as the one I'm scaling now."

Even more satisfying was watching that lie take the shine off his cocky smile.

"Is that a fact?"

Larissa gave a little shrug, then brushing an imaginary bit of lint off her black pencil skirt, used the brief pause to try and catch her breath. She never lied well, and given the dearth of mountains in her current love life, she wasn't too sure she could pull it off now.

"Excuse me," Conner said from the doorway. Larissa and Jason both turned. Larissa with a grateful look at the intervention, Jason with a glare. Conner's friendly smile didn't waver. "Perhaps you can delay the rest of this reunion?

The committee is on its way out but wanted a chance to talk with the two of you first, if you don't mind."

Larissa swept up her briefcase and with a quick tug at the hem of her black silk ruffled jacket, hurried toward the door. She slowed her rush when she realized she'd have to brush past Jason to get to the freedom on the other side.

Jason and his magic dick. Larissa lifted her chin and pretended she didn't feel its lure. Skirting carefully around him, she gave Conner a quick, grateful smile.

She also pretended she didn't hear Jason's low growl.

Knowing she should be focused on the committee, Larissa attempted to quickly sort through her tangled feelings. Why did Jason have to come back? What the hell did he need with a store? And why was he still so gorgeous? Shouldn't there be a rule for heartbreakers? That they were punished with a double chin or ten pounds for every year of misery they caused?

"Ms. Zahn? Conner was just filling us in on a few details. I didn't realize you and Mr. Cantrell knew each other," Ben said, breaking into her reverie.

"Quite well, as a matter of fact," Jason added, his voice still that same husky tone she heard so often in her dreams.

"Hardly at all, really," she dismissed just as quickly. "We met through Conner, actually. All things considered, I'd say Jason was practically a stranger."

A blatant lie. The room was lit up from the sparks flying between the two of them. She couldn't be the only one feeling it.

Conner, who should have seen the direction this was heading, steepled his fingers together and watched her with an enigmatic look. Jason just grinned, that devilish dimple flashing.

"Oh, I wouldn't say we were strangers, Larissa. Not after all we've been through together."

Conner smirked. The men on either side of him sat up a little straighter. They obviously sensed the vibes.

But Larissa's Romance Rule number three—learned the hard way—insisted that there be no airing of dirty laundry in public. It always, absolutely always, came back to bite you in the butt.

"So how long has it been since the two of you saw each other?" the pen-tapper asked.

"One year, eight months. Give or take a few days," Jason said, his tone so off-hand that it took Larissa a few beats to realize what he'd said. After a mental finger count, she realized he was exactly right.

Larissa had a smile on her face before she realized her lips had moved. He responded with a smile of his own, his gaze sweeping her body with a look so warm, she knew he was remembering her naked. Color washed over her cheeks and she gave herself a mental head slap. Proof positive why Jason was so bad for her. His sweet little comments made her feel like she was the most important person in his world. Right up until she remembered that she barely made his top ten list.

Which, she reminded herself as her own smile fell away, was just one of the reasons why he was so bad for her.

"Did the two of you go to school together?" Ben asked, his chubby face alight with curiosity. Larissa didn't know why he was so curious. It had nothing to do with either of their abilities to launch a store. But she answered anyway.

"No. I went to the local schools and Jason traveled."

"My parents were archaeologists," Jason interjected. "I was homeschooled on the road."

"But you hung out together? You had the same friends?"

"I used to hang out with Conner," Larissa said, her tone syrup-sweet. There went Jason's smile. "Jason's brother and Conner's were college roommates. Jason and I met at some party the Cartrights threw."

"Then what all is the *all* that you've been through together?" the irritating guy with the pen prodded, referring to Jason's earlier taunt.

They both ignored him. Larissa out of respect for the dirty laundry rule. Jason, she was sure, because he never answered anything that didn't suit him.

"I take it the two of you didn't realize you were competing for the same space?" Ben asked.

"No. It's been a couple years since Larissa and I had time to catch up, so this is a big surprise," Jason replied.

He shot Conner a look. Larissa couldn't believe everyone wasn't seeing through Jason's mellow demeanor. There was anger, impatience and a hint of worry in that blue-eyed glare. She understood the first two, but the latter? What did Jason have to worry about?

"And now that you know you both want the same thing?" Pen-tapper gave a sharklike grin, looking like the kind of guy who plunked down money to watch any form of violent sports. "Are you both still interested? Or is this one of those situations where you both say you want it, then after we spend hours assessing the situation and what's best for the hotel, one of you gets all sappy and backs down so the other doesn't get his or her panties in a twist?"

"Franklin!" Conner snapped.

"Hey, I think we have the right to know. We need to make a decision and I don't see much point in wasting time debating if one of them is going to step aside for the other."

His words ended in a buzz as the room did a little spin around Larissa's head. Both still interested? So Jason actually did want the store space? Why? For what? Did that mean he was really back to stay? She wasn't sure what panicked her more. The idea of battling against him for her dream space. Or knowing he was living in the same town again. It was hard enough to forget him when he was traipsing around the world. It'd be impossible to put him out of her mind if he was within touching distance.

But maybe, just maybe, she'd get the space…and he'd go away again. A girl could hope, right?

"Mr. Franklin, despite the tone of your questions, I do believe you have a good point. You're concerned with both your own time and what's best for the hotel," Larissa acknowledged.

She was proud of herself for sounding so reasonable when she wanted to smack all four men over the head with her purse. Conner for getting her into this, Franklin for being a jerk. Jason for all the memories and regrets beating through her. And Ben? Well, he was a guy and at this particular moment, they were obviously all on the same side.

"But you don't have anything to worry about," Jason interjected, obviously knowing exactly what she'd been about to say. "Despite our history, Larissa is right. She and I are practically strangers now. I want this space too much to let it go for old time's sake. And I'm sure she feels the same."

"Then you might be willing to negotiate?"

Larissa's stomach took a dive. Negotiate what? Rent? She could barely afford the amount Conner had told her. The promotional deal? The marketing tie-in with the hotel was the only reason she could justify the rent she could barely afford. What else could be negotiated?

"No," Jason said firmly. He didn't even look at her, instead keeping his gaze on Franklin. He still looked as kickback friendly as always. He was leaning against the window ledge, one foot crossed over the other and his hands in the front pockets of his jeans. He even had a friendly half smile on his face. But his eyes were hard, his jaw set. He wasn't taking any crap.

He flicked a quick glance her way. In that second, she realized he wasn't letting these guys give her any crap, either. She swallowed, warmth filling her heart.

"The terms were already presented and we agreed to them," Jason continued. "The decision is yours to make, of course. But neither of us will undercut or undermine the other so you can take advantage of the situation."

"No," Conner said before either of the other men could respond. "First of all, that's not how we do business at Cartright. And second, while the decision on which business will occupy the space is up to my associates, all terms and conditions are mine to make."

He stood, his associates reluctantly getting to their feet as well. Obviously, Ben had totally forgotten about his impending flight. "We'll discuss the situation, and I'll get you both the decision by tomorrow. But for now, I have a dinner appointment to get to. So we're going to take a look at the display while you both finish things up here."

Larissa gave a small shrug. Finish? She and Jason had finished a long time ago. Two years ago, in fact, when he'd taken his engagement ring and walked away.

THE SHOCK OF SEEING Larissa was starting to fade. The in-your-face lust seeing her always inspired was still flaming hot and strong, but years of adventures had taught Jason the wisdom in avoiding the kind of danger that led to certain doom.

And Larissa and him? Yep, definitely doomed.

"Wait, I'd like to see the storefront, too," he called out. He had no idea why. He didn't give a rat's ass what the store looked like. He didn't plan to spend any time in it. That was Peter's chore. But Larissa had seen it. Hell, she'd set up a display in it, apparently. So he'd better at least pretend he cared if he wanted to make a good impression.

"To be fair, why don't you give us five minutes to look over the display, then come on down," the guy named Ben suggested with a covetous look at Larissa.

Jason narrowed his eyes. Did this loser think by voting in her favor, he'd have a shot at making time with Larissa? She might have rotten taste in men, himself excluded, but she would never go out with a guy for a store space.

Jason eyed the pudgy guy's friendly face. Unless she was attracted to him?

Was that jealousy stabbing him in the gut?

Nah. He had no reason to be jealous. No rights where Larissa was concerned. They were over. Long over. So no, that couldn't be jealousy.

The green haze in his eyes said differently.

"The main hotel doors are all programmed to lock automatically. Because we're not open yet, we haven't brought in security guards so don't be surprised if you don't run into anyone. Feel free to explore as long as you like," Conner informed them. "Jason, if you'll give us a few minutes, you're welcome to stay behind and look around after we've gone. Larissa has the key to the store itself. I trust you'll lock it up and make sure things are secure before you leave."

"Sure. Yeah, I can do that. I'd love to look around," Jason lied. What the hell was there to look at? None of the stores were open. Hell, Daniel said they hadn't even brought in fixtures or inventory yet. Besides, unless the building was filled with potential clients, he wouldn't have a clue what he was checking out.

"I'll wait in here, too, if you don't mind," Larissa said. "I'd rather you get the full effect of the display and feel comfortable to honestly discuss it among yourselves. I'll go down after you've finished and gather up the materials, if that's okay?"

Ahh, there it was. His reason for waiting. Not because he wanted to spend more time with Larissa, although, man, was she looking hot. Her hair, that riotous mass of glossy black curls, was styled in a way that framed her face and accented those huge eyes. And that body? He shifted uncomfortably to ease the tightening denim. Smoking hot. Her skirt hugged her hips and was way too long, hitting her just below the knees and hiding legs he remembered as deliciously sleek. But the fabric cupped her butt just right. And her ruffled jacket looked soft and inviting, despite the long sleeves and lack of cleavage displayed.

But just because she looked great didn't mean he was hanging out to spend time with her. Nope, smart men didn't have to fall off the same cliff twice to know it was going to hurt.

They did, however, carefully assess the competition, looking for information and weaknesses that would let them win the game.

So. He was assessing. That's all.

"Thanks to both of you for coming in for the presentations. We appreciate it. And we'll let you know right away," Conner said, stopping in the doorway to give Larissa a quick hug. It was all Jason could do not to dive across the room and rip the guy's hands off of her. When they'd made their peace last year, Conner had claimed that even though he'd hoped for more, he and Larissa had only ever been friends. But maybe he'd lied?

Or maybe things had changed since then.

And maybe, Jason reminded himself with clenched teeth, it was none of his business anymore.

On his way out the door after Conner, Franklin gave Larissa a stiff smile, then shook Jason's hand encouragingly.

Ben looked like he wanted to drool all over her feet. He gave Jason a quick look, noted the scowl, and offered her his hand instead.

Smart man.

She might not be Jason's any longer, but he was pretty sure he'd have to beat the hell out of any guy who hit on her in front of him.

It was like a reflex or instinct or something. Totally unplanned and, well, realistically? Unwelcomed. Because he knew from painful experience that the last thing Larissa wanted was anything to do with his…what had she called it? Oh yeah, his pathetic, half-assed commitment-phobic posturing.

He'd asked her to marry him, hadn't he? So how could he be commitment-phobic? Which meant the rest of her accusations were equally unfounded and ridiculous.

Too bad she looked so damned good, though. She'd always been a cute kid. Tiny, like a fairy, with masses of black curls and brown eyes too big for her angular face. Her diminutive size and quiet nature had kept her off Jason's radar the first couple times they'd met. Hell, she'd still been in high school then. Way off-limits.

But her first summer home from college? Well, Jason Cantrell might be a little slow on the uptake sometimes, but he made up for it with enthusiasm. He'd taken one look at her golden legs in little cutoff shorts and he'd fallen hard and fast. Which pretty well described their entire courtship and, he was ashamed to admit, their first time in bed together.

She'd broken his heart.

And now she wanted to ruin his brilliant business plan.

Nope. Not gonna happen.

"So," he said slowly, leaning against the table and trying to look relaxed as he took a long, appreciative look at the woman fidgeting by the door.

"So?"

So, how was she doing?

So, what'd happened between her and Conner over the years?

So, why did she want to set up shop here, in a hotel?

So, when had she quit working for that old guy at the bookstore and what had she been doing since then?

"So, are you still single?" He winced as he heard the words, which had been nowhere on his list of approved questions.

From the look she gave him, it wasn't on her list, either.

"I can't believe you're interested in opening a store," she said, ignoring his question. "Are you leaving Can-Do Adventures?"

"Nope. Can-Do is doing great. We're in twenty-three countries now, touring every continent."

Her smile was fast and warm. You had to hand it to Larissa, she might hold grudges and have all sorts of insane ideas about relationships. But the woman was as sweet as they came, always ready to celebrate someone else's success and happiness.

"You're living the dream," she murmured, using his oft-repeated goal, as she gathered folders and diagrams to shove in her big leather bag. "Peter must be thrilled, too. I hope he's well."

Jason narrowed his eyes, trying to see if she was being sarcastic. Larissa had always had a subtle hand with the snark. But she looked genuine. Amazing, considering his brother had done everything he could to break the two of them up.

"He's as well as can be expected," he said with a shrug.

"Is something wrong?" Her words were politely concerned, but this time he saw the look of naughty glee in her eyes. Like she was imagining Peter stewing in a cannibal's cauldron.

"Yeah. He's been ordered to quit traveling. It won't be the same without him."

"I'm so sorry. Will he be okay?" she asked, stepping forward to put a consoling hand on his arm. Jason's body reacted like she'd rubbed up against him wearing only black stockings and a feather boa. Hard, hot and horny in an instant.

"He's terminal," Jason said, barely aware of his words as he tossed off the term he'd often used to razz his brother.

She blanched. Her fingers curled into his forearm, short nails biting the flesh. Jason's dick hardened even more as he flashed back to a memory of those same nails digging into his shoulder as he thrust into her welcoming body.

"Oh, Jason. I'm so sorry. Your parents must be heartbroken."

"Nah, Mom likes Meghan."

"Meghan?" She frowned. "What?"

Jason did a quick rewind and realized what she must have thought.

"Peter's getting married. It's a terminal case of commitment," he explained quickly, trying not to grin.

She pulled her hand away like he was covered in something gross. The disgusted look on her face echoed the action.

"You're impossible."

"Nope, sweetheart. How could you forget? I'm incredibly easy. At least, where you were concerned."

She didn't smile this time, but her cheeks turned a cute shade of pink. She made a show of looking at her watch.

"I think the committee should be finished with the storefront by now. I'm going to gather my display."

She turned away, bending to pick up a sleek-looking black

leather briefcase with red piping to match the shoes she was wearing. His eyes lingered on her feet, remembering the amazing torment she'd been able to give him with those toes. Was she wearing polish? He'd bet she was, something intense and sexy like red.

He wanted to find out almost as much as he wanted that store space.

"I'll go with you."

"You don't have to."

"Sure I do. You know where it is and you have the key," he reminded her.

"Fine," she said with a shrug. "You can use the time to explain why you're really here."

He could tell she was trying to look like she didn't care. But she was strangling that leather handle, so he figured he was bugging her.

Good. She was bugging him, too.

She headed for the door. Jason grabbed the koteka case he'd brought in as part of his pitch. He frowned at the long, worn cardboard of the dusty box. "I never got to show them my penis."

Well, that got her attention. Larissa turned to stare, choking back a laugh. "Literally? Or figuratively?"

"Both." He held up the box in an unspoken offer to show her. She gave him a long, considering look and shook her head. Guess she wasn't willing to see his figurative or literal penis.

"It's a koteka," he explained, stepping up to match his stride to hers as she headed down the hallway toward the elevators. "A penis sheath, actually. I brought it back from Papua New Guinea. It's been blessed by a medicine man and is supposed to impart virility and sexual prowess on the man who wears it."

"I thought you boys had little blue pills for that now," she said, stepping into the elevator and waiting until he'd joined her before punching the button for the lobby.

"The natives are a little behind in their pharmacology. Besides, this is better. It's magic."

"A magic dick, huh?" He didn't understand the amusement on her face, but loved the sound of Larissa's laugh as it bubbled out, bouncing off the stainless steel walls. Her look invited him to entertain her. He loved that look. He figured that was why she was so into books. She had that childlike quality of suspending disbelief and giving a story her undivided attention. He remembered a couple trips, he'd listened to the local's tales, then hurried back to his tent to write down the details so he could see that same look when he told his latest adventure story.

"Magic?" she prodded, her lips curved and her brow arched.

"The medicine man promised that the man who possesses this koteka will not only be sexually blessed, but that he'd have lifelong happiness with the woman he pleasured."

"Nice," she said with a sigh. Then she shook her head, as if she was refusing to fall under his spell. "But what does that have to do with the Cartright Hotel and its boutiques?"

"This hotel is a couples' gig, right? So I figured we'd showcase Can-Do with a museum of sorts. I've collected fertility figures and tools from all over the world. What better way to get the hotel patrons in the mood."

"You want to set up a sex shop for world travelers?"

"Ha. No. I want to set up a physical storefront for Can-Do. Something to lure travelers in via the hotel and the promotion Cartright promises. Along with some exclusive adventures found only through Cartright, I figure sex is the best way to entice people in to take a look."

"Leave it to you to reduce the wonders of traveling the

world down to sex," she muttered with a dismissive roll of her eyes.

"Haven't you heard? Sex sells, sweetheart."

And damned if Jason didn't have some he'd like to sell her.

4

BEFORE LARISSA DID MORE than blink, Jason shifted. He slapped his hands against the steel wall of the elevator, one on either side of her head. Larissa gave a squeaky little yelp. When had he gotten so fast?

She sucked in a breath. Her brain warned her to push him away. Her heart warned her to remember how badly he'd hurt her. Her body babbled hubba-da-hubba.

She almost looked down to make sure she hadn't melted into a puddle at his feet. He'd always affected her like this. Long before he'd had a clue, in fact.

He was clued in now, though.

His gaze swept over her heated cheeks, resting briefly on her lips before drifting slowly down, like a gentle caress, to her chest. The intensity of his look made Larissa want to look down and make sure her silk jacket was still closed sedately, hiding her red satin camisole.

The soft layers of fabric couldn't hide her body's reaction, though. She knew from the aching heaviness of her breasts that her nipples were in stand-up-and-pay-attention mode.

Just the way he liked them.

Jason's blue eyes glinted with a naughty sort of satisfaction when they met hers. His glance said he was amused, horny and hell-bent on pushing her to step up and meet his sexual challenge.

"So, are you in the market?" he asked, his words low and husky.

Her mouth watered. She swallowed, then had to swallow again before asking, "Market?"

"For sex."

Her thighs melted from the heat his words inspired. Her breath sped up and it was all she could do not to wrap her leg around his waist and press herself against his hard body.

"I'm not really in the mood for shopping," she lied.

"I'll bet I can change your mind."

She'd bet he could, too.

That was the problem with Jason. When he got this close, he made her want to throw away all her inhibitions—and her underwear—and give in to anything he asked.

When she was with him, she forgot what was important. She let go of her dreams. Her hopes for the life she'd grown up wishing for and never having. With Jason, she tossed aside the things she valued, like a stable home and family. Like romance and a career she loved. Like believing that she could be—deserved to be—the most important thing in someone's life. Important enough that he wanted to spend his life, all of it, not just random weekdays when he wasn't off having fun, with her.

Which meant she had to make sure he didn't get this close, she warned herself. With that in mind, she hauled out her fake smile again—oh, boy was it getting a lot of use today—and, steeling herself, pressed her hand against his chest.

Her fingers wanted to curl into the hard, warm flesh. Her palm tingled when it felt the soft dusting of hair there, where the top button gave way to the V-neck.

She forced herself to push him away, though.

"I've already sampled what you're selling," she reminded him. "And I'm afraid it's not worth the price."

Jason's eyes narrowed. He stood rock firm against her hand, not moving an inch.

Larissa's heart raced. Her throat dried. Had she gone too far? All of a sudden, she was vividly aware that she was alone with him. Not just in this elevator, but probably in the entire building. He was bigger than she was. Stronger and in every way, more powerful. She wasn't afraid he'd hurt her. At least, not her body.

But she was terrified that if she let him, he'd break her heart. Again.

Then his face relaxed. Underneath her palm, she felt the tension ease in his body. He gave her a quick smile, then with a one-shouldered shrug, moved back.

Her body chilled without the heat of his. She curled her fingers into her palm to ease the ache.

"You're missing out," he promised, assuming his usual pose by leaning back against the opposite wall of the elevator.

"Sex, sex, sex," Larissa groused, trying to sound like she hadn't just had a mental orgasm. "What is it with guys and sex today?"

"You mean I'm not your first?" he teased.

She pressed her lips together to hold back a smile. You had to hand it to him. Jason never copped an attitude when he was rejected. He just took it in stride.

Not that she'd rejected him often. At least, not in the beginning. From the moment Jason noticed she was female, all he'd had to do was give her a sexy look from those intense blue eyes and she'd dropped anything and everything. Including her pants.

Until the end.

Her shoulders drooped with the weight of the memory.

It was the end she had to keep in mind, here. That was real. The rest? Like all of Jason's adventures, the rest of their relationship had been a temporary fantasy.

"You're not even my first this hour," she finally answered, thinking of the pen-tapper and his desire for her to sex up her store plans. It was the truth, and thankfully let her sidestep the humiliation of admitting that she hadn't had a guy talk sex with her in over three months. Unless she counted that one bookstore customer who'd asked for a reference book on the health effects of Viagra. And she really didn't want to count him.

"The last hour?" he repeated. His words were measured, like he was weighing them carefully. "You and Conner had a little tryst before the meeting?"

"I didn't think you even knew what a tryst was," she quipped with a stiff smile as her stomach gave a little dip.

She gave Jason a careful look. She'd forgotten how jealous he got. At first, she'd thought it was kinda cute. Like he thought she was so gorgeous, he couldn't trust men around her. But then she'd realized that his jealousy meant he didn't trust her, either.

And as they'd found out, they couldn't have a relationship without trust.

Thankfully, the elevator reached the lobby so she could escape.

"The stores are over this way," she said, waving her hand toward the marble archway on the left that led to the boutiques. Their steps echoed loudly on the polished wood floors as they walked around a large statue of a naked couple entwined in a never-ending embrace. "That closed-in archway on the right will lead to the hotel's lobby and registration area when construction is finished. Conner took me through before he locked the doors. It's lovely."

"Lovely enough to justify the rent on the storefront?"

She slanted him a look. Neither of them had grown up with the wealth that Conner had, but they hadn't been poor, either. In the past, Jason's attitude toward money had always been "easy come, easy go." When had he started worrying about cost-effectiveness?

"I'm not an expert, but based on the other Cartright holdings and the luxury of the areas I toured, this will be a four-star hotel."

They stepped through the archway and into the long marble hall lined with upscale boutiques on both sides and planters overflowing with lush flowers, cushioned benches and romantic statuary in the center.

"Between the clientele, the caliber of the other stores already renting space here and the incredible promotion package Cartright is offering, the rent is a steal," she added as they passed stores that, while empty, displayed well-known names. Tiffany's, La Perla, MAC. "From what I understand, there's a waiting list for storefront openings. The only reason we're even being considered is that Conner wanted to bring in local merchants."

Why the hell was she trying to convince her competition of the worthiness of the prize?

"It sounds like you've done your homework" was all he said, though.

Stopping between a shop with a sign promising Godiva Chocolates and the storefront where she'd set up her display, she studied Jason's face. Why did he really want this space? It wasn't his style, nor would it lend itself to his business.

So what was he up to?

Before she could ask, he stepped forward to get the full effect of the window display she'd set up. Conner had left the doors open in welcome, and even though the space was virtually empty beyond that door, the effect was still warm and welcoming.

And, she thought with a soft sigh as she eyed the display, so very romantic. A pair of high-heeled ladies slippers were tucked alongside a stack of romance novels, topped with an antique blown glass perfume atomizer. A bouquet of roses tumbled in colorful profusion from a sterling silver vase and a handful of DVDs were splayed, like magazines, just beneath it.

From where they were standing, the display Larissa had set up on the checkout counter beckoned them, like a little finger wave, into the store. She knew she couldn't compete with Godiva, so she'd gone for the healthier romance treats. A cut glass bowl of strawberries, a bottle of champagne and an array of imported cheeses and crackers, all still in their wrappers. The effect, along with the rest of the merchandise, made her think of a romantic weekend tryst.

She just hoped it'd make Conner's partners think that way, too. Larissa nibbled on her thumbnail, nerves dancing up and down her spine again as she squinted, wondering if she should have left the ivory cashmere throw on the counter instead of moving it to the settee.

"Wow. This is…" Jason trailed off, taking a step back and crossing his arms over his chest to stare at the display in the window. "This is great. It's definitely not what I expected."

"You expected my display to suck?" she asked, giving him a frown.

Did it suck? Her eyes sped from item to item. Maybe she should have used her cell phone to take a picture and send to Chloe for a second opinion before she'd told the partners it was finished.

"No. I expect everything you do to be great," Jason said, interrupting her neurotic obsessing. His words were so offhand she knew he really meant them. Her shoulders softened. She wished she had half the faith in herself that he'd always shown.

Argh. Larissa's hands were halfway to her hair to tug at the curls. It was only the very real fear that if she did, her hair would frizz out and she'd look like Bozo the clown that kept her from grabbing hold and pulling.

She had to stop this. Every time Jason said something sweet, or gave her one of those sexy looks of his, she melted. Her mind was so filled with images of wrapping herself around his naked body that she forgot all the reasons why they'd split up.

He was bad for her. Like a chocolate fountain and bowl of strawberries were to a sugar addict, he was pure temptation. A temptation she needed to resist at all costs.

"I'm going to pack up," she muttered, hurrying through the mostly empty store toward the back room where she'd stashed her box. The sooner she got away from him, the better. First she had to go home. Then she had to call Conner and make sure she got this space. She'd even date Ben or add the sexy merchandise Franklin wanted if it meant she could seal the deal.

Not just because she wanted the space, although she did, so, so badly. She'd do anything—everything—in her power to make sure Jason didn't move back to town.

She had to.

AMUSED AT HOW FLUSTERED Larissa seemed, Jason sauntered along behind her. He poked at a candle, flicked a crystal teardrop on the wall sconce. Even though he knew it was rude, he smirked a little.

She'd practically melted at his feet in that elevator. Now she was rushing around like the devil was chasing her. Since he knew who she'd consigned horns, he figured he might as well enjoy the role.

"What are you doing here, a sort of general store? I thought you'd have a bookstore, to tell you the truth. I mean, you read incessantly," he called to her, as she scurried through a doorway in the back of the store. "Hell, you could have turned your apartment into a bookstore, what with every wall a bookcase and the stacks teetering on the floors and tables."

"It'll be a bookstore," she said as she came back into the room with a cardboard box held in her arms like a shield between them. "It'll just stock other things, too."

Jason frowned at the defensive note in her voice. What was up with that? He looked around, trying to see what it was about this stuff that'd embarrass her. He picked up a candle in a frosted glass jar, giving it a sniff. Nice. Flowery but not nauseating. He rubbed his fingers over a soft, fluffy blanket she'd thrown on the couch. Books, DVDs and CDs were stacked everywhere, along with some pretty statues and other girly things.

So, what was the problem?

"Is this a secondary location you're hoping to open here?" he probed.

"No."

His frown turned into a scowl. She'd already started planning for her bookstore when they'd been engaged. So what'd happened? Had it failed? Was that why she was so touchy?

"So, what've you been doing if not running your own store?"

"Working, of course." She shifted, her hair falling in a cloud of curls to hide her face. But he'd seen the color on her cheeks.

He narrowed his eyes.

"Working where?"

"At the bookstore, not that it's any of your business." Her chilly tone was at odds with the heat he could almost feel radiating off her face. It only took him a second to figure out why.

Shock zapped through Jason like a lightning bolt. She'd been so big on following her dream and had tried to lure him into that dreaming of the future thing, too. For a little while, he'd actually believed they could make things work, even though he'd known better. Half the reason they'd broken up was her need to be landlocked to a bookstore she swore would take all of her attention to make a success.

Well, maybe that was the half of the reason he hadn't told her. He was pretty sure she'd say the entire reason they'd broken up was that he was an insecure commitment-phobic asshole who couldn't make the long haul.

But they were focusing on her issues. Not his.

"You're still at old man Murphy's, aren't you? Working his bookstore? Same place you've been since high school?" he growled. "You never went out on your own? You never opened your own store? You're kidding, right?"

She'd always wanted to open her own bookstore. She'd always known that while her aunt loved her, the older woman had planned to leave her estate to her beloved cat charities. And Larissa was fine with that. She'd been determined to make her own way. She'd saved for years, stocking away part of her income and all of the insurance money she'd gotten when her parents had died. Having her own business was all she'd ever talked about.

He stared at the top of her forehead, the only part of her face he could see through the cloud of hair. She ignored him as she carefully wrapped a heart-shaped crystal dish in bubble wrap, then in paper.

Jason wanted to demand that she explain herself. He wanted to know why she hadn't grabbed her dreams before this.

But...what was the point?

They'd finished years ago. And just as soon as she got her stuff packed up, they'd be finished again.

He ignored the burning in his gut at that thought and shoved his hands into his pockets.

"Look, I've got things to do. You have Conner's keys with you, right? You can lock up after you've finished gathering your stuff."

Her head came up so fast, her hair practically floated around her shoulders. Brown eyes widened. Pale, full lips parted, then she pressed them tight together and sighed. Probably in relief.

"That's a great idea."

The overhead lights flickered. Jason glanced into the open space, then up at the skylight centered over the hotel's mini-mall. No storm. He stepped out of the store and looked up and down the bank of stores.

Weird.

The lights flared bright. Then the entire mall dove into blackness.

"What the hell..."

The loud crash of metal hitting marble screeched through the mall as the security bars slammed down to close off the entrance between the mall and the hotel.

Larissa screamed and jumped toward him, her hand clutching his arm. It was only instinct, he was sure. Still, he wrapped one arm around her shoulder to reassure her.

And to keep her from stomping on his toes with those killer heels of hers.

The darkness wrapped around them, terrifyingly heavy and dense. For just a second, she leaned into him. He felt her softly tremble. He loved the feel of having her in his arms again. Jason closed his eyes, reveling in her delicious scent. Before he could pull her closer, she stepped away and wrapped her arms around herself.

He had no reason to feel hurt. He wouldn't be upset if a woman he'd just met didn't want him giving her a comfort hug, would he? And Larissa had said it herself earlier. They were practically strangers.

His eyes started to adjust to the change in light. Which meant Larissa's were, too. Needing to hide the pathetically bereft look on his face, he strode over to a wall by the entrance to the store and flipped the light switch a couple times.

Nothing.

"Looks like the power's out," he said needlessly.

"What do you think happened?" she asked.

He could tell she was trying to sound calm, but there was a layer of panic in Larissa's voice. Why? She wasn't claustrophobic, so why was she so freaked about being stuck in here?

Or was it the company she was freaked about? Despite his irritation, he grinned. It was gratifying to know he still had such an effect on her. Especially since she seemed so determined to ignore her effect on him. He hadn't exactly been a monk in the last few years, but it'd been a long time since he'd made a woman nervous. Most of the gals he spent time with, in and out of bed, were a little harder, a little cooler. They knew the score and liked to play.

Then again, as he recalled, Larissa was pretty good with the game playing. Even with his ring on her finger, she'd kept her fingers in the dating pool. Peter had warned him that no pretty girl would sit around at home reading a book while her guy was off playing in the jungle. And hey, big brother had been right. Jason had come home from a trip and she'd been off yachting for the weekend. When he'd accused her of getting too friendly with Conner, a guy who they both knew damned well had a thing for her, she'd refused to deny it. Instead, she'd tossed his ring back in his face.

Gut burning, Jason tried to shake off the bitterness of the past. He needed to get out of here. Being around Larissa, all the memories and the temptation, felt like a punch to the gut.

"Maybe the electricity is on an automatic timer or something," he mused, looking around. "Don't worry about it. There's still enough light coming through the skylight for you to pack up, right?"

"Right," she murmured. "I'll hurry up and finish."

Neither of them mentioned his earlier intention to leave her to pack up alone. They both knew he wouldn't abandon her now. No longer carefully wrapping each item in packing paper, she started stacking things in the boxes as quickly as possible.

Jason strode over to the automatic doors that led from the boutique to a parking area. The doors didn't slide open when he stepped in front of them.

A tiny tendril of panic started winding its way through his gut. Maybe there wasn't an automatic timer. Jason's gaze shifted beyond the doors and his stomach sank.

"Shit," he muttered, staring out the heavy, brass-framed glass.

"What?" Larissa called, the concern in her voice rising to match the concern in his.

The hotel was high atop a hill, with a gorgeous bird's-eye view. The front of the building, he knew, was landscaped with large trees and flowering bushes, giving it the feel of a secluded oasis. But this side was still under construction.

Jason surveyed the cityscape. It looked deserted, bereft of all life. No color, no movement. Just...blackness. Other than the pale pinkish-orange of the setting sun, there wasn't a light to be seen.

He grabbed the keys and went through them until he found one that fit. He wiggled the key, then shook the door again. He narrowed his eyes, noting the solid steel bolts coming from the top and bottom of the door into the floor and ceiling. He shook the door again. The bolts held firm.

Shit.

"Jason?"

He rested his head briefly against the cool glass, wondering what he'd done to piss off Fate so much. Then, with a deep breath, he turned to face his ex-fiancée.

"So there's good news and bad news," he told her.

"The good?"

"The hotel and boutiques aren't on a timer."

She frowned, her gaze shifting over his shoulder to the view of the city. Horror widened her eyes as they met his again.

"Yeah, that's the bad. It looks like it's a city-wide blackout. Conner will be pleased to know his security measures work. The doors must've bolted shut when the power went off."

She shook her head, holding that soft fluffy blanket against her chest.

"You have a cell phone?" he asked, trying to remember Conner's number.

"I left mine in the car," she confessed. Through the faint light from the glass doors he could see her nibbling at the soft temptation of her bottom lip. Jason almost groaned. "Do you have one?" she asked.

"Dead."

"But there must be phones in the mall?" she said, looking around desperately.

"On the other side of the security bars," he remembered. "Nothing in here, though. Daniel said all the stores would be responsible for their own."

"We're stuck?" she asked, sounding like they were doomed.

"Yep."

Doomed might be right. Jason had climbed Mt. Everest in a snowstorm. He'd led a group of Girl Scouts out of the rainforest after an earthquake. He'd broken up a fight in a sleazy bar in Taiwan. But he'd never been this out of his element.

They had no supplies. He hadn't thought to bring a backpack and field rations to a business meeting. And he doubted, for all its professed powers, that the penis he had in that box was going to be of much help in this situation.

They had no means of communication. It was Friday night and the building was empty. Surely someone would miss them eventually. Conner would probably meet them in the morning to pick up the keys. But that was tomorrow.

At least they had shelter. Maybe there was a vending machine or something around for food. But Larissa had pretty much called it.

They were trapped.

Just the two of them. And the tempting softness of that blanket.

Jason had no idea what possessed him. He knew better. Hell, hadn't he lectured himself once already today? But... The devil made him do it, as his mother always said.

He gently pried the blanket from Larissa's fingers. Holding the whisper-soft fabric in one hand, he swept it around her shoulders, fisting both sides together to trap her in the cloudy white material.

"Guess we'll be spending tonight together, hmm." He leaned closer, his lips a hairbreadth from hers and asked, "What do you think we should do to pass the time?"

5

LARISSA KNEW EXACTLY what she was going to do to pass the time until they got out of here.

She was going to panic.

To avoid letting Jason know how freaked out she was and lose any semblance of control, she'd do it quietly. But she'd definitely be doing it.

She could already feel the mean fingers of anxiety grabbing at her, twisting her stomach in knots and making her woozy.

She couldn't be locked in. She had too much to do. She needed to call Conner and pitch her idea one more time. She had a column due Monday that she'd put aside this evening to write. She'd left spaghetti sauce out on the counter, defrosting. Being stuck here wasn't an option.

Especially not with Jason. He was kryptonite to her superhero. Chocolate éclairs to her diet. Tequila to her temperance vow. He was everything that tempted her. Every indulgence she secretly wished for, even though she knew he was so bad for her.

And her willpower to hold out against a temptation like him was limited, at best. She'd have been able to wave goodbye if they walked out now. She was sure of it. But after being trapped together? She'd mentally unzipped his pants with her teeth the minute she'd seen him. If they were stuck together, how long would her willpower last?

As if her internal struggle was written across her face, Jason smiled. His hands tightened on the blanket. The warmth of his fingers, where they brushed the delicate fabric of her jacket just over her breasts, seeped into her skin.

Her flesh warmed. Her vision blurred. Her head did a couple spins, like a carnival ride.

"Maybe we should—"

"We should find a way out," she blurted. She tried to hide the breathlessness of her words by shifting, tugging the soft fabric of the blanket from his hands. She stepped backward so fast her cute red heels slipped on the marble floor. She windmilled, trying to regain balance.

Jason grabbed both of her arms, keeping her from sliding across the floor on her butt.

"Falling at my feet?" he teased.

"Lucky for me, you keep saving me from that humiliation," she retorted, her cheeks on fire. She made sure she was steady, then quickly, but carefully, stepped away.

"You okay?"

"I'm fine," she said, tugging her jacket into place. Then with reluctant courtesy, she gave him a look from under her lashes and murmured, "Thank you."

"Sure. Can't have you getting hurt. It's not like we can call for help, and as much as I'd love to play doctor with you, I don't have a first aid kit handy."

Larissa's lips twitched. Then she remembered, she was immune to his charm.

"We're really stuck?" she asked, hoping he'd tell her he had some clever escape planned.

"Until the power comes back on. Or until tomorrow at the latest," he said instead.

Locked in, all night, with Jason? Larissa's heart thudded against her chest. "What about a security guard? Or Peter? Won't he be looking for you?"

Jason shook his head. "Nah. Remember what Conner said? They don't have a security team in place yet. Conner figured the locks would be enough for now. And now that Peter's got Meghan, he doesn't really care what I'm doing."

Her heart was thudding in her head now, pounding a sensual beat of warning against her brain.

"There has to be a way out," she said quickly. She knew she sounded a little desperate but she didn't care. Desperate times called for freaking out. "Did you try all the keys?"

"The only key that fit is in the lock now," he replied calmly. "It won't open the security bolts, though. I'm assuming they are a part of the theft deterrent system. They probably require a code or special passkey or something."

That made sense. Larissa turned the key anyhow. It twisted. She heard the locks disengage. But the bolts didn't move.

She grabbed the etched brass handles of the door and shook it as hard as she could, ignoring Jason's laugh behind her.

Echoing his earlier move, she rested her forehead against the glass and tried to gather her thoughts.

They were too scattered, though. Hearing footsteps, she turned to see that Jason was halfway down the mall.

"Where are you going?" she called to his retreating back.

"While you bruise your fists on the doors, I'm going to scout things out. See if I can find food, water or maybe an alternate exit that those keys might open." He glanced back and gave her a wink. "Don't scuff those pretty shoes kicking the door, though."

Leave it to him to go into super scout mode while she hyperventilated. And yes, she frowned, she had considered kicking the stupid door. This was exactly the reason she'd hated taking trips with him. He'd always babied them down for her, and she'd still come off as a total incompetent.

She hated that feeling.

"Maybe you'd rather I use them to kick your—"

"Temper, temper," he chided. He stopped at an unmarked, solid door between two glass-fronted stores and gave her a patient look. "You wanna wait here or come with me?"

And there it was, the question that had defined their relationship.

Only this time, Larissa didn't have to think about the choices. She folded the blanket over her arm, stopping at the still open door to her—because dammit, after all of this, it'd damned well better end up hers—store and tossed it in a box. Then, her still unscuffed heels clattering loudly over the marble floor, she hurried to Jason's side.

"What if we crawled through the air vents," she suggested, noticing one high above the doors, halfway toward the vaulted ceiling.

"That'd be a no," Jason told her as he opened the unmarked door for her to enter first.

"Why?" she asked. "You climb mountains and shimmy up trees for coconuts. But you won't crawl through a suburban vent?"

"That vent would only take us to some other part of the hotel. Did you want to move to a room with a bed, perhaps?"

Hell, no.

Larissa hurried through the doorway into the dark hall. She didn't want to be a chicken, but as soon as Jason let go of that door, what little light there was would vanish. Not that she was afraid of the dark, but wandering through a strange place in absolute darkness with Jason felt like a really bad idea to her. Who knew what she might accidentally touch.

"We're going to have trouble finding anything we need without some sort of light," Jason said, echoing the saner part of her thoughts. "Maybe if we prop the door open, we'll be able to see."

Larissa arched a doubtful brow. She could barely make out anything halfway down the hall now.

"I don't suppose you keep a little flashlight in your purse," he mused.

"No." Then remembering, she turned back to face him. "I do have a book of matches I got as a favor from the wedding I attended last weekend, though."

His face was in shadows and the wince was infinitesimal, but she still caught it.

"They're matches, Jason. Not marriage cooties."

He gave a short, rueful laugh and shrugged. "Nothing personal."

"Of course not. As far as I know, I was the closest you ever got to a wife. So, there's no reason for me to take your feelings about it personally."

Impatient, Larissa brushed past Jason, pretending that the feel of his body against hers didn't make her want to close that door and let the dark keep their secrets.

"Where are you going?" he asked.

"To get the cootie matches," she tossed over her shoulder as she stalked away from him.

She was still stomping when she reached her purse, where she'd left it on the counter of her soon-to-be store. She didn't unzip the leather bag yet, though. Instead she draped her arms across the countertop and laid her forehead against the cool marble, trying to chill out.

"Keep your eyes on the prize," she lectured herself. She

used a couple more deep belly-breaths to get her thoughts in order.

Being trapped was definitely high on her sucky list. And being trapped with Jason was even higher, right under flood, famine and worldwide illiteracy. But that wasn't the big picture, it was simply a tiny roadblock. She just had to remember that.

The priority here was that she get the store. Which meant that Jason couldn't get it. So if she was going to be stuck here—with him, anyhow—she might as well find some way of turning it to her advantage.

It was all about having the right attitude. Being bitchy and defensive would get her nowhere. If anything, losing control like that just meant that she was giving Jason that much more power, even if he didn't realize it. And knowing Jason, he probably did, and would use it to keep the upper hand. She already had enough to deal with fighting off her attraction to him.

So just like she'd done earlier, when she'd put a lid on her snarky attitude with Conner's partner, she'd paste on a pleasant smile and put her energy into sealing the deal. She'd either convince Jason that she was more deserving of the store or she'd find enough out about why he wanted it and use that to convince him to go in a different direction.

Easy peasy.

And how pathetic was it to lie to oneself? Rolling her eyes, but back in control, she got the matches from her purse and turned toward the doorway. Her gaze landed on the box of merchandise she'd packed away.

A wide smile curved her lips and she knelt down to unwrap one of the scented candles. See. Chill out and get her head on straight and things were already going her way.

She lit the decadently scented soy wax and headed back to join Jason. She wasn't surprised to see he hadn't waited.

One hand cupped around the flame to keep it safe, she made her way down the hall, pretending she wasn't wigged out by the long, spidery shadows her fingers cast on the walls.

There were three doors at the end of the hall. Jason had propped one open with a chair. She could hear the occasional thump and four-letter word, so she knew he was in there. Pausing in the doorway, she squinted through the dark.

"Score," Jason said, obviously hearing her less than stealthy entrance. "It looks like the construction workers keep some food in here. Roach coach sandwiches, bottled water, a little of this and that."

Larissa's eyes adjusted, so she could make out the dim outline of tables, chairs and counters. The candlelight reflected off the door of the stainless steel refrigerator Jason was looking into. He glanced over his shoulder and gave an approving nod toward the candle.

"Clever. Part of your inventory?"

"Yes. It's the Passionflower by Moonlight scent. Chloe makes them," she told him as she stepped farther into the room. Holding the candle high, she looked around and tried to tell herself that this was the comfy space where she'd be having lunches soon. And not a creepy potential scene from every horror movie that ever started with a blackout.

"Chloe made that candle?" His arms full of what looked like food, Jason let the refrigerator door swing shut. "I thought all she made was trouble. How's she doing now?"

"She's good. Busy with her many businesses, yet still finding time for trouble," Larissa said with a shrug. Jason and Chloe had gotten along really well, kind of like brother and sister with a mutual passion for smart-ass dialogue, movies that blew things up and their love for Larissa herself. Which probably accounted for why Chloe had taken their breakup so personally.

"I'm glad. Both that she's doing good and that she hasn't lost that troublemaker side. Tell her hi for me, okay?"

Tell her that the guy with the magic dick said hi? Chloe would love that. "I'll tell her. I doubt she's going to want to hear it, though."

Jason emptied his armload onto a table next to a pile of stuff Larissa hadn't noticed before. She joined him to see what he'd collected. Some bottles of water, a brick of unopened cheese, sandwiches in plastic, a couple of apples and a large bag of chips. There was also a roll of paper towels.

"At least we won't get hungry," she commented. "Wasn't there a vending machine, though?"

"Yup. But it's digital and it went down with the power. I'll leave some cash and a note to cover this food, though."

"Well, aren't you both responsible and resourceful," she teased.

"Tricks of the trade," he dismissed with a modest shrug. "So why won't Chloe want my greeting? I thought she liked me."

"Sure," Larissa agreed, leaving her candle on the table as she started rooting through cupboards and drawers to see what she could add to his stash. "She liked you when we were a couple."

"She doesn't like me anymore?" He sounded like a pouting little boy who'd just been told Santa wasn't real.

Larissa added a sleeve of saltine crackers and, oh yeah, a handful of chocolate bars to the stash. "Well, let's put it this way. She burned your effigy in a bonfire the Halloween after we split up."

"Ouch."

"You were naked," Larissa told him, only gloating a little. "And you were really, really small. If you know what I mean."

Grimacing, Jason's hand twitched toward the fly of his

jeans. Larissa turned away to hide her smirk. Seeing a box on the floor next to one of the cabinets, she brought it over to carry their booty.

She sighed at the pile of food. They wouldn't really need to eat that, would they? Someone had to come for them soon. Maybe? Hopefully?

Not likely. Her shoulders sagged as she started packing food into the box.

"Was this at her annual Halloween bash? The one that usually has a guest list of, oh, a hundred people?"

"It was closer to one-fifty that year."

He sighed.

"Any anonymity?"

"Well, she labeled the effigy with your name and recited a poem before she tossed it into the flames. So, nope." The box filled, Larissa lifted it, then glanced at the candle on the table. She couldn't carry both. Before she could figure it out, Jason reached around her to take the box from her arms. His hands left heated little tingles of awareness as they brushed hers, his arms practically embracing her from the side. Larissa swallowed, trying to clear the lump from her throat.

She was glad he had a hold of the box since she'd probably have dropped it at his feet otherwise.

"I'm sorry I missed the event," he said in a husky tone she knew had nothing to do with Chloe or effigies. But it had everything to do with fire. Her eyes wandered over his face, all intriguing shadows and angles in the candlelight. God, the man was gorgeous. Even clearly irritated, he still looked good enough to lick from head to toe.

"You can probably catch it on YouTube," she said breathlessly. She watched closely, hoping to see anger on his face. That would go such a long way toward making him less drool-worthy.

Instead he threw back his head and laughed. The sound echoed through the dark room, wrapping around her like a good-natured hug. Damn him. Why couldn't he be a full-time jerk? It'd be so much easier to dislike him.

"I'LL HAVE TO LOOK IT UP," Jason said, trying to control his laughter. He probably should be irritated to be publicly mocked, but as long as Larissa wasn't the one commenting on his...size, he figured it was just good fun. "Leave it to Chloe to find an original and creative insult."

"She's a wonder," Larissa agreed with a smile that said she'd probably bookmarked that YouTube page. She glanced around the break room. "It looked like we've gotten everything useful, doesn't it?"

She lifted the candle and, hand curved to protect the flame, headed toward the door.

"Did you see what the other rooms were already?" she asked.

"Janitor's closet and storage," he said, hefting the box a little higher and following her. "I couldn't see much without light, but from what I could make out, the storage room has a series of lockers, all secured. And unless we want to scrub floors, there wasn't much in the janitor's closet, either. I didn't find any bathrooms, though. That could be an issue."

This was the problem with being trapped in an urban setting instead of a remote island somewhere. Sure, they had shelter and didn't have to climb trees for their coconut dinner. But he didn't think Conner would appreciate it if Jason peed on those pricey plants lining the center of that mall.

"Actually, there's a public restroom in the hall across the mall, but Conner mentioned that it's not outfitted with toilets yet. But there are private bathrooms in each of the stores. I checked and the one in my store isn't locked."

"My store," Jason muttered with a frown. Why was she so sure she'd get the space? He had a much stronger track record and already had a successful business. She had a fluffy romantic dream. And, he had to admit, the nicest ass he'd ever seen.

He wanted to ask if she was dating Conner now, but figured she'd blow up like she had the last time he'd asked that question. But that was probably why she was so confident that she'd edge him out. Because she had the inside track.

Jason's gut burned at the idea of anyone other than him being with Larissa. The idea of her with Conner, a guy who could offer her the world, plus her perfect store space, made the burn flame even higher.

And those guys with Conner had definitely been checking her out. Which meant that even if they tried to spout some crap about professionalism in choosing, they were leaning her way.

Despite their history, Jason didn't want to hurt her and take away her dream. But he needed that store. The future of Can-Do was on the line. Despite his friendship with Daniel, Conner was obviously going to be on Larissa's side. And given that his ass didn't look nearly as good in a skirt, Jason had absolutely no way of influencing the other guys on the committee.

Which left Larissa. Jason eyed the way her jacket ruffled across those curvy hips. His gaze slid down the narrow black skirt covering way too much of her legs, then dropped to those sexy little shoes in do-me red.

They were stuck together for the next little while, so even though she probably wanted to, she couldn't run away. And as long as he kept his eye on the prize—which was scoring that store space—he could dial back his predator instincts and try and be a gentleman long enough to find a way to talk her out of taking such a huge business risk. Diplomacy and circumspection. He could handle that.

At least, he thought he could.

"It sounds like all our needs are covered, then," he said, referring to his concern over a bathroom.

When they reached the store, he dumped the box on the counter. Larissa set the candle down. He watched her cast a look around the store, kind of like those looks moms gave to their funny-looking newborn babies. Love, pride and a blind sort of surety that it was the greatest-looking thing in the world. He squinted a look at the bare walls and modern fixtures and shrugged.

It definitely wasn't his style, that was for sure. But he wouldn't have thought it to be Larissa's, either.

"You really like this space?" he asked. "I mean, I thought you wanted your bookstore to be in one of those fancy old houses. Something with a lot of character and, what was it? Charm?"

"Well, sure, that's what I wanted." She looked both surprised and cautious. "But that was before. Now I know that to make my dream a reality, I have to make certain... adjustments."

"You? Adjust? You're kidding, right?" Jason winced. That hadn't been very diplomatic.

"I can adjust," she protested, crossing her arms across her chest. The lift of her chin and her tone were both defensive. "Unlike some people who refuse to compromise, I'm excellent at adjusting and doing whatever it takes to make something work."

"And I'm not?"

"I didn't say that."

"You implied it."

"No." She shook her head, sending her curls bouncing

over her shoulders. "I said I've adjusted and worked on perfecting my plans for the future. And since you're considering totally changing how you operate your business by trying to shoehorn it into a store, you're obviously willing to adjust."

"From the sound of it, you don't think much of my plan, though."

So much for circumspection. But if there was one thing Jason had always hated, it was being judged. It made him feel like he had to prove something. And since whipping it out and showing off his size wasn't the answer, he'd have to find another way.

He just wasn't sure what, since he had plenty of doubts about this crazy scheme. But he wasn't telling her that. He'd learned early on that life was all about impressions. He kept a confident, assured demeanor, whether he got lost guiding a tour through the Amazon or if he got up in the middle of the night to find the group's campsite surrounded by hyenas. If he acted like he had his shit together, people believed he did. And sooner or later, the act became reality.

"I didn't say what I thought of your ideas, one way or the other," she protested. "I think your business is just that, yours. You've devoted enough of your life to it—you should know what will work or not."

"But you've devoted a lot of your life to learning business." He strode over until he was just inches away. She lifted her chin and glared, but didn't give way. God, he loved it when she got all spunky and brave. "You take classes, read books, made those business plans. Don't you have an opinion on the wisdom of my plans?"

He had no idea why he was doing this. It was some twisted form of masochism. Or maybe he just needed her to say something strong enough to piss him off, since he was having rotten luck convincing himself to keep his hands off of her.

"What difference does it make if I think changing your business is a good idea or not?" she challenged, looking more curious than pissed. "My opinion never mattered to you before."

"Of course it did," he countered. Then he grinned wickedly and gave in to temptation. He reached out to lift one of those soft curls from her shoulder and rubbed the silky length between his fingers.

She stiffened, like she wanted to pull away but didn't want him to know he was getting to her. Good. He wanted her edgy. He wanted her to reach the same level of sexual hyper-awareness that he was at. He stared at her lips, remembering their softness and sweet flavor.

And how long it'd been since he'd had a taste.

"You don't really need my thoughts. I'm sure you can see just as well as I can that this space is much better suited to my store than your jungle adventures."

"Right," Jason said agreeably, like he wasn't irritated. He shifted to the right, trapping her between his body and the counter. "Better suited. Because it's just about appearances, right? And yet, one of us here has spent the last four years dreaming, planning and talking about a perfect dream. The other of us has been living the dream as a work-in-progress. Which one do you think really counts?"

6

"It's about more than appearances," Larissa defended. "Not all businesses can be built on the concept of spending each day playing, you know. Some of us want to make sure everything is just right before we commit our energy, reputation and finances."

She gave him a pointed look just this side of a smirk. "How'd you start your business again? Wasn't it by borrowing money from your mom so you could take a couple of drunken frat boys kayaking?"

"You're just jealous," Jason teased, his body so close to hers she could feel the heat radiating off his chest.

"Aren't you the jealous one?" she challenged, knowing she was stepping into dangerous territory but willing to risk it if it meant he'd back off.

The teasing look on his face faded, replaced by an intensity that made her stomach take a nosedive. She winced, waiting for the explosion. But it didn't come. Instead, right there before her eyes, he seemed to gather control and pull himself together.

He leaned closer to say, "Sweetheart, the only reason for me to be jealous is if you've found some guy who can make you explode in sexual delight the way I did."

He paused, as if waiting for her to fill him in on her incredible sex life. When she just pressed her lips together, he grinned.

"See, no reason to be jealous," he taunted.

That he was right made her furious. Pulse racing, she stared into Jason's blue eyes. His usual cocky amusement was there, yes. But so was desire. Hot and intense, with the promise of all sorts of orgasmic pleasure.

Oh yeah, he wanted her. She shivered a little and forced herself to pretend her nipples weren't aching and that her panties hadn't suddenly become damp. Her fingers trembled with the need to touch him. Just one more time, to slide her fingers over the hard muscles of his chest. To wrap her hands around the thick muscles of his arms. To...

No! She had to stop this. He gave her a sexy look and she instantly turned into a puddle of lust?

Why did he always get to be the one in control? Why did she always fall, panting at his feet? When did her dreams come true, the ones where *he* fell at *her* feet?

What she'd do once he was groveling at her toes depended, of course, on which dream she happened to be entertaining at the time.

There was the power dream, where she left him in a pathetic heap wanting her like crazy while she turned her back and walked away.

And then there was the sexy dream. Where she made him her love slave and he, following her orders, kissed his way up her leg until things got interesting.

"Maybe you should move back a little," she said, squirming and trying to hide her breathlessness. "Without AC, it's getting pretty hot and stuffy in here."

"You think that's the lack of AC, babe?" He shook his head, a few strands of sun-kissed hair falling across his forehead. "What kind of guy are you seeing that you'd confuse horniness with humidity? Has your love life become that boring?"

What love life? The only sexual variety she got these days was in choosing between her D-cell powered friend and the shower massage. Not that Jason needed to know that.

Especially when she was sure his love life was full and varied. Jason was any woman's perfect man. Gorgeous and sexy with a hard body that promised endless hours of pleasurable exploration. A fun, engaging personality that made good on the charm his smile promised. And then there was that dangerous hint of bad boy that any woman with man-radar could tell meant he knew all the naughty tricks, even if he'd only stick around long enough for one round of show-and-tell.

"I'm sure it's the lack of AC. Either that, or your ego has become its own heat source," she snapped, blinking away the sting of tears. Frustration, she told herself. It had to be that and not some insane form of jealousy. She tried to move around him, but he sidestepped to block her escape.

"My ego does provide a lot of heat," he agreed. "But it's fueled by plenty of references."

Larissa rolled her eyes. That was enough. Needing some breathing room, she pressed her hands to his chest to push him away. He didn't budge.

He did make a little growly sound of appreciation in the back of his throat though.

She yanked her hands back.

"You'd better watch yourself," he teased, as if he could read her thoughts. "We're not only fighting the lure of candlelight but we've got super-koteka there, giving off all that sexual mojo."

"Right, with all that temptation, there's no way I'll be able to control myself," she replied, her mouth getting ahead of her brain again. "Because you're such a stud and all."

She immediately wanted to grab the words back. Not because she was a verbal wimp. Nope, she wanted them back because she was another kind of wimp. The look on Jason's face, intense, focused and a little pissed, sent warning sirens off in her mind. That look reminded her, in no uncertain terms, that she was a complete sexual wimp. The kind who couldn't say no to temptation.

That was his "dare me" look. The look that he got when he went off to climb death-defying mountains. When he'd jumped out of a perfectly good airplane. When he wanted to make love.

Eek, she silently squeaked.

"I don't suppose you're considering skydiving," she asked desperately.

"Not even close," he said, stepping closer. Close enough that the heat from his body was probably steaming away any wrinkles in her silk jacket.

"Mountain climbing? A trip down a crocodile-infested river in a canoe?"

"I had something a little more exciting in mind," he confessed, his words husky as took her hand and lifted it to his mouth.

Her knees nearly buckled. Of course he had something else in mind.

"Rappelling in the Painted Desert?" she suggested softly, remembering the time he'd convinced her that dropping herself off the side of a mountain would be fun. He'd used sex in that argument, too.

His grin told her that his memories of that trip were just as hot as hers. Larissa's stomach gave a slow, twisty dive. She pressed her thighs together to stop the trembling, but the movement only added to the wet need pulsating between her legs.

"You know what I remember?" he asked quietly.

How her screams of ecstasy had echoed through the canyon the night they'd camped at the base of the mountain?

"What?" she whispered, her eyes glued to his lips. Her fingers ached with the need to touch him. To run her hands over his chest and feel the heat of his bare skin beneath her palms.

"I remember that you babble when you're nervous." He shifted, angling his body lower, so his face was level with hers. "So what's up, Larissa? You nervous about something?"

"Uncomfortable isn't the same as nervous," she said, sidestepping the issue. Because even though they both knew damned well she was nervous, she wasn't about to admit it.

"What's to be uncomfortable about?"

The distinct possibility of exploding from sexual overload. Probably better to keep that to herself, though.

"You're kidding, right? We're trapped inside an unfinished mall with borrowed food, no air conditioning and no way to tell anyone in the outside world we're here," she growled, frustration rising with each word until she hit a dog-calling pitch. Just in case that wasn't enough, she threw her arms in the air to emphasize her aggravation. "I'm trying to launch a new career and finally find the perfect venue that fits my dream to a tee. And what happens? You show up. You. Of all freaking people."

"Were there other freaking people you'd rather be trapped with?" he asked, taking both of her hands in his. Probably to keep their irritated punctuations from poking him in the eye.

"I'd rather not be trapped at all." She tried to tug her hands away. He didn't let go.

"Well, we are, so we might as well take advantage of the situation, right?"

Wrong. Wrong, wrong, wrong. Shaking her head, Larissa tried to find the words to protest. But his fingers were rubbing over hers in soft, gentle swirls that made her insides go gooey. He lifted her fingers to his mouth and brushed a warm kiss over her knuckles. She almost whimpered as he stared over her hands, his eyes filled with wicked temptation.

"You never answered my question," Jason said, his words husky and low.

"What question?"

"Are you single?" He pressed her hands to his chest, then curved his along her waist.

"Does it matter?"

"Yeah," he said, his mouth coming closer and closer. "Yeah, it does matter."

"Why?" she breathed, her words a whisper against his lips.

"Because you're going to feel really bad making time with me if there is some poor schmuck waiting at home for you," he said just before his mouth took hers.

She wanted to protest. In a heartbeat, her mind was ready to pitch an entire argument about assumptions and cockiness. But, as always when it came to Jason, her body overruled her brain.

Besides, given that just the soft press of his lips to hers had her melting, she was pretty sure his cocky assumption was right. The man had always had a special way with the cock.

His mouth teased. His lips were soft, gently rubbing over hers then slipping away. Tiny little kisses that had her panting. Wanting, needing, more.

She clutched his arms, her fingers clinging to his rock-hard biceps. Passion she hadn't felt in years exploded, swirling through her body. Her nipples ached, pressing through the layers of fabric as if pleading for his attention. The tight, hot bud of desire pulsed between her thighs, begging for release. She shifted her hips, trying to press herself to the hard length of his thigh. She tried to slide her right foot along the strong muscles of his calf, but couldn't lift it more than a half-foot.

She bit back a frustrated groan. Useless. The tight A-line of her skirt was as good as a chastity belt, keeping her thighs locked together. She didn't know whether to cry or celebrate. The skirt was probably the only thing keeping her from rubbing against him like a cat in heat.

But knowing she couldn't take her pleasure gave her a freedom she wouldn't have allowed otherwise. Using it like a safety net, she gave herself permission to have as much fun as possible with her thighs closed.

Still pressed against his chest where he'd left them, her fingers relaxed. For just a second she reveled in the feel of his heart beating beneath her palms. She smoothed her hands over the hard planes of his chest, the soft cotton of his shirt a delicious contrast. Needing to see if the body she'd reveled in memorizing still felt the same, she slipped her hands up to his shoulders, then down the hard, rounded muscles of his biceps. She moaned in the back of her throat.

His body was a work of art. A tool he'd honed to perfection on his long treks up mountains, over waterfalls and into jungles. A tool, she remembered, that he wielded with precision when it came to lovemaking.

Their kiss intensified. She sipped at the rich taste of him, sucking his tongue deeper into her mouth. His moan filled her with sensual power.

Romance was her priority. It was her life.

But right now, in this moment, she'd be happy with sex. Because Jason's tool was the best she'd ever had. And she'd love to use it, just one more time.

Oh, God, she tasted good. Like strawberries and cream, drizzled in chocolate with just a hint of something alcoholic that would knock him on his ass before he realized it.

Jason's entire being was in conflict. His body was loving the feel of Larissa's sweet little curves pressed against him again. His brain was doing that mocking head shake, clearly not impressed with his inability to stick with the plan. He was just supposed to intimidate her a little, then convince her to back off of this store idea. And some other part of him, he'd call it his heart because his soul sounded so drippy, that part gave a big ole sigh of relief, as if it'd just come home after a long, lonely trek.

Like he did anything that threatened to get in the way of his pleasure, Jason ignored it.

Kissing Larissa was much more important. He slipped his hands through the tangled jungle of her curls, loving the silky way her hair grabbed at his fingers. Like she was holding onto him, willing him to get closer. His mouth slanted, taking their kiss deeper. Tongues danced, smooth and sleek, against each other. Shifting his fingers, he pressed them against the back of her head, pulling her tighter against his body.

Her breasts brushed against his chest softly. His dick hardened like steel, the length of it throbbing painfully against his zipper.

He told himself to behave. A kiss. He was only giving in to the desire to kiss her. Just one taste, after such a long time of going without.

Then she gave a soft, purring kind of moan and pressed a little harder, her breasts flattening against his beating heart.

Screw behaving.

He slipped one hand from her hair and brushed his fingers gently down the length of her neck. He skimmed the soft ruffled fabric of her collar until he reached the top button that held the jacket closed.

Her breath caught, the action pressing the lush curve of her breast against his fingers. Jason felt the hesitation in her kiss. Before she had time to solidify her doubt and tell him to stop, he brushed his fingers over the tip of her breast. Her nipple pebbled against the back of his fingers. In gentle, barely touching her sweeps, he brushed his knuckles across the peak once. Twice, then again a third time.

She groaned, nipping at his lower lip in a sharp little bite that sent a shaft of desire all the way to the tip of his dick. Without thinking, Jason pulled his other hand from her hair and slid it down to cup her ass, lifting her tight against his painfully hard length.

One-handed, he made quick work of the tiny, fabric covered buttons of her jacket until he reached the last one at her waist. He pushed the fabric off one shoulder and pulled his mouth from hers. Her protest was a high-pitched moan.

He buried his face in the curve of her neck to breathe in her scent—soft floral and a sweetness that was all Larissa. His fingers traced the lacy edge of her camisole, knowing she'd worn the sexy little piece of lingerie for herself since that jacket thing modestly covered all the good stuff.

He had to see. Had to know if she looked as good as he remembered.

Jason pulled back a little, taking in the sight with hooded eyes. Lush breasts, surprising given her tiny body, spilled over a frothy concoction of satin and lace. He couldn't tell the exact color in the candlelight, something between a red and a pink. Like raspberries.

He swallowed.

Damned if she didn't look even better than he remembered.

"I love that you wear this kind of thing," he whispered,

giving in to the need to press damp, open-mouthed kisses along her throat.

Her head fell back to give him greater access as she murmured, "What kind of thing? Underwear?"

"Underwear is plain and cotton. Kind of like vanilla. Useful but not really exciting," he decided, his teeth snagging one tiny satin strap and tugging it aside so her shoulder was bare. That pulled the pale fabric of the camisole tighter against her breasts, drawing it taut over the pouty points. He swallowed hard.

"There's nothing vanilla about you, or the sexy little things you wear."

Their height difference a challenge he'd solved years back, he looked around quickly, then wrapped his hands around her waist and effortlessly lifted. Her hands gripped his shoulders for balance as he set her on the counter.

"Jason—"

He could see the sexual fog clearing from her eyes, concern and way too much sanity starting to shine in those dark depths.

Nope, definitely not the look he wanted.

Quickly, he kissed her again. A swipe of his tongue over her lips was all it took to get her to open that delicious mouth to him. Her lips were warm and inviting, even though her hands on his shoulders pressed against him like she was making sure he didn't get any closer.

A challenge?

Perfect.

He stepped up his game, taking the kiss deeper as he slipped his tongue in, out, then in again to mimic the slow, heady pleasure he'd have sliding the hard length of his dick into the welcoming warmth of her body.

His hand swept down her smooth arm to her elbow, then slid back up to curve down the side of her torso. Her breath caught. He could feel her anticipation build as the side of his hand brushed against the heavy weight of her breast.

Her gasping little moan sent a shaft of desire straight through his body. Muscles taut, he reminded himself not to get carried away. This was just a little fun. A little kiss for old times' sake. He was in control here.

He moved his hand slowly, oh-so-slowly, back up the same path along her torso. But this time, his palm cupped her breast. Barely touching, just a hint of pressure, as if he was sensing the delicious weight rather than holding it.

Her fingernails dug into his biceps.

Screw control.

He shifted, taking her breast into his hand. The hardened tip nudged his palm. He curved his fingers under the lace of her silky little top so he was gripping it. It took all his restraint not to give it one swift rip so he could get to the barely hidden treasure. But destroying Larissa's underwear would probably ruin the mood. At least, for her.

Instead he dipped deeper, rubbing the backs of his knuckles over the hard bud. It felt like pebbled velvet. He wanted—needed—to see more.

He slowly, reluctantly, pulled his mouth from hers. He hated to leave that delicious pleasure, but his need was too high. He took a second to take in her face, all sharp angles and those huge, huge eyes staring back languidly. Then he dropped his gaze to her candlelit chest.

Her skin was so pale, even in the flickering light, he could see the faint pattern of veins as her heart beat a rapid tattoo right above her silky top.

His body tense, his nerve endings all zinging in anticipation, he slowly used one finger to slide a strap down her arm. The top dropped a little. He held his breath, but the lace caught on her beaded nipple. He could see the rosy point through the delicate threads like a ripe raspberry hidden by frothy sugar. A deliciously teasing temptation.

Concentration narrowing to a pinpoint, he rubbed the tip of his forefinger over the lace. Her nipple puckered even tighter. Her breath shuddered, making her breast bounce gently against his skin.

Slowly, all of his moves careful and deliberate, he settled her knees to one side of his thighs. Then he leaned closer so Larissa had to tilt backward, her hands propping her up in a half sitting, half lying position.

"I dream of you," he confessed beneath his breath just before taking that plump tip into his mouth. His tongue swirled as he gently sucked on her flesh. She tasted so good. The lace added an extra layer of surreal delight to the experience. Between the candlelight and the lack of any sound other than Larissa's gentle moans, it was like he was in a dream.

A very tasty, very erotic, very tempting dream that made him wish for things he'd long since given up as impossible.

Like sweet Larissa.

Bittersweet pain layered over the fervent delight pounding through his body as he remembered that, as good as she tasted, as much as he wanted her, this road was a dead end. Larissa was a forever girl and he was all about the present moment.

He rasped his tongue over her burgeoning flesh. His muscles tensed at Larissa's gasp. She was so responsive, her body so tuned in to his own desires, it was like his wildest dream was coming true right before his eyes. And right under his tongue.

So if the present moment was all he could get, he'd wring every drop of pleasure from it he could.

Focused on that, he pushed the lace away with his tongue

while his other hand slid the opposite strap down her arm. The fabric dropped, framing her breasts in a silken cradle for his enjoyment.

His fingers traced a delicate pattern over one breast, sliding over the tip so she gasped, then cupping and holding the weight up for his kisses. Gently at first, he brushed his lips over one tip, then the other. His kisses got hotter. His teeth nipped, his fingers plucked the delicate flesh into tighter pebbles of delight.

More, his body shouted.

He slid his tongue up her slender throat, then took her mouth in a voracious, hot and wet kiss. Teeth, tongue and lips slid together in a wild dance. Knowing he was pushing his luck, hoping she was turned on enough to let him, he slipped one hand along her side until he found the button and zipper holding her straight jacket masquerading as a skirt closed. A flick of his fingers and he loosed the fabric.

His mouth still on hers, he used his torso to press her backward so she lay lengthwise down the counter. Her hands roamed his shoulders before she slid one inside the open collar of his shirt. Her fingernails scraped a trail of ecstasy along his chest and she gave a low purr that vibrated through his body like thunder.

With open-mouthed kisses, he made his way down to her chest. Unable to help himself, he stopped to pay special homage with a flick of his tongue to each straining nipple before kissing his way down the curve of her breasts to her stomach. He nibbled at the soft flesh, his hands going to the loosened waistband of her skirt. As if she'd just realized what he'd done, her body tensed. He pulled one hand from the skirt, sliding his palm in the opposite direction of his mouth until he cupped her breast, his fingers creating a sensual distraction.

It was only when he felt her relax again, her muscles

softening, her focus on the pleasure he was giving her instead of worrying about what he was up to, that he pressed his kisses lower. He nudged the skirt down to bare her belly, kissing the sweet indention before swirling his tongue in, then out. A little shudder rocked through her body, sending a shaft of pleasure through him.

He kissed lower, taking the skirt down as he went. When the fabric caught at her hips, he winced, knowing his sneaky plan of descent was in jeopardy. Larissa shifted. He moved fast, sliding her skirt off her legs in a single swift tug. Before it hit the floor he had his fingers inside her panties.

Knowing she could call it quits at any time, he went right for the gusto. Draping her knees over his shoulders, he spread her legs wide.

She gave a high, keening cry of pleasure when he rubbed his thumb along her swollen clit and he knew he had her. Tension poured from his shoulders and he let himself relax and give over to the moment.

A tiny scrap of lace masqueraded as her panties. He didn't waste time pulling them off her hips. It was faster, easier, to slide it aside so he could have full access to her wet delight.

His fingers slid into her tight sheath, swirling and dancing to the rhythm of her hips as she rose to meet his thrusting digits. He breathed in her musky scent and groaned, then licked her like an ice cream cone.

Already primed, she went off like a rocket. A cry of shocked pleasure ripped through her. She grabbed his shoulders, whether for traction as she raised her hips or to make sure he didn't stop, he didn't know. Didn't care.

He sucked the dewy fold between his teeth.

"Oh, God," she gasped hoarsely.

He nipped, then soothed her with his tongue. Her *Oh, God* became a chanting entreaty.

His fingers found her rhythm. His tongue matched it. Knowing she was right there on the edge, he reached up to give her nipple a little tug.

She exploded. Her chants became a keening cry of ecstasy. Her body tensed, as if she were holding on to the orgasm as tight as she could. Then she surrendered, her hips falling back to the counter and her entire body relaxed.

Shudders, tiny little tremors, quaked through her body. The sound of her labored gasps echoed through the room, music to his ears. The sharp bite of her fingernails in his shoulders eased. Consciously or not, she rubbed the tips of her fingers over the flesh she'd just gripped so tightly as if trying to ease the sting.

He wanted her like crazy. He needed the feel of her hot, tight body sheathing his. Milking the pleasure from him until he was spent. His dick throbbed painfully, begging for release.

Jason dropped his head against her belly, his face pressed to the smooth warmth. He knew what was in his wallet down to the exact dollar, the placement of every credit card because he'd watched customs dig through it just that morning.

And nowhere in there, or anywhere else on his person, was anything resembling a condom. He wanted to scream in frustration.

He licked his lips and lifted his head, smiling at the sight of her, all mussed and heavy eyed. Color warmed her to a soft rosy shade, from her cheeks to her tasty nipples.

Regret twined with frustration at the sight. In that second, he wished everything could be different. That he could be different. He wanted to promise her anything if it'd give them another chance.

But he'd done that once already. And the results had pretty much sucked.

So all he said was, "Yum."

7

Yum?

Her head spinning, Larissa didn't know if she was supposed to thank him for the climax, or, well, thank him for stopping.

Her body was still shaking with pleasure, orgasmic aftertremors shuddering through her as Jason pressed another kiss to her hypersensitive belly before pulling away from her.

He gave a pained wince as he straightened. Her gaze automatically dropped to his crotch, where his erection was looking like The Incredible Hulk, ready to rip itself free of his jeans.

She licked her lips. Oh, yeah. Yum, indeed.

He pulled away, his back cracking through the room like a slap, pulling her out of her sexual fog.

Of course his body was protesting. He was sporting a redwood-sized hard-on.

Before, she'd have played *this for that*. Because the man was so freaking amazing at this, she loved giving him that.

But this wasn't before. And the only thing they'd ever

had that was real between them was sex. A fact she needed to remember.

Suddenly very aware of how naked she was, in more ways than one, Larissa sat upright, pulling her camisole straps back over her shoulders and adjusting her panties. Avoiding his eyes, she slipped her legs to the edge of the counter, but before she could hop down, Jason reached out. His hands wrapped around her waist, so big and warm, and he lifted her gently to her feet.

Tears stung her eyes. Why did he have to be so damned sweet? Couldn't he just be incredible in bed? Just be good at the sex stuff and useless at melting her heart? She wanted to punch him in the arm, he made her so angry. He was everything she wanted in a man. But he was everything she didn't want, too.

"That was a mistake," she muttered, looking around for her skirt and jacket, hoping they'd offer some modesty. Her jacket was there hanging on the edge of the counter. She snagged it and shoved her arms into the sleeves so hard she was surprised she didn't rip the delicate fabric.

"Am I supposed to apologize?" Jason asked with a laugh that stopped somewhere between pain and irritation. "You weren't shoving my head away, babe. So I figured you were having yourself a pretty good time. If I had a condom, I'm betting we'd be making each other see stars right about now."

Just as angry with herself as she was with him, Larissa shrugged. After a quick glare at the useless chastity belt of a skirt, she scooped it up. It only took a second to decide that wiggling into it would only make the situation worse, so she snagged the soft blanket that had started all this trouble and wrapped it around herself.

"What are you doing?"

"I'm going to get dressed," she said, clutching her skirt

in her fist and heading to the bathroom at the back of the store. Realizing she'd be dressing in a strange pitch black room, she hesitated.

Jason heaved a loud sigh and, walking so stiffly she winced with guilt, he scooped another candle from box and handed it to her. "I don't have the cootie matches so you're on your own for getting it lit."

Larissa pulled her gaze from the long, hard length pressing in painful relief against his zipper before she did something crazy, like drop the blanket. But darn it, she'd been raised with the concept of one good turn deserves another, and if she'd ever seen something worth turning, it was straining that zipper.

No. Their little sexual reunion had been a mistake. A wonderful, mind blowing, deliciously wonderful mistake. Compounding one mistake with another would be crazy. Feel and taste great, but still… "No!"

"Huh?"

"Nothing." She grimaced, then gave him an apologetic look and took the candle. Not willing to bend over and dig through the box, given the naked state of her butt, even covered with a fluffy blanket, she tilted the other candle until the fresh wick took flame.

Sex, even great sex, wasn't worth giving up her romantic values for. She'd tried that once—with Jason himself, as a matter of fact—and it'd bitten her in the ass. No, romance was something that would last. It was a give and take, a careful consideration of the other person's needs and a desire to do special little things to make them feel good. Romance was about the little things that said you wanted to build a beautiful future together.

And while she might stretch that definition by pretending she was being considerate in wanting to take care of his needs and desires, there was nothing little about his thing.

She and Jason? Sure he had his romantic moments, like when he'd helped her down from the counter. He had it in him to be sweet and thoughtful. He was a gentleman without making a big deal of it.

But she'd tried to convince herself once that those moments made for a romantic relationship. And usually then, like now, she was doing the convincing while her body was still rocking the wild afterglow of an orgasm.

The reality was, they had no future beyond this power outage.

Pretending that didn't bother her, Larissa took her candle and skirt and hurried her blanket-covered butt to the back room. Once there, she sucked in a deep breath to try and control the tears that'd suddenly flooded her eyes.

She was being silly. It was just emotional overload brought on by the best orgasm she'd had in two years. Nothing to cry about. Well, other than the fact that this just proved that all her orgasms over the last almost-two years had been pretty pathetic.

She put the candle on the bathroom counter, taking care that it was safe. Setting the place on fire was probably a bad idea, given that she had no clue if the alarms became inactive without power.

A quick shake told her the wrinkles were now a permanent feature of her skirt. No matter, it wasn't like she'd ever wear it again anyway.

She stepped into the skirt and with a wiggle of her hips, slid it into place. She avoided looking in the mirror, knowing her candlelit face would tell her way more than she was willing to handle.

Instead, she gathered the blanket and candle again, and

with a deep breath and quick lecture, rejoined Jason in the store.

Except... She looked around. He wasn't there.

"Jason?"

Fear tickled her spine. Visions of horror movies filled her head. It was always the idiot girl who had irresponsible sex that got whacked by the ax-wielding maniac. But was it really irresponsible? They hadn't had actual intercourse, after all. The only potential danger was to her heart, not her health.

Right. Larissa rolled her eyes. She'd try that argument out on the ax-wielder and let him provide a moral compass.

"Jason," she yelled, tossing the blanket on the settee and hurrying to the front of the store.

No response.

Nerves screaming, she looked around for a weapon. Nothing. Then she spied the long, dusty box Jason had tossed on the bench outside the store. Hurrying over, she flipped the lid open and with a grimace, grabbed the three-foot long wooden dick.

It was smooth and weirdly warm beneath her fingers. And heavier than she'd have guessed. Guys hung this from their dicks? Talk about a workout.

Pretending it was just a stick, not an ode to the fragility of the male ego, she hefted it over one shoulder and lifted the candle high in her other hand.

Swallowing hard, she forced herself to walk down the hallway toward the hotel.

"Jason," she called again tentatively.

Her voice sounded like a mouse's squeak. Pathetic.

"Jason?" she yelled this time.

Was that a sound? She stopped so she could hear without the sound of her high heels tapping against the floor to distract her.

Larissa put the candle down on one of the center display counters so she could get a better grip on the dick in case she needed it as a weapon. For the first time, she was glad it was a big dick.

Swallowing the balled up terror stuck in her throat, she took a deep breath and turned the corner.

"That works better with a body in it."

Larissa jumped, screaming. Spinning around, she wielded the wooden dick like a baseball bat, ready to smack the head off the ax-wielder.

Lightning fast, the man jumped backward just before it cracked him in the face. Jason's laughter roared, echoing and bouncing mockingly off the high ceilings.

She could barely make out his features in the dark, which meant he couldn't see her glare, either. But she still offered her death-stare as he bent at the waist, his fists on his thighs because he was howling like a baboon.

"Don't choke on your hilarity," she muttered.

"I'm sorry. But what'd you think you were going to do? Beat me with a hollow stick because I got under your skirt?"

Deciding that sounded more reasonable than the ax-murderer theory, she just shrugged.

"Where'd you go?" she asked, still out of breath as she pressed her hand against her chest to keep her heart from exploding.

Still grinning like a naughty little boy, he pointed at the hotel's entrance to the mall. "I remembered seeing phones by the elevators when we came through. I wanted to see if they worked."

Larissa's chin shot up. The first thing he thought of after sexing her up was an escape route? Wasn't that so freaking typical.

"And?" she asked coolly. It didn't matter. It wasn't like she was hoping he'd stay around or anything.

She suddenly realized she was still clutching the dick, her fingers gripping it so tight that if it'd been a man, it would have twisted clean off. She tossed it to Jason, who easily caught it. To his credit, he didn't say a word, either.

"And they are on a closed-circuit system, only connecting within the hotel itself," he said with a shrug. "I double checked all the doors on that end. Nada. We're still stuck."

"This must be your worst nightmare. Stuck in one place, unable to run off and play when you get bored."

"What's that supposed to mean?"

She remembered his disgust the time she'd confessed that she thought all his trips were his way of escaping the responsibility of their relationship. It'd been their last argument before their breakup. Well, the last one before he'd accused her of cheating on him, of course.

But even then, he hadn't sounded this angry.

Nibbling on her bottom lip, she stared. His face was a study of shadows, giving him an intimidating look she'd never associated with Jason. Before, he'd always been a sexy, fun, sanity-threatening charmer. Someone dangerous to her heart, but otherwise completely safe.

But now? Her heart was still pounding but not from any ax fears. Looming over her, his shoulders twice the width of hers, he looked like he'd be able to kick any ax-murder's butt.

And wasn't that a turn on. Heart still beating way too fast, she turned away to retrieve her candle.

"Larissa?"

"I'm hungry," she said, ignoring his question. He gave her a long look, then shrugged. It was his way of letting her know he saw the game but was willing to let her play.

He fell into step beside her as she hurried back to the store.

"I just ate, but I could go for seconds." Between his mild expression and even tone, it took her a few beats to get the innuendo.

"Cute," she dismissed as if the idea of his tongue between her legs again didn't make her clitoris quiver. She hurried over to the box of food.

She pulled out a couple of sandwiches, a sleeve of cookies and some fruit. With a quick scan, she decided to eat at the bench outside the store instead of at the counter. No point giving Jason any more fuel to tease her over.

"I forgot how hungry you got after sex," he mused, leaning against the arched doorway watching.

"We didn't have sex," she corrected meticulously.

"It tasted like sex to me."

What was she supposed to say to that? Denying it was churlish. Or was it? This was why she wrote rules for romance. Not for sex. Romance was easier to figure out.

She decided that ignoring any references to sex was the only way to handle this situation. At least, it was if she didn't want to end up in that same position again—on her back, legs wrapped around his shoulders.

And she was doing her best to pretend that's not exactly what she wanted.

"ARE YOU HUNGRY? Did you want a sandwich or some fruit?" Larissa asked, giving him a wide berth as she headed out of the store toward the center of the mall. He watched her hips swing temptingly in that damned skirt again, and sighed. She was clearly unwilling to discuss what he'd already eaten. Since he had no clue what to say, either, he let it go.

They'd just go back to pretending all this sexual tension zinging through the hot, heavy air was brought on by the storm outside. One thing you could always count on with Larissa, she was good at keeping those little fantasies alive.

He watched her choose a leather bench situated in the center of the mall, huge frothy green plants flanking her on either side. With the growing humidity and greenery, it was starting to feel like lunch in the tropics. Larissa set the candle on the center of the bench, then placed food around it like a candlelit picnic.

"Jason?" she asked with a frown, reminding him of her invitation to eat. He glanced at his watch. Seven-thirty. Only a couple hours since the power had blown, but long enough that he was pretty sure they were stuck for the night. Might as well fuel up.

"Sure, thanks." Unsure of his next move, or even his next thought, he slowly straightened from the doorway and sauntered over. He took a few seconds to wrap the koteka in its cotton cloth again before shutting it away in its box. Then he slid the box beneath the bench and sat across from her, the food a safe barrier between them.

"So tell me what you've been up to," he said after a couple bites of mediocre ham and swiss on rye. It needed mustard. He'd eaten tree-bark stew and beetles in his time, so the fact that this sandwich basically sucked was ignorable. But ignoring was easier with a distraction. "I thought you'd have your bookstore long before now. What's the deal?"

She gave him a long look. He could almost see the mental debate going on behind those pretty brown eyes. Did she take him up on the safe, innocuous conversation topic? Or did she risk ignoring it, knowing he'd bring the discussion back to something more dangerous, like how much better she'd tasted than this sandwich.

For a few seconds, he wasn't sure if she was going to

answer or not. Finally she gave a little shrug and set the sandwich down in exchange for an apple.

"I realized that I'd be able to build a more successful store, have a better chance at success, if I laid a stronger foundation. So I took some classes, worked on a few sidelines that will enhance the reputation of the store and bring in more customers."

He shook his head, both impressed by how smart she was at business stuff and baffled that she could wait so long to go for something she wanted.

"You already have a degree in English. So what kind of classes did you need?" he asked.

Her mouth full of apple, she gave herself time to finish chewing before explaining, "Marketing, business and some computer courses."

All that to sell a few books? His confusion must have shown on his face because she leaned forward to explain.

"Bookstores are an endangered species these days. I knew I had to change with the market, and to do that I needed a stronger skill set and a better handle on marketing. The business classes just made sense. After all, I'll be running my own and it pays to know how to do it correctly from the get-go."

"Can-Do is doing great, and I never had to take a bunch of classes," he said, his spine stiffening. He didn't know why Larissa's intellectual approach always made him feel defensive. Maybe because he tended to fly by the seat of his pants instead of obsessing beforehand. Which usually worked out just fine.

Except when it didn't, and his business was in jeopardy.

Like now.

He snapped off a bite of his sandwich, grinding it between his teeth.

"Can-Do is a specialty business that's been built on your charm and reputation," Larissa said, her tone dismissive as if she hadn't just given him a huge compliment. "You honed in on a niche market and made it your own. Between your reputation and your connections, you're obviously going to succeed."

Jason frowned, wondering if she actually thought he was a success and not just a lucky asshole.

"Unless, of course, you do something crazy and ruin it," she added, taking another bite of her apple.

Tossing the tasteless sandwich aside, Jason leaned back on the bench and folded his arms over his chest.

"What's that supposed to mean?"

"Huh?" She'd tucked the apple core on a napkin and was now wiping her fingers with another. "What? Oh, you mean ruining the business?"

"Right. What makes you think I'm ruining my business?"

Larissa rolled her eyes. "I didn't say you were. I said you were a success and would stay that way."

"Unless I ruined it," he ground out.

"Feeling a little defensive?" she guessed, poking at her sandwich again before taking a tiny bite.

He gave her a long stare.

"All I meant was that even successes can fail if they aren't careful. You've built a consistent message with Can-Do. Adventures with a smile. Fun trips, affordable deals, appealing locales."

She waited for him to nod, which he finally did with a short jerk of his chin. He felt like she was luring him into a corner, waiting to spring the trapped door open so he landed on his ass.

"You've got a solid brand. You always were good about keeping your customer database current, so I'm sure you have a list you can tap anytime to tempt them with some special trip or other."

He shrugged one shoulder. "Yeah. That's all SOP. Actually, you're the one who setup our database way back when," he reminded her. "We've added a few search options. We can pull up preferences, like time of year, continents and even travel style. It is pretty solid."

"See," she said. "You've got it handled."

He'd feel a lot better if she'd met his eyes when she'd said that.

"But?"

"But, what?"

"But you think I'm screwing something up. You're tap dancing around it, but I can tell. So spill, what's the problem?"

Larissa avoided his eyes, instead making a show of rewrapping her barely eaten sandwich. She tore open the sleeve of cookies and chose one with delicate precision.

Jason wanted to grab the cookie and send it skittering across the floor, but he knew it wouldn't make her talk any faster. Larissa was gathering her thoughts, marshalling her arguments and adjusting her presentation.

Why couldn't she just blurt it out, tell him what she thought the problem was? It wasn't like he was unreasonable. He'd hear her out. He welcomed insight and constructive criticism, dammit.

Not that there was anything wrong with his plans. He knew his business best. But it would be entertaining to hear whatever crazy problem she'd dreamed up.

If she ever got around to telling him. He bounced his fist off his thigh impatiently. The girl spent more time in her head than she did in real life.

She drove him nuts.

He watched her nibble her way around the circumference

of the cookie. Her teeth took tiny little bites of the crisp chocolate studded wafer. Her pink tongue glistened as she licked a crumb off her lip. He swallowed hard. His dick stirred resentfully, since it was still suffering from painfully unrequited sexual frustration.

Oh yeah, she drove him totally frigging nuts.

"Well, I've already said that I think you've created a solid business," she finally said.

Jason's fist bounced harder.

"And I haven't been following your business the last few years or anything, but from what I know, you're one of the best at what you do. So if you had to make adjustments, you could. Unquestionably."

She took another tiny bite of that cookie. A piece broke away, dropping into the deep vee of her partially rebuttoned jacket. He imagined licking that crumb off her cleavage and felt a light sweat break out on his forehead.

"Adjustments? Why would I have to adjust anything?"

Besides the erection pressing painfully against his belly. A slight shift to the left would ease the pressure, but groping himself seemed a little inappropriate.

"Well…"

"Well, what?"

She wrinkled her nose, grabbing another cookie from the sleeve. She bit it in half with a snap.

"Well, you're obviously already making adjustments, aren't you? You're looking at shifting from depending on your reputation and word-of-mouth to setting up shop in a hotel mall." She glanced down to brush crumbs from her lap and noticed the bit of cookie nestled in her cleavage. With one finger, she scooped it out. It was all he could do not to grab her wrist and carry that delicious crumb to his own mouth.

She glanced back up and caught the look on his face.

Even in the dim light, he could see her fingers tremble as she tossed the crumb onto the napkin along with her apple core.

"So if you're already adjusting, you must have a reason, right?"

He could barely hear her over the rush of lust buzzing around his head. Heads. Then her words filtered through the hunger and he blinked.

"Sure. I wouldn't do it without a good reason."

"And?" This time she was the one doing the prompting.

"And I told you. Peter is settling down. He's cutting his trips down to a dozen or so a year."

"So why change things? Your trips pay for your expenses, right? So you're financially secure. And if Peter's not traveling with Can-Do, won't he get another job?"

"Sure. He's already got a job lined up." He ignored the part about financial security.

"So why tie yourself to a storefront? That kind of long-term anchor seems at odds with the business you've built." Her words were neutral. But her eyes shone with a fervid curiosity.

He couldn't blame her. After all, his refusal to change was one of the core reasons they'd split up. That, and her dating another man. Jason had sometimes wondered if she'd gone out with Conner to push his buttons and force him to choose between her and his traveling.

Jason just stared, his face impassive as he debated answering. It wasn't like his financial responsibilities were a secret, but she didn't know how bad the situation with his mom had become over the last few years. And he didn't like to talk about it. Or to admit, even in a roundabout way, that there was something dragging on his dreams and calling the shots from behind the scenes. It did major damage to his self-image of a free and easy kind of guy.

That, and thinking about it usually made him want to beat the hell out of something.

8

LARISSA'S BODY WAS SO TENSE, she felt like she was going to have bruises. She didn't know what was going on in Jason's head, but he looked furious.

She shouldn't have talked to him about business.

Her stomach cramped and tension danced in little black dots in front of her eyes.

They were locked in here for who knew how long and now he was pissed. A tiny trickle of sweat slid down her back. The room, so cool when they'd come in, was starting to take on the damp heat typical of a South Carolina evening storm. And now she could add an angry ex-lover to the mix, just for a little extra discomfort.

She wished they could go back to before, when it'd only been shock and sexual tension filling the air between them.

She should have kept her mouth shut. She knew better. Larissa's romance rule number five: Men are like glaciers—frozen solid and slow to change. Trying to resculpt one was a lesson in frustration, so why bother?

She'd learned that the hard way when she'd thought he'd actually be able to commit to a relationship between them.

Instead, he'd found the first excuse to bail, running back to his freedom as fast as he could.

It wasn't until she saw the crumbs falling from between her fingers onto the leather bench that she realized she'd crushed her cookie.

She grimaced, opening her hand to stare in dismay at the mess. Chocolate, even the kind in crappy mass-produced cookies, deserved more respect.

"Look, forget I asked, okay?" she blurted out, needing to fill the silence. "Obviously you've been running Can-Do for a long time and you know what works and what won't."

Like watching an ice cube melt in the hot sun, the taut line of his shoulders slowly eased and his face relaxed. Then he shrugged and looked away with a deep sigh.

"No. I'm the one who pushed the subject. Which means you deserve to have it answered."

Her mouth dropped.

"Who are you and what'd you do with Jason Cantrell?" she asked.

That dispelled the last of the tension. He laughed and reached over to take her crumb-filled hand. He locked his gaze on hers. His blue eyes filled with mischief as he turned her hand over to shake the crumbs into a napkin. Crumpling it, he then lifted her palm to his mouth and licked the melted chocolate from her skin.

His tongue was hot. Fire flamed low in her belly, making her suddenly damp lips tremble with need. His tongue slid fingers of her free hand into a fist, nails cutting into the skin, and tried to convince herself that jumping him was a really, really bad idea for a really long list of reasons.

They had no future.

She'd hate herself in the morning if she gave in to meaningless sex.

He'd walked away from her once already and broke her heart.

They didn't have a condom.

His tongue swirled over the soft, meaty flesh between her thumb and her forefinger, then he sucked softly.

Her list went up in flames as her brain shut down. Her breath shuddered, molten heat making her thighs damp. Two more seconds of this and she'd rip her own clothes off and climb all over him.

"I thought you were going to answer my question," she gasped.

His mouth paused its delectable torment to frown at her words. She used his hesitation to pull her hand away, tucking it under her hip to hide it until the tingling stopped.

The look of sexy mischief left his eyes just before Jason looked away. She winced, then told herself to stop being such a wimp. She wasn't trying to fix his business or find a way for him to stick around this time. She was just asking a simple question—one that he'd insisted he was going to answer. It wasn't like she was breaking any rules.

"Peter's going to get a regular job, sure," Jason finally said. "But he's like me. It'll drive him nuts after awhile. I know he thinks this is going to work out for him, the settling down and staying in one place. But it can't last."

"You're saying there is no way your brother, who loves this woman enough to marry her, will be happy spending his life with her?" Larissa snapped, knowing she was projecting but not caring. Unable to stay still, she started pacing the seven-foot distance between the bench and the storefront.

"You realize this isn't about us, right?" he chimed in, sounding bored as he leaned back, his elbows on the side of the bench.

"I'm just saying, how can a marriage work if one of the two people involved is going to be miserable? Wasn't it Peter who pointed out that little fact when we got engaged? Didn't he say that you'd hate being stuck and eventually hate me for making you stay around?" The words were bitter on her tongue. She stopped pacing to plant her fists on her hips and glare. "So how is it going to be different for Mr. Know It All? How is his marriage going to survive?"

"I don't give a shit what happens to Peter's marriage," Jason snapped, no longer looking relaxed as he sat up straight and returned her glare. "I need to make sure there is a large enough steady income to keep my mom in the assisted living home and off state assistance."

Larissa's anger drained so fast, it should have been accompanied by a sucking sound. Her cheeks warmed and her eyes burned. She hadn't known his mom was in a home. Iris Cantrell had had a stroke while on an archeological dig five years ago. Her husband had gotten her medical care as fast as possible, but she'd been permanently affected and unable to care for herself ever since. The last Larissa had known, Iris and Lawrence had retired here in South Carolina.

"I'm sorry. I didn't realize she was doing so poorly. I guess your dad can't take care of her on his own any longer?" Larissa asked quietly.

"Dad wasn't cut out to play nursemaid, apparently," Jason said, rising to take over her pacing track. "After her second stroke, she was a lot more dependent. Dad couldn't handle it. Right before we split up, actually, he filed for divorce. They never had much, since all their money went back into their research. He left her the house, but took what little cash they had."

Why hadn't he told her? Turned to her? Despite her own feeling of rejection, Larissa reached out a hand in support, wanting to offer something, anything, to ease the pain and anger in his voice. But his back was to her as he stared at the dark, empty wall of stores.

Before she could think of anything to say, he took a loud breath, then shrugged like he was shaking off his emotions. When he turned back to her, his face was calm. But she could still see the pain in his eyes.

"So that's why I need to keep Can-Do Adventures kicking ass. There are responsibilities. And for now, they fall to me to handle. Peter will be back full time eventually. That's not a reflection on his marriage, simply a fact. We Cantrell men are just made that way."

"And his wife?"

"Meghan's cool," Jason judged, looking uncomfortable. "I guess they've talked about it. She'll travel a little, too. She says she'll be okay with whatever Peter does."

Unlike Larissa.

It was a damned good thing she wasn't in love with Jason any longer. And just as soon as her heart stopped crumbling like that stupid cookie, she'd work on being grateful.

"So what about you?" Jason asked, rocking back on his heels, hands in his pockets, looking so casual that it would be easy to overlook his tight face and hunched shoulders. "You still haven't explained why you're still at the same bookstore. What happened to all your dreams? I can't believe you'd wait this long and change them that much."

His words poured out so fast, she knew he was using them like a shield. Like her advice, or even her company for anything more than a few weeks, Jason didn't want her sympathy.

She swallowed the ball of misery that'd welled up in her throat and made a show of gathering their dinner leftovers to hide her face so he wouldn't see the pain burning in her eyes.

"You're not going to share?" he asked after a painful silence.

"There isn't much to share," she said tonelessly as she

walked a few feet over to a trash can to toss everything, eaten or not. "I already told you that I'd decided to take some classes, solidify my foundation and perfect my business plan before I made a big move."

Shoulders knotted, she debated returning to the bench or finding somewhere to hide until she had a grip on her crazy, out-of-control emotions. But it was getting hotter by the minute, the air a physical thing now, like a heavy, damp blanket laying over the mall. If it was this warm out here in the open mall, she knew the heat would be worse hiding in the store.

"So you've spent the last two years going to school?" Jason prodded.

He wouldn't let her run and hide. He'd fessed up, and he would insist she do the same. So Larissa returned to the pool of candlelight surrounding the bench. She didn't sit, though.

"I've been building a foundation," she corrected. "I'm known as one of the leading authorities on romance in the country now."

His mouth dropped. Actually grateful for a way to break the emotional ice, she asked in a teasing tone. "What's with the shock? You don't think I'm qualified?"

He opened his mouth, then shut it and shrugged. "I have no idea. I don't even know what that means. Are you famous or something?"

She gave a little laugh. "Not famous, really. I started an online column a few years back called Romance Rules. It turned into a big hit. It was syndicated, then picked up by *Cosmopolitan* magazine."

Jason's eyes widened.

"I thought that was more about sex and fashion than hearts and flowers."

"I provide contrast and balance," she informed him with a

big smile. "Actually, I'm really proud of how well it's going. I was nervous at first. I mean, like you say, their platform is pretty much living the sexy life. But we quickly found out that even sexy lives need romance. Now I'm a hit."

She was proud of how she'd made that distinction. That women could have full, exciting sex lives that made them feel loved and wanted and needed. After all, that's what romance boiled down to in her opinion. Feeling special because of love.

"So you have all that going for you," he said with a proud grin. "That's great. I'm going to have to pick up one of those magazines and see what you're advising."

Larissa gave him a slow, shy smile. She'd had this secret fantasy once. Or twice. Or every time she wrote an article—that Jason might randomly pick up the magazine while waiting in an airport or doctors office and see her name. He'd be curious, then awed at her advice column. And he'd see all the things he'd done wrong in their relationship and hurry back to fix them.

A crazy fantasy. Especially since she knew he only read travel pieces and spy novels.

"But why open a store here if you've got that going on?" he asked. "If you're going to keep a store and that romance thing, I'd think you'd stay in the house the bookstore is already in. You always seemed to love that place."

She crashed back to earth with a mental thud as she realized his interest was really all about the store, not her.

"The Victorian is fine," she explained, her tone a little chilly. "It's gorgeous and wonderfully preserved. Mr. Murphy has even made a number of renovations based on my suggestions. The dining room and back parlor were combined to create a café. It does a nice amount of business, and there are four bookclubs that meet there monthly."

She babbled on for another few minutes about the glory

and wonder of Murphy's Books before she noticed the little smile on Jason's face.

Her voice trailed off as she struggled to read that smile. "What?" she asked.

"You love that store. I get it. What I don't get is why you're still there. You're a nationwide romance authority. You've got two degrees, what I'm sure is the best business plan in existence and unless you've gone crazy, you had a decent chunk of money to fund whatever plans you had."

"So?"

"So I'm confused. I asked you before but you haven't answered me. Why haven't you left the store to start your own gig long before this? Or why haven't you simply bought old man Murphy out, like you said you were going to two years ago and made that store your own?"

JASON WAS SURPRISED at how much he needed to know that answer. It wasn't like she'd been under contract to follow through with her plans, even though those damned plans had been a major player in their breakup.

"As wonderful as it is, it doesn't fit the image I want to create," she confessed, sitting on the bench and giving him a dreamy sort of look. "A dedicated bookstore is a wonderful thing, but I don't want to focus solely on books. I want to expand to all things romantic. That's the name of my store, by the way, Isn't It Romantic."

"Cute." And it was. In a fluffy, girly kind of way. From a guy's angle, she'd bet it was a little hive-inducing. "So it's a girl store? I'd have thought females would swoon over Murphy's place. It's got all that quaint architecture and history and character. But if you don't want to do it there, why not open in a typical mall?"

His *why here?* was unspoken but clear.

"The Victorian is in a smaller neighborhood and brings in local patrons but won't ever get the kind of foot traffic The Cartright will bring in," she said, looking around the space like she was seeing it filled with rich shoppers, their fists filled with credit cards as they stampeded toward her doors. "This location will not only bring in guest shoppers from all over the country, but the local businesses will patronize it as well. The median income of the shoppers here will be much higher than the average mall, too."

He frowned. Was he the only one who saw the glitch in her plan?

"Don't take this wrong, but these stores…" He waved his hand to indicate the closed doors lining the mall walkway. "Tiffany, Louis Vuitton, Apple. These are all pretty high dollar, right?"

"So?" she snapped. "Isn't that why you want to make a sex museum here? To attract the high dollar customers?"

"It's not a sex museum," he corrected with a grin, glad she remembered his plans. "It's an opportunity to partake in exclusive couples' weekend adventures."

"Whatever," she dismissed. "This place is perfect for all the reasons I've already told you. And clearly, my window display would look better next to Tiffany's glitter than your penis stick."

His grin widened. She had a good point. Not that he'd give up his claim, but that koteka was a pretty beat up piece of wood. Propping it in a window next to a bunch of diamonds was a little pathetic.

"Regardless of which one of our windows would look better next to the diamonds, I'm still confused."

"About?"

"Daniel told me they'd just made the decision to hold one space for a local friend a month ago. You couldn't have been planning on this location for all that time."

Larissa's smile faded. She looked down at her skirt, brushing at the fabric like she was trying to smooth out the wrinkles with her palm.

"I'd get it if you'd opened at a different location and were looking to move up," he said. "But you're just getting rolling. So what's the deal? Why the delay in starting your own business?"

She'd always used the store as a reason not to travel with him.

Had it all been bullshit?

Had all those middle-of-the-night doubts about his career choice been brought on by a lie?

"I told you—"

"Right," he interrupted. "You had to build a stronger foundation. Which sounds great. But that's not what you said you were going to do a couple of years ago." When they'd broke up over it, dammit. "You said you needed to focus on getting your shit together so you could buy Murphy's store."

She clamped her arms across her belly. He wondered if she knew her jacket was still unbuttoned enough to make that move a gorgeous temptation as the candlelight flickered over the curves of her breasts.

Jason tore his gaze away, forcing himself to keep his eyes on her face. That's where he'd find answers. Looking for them in the other parts of her body only led to trouble.

"I didn't buy the store right after we split up because…" She stared past his shoulder for a second like she was trying to figure out exactly what to say. Or how to say it. Then she gave a little one-shouldered shrug that played havoc on his intention to keep his eyes on her face. "I wasn't in a good place, emotionally, after we split up. It took me awhile to be sure of myself. Of my dream. I'd already lost one of the most important things in my life. I didn't want to blow the other."

Jason winced. He'd have rather she kicked him in the gut with those high heels of hers. He hated that he'd hurt her, even though she'd been the one to cheat. Yeah, he might have mentally called her all manner of horrible names at the time, but that didn't mean he hadn't known that she had to have been miserable with him if she was going to do something that drastic. Before, he'd have sworn that cheating wasn't in Larissa's repertoire.

But he'd been so pissed, so worried he'd do something violent, he'd walked off when she'd refused to explain. So this was the first chance he'd had to deal with the aftermath of their breakup, face to face.

It didn't feel any better now than it would have then.

Obviously uncomfortable with sharing as much as she had—or with his pained silence—Larissa sprang to her feet. Before she could go anywhere, he stepped forward, blocking her path. He didn't know what he wanted to say to her. Hell, he didn't even know what he wanted from her. A chance to worship her body for a few hours, sure. But she wasn't the type of girl to offer up a free ride. And he wouldn't have... liked her as much if she were. From the time they were kids, he'd had a thing for her. But he'd ignored it. Mostly because of just that reason. Larissa was a good girl.

Which was why he'd asked her to marry him. Because a guy didn't do all those lustful and wild things to a good girl unless he planned to do right by her, too.

He'd have probably done them both a favor if he'd just seduced her without offering up a lot of promises he'd known he couldn't keep.

"Jason, I'd like to pass, please," she said quietly.

"Wait a second," he said. He still didn't know what to say. He just knew he had to say something.

So he spoke from the heart. Or somewhere close by.

"Look, we both made mistakes before. But, you know, I miss you," he admitted quietly. Her eyes rounded so wide, her lush eyelashes almost touched her brows.

Taking that as a good sign, Jason stepped closer, trailing one finger along the smooth skin of her cheek before slipping his knuckle under her chin to lift her face to his.

She didn't slap him away. Another good sign.

"I'm not claiming monkhood or anything, but I haven't had a relationship since we split," he confessed. "I've never found anyone I wanted to be with like I want you. Never cared about anyone else enough to want to spend the time or effort to build something."

Her tongue slipped out to wet her lips, making his fingers clench. She stared into his eyes as if she were trying to see into his soul. He shifted, a little uncomfortable at that idea. After all, even he didn't know what was in there.

"So? What do you think?" he asked, cringing inwardly at his awkwardness. He'd had more finesse in grade school. But that look on Larissa's face, so searching and honest, made him fumble.

"Think? About what, exactly?"

"About us. You and me. Spending some time together," he clarified, starting to regain his verbal footing. "After we're out of here, I mean."

She blinked a couple times, a tiny wrinkle forming between her eyebrows. Tilting her head to one side, she asked, "Like...what? Dating?"

"Right," he said, relieved that she'd waded through his fumbling to get to the heart of his suggestion. "Date, hang out, get cozy."

He slid his hand around to cup her chip, marveling at how soft her skin was beneath his fingers. Leaning down, he held her eyes as he brushed a whisper soft kiss over her lips.

The frown didn't go away, though.

"What do you think?" he asked, trying a second kiss, this one with a little more pressure.

She moved her head back. Just enough to break contact with his mouth. She didn't pull her chin from his hand, though. That was a good sign, right?

"So you want to go back to what we had before, without the commitment. We date. When you're in town. We hang out. When you have time. And we get cozy. When you're horny."

Jason narrowed his eyes. Was she pissed? He couldn't read her tone. Her face was blank.

"We can get cozy when you're horny, too," he promised trying out his most charming smile.

She didn't smile back.

"Well?" he encouraged. He knew he should wait. He should have been more tactful, maybe a little more seductive. He should have started by asking for a date, not lining it all up like that.

But still, maybe she'd say yes.

Holding his breath, he waited. Larissa gave him a long, indecipherable look. The she slowly shook her head. Shoulders low, she pressed her lips together before saying, "I don't think it'd be a good idea. I doubt either one of us has changed what we want out of life. Or out of a relationship. So why go through the misery and disappointment all over again?"

"It doesn't have to be misery if we know from the get go what the game plan is," Jason objected, even though he knew she was right. But, dammit, he didn't want her to be. He wanted it all. His career and freedom. And the woman he...cared a great deal about.

He winced, knowing if she could hear his thoughts she'd give him that arched look of hers as if to say, see, *I told you so*.

"I need a break," she said, looking around, flustered.

"And what do you suggest I do while you hole up in the store?" he snapped, even though he knew he was more angry with himself than her.

She bent gracefully and lifted the candle, then handed it to him.

"Why don't you go explore the mall, or break into the hotel or even try climbing the walls to find a way out of here. If it helps, pretend I agreed to another of your non-committal relationships. That should inspire you fast enough."

9

LARISSA WANTED TO PAT HERSELF on the back.

She hadn't kicked Jason in the balls like she'd wanted.

She hadn't thrown anything when she stepped into the softly lit store.

And she hadn't screamed. At least, she hadn't until she'd reached the bathroom at the very back of the store. And then she did her screaming into the blanket she'd grabbed on her way back.

All things considered, it was an excellent show of self-control.

That she'd been locked in the bathroom for ten minutes and couldn't bring herself to go back out might not be so brave. But dammit, it wasn't every day a girl had an invitation for a romance-less, non-committal, non-relationship filled with lots of hot, steamy sex.

She closed her eyes and leaned her forehead against the cool door, breathing in the faint scent of fresh paint.

"Maybe if I hide in here long enough, Jason will actually find an escape route," she muttered. Or maybe, hopefully, she'd overcome the urge to run out there, throw herself in his arms and agree to anything he wanted as long as she was the only girl he was cozying up with.

What'd she said to Chloe just this afternoon? That she didn't believe in gratuitous sex. That without emotion and commitment, sex was a shallow thing. What kind of evil universe did she live in that it'd test her like this?

"Chloe's gonna laugh her ass off when she hears about this," Larissa told herself. "And probably suggest I get therapy when she hears I'm having conversations with myself."

Finally, more because she didn't want Jason to come looking for her and find her hiding in a bathroom than any sense of bravery or ability to handle the situation, she turned the doorknob. Taking her flickering candle, she returned to the damply humid darkness of the store, looking around as she went.

No Jason.

She went to the arched entrance and held her candle high.

No Jason.

She thought about calling out. But she didn't want him back that badly.

His penis box was still tucked under the bench, though, so she figured he hadn't escaped yet.

Not caring if an ax murderer showed up this time, she set her candle on the checkout counter and looked around. She needed to distract herself or she'd go insane. She pulled her briefcase over and emptied the contents so she could sort and tidy it, figuring there had to be something in here she could work on.

An hour later, she'd revised her brochure, noting in the margins changes she'd like to make. She'd written a thank you letter to Conner, Ben and Franklin, accepting their imaginarily generous offer. She pulled out her business plan, intending to go through and revise it now that she'd spent time—*way too much time*—in the actual store space.

She had to admit, she was a little intimidated by the stature of the stores around her. Could she pull this off? Was Isn't It Romantic a big enough idea to justify her spot in this mall?

"Sure it is. You're one of a kind. You're in *Cosmo*, for crying out loud," she assured herself. Besides, what was it Conner had suggested?

"Romance à la Cartright?" She wrinkled her nose. "Stupid idea."

That wasn't part of the deal, was it? She jotted down a note to make sure he'd been joking. But it was flattering to be asked, right? That proved she was a strong enough contender for the space.

"Not like some travel agency," she muttered.

She flipped through the pages of her business plan. But she couldn't concentrate.

Where the hell was Jason?

Larissa looked around, but there was no sign of life in the dark emptiness beyond her doorway. She listened, but could only hear a pounding splatter of rain hitting the mall entry windows.

She breathed in the muggy air. If she had to be trapped like this, she wished there could have at least been a little window somewhere she could open to ventilate some of this hot air out.

Was he coming back?

Not that she cared, really. But if he wasn't, she could take off her jacket and skirt and curl up on the cool marble floor to get comfortable.

Leave it to Jason to make being trapped without electricity or outside contact even more miserable. Thoroughly disgusted with the entire situation, she tossed her notebook and pen down. They slid across the counter, stopping just short of toppling off the other side.

"This is ridiculous."

Larissa bit her lip, trying to decide what to do. She picked up the almost-burned down candle and walked to the door, looking out to the right, then the left.

No Jason.

She shrugged. She'd be damned if she'd call for him.

And she was dying of heat exhaustion here.

Trying to ignore the tiny skitter of fear tracking up and down her spine, she turned back into the store and considered. Then, looking over her shoulder again to make sure Jason hadn't sneaked up behind her, she made quick work of what was left of her jacket's buttons. She shrugged it off, then looked around and hung it from one of the wall sconces so the silk wouldn't wrinkle any worse.

She bent down to unbuckle the straps of her darling red patent-leather mary-janes, sighing in pleasure as she slipped her sweaty feet out of the tight shoes. She wiggled her toes a few times, then planted her feet flat on the floor, trying to absorb some of the coolness from the chilly stone.

Close, but she wasn't quite comfortable yet.

Nerves giving her goose bumps despite the heat, she hurried back to the doorway to look around again. No sign of Jason's candle or Jason himself.

Not that it mattered. She'd told him to take a hike and she was sure he would. He'd never stuck around to fight for their relationship when it'd mattered. So why would he hang around to argue for some random cozy times now?

"No obsessing," she chided herself.

Then, one eye on the door, she quickly shimmied out of her skirt. She sighed in pleasure as the air, even as moist and warm as it was, cooled her legs.

She wrapped the blanket around her hips, tucking in one end of the fluffy fabric to hold it in place. Not the perfect answer, but definitely more comfortable than her skirt and this way her modesty was safe.

She glanced at her lace and satin covered breasts and shrugged. Okay, so her modesty was *almost* safe.

Not that it mattered. "He's probably gnawed his way through a wall somewhere and is hightailing it off to the Amazon by now."

Sick and crazy with the constant silence, Larissa looked around. She had a stack of mood music CDs in her box of goodies. But nothing to play them on.

Needing noise, she started humming as she squatted down by the box to flip through the CDs.

"Hmm, hmm, *time for me to go home,*" she hummed. *"Getting late, dark outside."*

She set the CDs aside and pulled out the variety of Chloe's specialty boxes she'd brought to display. Even in the dim candlelight, the packaging screamed romance. Embossed lettering, shiny ribbon and gold foil stripes. Pretty.

"I need to be with myself," she continued to sing quietly as she pried open one box labeled *Sweet Sensuality*. *"Clarity, peace, serenity."*

Into her hands poured the makings of a very romantic, very sexy evening. Chocolate body paint, love dice, fluffy feathers on a stick, a very ambitious number of condoms and yet another candle. Larissa didn't have to lift the glass jar to her nose to know what scent it was. Black Cherry Vanilla wafted around her.

She closed her eyes. She hadn't smelled that in years. It'd been her favorite, the scent she'd always lit for her romantic evenings with Jason.

Beginning with their first night together. After years of secretly crushing on him, pretending to be happy being just a friend, Jason had finally asked her out. She'd seen it as her very own romance novel, albeit a very sexy one. She'd worn a tiny excuse for a dress, one that had narrow straps and a beaded bodice that let her go braless.

The night, and Jason, had been straight out of a romance novel. They'd gone to dinner. They'd hit the clubs and danced. They'd barely drank, already intoxicated on each other. And when Jason had walked her to the door, she'd invited him in. And lit her candle.

And, while he got comfortable on the couch thinking he was going to get a snack, she'd stripped naked. And given him a whole lot more to eat.

It'd been the beginning of her very own fairy tale. Her hot, sexy prince had swept her off her feet. The sex... Larissa fanned her hand in front of her face, feeling her skin heat up. The sex had been incredible. Better, even, than all the romance novel sex she'd ever read about.

But it'd been all flash and no substance. Not real romance. Because even then, when things had been so incredible, she'd known it wouldn't—couldn't—last. That he wouldn't stick around.

She glanced at the goodies in her hand, regretting for an instant that as great as the sex had been, they'd never gotten naughty. No chocolate body paint, no whipped cream bikini, no kinky games.

Who knew how much more incredible sex could have been with a little adventure added in? Maybe if Jason had actually loved her, had trusted her, they'd have had a chance to find out.

If he'd trusted her, he wouldn't have thought twice about her dinner with Conner. She'd done it hundreds of times before they were engaged. Why would she stop simply because she and Jason were a couple? It hadn't been anything other than two friends having a meal. Granted, the meal had been on Conner's yacht, but that was just a Conner thing.

She'd been such an idiot. Even after their huge breakup

fight, when Jason had accused her of all kinds of ugliness with Conner, she'd hoped—believed—that he'd come back to her.

That's how it always happened in the books. But he hadn't. Jason had hit the road, obviously thrilled to be free and unencumbered again. She'd waited. And waited. But he hadn't returned.

Finally, she'd had to accept that he really wasn't her hero, after all. Or that she wasn't romance material.

Hence, the birth of her romance rules. Because with a solid outline, she could make sure her next relationship was one she could count on.

"He's just the guy who broke my heart," she murmured, standing carefully, as if moving too fast would set off a crying jag. Larissa set the candle and the rest of the goodies back in the box. All, except the condoms. She stared at that string of possibilities, the images of her and Jason's naked body wrapped around each other flashing through her head.

She fingered the condoms, her thumb sliding over the slick foil. She should leave them in the box. She should put them back in the planter out front. Better yet, flush them all down the toilet so they wouldn't tempt her.

She swallowed, trying to calm her racing pulse.

"That looks a lot more comfortable."

Larissa's scream echoed through the almost empty room. The string of condoms flew out of her hand. She was glad she was barefoot, since she jumped at least a foot high before spinning around. Her fist clutched the blanket to keep it from coming loose.

This time Jason didn't laugh at her reaction. He just set his almost gutted candle on the counter next to hers and waited for her to regain her composure.

"Where'd you come from?" she asked as soon as her

voice worked again. It was like he'd been conjured up by her horny thoughts.

"A twinkle in my daddy's eye," he said. His words were light, but he sounded tired.

"I've heard twinkles are dangerous," she said slowly, trying to read his expression in the dim light. Something was...off. She didn't know what was wrong with him, but something was. It wasn't like he'd be upset over her turning down his oh-so-romantic proposal, so it had to be something else.

The sight of him, so sexy as he stood in the doorway, made her melt a little. Was it wrong to want one more memory? To want a little of that adventurous sex to remember him by?

"Twinkles are usually nothing but trouble," he confirmed as he stepped farther into the store. He shoved his hands into the front pockets of his jeans and looked around.

Larissa looked around, too, trying to figure out what he was seeing. Then she stepped closer. His furrowed brow and down-turned lips made her want to give him a hug.

She waited for him to say something else. Anything else.

Silence. She was so freaking tired of silence.

Finally, she couldn't stand it. She hated seeing him hurting. So she laid a hand on his arm and asked, "What's the matter?"

His wince was infinitesimal, so small that if she hadn't been touching him, she wouldn't have caught it.

"Nothing."

"Right," she agreed. "That's why you look like someone just shredded your passport."

He didn't even crack a smile.

"Did you find out we're really stuck here all weekend?" she asked, panicking a little. Not so much at the idea of being trapped for the entire weekend—was there enough food or would they have to resort to the body paint? No, what really scared her was how appealing the idea suddenly was.

"Nah. Like I said, Conner will be here before noon tomorrow."

Larissa pursed her lips, then decided that circumstances justified calling out the big guns.

She stepped a little closer, not touching him but close enough to feel the heat radiating off his body.

She gave a deep sigh, knowing the move would challenge the lace of her camisole.

And she gave him the look. Chin down, puppy dog eyes through the fringe of her lashes and her lower lip protruding just a little.

He burst out laughing. "God, that's pathetic."

"Got you to laugh, though," Larissa pointed out with a grin. Tucking her hair behind her ear, she tilted her head and asked quietly, "Seriously. What's wrong?"

"I guess I need to apologize," he finally muttered. He dropped his gaze, staring at her bare toes instead of her face.

Larissa couldn't have been more shocked if he'd announced he was planning a sex change operation. Or, to be honest, more horrified. Jason never apologized. He'd never felt he'd done anything that warranted saying the word "sorry."

But he did now? What had he done that she didn't know about? She thought of all those nights he'd spent away from her and her heart whimpered.

Suddenly she realized how blindsided and miserable he must have felt when he thought she'd cheated on him with Conner. It was like someone was ripping her guts out through her heart.

"Why?" she said when she found her voice.

"We never should have gotten engaged. I should have known it'd end like it did."

Anger slowly seeped through her bloodstream. Even though she'd had a million doubts herself, it still infuriated her to hear that Jason hadn't had any faith in them.

So pissed she was surprised steam wasn't pouring out her ears, Larissa slapped her arms over her chest and tilted her chin. "Really? Why? How were we doomed to failure?"

"Not us. Me."

Her steam sputtered.

"I thought there were two of us in that relationship."

"Yeah, but you're not all messed up."

"And..." She shook her head, really confused. Jason had always been the epitome of confidence. What had happened? "What messed you up?"

"My father."

Wincing, Larissa remembered his earlier confession about his father walking out on his mom. Jason had always identified with his father. And, on the surface, the men were a lot alike. Charming and easygoing. Upbeat and friendly. But underneath, Louis Cantrell had seemed more focused on his own goals, his own plans, than the good of anyone else. Unlike Jason, who seemed to put his entire family before his own wants.

"You're not your father, Jason."

"I'm his son. You know as well as anyone how like him I am," he countered. His words held a bitterness she'd never heard before. "Hell, aren't we the perfect example of just how much like him I am? I hurt you like he hurt my mom. What's the diff?"

"The difference is that you are the one who's taking care of your mom." She risked her own peace of mind to offer the small comfort of laying her hand on his warm, muscled arm. God, he felt good. Swallowing, she forced herself to continue. "You were faced with the same choices as your dad, but you went a different route. Even now, you're willing to sideline your own goals to make sure your family is taken care of. Your dad never did that. Do you think, when you were kids, that he'd have stayed home if you boys couldn't go on digs with him?"

Jason's brow creased, then he gave a sigh.

"Probably not," he muttered. "But that doesn't mean I'm not like him."

Unable to help herself, she patted his arm again. The muscles were hard and inviting beneath her fingers. He looked like the sexiest thing to wear jeans. He sounded like a hurt little boy. He was the strongest man she knew, and the most caring.

She really, really wished she could think he was the jerk he now thought his father was. Then dismissing her feelings for him would be easier. Leftover feelings, sure. Just a little unfinished business, she assured herself. A little hot, sexy unfinished business.

Larissa sighed. She looked away, giving herself a second to make sure she wasn't about to make a huge mistake.

Did it matter, though? She wanted this. She missed this so much. So if it was a mistake, well, she'd just add it to the rest of the things she regretted about her and Jason.

She looked at him again. The shadows painted dark slashes and angles on his face, showing her depths she'd never realized he had. Depths she wished she didn't know about now, since they only added to his appeal. Since she'd already read their romance story, she knew how it ended.

She knew she was crazy to want to open those pages again. But she didn't care.

JASON FOUGHT THE URGE to turn and run from the room. He couldn't believe he'd told her his dirty little secret. He'd come back to make sure she was set for the night before he found a corner to crash in. Not to dump all his emotional crap at her feet.

And he definitely hadn't figured it for a ploy to play his way back into her good graces.

But he couldn't move. The soft pressure of her hand on his arm was as effective a trap as those big-ass locks holding them inside the building.

"Our doom aside, do you really think your parents had a horrible relationship?" she asked, her tone making it clear she was humoring his melodrama. "Despite the rotten way your father left, didn't your parents have almost thirty years together that didn't suck?"

Jason frowned. "What difference does that make? Those thirty years were easy times. He couldn't hack being there when it counted."

"And I thought I was the 'all or nothing' romantic in this relationship," she said with a small shake of her head. She lifted her hand off his arm, leaving him chilled and lonely. She gave him a long, considering look. Like she was already regretting whatever she was about to do.

Then, tightening the knot of her blanket, she hitched her fluffy bastion of modesty a little higher and turned, giving him a tempting view of the silky skin of her back and smooth shoulders.

He wanted to touch her. To slide his hands over her skin and lose himself in the welcoming warmth of her body. He hated all this emotional crap. Drama should stay on the big screen, not foist itself on real life. At least, not on his life.

Resigned, Jason watched Larissa walk away. He should be used to seeing the back of her by now. But she didn't retreat into whatever hidey-hole she'd claimed in the backroom. He frowned, watching her slowly pace the far wall, staring at the floor like she was searching for something.

He glanced down, but couldn't see a thing. The darkness swallowed her feet, making her look like she was floating in that blanket. Apparently she found it, though, because she knelt down and swept her hand across the floor.

He frowned, trying to make out what it was. She tucked her hand into the folds of her blanket, though, as she made her way back across the room to stop inches from him.

His body heated, his mind went blank for just a second as her scent wrapped around him in the warm air. His fingers itched to touch her. His mouth watered to taste her. His dick...well, it went without saying what it wanted to do. Same thing it always wanted whenever Larissa was around.

Looking as heartbreakingly serious as she had the night she'd told him they were over, Larissa stared into his eyes. Jason swallowed. He'd broken his arm when he was a kid riding his bike. Then, years later, he'd rebroke it in the same place. It hadn't hurt any less the second time around.

He wasn't in love with Larissa. He couldn't be. Wouldn't let himself be. But damned if he wanted his heart kicked a second time around.

He tried to think of something to say to shift the mood. A joke or clever comment. But before he could come up with anything, she held out her hand.

Jason winced before he remembered that she couldn't be holding his ring again, she'd given that back once already.

He looked down. He blinked, giving his head a little shake to reengage his brain.

Even in the flickering candlelight, the foil shape was unmistakable.

"A condom?" he asked, still needing confirmation.

She opened her fingers, letting a string of at least a dozen of those little rubber beauties trail over her palm.

He grinned at her faith in his prowess. Damned if he wouldn't do his best not to let her down.

"If this is a dream," he begged, as he took the foil-wrapped keys to heaven, "don't wake me up."

"How about I keep you up?" she offered with a teasingly wicked little smile.

The sight of that look, her sparkling eyes and sweet smirk, was like a punch in the gut. He hadn't realized how much he'd missed that look. Missed her. Until now.

"I thought you said you didn't want to do the cozy friends with benefits thing," he reluctantly reminded her. His dick throbbed in protest. Like it wanted to scream out, no! We're so close, don't blow it.

The wicked look left her face, leaving a bittersweet smile. She tilted her head so a curtain of black curls swept across her shoulder, brushing the lace of her camisole.

"That's not what this is. I'm not opening the door to a future between us, even a cozy non-committed one." She touched a finger to the foil wrappers. "I know we can't be what each other needs. But for right now, right here, we can be what each other wants."

"And that's enough?"

"It can be," she said quietly.

"So this is just for the night?"

"Tonight," she confirmed. "Or as long as the condoms last."

Jason fought a frown. A part of him—a part he didn't even recognize—wanted to scream *hell, no*. Maybe they had no future, given all their issues. But what was between them was more than easy sex.

Maybe he had issues with commitment, but what he and Larissa had been to each other had been pretty damn special. Too special to cheapen with a night of rolling around in an empty building lust.

He stared into her dark eyes, trying to read what was going through her head. This was just what he'd wanted. To be with her without the pressure and expectations and guilt. To enjoy the incredible intensity of their passion.

And she was offering it up, commitment-free.

Why did that feel so wrong?

Telling himself to quit being a dork, Jason gave in to his body's demands. The tips of his fingers caressed her bare shoulder, reveling in the silken texture of her skin. He bent his head, pressing his lips to that same spot and breathing in her delicious scent.

"Then we'd better get to it, then," he said, his voice husky with desire as he tossed the foil wrappers onto the counter, in easy reach. "We've got a lot of condoms to go through."

10

Jason lost himself in the taste of Larissa's mouth. Their lips slid together, soft and sweet. He loved how her fingers dug into his shoulders. Like she couldn't get enough.

A part of him, the part quickly getting drowned out, wished they had a chance for more. Wished she'd agreed to give his idea a chance. If she was willing to have one night of commitment-free fun, why not a bunch of nights?

But if all he could get was this night, he'd make damned sure it was one she never forgot.

With that in mind, he swept his tongue over her lips in a gentle caress. She tasted so sweet, so tempting. He wanted to keep it gentle, to build and tease. But her warmth pulled him in.

He nipped at her lower lip, a gentle little bite. Her gasp gave him entrance to her mouth. Lips sliding together, their tongues danced a hot, fast rhythm.

He rolled her nipple between his thumb and forefinger, loving how she shuddered in pleasure. He'd climbed mountains, jumped from planes and rappelled down cliffs. But nothing made him feel more manly than the response Larissa gave him. He scraped his thumbnail over the turgid tip of her breast, making her moan.

He wanted to climb inside her, to be a part of her and hear her not just moan, but scream his name. He wanted it so bad, he was afraid he'd do anything, say anything and definitely promise any damned thing, just to have her.

Which was what had gotten him in trouble before.

Remembering, Jason forced himself to slow down. He softened the kiss until they were barely nibbling at each other's lips, then shifted to her cheek before taking a slow, meandering journey down her throat.

Yeah. He was still in control. It was all good.

He breathed in her scent, made all the stronger in the dark for some reason. Spicy sweet and sexy as hell.

Control, Cantrell, he lectured. Keep it light and fun.

"I can't believe you carry condoms," he said, laughing against her shoulder. "I have to admit, it doesn't quite jive with the romance authority image I had in my head."

"There's nothing romantic about getting all riled up and having to quit just before the payoff," she reminded him as she swept her fingers up, then down his spine in a way that made him want to arch his back and purr like a cat.

"Speaking from recent experience, I'd have to agree," he said with a low laugh.

Her hand slipped lower, nails scraping gently at the small of his back through his shirt. He automatically shifted his pelvis forward, pressing his erection into her belly.

"So what other secrets are you keeping as the romance authority?" he teased, pressing little kisses down her arm until he reached her wrist. He took her hand in his and turned it over to place a warm, moist kiss in the center of her palm. He smiled when her fingers trembled in his.

"What makes you think I have secrets?" she breathed.

"All women have secrets." He lifted her knuckles to his lips, then pressed her hand flat against his belly. Her fingers slid between the buttons of his shirt, teasing his stomach.

"If I do," she told him after a just-a-beat-too-long pause. "Then they're obviously more romantic to keep to myself."

He wondered what she'd really wanted to say, then told himself it didn't matter. They were in for a night of incredible physical intimacy. They definitely didn't want to delve into that emotional intimacy crap.

"You would know, since you're the romance authority," he mused. "That sounds serious. Like you're in charge. You're obviously not wearing leather panties."

"That doesn't mean I won't take charge," she said.

Jason stopped kissing her throat long enough to give her a grin.

"What?" she asked.

"I'm not saying you're passive or anything, sweetheart. But I know your moves, remember."

"Is that so?"

"It is."

"Well, we'll just see about that," she promised, stepping out of his arms. "My turn, hotshot."

Grinning, Jason stepped back and raised both hands in surrender. He also knew which buttons to push. All it took was a hint that she was a little too sweet and Larissa would insist on proving him wrong. To his never-ending delight.

His grin dimmed a little as she turned away with a swirl of that fuzzy covering of hers, giving him a fluffy covered view of her behind when she bent over that box she'd hauled in.

When she turned back, she had a candle in one hand, which didn't much interest him except to ensure he could still see her as they pleasured each other. But the jar in her other hand...

His jaw dropped. Heat pounded a beat in his head as he

realized what she was holding. He thought she'd drop the blanket and start stripping his shirt off.

Talk about hitting the jackpot.

"Body paint?" he confirmed, squinting at the label. "We're having a little preloving snack?"

"Not we."

His brow arched. She set the candle on the counter, then with a flick of her fingers, let the blanket fall to the floor. Her body glowed as the golden light shimmered off her tiny little panties and satiny lace top.

Jason's blood poured out of his head. His breath shuddered and his mouth went dry.

"Just me?" he pleaded.

With a naughty look, she shook her head. Then she took the cootie matches and lit her new candle. A rich aroma instantly filled the air. Already turned on, Jason's dick got painfully hard at the smell. It was the scent of lovemaking. Of him and Larissa. Hot. Wild. Intense.

She set the chocolate over the candle flame, balancing it on the edges of the jar.

"How long will it take to get hot?"

"It's going to get hot fast," she promised. He shifted, trying to ease the stranglehold his jeans had on his pride.

As good as her word, Larissa stepped in front of him, using her fingernails to lightly scrape her way down his chest to his belly. Jason sucked in his gut. With a hard tug, she pulled his shirt from the waistband of his jeans and made quick work of the buttons. He shrugged it off, then reached out to wrap one hand around her waist to pull her closer as his other closed over the soft weight of her breast.

Before he could have too much fun, though, she pulled out of his arms. She gave him a teasing look and wiggled her brows, making her look like a naughty little fairy.

"Nope, no distracting me," she chided. "I'm hungry."

"I'm hungry, too," he countered with a laugh, anticipation building higher as she checked the jar of chocolate. She gave it a quick swirl, but apparently wasn't satisfied since she set it back over the flame.

"Isn't there some saying about ladies first?" she asked, walking back to him with a sexy little strut that made his mouth water. Her legs glowed gold in the light, the silky fabric of her camisole sliding temptingly over her breasts and emphasizing her tiny waist.

"You came first earlier," he added with a wicked grin.

"Well, now I get to return that favor," she promised.

She reached out to tap her fingernail on his buckle. Jason sucked in a breath, anticipating her next move and waiting for her to unhook the belt. But she didn't. Instead she scraped her fingernail over his zipper, making his already straining erection hit concrete hardness in a heartbeat.

"Strip," she ordered softly.

She looked so sweet. She sounded so innocent. It took him three seconds for her words to penetrate.

"Me, strip?"

"You. Strip for me."

His mouth went dry. He wasn't big on performances, other than the ones he could do between her legs.

He eyed the stubborn tilt of her chin and the impish look in her dark eyes and knew she would insist. And he'd thought her innocent? That romance authority thing was definitely going to her head.

Feeling like a Chippendales reject, Jason grimaced, then unbuckled his belt. Just as his fingers unsnapped his jeans, Larissa hummed a little bump and grind ditty low in her throat.

"Shit," he muttered. Then, seeing the amusement in her eyes, he grinned. She hummed some more. Picking up the beat, he jacked his hips to the left and unzipped. Jacked his hips to the right and kicked off his right shoe. Back to the left for the other shoe.

Stopping to awkwardly yank off his socks, he grinned when Larissa's mood music took on a quicker tempo. When he straightened, though, she slowed it back down to the traditional stripping beat.

"Where'd you learn that tune?" he asked.

"I'll tell you after you're naked," she promised, her words low and husky.

There was nothing to do but go for it, then. He slid his fingers under the waistband of his jeans, catching his boxers as well, and pushed, making sure he didn't damage the star of the show as he went.

With a quick kick, he shucked the pants off his legs and, getting into the moment, did an awkward dance move that was something between the Macarena without the hand moves and an electric slide.

"A dancer, I'm not," he said when he faced her again.

"You're the best naked dancer I've ever seen," she said, giggling a little.

"Isn't this where you slip a dollar into my G-string?" he asked with a laugh when she clapped.

"You're not wearing one," she replied, her words a purr of approval. She lifted the jar of chocolate and gave it a swirl, then offered him a big smile. "But I can paint one on for you."

Jason stopped laughing.

His pulse sped up, desire coiling tight at the thought of how she'd look licking that chocolate off his body. Of how he'd feel.

She uncapped the jar and stepped closer. The scent of milk chocolate, rich and sweet, filled the room. His mouth watered.

Then she dipped her finger into the jar. With her eyes locked on his, she placed her chocolate covered digit into her mouth and sucked. Jason almost exploded. His erection throbbed against his bare belly, begging for attention.

With two fingers, she scooped out more chocolate. Then, with a smile that made her look like a wickedly naughty fairy, she wiped the chocolate down his chest. The warm sticky liquid dripped, but Jason didn't look at it. His eyes were riveted on her.

She dipped again, this time painting the chocolate across his belly. Jason sucked in a breath, his heart pounding a loud rhythm in his head. He waited, desperately hoping.

She didn't disappoint him. Larissa's fourth foray into the chocolate jar covered four fingers. She released his gaze as her eyes dropped down his body. He followed her movements, watching her hand as she wrapped the warm treat around his throbbing cock.

Like she wasn't driving him insane, she concentrated on rubbing the chocolate over the rounded knob, then sliding her fingers up his shaft, then back down. Jason swallowed a groan. She swirled another layer of the rapidly cooling dessert over the head of his erection as if it needed double-dipping goodness.

She stepped closer, so close she was almost, but not quite, pressed against him. She gave him a wink, then nibbled licking little bites of the sweet confection off his chest. Jason sighed with pleasure.

He curved his fingers over her breasts, loving the weight, the soft cushion of them in his hands as she tasted her way over his chest. She shifted, nibbling lower. He watched her through slitted eyes, as turned on by the look of delight on her flushed face as he was by what she was doing to his body.

When she dropped to her knees in front of him, Jason was pretty sure he'd just died and was about to see heaven.

Then she blew on his dick. Warm air swirled around it. The feeling of her breath and the hardening chocolate made him groan out loud. He tunneled his fingers into her hair, needing to hold on. Needing to feel like he had some kind of control.

She leaned forward, her pink tongue licking him like there was no tomorrow. He shuddered. She cupped his butt with both of her hands, going to town on the chocolate as she sucked, nibbled and licked him clean. Jason was pretty sure he'd pass out if she didn't stop soon. Pass out or explode all over her. And he had other plans for his explosion.

Desperately, he tightened his fingers in her curls and pulled her head back.

"My turn," he insisted.

LARISSA RELUCTANTLY LET Jason pull her to her feet, licking bits of chocolate off her lips as she rose. Sweetness filled her mouth, desire burned through her body. She leaned forward to nibble at the chocolate still smeared on his chest, starving for his taste and unwilling to be deprived of a single bite.

He didn't give her time for more than a nibble, though. Apparently at his limit, he swung her into his arms, then kicked the blanket out flat on the floor before kneeling down on it.

His arms still holding her tight, Jason kissed her. Hot and wild, it was like he was starving. For her. Larissa's heart raced, as much at the idea of him wanting her so much as the passion that his kiss incited.

Slowly, gently, he lowered her to the blanket. The soft fluffy fabric brushed erotically against her back, a vivid contrast to the hard strength of his body brushing against the front of her.

Making quick work of her camisole and panties, he slid down her body, the rough hair on his leg scraping erotically over the softer flesh of her inner thighs. His mouth took her nipple, sucking and nipping in delicious torment.

His hand skimmed her hips and he shifted so he could curve his fingers deep inside her, tweaking and teasing her wet sex.

His fingers swirled, his mouth sucked. Her mind spun. She couldn't think. It was all too incredible, too wild.

He rubbed his thumb against her sweet spot, making her moan. Stars exploded behind her eyes as a tiny climax ripped through her body.

Larissa shifted, lifting her hips higher, silently begging for more.

"You want me?" he asked, obviously wanting her pleas to be a little louder.

"I want you," she gasped as his thumb pressed again, his fingers dancing in and out, in and out. He played her like he was a master and she was a finely tuned instrument crafted just for his pleasure.

She clenched her thighs, trying to hold his hand still. He wouldn't let her. Her body bucked against his fingers as another orgasm flashed through her.

Jason gently coaxed her back down to earth with soft fingers and tiny kisses. Her head thrown back, eyes closed as the pleasure still shimmered through her body, she felt him move away. Heard the rip of a foil wrapper. Anticipation tightened, her thighs quivered.

She shifted, opening heavy eyes to watch Jason position himself between her legs. She bent her knees, offering herself in silent supplication.

He plunged. She gasped, quaking at the sudden impact. Pleasure screamed through Larissa's body. She arched her back, trying to take him in deeper.

"More," she gasped, trying to breathe as the power of her climax teased and tormented her, just out of reach. "I need more."

Jason shifted lower, his hands slipping under her knees to lift her legs over his shoulders. Larissa's eyes flew open. He shifted higher, lifting the small of her back off the floor. She whimpered at the change in pressure, feeling like he was filling her like never before. Pounding deeper, harder. His face was in shadows as he gripped her thighs, but she knew he was staring down at her. At them.

The idea of it, of him watching their bodies slide together, sent her over the edge. Passion coiled tight in her belly, then released as a huge orgasm washed over her. Larissa's head tilted back and she lifted her body onto her shoulder blades to meet Jason's thrusts.

She whimpered, stars flashing behind her closed eyes as one orgasm after another pounded through her. Her body exploded in delight, her thighs clenching tight as if she could wring every drop of pleasure from him.

Make every drop last.

Because it was the last. This was too good. Too delicious. Even as her body gloried in the incredible feelings, her heart wept at the reality. Desperation added a sharp bite, an edge of pain that only intensified her passion.

If this was it, she'd take as much as she could.

JASON DROVE INTO LARISSA'S BODY, plunging deep and hard.

He jerked, growling so low in his throat, Larissa swore she felt rather than heard him. Needing to watch his pleasure, she pried her eyes open to stare at his taut face. He stared back. His blue eyes glittered, his breath came in pants.

He was so close.

Wanting to push him over the edge, needing to know she had that much power, she scraped her fingernails up her belly to cup her own breasts. He jerked.

She swirled her index fingers around her areolas. He lost rhythm and gasped.

She tweaked her nipples between her thumbs and forefingers. Zinging shots of electric delight zipped through his body, sending him spiraling out of control.

Jason threw back his head and exploded.

He was dimly aware that his climax had sent Larissa over the edge of pleasure once more. This time she gave a high whimper that ended on a cry as he shifted so fast she didn't know he'd moved until his mouth nipped at her inner thigh.

She screamed. Her body convulsed. Her breath came in pants as she came in waves.

He loved it. Loved her.

Breathing hard, Jason tried to stop his head from spinning out of control as the aftershocks of his orgasm pounded through him like a four-point-five earthquake.

Holy shit. He tossed back his head, shaking his sweat-dampened hair off his face with a shudder of pleasure. Had it always been this good? Why the hell had he ever left her bed? His brain was severely lacking blood, so he couldn't remember a thing. But whatever the reason, he'd obviously been an idiot.

And he had no idea how to fix things. Especially now that Larissa only wanted him for his body.

LARISSA COULD BARELY BREATHE. Passionate aftershocks still quaked through her. She was pretty sure time had passed since Jason had blown her mind. Five minutes, ten, four days. Something like that.

She gave an exhausted sigh. Like it was some kind of

signal, he groaned, then moved off of her, sliding behind her as she curled onto her side.

After shifting to take care of the condom, Jason cuddled her close, her back tight against his front, his arms crossed over her stomach. He nuzzled her hair off the back of her neck to scatter soft kisses across her shoulder.

"You really are the romance authority," he said, a hint of laughter in his words.

"There's more to romance than good sex," she said, exhaustion pulling the automatic response from her. If his arms hadn't been holding hers in place, she'd have slapped her hand over her mouth. This wasn't time to climb on her soapbox. Especially since any romance lecture she'd offer would be hypocritical.

"But as good as the sex is, the romance adds a sweet layer to it, right? Kind of like we are hot together regardless, incredibly hot. But adding a little chocolate? Baby, that layer sent us into the stratosphere." He laughed and pressed another kiss over the back of her neck. "Only you could make sexy that sweet. Only you keep me awake at night, desperate for just one more taste."

Larissa's heart melted a little. She didn't know what to do, what to think.

"You know romance better than you give yourself credit for," she murmured softly. Better, actually, than she'd ever given him credit for. It had been easier to perch on her high horse and judge Jason than to shift her own perceptions. Or to admit that maybe it wasn't that they were lacking romance in their relationship, but that the romance she wanted just didn't exist.

That he made her remember all of his good points wasn't just the problem. It was that he made her doubt her own beliefs about romance. He could act so romantic. But the reality was, what they had between them was the epitome of gratuitous sex.

Maybe this sex thing had been a mistake. Because now she wanted things all over again. Things she knew she couldn't have unless she was willing to settle.

Again.

With a sweep of her lashes to hide the distress in her eyes, Larissa focused on gliding her hand over the tempting hardness of his bicep where it crossed over her chest, willing to sacrifice herself to a night of incredible, mind-blowing and meaningless sex to distract herself from that painful little truth.

Because facing it meant questioning her entire belief system.

And she wasn't willing to consider that for someone who wouldn't stick around.

Since Chloe wasn't there, Larissa would never have to admit to being a straight up liar. Instead, she promised herself that since tonight was her own final fantasy, she could do whatever she wanted.

And she wanted to do Jason. Again and again and again.

Rolling over to face him, Larissa scraped her teeth over his nipple. He groaned and his fingers tightened on her butt, pulled her tighter against him.

"Is there more chocolate?" he asked, his breath hot and moist against her throat as he lifted her over his body.

"Enough," she said, gasping as he took her nipple into his mouth. He teased and tormented. Larissa had thought she was satisfied. No, she knew she had been satisfied.

But a whole new need exploded inside her. One that demanded she have him. As much of him, as fast as possible.

As they twined together, their passion climbed higher, flamed hotter.

And the power of their coming together made it easy for her to ignore the tears soaking into her hair.

11

THE AIR WAS HOT AND WET, almost dripping with humidity. Jason's body felt like liquid, he was so relaxed. Curled around Larissa, he sighed and let the pleasure wash over him. It wasn't like he didn't have a whole slew of incredible memories of their times together. Hell, he hauled the memories out every once in awhile just to torment himself.

But this time? It'd been intense. It'd been wild. It'd been like Larissa had tossed aside her inhibitions to kick things up a few—or few dozen—degrees.

He did a quick inventory, trying to assess how long it'd be before all his parts were ready to give it another go.

Then his stomach growled.

Larissa giggled.

"I thought you were asleep," he murmured, brushing a kiss over her hair.

"It's too hot and sticky to sleep," she said with a sigh, turning in his arms. Her body slid damply against his, proving her point.

And turning him on.

Again.

Yep, his parts were definitely considering coming out to

play. Maybe he should get an image of the Energizer bunny tattooed on his ass.

"What'd you have in mind if you're not interested in sleep?" he asked, his hand tracing a swirling pattern on the slick skin of her hip. He was tempted to slide his fingers down and see what else was slick and wet, but before he could decide if his body would do justice to his thoughts, his stomach growled again.

"Maybe you should have eaten that sandwich earlier instead of taking off like that," she teased with a laugh. "Where'd you go, anyway?"

"The janitor's closet," he joked. Actually he'd returned to the lunch room to give them both some space.

It wasn't the aftertaste of that nasty sandwich that made Jason's stomach turn, but a flashback of their dinnertime discussion. His having to admit his father's deficiencies, Larissa shooting his proposition down, the realization of just how bad he'd hurt her.

Definitely unappetizing at the time, and even worse in reruns. He'd rather lick the chocolate jar than try that again.

"You don't really think you're like your father, do you?" Larissa asked quietly, not meeting his eyes but instead staring at her fingers as they traced a damp pattern on his chest.

"It doesn't matter," he dismissed quickly, wondering if she'd read his mind. "We're here, naked and have at least a dozen condoms left. Why waste time talking about my family?"

"Well, you are the one who brought it up earlier," she added sweetly. So sweetly that he knew she wasn't going to just let the topic go.

Jason stiffened. At least his spine did. Not anything interesting unfortunately. Steeling himself against a discussion he didn't want but could see Larissa leading up to, he tried to think of a distraction.

The lack of stiffness in his happy parts didn't bode well for his favorite method of changing the subject.

"I'm just saying," she continued, her fingers tracing lower and lower. He tried to focus on the soft caress. "You're obviously pissed off at your dad. And with good reason. But have you talked to him? I mean, you two were so close, Jason. I hate to think of you losing a relationship that means so much to you."

"Maybe," Jason muttered. He didn't know what to say—he'd thought the same thing.

"To tell you the truth…" Her voice dropped. So did her hand. He figured he'd focus on the hand. "Your parents intimidated me. A lot, really. I mean, they were totally on the same page. They had the same goals in life and the same interests. But I sort of wondered, didn't your mom ever have other dreams? Other things she wanted in life?"

Sure. His mom had talked a lot, especially as they got older, about settling down for longer periods of time. She'd wanted to plant a garden. To see movies and go out to dinner. But that hadn't been in his dad's plan.

Too bad she'd had to have a stroke to get them. Jason dismissed the thought as stupid, but a part of him wondered if maybe she hadn't been a little relieved to finally have an acceptable excuse to not follow his father on yet another dig.

"I guess it's okay to tell you now, I worried that you'd expect the same from me. That absolute commitment…" Her words trailed off. Jason didn't need to see her face to figure out what she was probably thinking. Maybe he had. And maybe she was right. Hadn't he thought that if she'd just come with him on his travels, she wouldn't have had time to stay home and date other guys? Stupid thought, yes. But he'd had it all the same.

"Nope," he said. Then, not sure why but unable to keep the words quiet, he added, "I mean, I really did enjoy having you along. It was always cool showing you the places I loved, sharing my excitement. But I never expected you to give up your own plans, your own dreams, for mine."

He just wished they could have meshed their dreams together a little better. With his arms wrapped tight around the only woman he'd ever loved, Jason stared off into the dark. Peter was like their dad that way. He expected total devotion. He insisted on bringing Meghan on trips. As many as possible. He always used to warn Jason that he and Larissa were doomed because she wasn't into adventure. Sure, she'd liked the more romantic treks, the ones with a night or two in an exotic hotel or a hut on the beach. According to Peter, once in awhile wasn't good enough. It was all or nothing for the Cantrell men.

Since their dad had seemed to be the same way—although Jason hadn't ever actually asked him—he'd assumed Peter's assessment of the Cantrell men's code was right.

Which was probably why Jason had ended up with nothing.

He nuzzled Larissa's hair with a sigh. Even knowing those things, he couldn't imagine doing it any differently. Larissa deserved her own, incredible life. Proof positive was how she'd built such a great name for herself as a romance expert. Could she have, would she have, done that if they'd been together? Or would he have stifled her instead?

"I guess it doesn't matter in the long run," he muttered, thinking more of his own relationship than his parents'.

"Sure it does. I mean, they made it for a long time, didn't they?" she mused. "That says a lot. They must have had a lot of passion between them."

"What?" he yelped, both grossed out and grateful for the distraction.

"Not the naked kind," she laughed. "You know, more like friendship. Caring and excitement. That kind of thing."

"They were, you know, parents. It wasn't like I was watching their relationship or anything."

Or seeing them as people in their own right, he realized with a frown.

"Were there any hints of a problem before your mom had her stroke?" she asked, finally looking up to meet his eyes. Unfortunately her fingers stopped their sweet distraction, so he had to focus on her.

"I don't know," he said, shrugging one shoulder. "Is it getting stuffy in here? Maybe we should move into the mall. It's a bigger space, more circulation."

"Right, walk out there," she said with a laugh. "No way. What if the electricity comes back on, including the security cameras?"

Jason imagined a bunch of security geeks watching the video of him and Larissa getting wild with the chocolate and decided the first thing he'd do when someone let them out of here would be to destroy those tapes. Before Conner saw them, of course.

"Aren't there cameras in the stores?" Despite his anger at the idea of their private moments being recorded, he'd gladly dance naked for one as a thank you for the subject change.

"No. In-store security is the store's responsibility. Didn't Conner tell you that?"

"I didn't talk to Conner, I talked to Daniel. And to tell you the truth, I didn't listen to half the crap he said. I knew the space was what I wanted. I figure I'd leave the details to Peter."

She hummed a little low in her throat. Like she had something to say about that, but in the interest of keeping the naked peace, she was refraining.

Grateful, Jason brushed a kiss over her bare shoulder and curled her tighter in his arms.

"So do you see your mom often now that she's in a home?" Larissa asked, stubbornly returning to her torment...that was, the topic. She was like one of those little dogs. All cute and fluffy looking, but stubborn as hell when she got her tiny little teeth into something. And too sweet to kick out of his way.

"Often enough," he finally admitted. He hated it, though. It was hard enough seeing his mom as a single person instead of part of a parental unit. It was harder still seeing how broken she'd become. "I drop in. You know, when I'm home and stuff."

Why couldn't Larissa feel how uncomfortable he was? Or maybe she did and she was ignoring it. Was this one of those stupid *for his own good* discussions? The last one of those they'd had ended with the word goodbye.

"Is she excited about Peter's upcoming wedding?"

Why were they talking about his family? Tension curled so tight in his body, his toes ached. He couldn't deal with this. Why couldn't Larissa just stick with pillow talk or compare him to her other sexual conquests? Why did it always have to come around to serious shit that made him want to run screaming from the room?

"Mom's not too focused these days, but it really doesn't matter," he dismissed, wishing he wasn't lying.

"How can it not matter?" she asked. From her puzzled look and the innocent tone, he knew she was seriously confused. Not trying to scrape her fingernails over the chalkboard of his soul.

"It just doesn't, okay." Jason sat up, careful to make it look casual and not like he was trying to jump away.

"Okay," she said slowly. He'd used that same tone once when he'd woke up on safari to find a lion prowling his camp. He knew what that tone meant.

He wanted to get in her face and make her acknowledge that he wasn't bullshitting with her excuses. That he wasn't an emotional commitment-phobic mess with parental issues.

That if anyone would know what mattered—in his past, his present and his damned future—it'd be him, wouldn't it? Yes, dammit, it would.

But that might come off as a *little* defensive.

"I need food," he declared instead, glancing at his watch. "It's almost midnight. Definitely time for a snack."

He didn't even try to lie to himself that he wasn't running away. From his thoughts. From the answers. And yes, maybe he wanted to get away from Larissa, too.

Things had been a lot better when they'd been having sex.

He got to his feet so fast, she almost tumbled off the blanket. With a sheepish apology, he reached out a hand to help her into a sitting position.

"Did you want anything?" he offered, a gentleman to the last, even while running like a pansy girl.

"Maybe some water from the fridge. It might still be cool in there, don't you think?"

Heading out of the store, he gave a noncommittal shrug, not wanting to have to make a decision right now, even on something as simple as his opinion.

"Aren't you going to put on your pants?" she asked. Her look said she knew exactly what he was doing, but she laughed it off. Obviously she didn't want to fight naked any more than he did.

His shoulders itched uncomfortably at the idea of someone—anyone—knowing him that well. It was definitely time to take a break.

Jason glanced at his crumpled jeans in the corner. Just the thought of putting thick denim on in this heat made him cringe. Then he looked down at his body, still sporting splotches of chocolate and wrinkled his nose. "I think I'll hit the bathroom to wash up instead."

She pointed questioningly to his boxers, hanging like a banner off one of the light fixtures.

"Why bother?" he decided as he bent over to give her a kiss before heading out into the mall. "I'm just going to get naked and have my way with you again as soon as I get back."

"There's a bathroom right here," she said, gesturing with one hand toward the back of the store.

Jason felt like there was a rope tightening around his neck. Swallowing past the constriction, he shook his head.

"Nah, there's a bigger one out here. More room to, um, de-chocolate myself and stuff."

"Then don't you at least need a candle?" she called after him as he hurried out.

"Nah, I know where all my stuff is."

Now to get it all put back where it belonged. Hidden away, behind firm emotional barriers. The same place any other well-adjusted man would put it.

HER ARMS WRAPPED AROUND her bent legs, Larissa laid her cheek on her knees and watched Jason's very fine, very naked butt leave.

She didn't know why she was wasting her time wishing he'd open up and actually talk to her. This night wasn't about rekindling their romance. It was simply the consequences of being trapped together and really, really horny.

That was all. She just had to keep those facts in mind and she'd be fine.

Straightening and hooking her elbow to the outside of the opposite knee, Larissa stretched until her back cracked. Then she switched in the other direction. She arched her neck one way, then the other, then back to release tension she hadn't realized she was holding.

"You'd think hot sex and multiple orgasms would have loosened me up," she muttered to herself. And maybe they would have, if it hadn't been for that undertone of angst making her so edgy.

Larissa straightened her legs, arched her toes and stretched her body flat until her fingers gripped her ankles.

"Good thing we're not a couple," she told her knees.

And it was. She was glad she didn't have to do this emotional dance any longer. They weren't a couple, so she didn't need to fixate over what she said and if he was pissed because she'd said it.

No longer would she freak out after attempting to get Jason to emotionally open up. To admit that there was more to him—to them—than surface jokes and great sex.

So she was glad that she wasn't dealing with all of that.

"Nope, all I'm doing is enjoying some great sex to pass the time," she said to the room at large, wondering if her words could really be considered lies if nobody was there to hear and she personally knew she was spouting bullshit. Kinda like the tree in the woods enigma.

Trying to distract herself from the pending depression she felt looming around her like an extra layer of sticky-hot humidity, Larissa imagined Jason's trek through the mall.

Talk about out of his element. He was in a mall instead of some remote jungle.

And, of course, there was the naked thing.

Focusing on the idea of Jason, naked, was the best distraction ever.

He was waltzing naked in front of the likes of Tiffany, MAC and the finest French undies known to women. She giggled at the image, then lay back on the marble floor and tried to soak up some of the coolness of the stone. Eyes closed, she imagined his naked journey and wondered, could she be that comfortable in her nudity?

Not likely, she snorted. She doubted she could step into those stores in anything less than her best dress and most expensive shoes.

She remembered the last time she'd tried to shop in La Perla. The salesman had been so snooty, she'd ended up leaving without buying a thing. Then, out of pure defiance, she'd headed straight to Victoria's Secret and loaded up on panties.

She sure hoped that sales guy didn't end up working at this location. She could just imagine him staring down his nose at her store while he fondled a mannequin's garter belt. He'd definitely consider her offerings too pedestrian to be within gawking distance of his lacy merchandise.

Her grin faded. She glanced at her briefcase, with its carefully detailed business plan. Her eyes shifted to the box of merchandise. Cute stuff. Fun stuff. Pure romance, both sweet and sexy.

It'd work in the bookstore. She could imagine the items scattered around the Victorian, how she'd display them in the rooms. Those kits Chloe made would be perfect in the kitchen with a little sign that suggested the customers cook up a little fun.

She'd repurpose one of the small, cramped parlors with a plush chair and wide-screen television. Maybe a pair of fluffy bunny slippers and a luxurious blanket. She rubbed her fingers over the one currently providing a cushion between her butt and the hard marble. She'd fill the shelves with the romance DVDs she'd sell.

Larissa shook her head, blinking fast to erase the image from her mind.

That was yesterday's dream. A dream that depended on her convincing people to stick around, on her ability to lure customers back to the store time and time again. The only way to keep an independent bookstore in business, let alone a specialty store like she'd want, was customer loyalty. And Larissa had learned the hard way that loyalty in the long term was a myth.

That was why this deal was so perfect. Here, in a hotel, she didn't need to worry about returning customers, since the nature of the location meant the people always changed. Here, she could create an image, expand her role as the romance expert, and nobody would be around long enough to discover it was all a sham.

And she was going to make it work, even if she had to march her department-store-dress-wearing-self into La Perla and face down the snobbiest of the snobs.

She wished Jason would hurry back and distract her from these horrible, soul-baring thoughts. This was why sleep was so important. Not for health reasons, but because these intense, heart-wrenching thoughts always surfaced at two in the morning.

Shoving her damp, humidity frizzed hair off her shoulder, she had to admit, it was so sticky and uncomfortable in here, she wouldn't have been able to sleep anyway. Which meant Jason should be here to distract her, dammit.

Leave it to Jason to go missing when she needed him. Larissa got to her feet and, feeling really naked, looked around for something to wear. She started to perspire at just the thought of wrapping that blanket around herself again. Just as she was wishing the rain would cut through the humidity, or that the windows were breakable, she spied Jason's shirt.

That'd work. She'd just hooked a couple of the buttons when she heard a noise.

Her heart raced.

Ax murderer?

"You'll never guess what I found," Jason said as he came through the entryway.

She sighed a little, her body going into a full-on meltdown at the way the candlelight flickered temptingly over his body. Her eyes slid down the wide expanse of golden shoulders, muscled and glistening. His arms, the same arms she'd gripped so tightly as he drove her over the edge of screaming passion, were curved around…something. She didn't care what. She was just irritated that whatever he held obscured her view of the happy trail aimed down his washboard abs.

Her eyes dropped to the main event.

Even at rest, it made for an impressive show.

Larissa ran her tongue over her lower lip, determined to get another taste. Which meant she had to keep those pesky little observances and personal comments to herself.

Screw romantic connections. She wanted good sex.

"Larissa?"

"Huh?"

"You okay?"

She dragged her eyes back up his body to meet his questioning gaze. He looked so sweet. His hair fell across his forehead, giving him a sexy little bad boy look. She couldn't see the expression in his eyes, but his half-smile was teasing. His stance just a little cocky.

Why was he everything she wanted in a man? And why was most of it locked up so tight inside him that he had no trouble denying it. Even to himself.

She swallowed, hard. Sex, she chanted silently. Remember the sex.

"Yes. Of course. I'm fine."

He gave her a long look, like he was trying to see inside her head and figure out why she was lying. That he knew she was lying was a given.

"Did you want to hear what I found?"

"Sure." Her fingers wrapped around the open plackets of his shirt, tugging them closed. She suddenly felt both overdressed and much too vulnerable.

"What if I told you I found a way out?"

Well, that yanked her right out of Fantasyland. Were they done with the sex? Had she wasted half their sex time trying to get him to admit he had a heart? Larissa's lower lip protruded.

"Really? You found a way out?"

"No," he said with a laugh. "But I did think that'd be your first response. You know, given how you kept going on earlier about getting out of here."

"Sure. Because now that we've gotten naked together, I was hoping you'd hurry up and find that secret way out." Larissa's return smile was a little stiff. So was her middle finger, but she kept that hidden in the fabric of his shirt.

He stopped laughing, his smile dimming a little. "Me, too. But only because I'd rather finish our naked times in a bed than on that floor. But I'm willing to pull the gentleman card and offer to take the bottom for the next few rounds."

Larissa gave him the laugh he wanted. And she didn't point out that their naked times were restricted to this night, this place and this once. He knew that already. But like so much else that Jason knew, he'd rather pretend it wasn't there.

"So what did you find if not a secret passage out of here?" she asked lightly.

"The answer to all your fantasies."

"Johnny Depp is here?"

Jason kept his eye roll small, instead raising his hand to shake the contents a little. Larissa squinted, trying to figure out what he had. It was hard to focus, though, since his shaking sent things swaying.

"It's a bowl?"

"And...?"

"It's a bowl of something that's making a lot of noise?"

He walked slowly forward, his steps reminding her of a stalking animal. A tiny skittering of nerves danced up Larissa's spine. With his eyes on her, she felt frozen in place. Her breasts rose and fell quickly beneath the soft denim shirt. He stopped inches away and, his gaze still locked on hers, lowered the bowl. It was still too high for her to see what was in it, though. Not that it mattered. She couldn't tear her gaze away from his hypnotic blue eyes.

His fingers traced just inside the unbuttoned edges of her—or really, his—shirt, his knuckle skimming her flesh and making her shiver as he left a heated trail. She pressed her thighs together, desire coiling tight between her legs at his touch.

His other hand slipped around behind her. She barely noticed as he skimmed the back of his hand under the shirt.

Then he pressed the icy cold bowl to her back.

Larissa jumped, gasping out a tiny scream.

"I found ice," he said, laughing as he showed her the bowl. "It's melting fast, but there were a few trays in the break room freezer."

"Oh," she breathed, wrapping both hands around the metal container and closing her eyes at the wonderful chill that poured through her palms. "So nice."

"You wanted cool water, I figured this might work."

"Did you bring a glass?" she asked, looking around to see if she'd missed it. Not seeing one, she shrugged and lifted the bowl to her lips, sipping the ice cold water. "Mmm."

She took a deeper drink. Big mistake. The large bowl wasn't made to drink from, so the water slopped over the sides. His eyes narrowed. Rivulets streamed down her chin and over her throat.

Jason gave a low groan.

Despite the ice, Larissa's body started to burn.

He took the bowl from her and, his eyes locked on hers, took a drink. He barely swallowed though. Brow furrowed, she watched him set the bowl on the counter, then he skimmed his hands under the shirt, up her torso and cupped her breasts. His fingers squeezed gently. Larissa's head fell back and she took a deep breath so the fabric of the shirt separated. He released one breast to flick open the few buttons, then bent down and wrapped his lips around her hardening nipple.

"Omigosh," she breathed, shocked at the intensity of the feelings pouring through her. His mouth was hot. The ice was cold. The contrasts were incredible.

Icy water dripped down her breast, over her stomach. He grabbed another ice cube and slid it along her hip. She listened, surprised it didn't sizzle on her hot body.

Then he pressed his palm against the wet heat of her mound. The ice made her thighs clench automatically. Her gasp ricocheted off the walls. After a quick nip of his teeth on her tight nipple, he kissed the underside of her breast, then skimmed down her torso, open mouthed, until he was kneeling in front of her. Her legs wobbled. He wrapped one arm around her hips to help support her as he nudged her thighs apart.

He stared into her eyes, a dark promise of delight in the

blue depths of his as he popped the ice cube into his mouth. Holding her gaze until the last second, he licked his freezing tongue over her already swollen and well-pleasured sex. The chill was incredible. Invigorating and seductive.

Then his fingers slipped inside her. First one, swirling and plunging. Then two. He sucked harder. Her body shook. He sent her up so fast, so hard, she couldn't think straight. All she could do was dig her fingers into his shoulders and hold on for the ride.

Her climax was wild and intense. Her body rocked against his mouth. She shivered at the power he had over her, but couldn't find it in her to care. If the man could play that kind of magic on her body, he was welcome to do it anytime.

After a few seconds, she decided turnabout was only fair. When she knew her knees would support her, she stepped away.

And reached for the bowl.

"Whatchya doin'?" he asked in a raspy tone.

"Paying you back," she promised just before she slipped a couple pieces of melting ice into her mouth and knelt in front of him.

As far as distractions went, an iced-down blow job was top of the list for keeping her focus off her breaking heart.

12

WAKING SLOWLY AND THROWING OFF the groggy fog of a couple hours sleep, Larissa stretched her arms overhead, trying to work a few of the kinks out of her sore body. Who knew an ice cube blow job could be that exhausting. She gave a luxuriant smile, feminine power pouring through her and bringing almost as much pleasure as her earlier orgasms.

Okay, maybe not nearly as much. But a lot of pleasure. She grinned, loving this feeling. Missing how good it was to be not just a woman, but a sexual being.

She glanced around, looking for the man to thank for the experience. Nada. Maybe he was in the bathroom?

She stood, wincing as her thighs screamed. Wow, it'd been a long time since her body had been a sexual being. Having really, *really* good sex used muscles she'd forgotten she had. She took a couple mincing steps, groaning a little. She looked around, glad Jason wasn't here to witness her lack of grace.

And speaking of really, really good sex…and Jason—where was he?

Her pleasure fading a little, she glanced at the open bathroom door and didn't see any candlelight. She frowned, noting that his jeans and shirt were still crumpled on the ground. But his boxers weren't flying from the sconce any longer.

Which meant he was at least semi-dressed. Wherever he was.

Apparently she was the only one who was having trouble walking after their sexy times.

As usual.

Larissa bent over, grabbing Jason's shirt off the floor and shrugging it on. She shoved the buttons through the holes, her teeth clenched.

His scent wrapped around her as warmly as the fabric. She fingered the cuffs, then shoved them up her arms as she stomped toward the front of the store to glare out into the mall.

Seriously. It was the middle of the night. Where the hell was he? Why couldn't he stick around for just a little while? Hadn't the night been incredible for him, too? Hadn't he groaned and moaned and had a wild old time? Hadn't it been worth sleeping in each other's arms for at least a few hours? She squinted at her watch, noting it was half past three in the morning. She wondered how many minutes he'd held out after she'd dropped into sleep before heading off. Five? Maybe ten?

Shoulders hunched, she stared down one side of the mall, then the other. She twisted her fingers together. She could go look for him. But that would make her look desperate, wouldn't it? Or was it more pathetic to be found waiting here for him like a lovesick girl, her happiness hinging on his return.

Larissa tilted her head back, staring at the ceiling and blinking fast to clear the tears from her eyes. How did she end up here again? Had she learned nothing in the last few years? Was she so pathetic that she couldn't resist Jason's magic dick? Or was this a sad little romantic fairy tale she kept falling into, thinking that somehow, some way, they had a future. Together.

Larissa crossed her arms over her chest, pacing back and forth in the doorway.

This was supposed to have been one last fling. A chance to do all those naughty things she'd missed out on the last time with Jason, but to do them the smart way. Knowing it was just sex, she would not only have her fun, but finally put to rest her internal struggle with that one question... Could she settle for a relationship that was all about sex, knowing there was no emotion involved?

Larissa's pacing had brought her to the back of the store, to their love nest. The mohair blanket was balled into a soft bundle, Jason's clothes were strewn against the wall and an empty chocolate jar tilted on its side like a drunken soldier.

All evidence of decadent, intensely satisfying sex.

The only thing missing, as usual, was Jason himself.

Which said it all.

Larissa shook her head, the stomping sound of her bare feet against the marble taking her pacing to an angrier level. She really was pathetic. She couldn't believe she'd actually believed, somewhere deep in the hidden recesses of her heart, that he'd take one look at her again and fall in love.

Or that if they gave in to their passion, he'd give up wanting to do all that traveling and wish he could build a life with her.

Larissa clenched her fists and growled. Because believing all that crap had worked so well for her the first time.

She stopped mid-pace to stare at the counter where Jason had stripped her bare the first time last night. A tear trickled down her cheek. Talk about a sucky time to face reality. At least last time, she'd had Conner there to distract her. She should be grateful he was nearby for this round, too.

"Hey, looking for me?"

Larissa spun to face Jason, who stood there looking like sexy temptation, his boxers thankfully covering those tempting magic parts. He had a large, Maglite-type flashlight in one hand and a few bottles of water in his other.

"No," she told him in a distant tone as she surreptitiously wiped her cheek and wished, not for the first time, that he'd made it easier and just stayed away. "I was just getting a feel for the floor footage. It made sense to get to know the area since I'll be working here."

His smile downgraded. "What's wrong?"

"Why would anything be wrong?"

"Number one, you sound irritated. Number two, you're talking all formal again. And three, you haven't come over here to kiss me or slide your hand down my boxers. So something's obviously bothering you."

Larissa opened her mouth, wanting to point out that there was more between them than just sex. Then she closed it. Because, truthfully, there wasn't.

"Nope," she replied with a friendly, totally fake, smile. "Nothing's wrong. Like I said, I was doing a little planning. Getting comfortable in the space, you know?"

"Comfortable?" Responding to her anger by dumping his armload of stuff on the counter, he turned to face her with his arms clamped over his deliciously bare chest. "Yeah. You seem really relaxed and mellow here."

"I'm focusing on business. You know how that goes, don't you? Of course you do," she continued, finally losing her grip on that emotional control. "You know all about how important it is to put work first. You're the king of business first, aren't you?"

"Why would you be thinking business after the way

we've spent the last few hours?" He narrowed his eyes, getting that same wigged-out look on his face that he'd had earlier, before he'd gone on his ice run. "Or was it only some twisted way of trying to talk me out of competing for the storefront here?"

Larissa's lingering tears disappeared.

He actually thought that after everything that had happened between them, she'd be standing here trying to figure out how to screw him over? Her? Screw *him* over?

A voice in the back of her head pointed out that if she'd thought she could influence him, she'd probably have tried. Not on her knees perhaps, but still…

Yet more proof that Jason wasn't the man for her. She grabbed onto that realization, and the stirring anger, and held on tight. She needed to emotionally step back and, as usual, he'd just given her the opening.

"So where were you off to?" she asked. "Still trying to find a way out?"

"Just exploring."

"What's left to explore? I'd have thought you'd seen it all by now."

"Sometimes it's fun to check it out again. See if you missed anything the first time."

She rolled her eyes.

"I doubt you missed anything. There's this small mall area, a lunchroom, janitor's closet and storeroom. What the hell else is there to see?" she asked, ignoring the double entendre. "That was the third time you disappeared since we've been here."

"Not that you were counting or anything?"

Glad the darkness hid her blush, Larissa just shrugged. "Hey, at least I can always count on you leaving."

"Where the hell was I going to go?" he snapped, starting to sound impatient. "You said it yourself. We're trapped."

"Your own version of hell," she quipped.

"You keep saying things like that. What's it supposed to mean?" He punctuated the question with a fist in the air, like he was so frustrated that he had to hit something.

She rolled her eyes. "You've said it yourself. You can't stand to stay in one place."

"Adventures are pretty boring if they are done in one place, don't you think?"

"Life should be more than an adventure, shouldn't it?"

He gave her a penetrating look and shook his head. "What's the deal? You're taking my business so personally. Like it's all about you or something."

"Of course it's not about me," she defended. Then, before she knew it, the words escaped, "But if you really cared, you'd have given enough of a damn to actually consider me."

Jason shook his head, making her feel even more pathetic. He was like an emotional magnifying glass, damn him. She pressed her hand to her stomach, suddenly wanting to throw up.

"I don't get it, Larissa. You've got this insane inferiority complex. You're smart. You're sexy. You're sweet and gorgeous and talented. But when you say shit like that, it's like you're insecure or something. What's the deal?"

What? Like she was supposed to drag out her bag of neurosis and spread it across the floor for him to poke through? Hardly. Larissa shook her head.

"If I was all that, why did you leave me?" she asked. Horrified, she clamped her lips together and wished the words back. Oh, God. That's not what she'd meant to say. She'd never, ever meant to ask him that. Her pride, and her heart, didn't need the agony.

"What?" She didn't need the sputtering light of the candle to see the shock on his face. His tone was clear enough.

"You left," she said quietly. She wanted to get up and run away instead. But where? She was trapped, both literally and figuratively. "You took my engagement ring and you walked out."

"You went out with Conner," he replied, for the first time sounding hurt instead of cockily irritated. "Then when I got pissed about it, you handed me the ring and told me to leave. What the hell was I supposed to do?"

The heat of her glare combined with the tears wetting her lashes made it feel like there was steam billowing from her eyes. Fury, fear, pain, they all mixed together to tangle her thoughts and make her want to scream.

She didn't know what she'd wanted him to do. To convince her that they could make it? To refuse to let her end things? To freaking fight and prove he loved her enough to want to stick around?

Yeah. She'd wanted all of that. But she'd also wanted him to leave. To take the broken dreams of a perfect romance and constant heartache of failure and go. Because she'd been sure it would be easier to live, to succeed and believe in herself, if she wasn't always waiting for him to realize she wasn't enough for him and leave on his own.

Horrified at the realization, she clamped her lips tight together to keep from crying out.

"That's all in the past," she said quickly, thankful that her voice was only a little choked up. "I'm sorry I brought it up. Let's talk about now, instead."

"Now?" he said suspiciously.

"Sure." She floundered, mentally flailing around trying to find something safe about now. Desperate, she glommed onto what he'd said earlier. "Let's talk about the store and how much better your business would do if you set it up in a different location."

"I knew it," he said. "You do want me up to change my plans, don't you?"

Larissa threw her hands in the air. "Of course you should change your plans. They're crazy. They don't fit your business model, nor this location."

"My plans aren't any crazier than yours. You're trying to fluff up a pussycat and make it into a tiger. Your idea isn't tiger-worthy, Larissa."

She felt like a million needles were stabbing her in the heart.

"What kind of stupid thing is that to say?" she asked, blinking the black spots away.

Jason shook his head, then strode over to grab up his jeans and shove his legs into them. Avoiding her eyes, he yanked the zipper up with such force that Larissa winced, glad she had finished playing with the package, since he probably just damaged it.

"Forget it," he finally said as he snapped his pants.

"No. You meant something with that stupid cat analogy. Maybe you can put it in English so it's clear what you mean," she challenged, shoving her chin out to keep it from trembling.

"Let's not do this, Larissa." He backed away, shaking his head and sounding tired. She ignored his tone, focusing instead on the fact that, as usual, he was running from her.

"Why? Because it might hurt our non-relationship to be honest with each other? Why don't you tell me how you really feel? You know, like you never did when we were together."

Well, that got his attention off his fly.

"Aren't you the one hiding?" he asked, his tone somewhere between taunting and pitying. "Using this as yet another excuse to run away from your dream? You could be living the life you always talked about, but you keep holding out until the perfect time. The perfect scenario. How long is it going to take before you accept that life isn't perfect?"

Her heart pounded so loud, she was surprised it didn't echo through the empty room. Larissa stared, blinking a few times to process his question.

When the answer hit her, she felt like she'd been punched in the gut.

He was right. She looked around the opulent store and all of the doubts that she'd had about fitting in here, and at the mall, crashed over her. Her perfect dream was to take over the bookstore. But she'd set that dream aside for this one.

Why? Because she'd created that dream when she was with Jason. She realized that whenever she thought about the bookstore, her image was of herself, married to Jason. Waiting and nurturing her business while he traveled. Raising their children in that darling location after they'd bought the house next door to live in.

Jason was such an integral part of that future, she'd had to give it up when he was no longer a part of her life.

Larissa swallowed back the pain that lodged in her throat and gave Jason a nonchalant shrug.

"I know life isn't perfect," she said, forcing the words out. "But at least I'm smart enough to know what I'm capable of instead of diving in over my head because I'm too cocky to be realistic."

"Does this circle back to your brilliant assessment of how I should be running my business?"

"You mean ruining your business?"

"How's that unlike what you're doing? You're going to give up a great location where you're already established, all to chase a bit of glitter and gloss?"

"At least I understand the wisdom of making a plan

instead of diving in with both feet and crossing my fingers I don't break my ankles when I hit bottom," she snapped.

"Yep, that's you. The queen of the plan. You're so busy planning, you don't live. You spend so much time dreaming about what could be, you never actually live in the moment," he told her.

"What are you? A self-help guru all of a sudden?" she challenged, her shoulders stiffening defensively. "Live in the moment? Where do you get that crap?"

"From you," he barked.

They both slammed their mouths shut so fast and tight, the sound of teeth snapping echoed in the room.

"You know this isn't right for you. Your idea is cute. It's romantic and fun and clever, yes. But it's not high end. You can try and make it work here," he said, waving his hand around the store. "But it'll never fit in. Not really. Not the way you want it to."

Was he talking about her business? Or their failed relationship? She'd never realized how alike the two things were. Larissa hated him for saying out loud all the things she'd been secretly worrying about.

"I'll fit just fine," she defended weakly. "At least I'll do better than you would. You're talking about putting a travel agency into a mall that caters to the wealthy and pampered. How does that tie in with the theme and message Cartright is trying to put together here?"

The air changed. Humid and tense turned to hot and ugly in the blink of Jason's blue eyes. Larissa gulped, mentally kicking herself.

"Cartright. You mean Conner, don't you?"

Oh shit. He was so pissed. Larissa wished she could hide somewhere, but there was nowhere to go. Between his clenched jaw, his narrowed eyes and the waves of fury emanating off of him, she figured this was a smart time to shift gears. Not to back pedal, but maybe to stop poking him in the eye with a sharp stick.

"It doesn't matter," she forced herself to say with a jerk of her shoulders. "That's the past, right?"

"Right. The past. So I should just forget that while we were engaged, you spent the weekend yachting with another man?"

She was so freaking sick and tired of carrying that unfair blame that she finally snapped, giving a little scream and tugging on her hair. Damn him for not trusting her, even after all this time.

"Another man, and twenty other friends," she said through clenched teeth.

Looking shocked—whether from her scream or her words, she didn't care—Jason frowned, crossing his arms over his still bare, and oh, God help her, still tempting chest.

"You never told me there were other people there," he accused, stepping closer so he towered over her.

"You never asked," she offered back, her tone so saccharine sweet, sugar could have dripped on her toes.

"I shouldn't have had to ask. A simple sentence from you and we wouldn't have had a fight." He glared down at her, his hands now fisted on his hips. "We wouldn't have split up."

Larissa shook her head so fast, her humidity-dampened curls smacked her in the cheeks. "We'd have still split up. You didn't trust me. You believed I'd cheat on you. Why should I bother to defend myself if you didn't love me enough to have faith? Faith in me. Faith in us."

FAITH? WHAT THE HELL was Larissa talking about? Jason shook his head, wondering how much long-term damage reading all those romance books had done. She actually thought he was supposed to have faith, even in the face of proof to the contrary? She really did believe in fairy tales.

"That's such bullshit," he replied, fury pounding through his head. He didn't know if he wanted to believe her or wanted her to be lying.

"No," she snapped. "That's such reality. You never cared enough to trust me and you never cared enough to stick around. We had no future."

Yeah, he'd rather she was lying. Lying would mean she'd had faith in him and was just trying to hurt him back. Lying would mean that she'd believed in them. That she'd really loved him.

"You could have come on the trips with me," he added, struggling to pull his thoughts past the anger pounding against his temples. "I asked you plenty of times. It wasn't my fault you had to mind the store or some other crappy excuse."

"You think my reasons for not dropping everything in my life and running off to play Jane of the Jungle with you were crappy excuses?"

Jason shoved his hand through his hair, then gave a whatever shrug. He should have left it alone. So she was irritated. Trying to find out why only led to these dreaded emotional time-sucks, *discussions*.

He hated discussions.

But at least she didn't sound snotty anymore.

He was man enough to admit, he didn't know women well enough to know if that was a good thing or not.

"I think you could have made more changes. A few concessions," he admitted finally, hoping to derail any future discussing. If he could bury his anger, she could skip the discussion. It was only fair. "I mean, if you'd had your way, I'd have done all the changing while you called the shots."

She narrowed eyes that suddenly looked like they could

flame-broil him. "Let me get this straight. In your opinion, we split up over a power play?"

Starting to feel stupid standing there in his underwear, Jason clamped his arms over his chest and nodded. "Yeah, that about fits. It was your way or the highway. And when I wouldn't change, you went out with someone you thought would fit your pre-determined role of the perfect guy."

"Well, it's a good thing you know all the highways and byways, then, isn't it? So you didn't get lost as you ran out the door."

"Ha ha. Why don't you drop the sarcasm and get serious?"

Jason winced, wondering if he were hearing things as the words echoed in the suddenly still room. He wanted the words back even more than he wanted his pants.

"Serious?" She slowly advanced, looking like a vengeful fairy about to curse him. "And you thought it was all about a power play? I tried to talk seriously with you for a year. To work out a way that we could have a future together. That we could grow and build a life. But all you wanted to do was keep going out to play. And you want me to get serious?"

"See, all of that crap sounds boring. It sounds like hell. Who wants a life of growing and building? That's work," he snapped. So much for burying the anger. He shook his head, wondering how so much stuffiness could be packed into such a sexy body. "Life should be fun. An adventure, a good time. Life's about more than dreaming and working, Larissa."

He waited for her defensive response. For her to tell him all the reasons why he was wrong. His shoulders tensed as he prepped for the blow.

But...nothing. She gave him a long look, then just shook her head and turned to walk away.

"Where are you going?" he called, wincing and hoping he hadn't hurt her. God, what was wrong with him? He'd made plenty of mistakes. Who was he to lecture Larissa on how to live life?

"Does it matter?"

"Does this mean we're not going to fight?"

"Why would we?" She stopped and gave him a look over her shoulder. It was one of those casual, barely interested half smile looks. "It's not like it matters, right?"

With that, she headed off into the dark. Jason stood there, his feet rooted on the floor, as he tried to sort through his reactions.

Shock. How could she say it didn't matter? He knew it did. It was the core reason for their splitting up, so of course it mattered. But she sounded like she didn't even care.

Hurt. Why would she sleep with him if she hadn't cared? Larissa wasn't the purely physical type. She had to feel something to get naked with a guy. Dammit, he'd felt her expectations. He'd heard the silent wishes and hopes and dreams she'd laid at his feet.

Anger. Who the hell was she to decide that their relationship wasn't worth fighting for?

Jason let all of those emotions propel him as he stormed down the mall to pace until he regained control. Ten minutes later, he headed back to the store to find her and finish this discussion. But Larissa wasn't there. The candle was down to the bottom of the jar, just a black wick in a pool of scented liquid. Her bag and shoes were right where she'd left them, so he knew she hadn't discovered some secret escape hatch.

He found her at the far end of the mall by the wall of glass and entry doors. She was curled up on one of the benches, her hands cushioning her head as she stared out at the stormy sky.

"So, what's the game?" he asked as he reached her.

She must have heard him coming, because she didn't seem startled. She didn't even turn her head to look at him when she shrugged and answered, "Again, why would I bother with a game? Like I said, it doesn't matter any longer."

"How can you say it doesn't matter?"

This time she did look at him. Her face was set. He could see something in her eyes, but the light was too dim for him to tell if it was hurt, resignation or anger.

"We're not a couple. We're not together. We have no future. So, given all of those reasons, I feel totally justified in saying it just doesn't matter."

"What about last night?" He sounded like a girl but he didn't care.

"What about last night?"

"Didn't that mean anything to you? We spent hours having the best sex either of us have ever had—or are ever likely to have again. We blew each other's minds. It was fucking incredible." His voice was echoing loudly off the walls now, but Jason didn't bother to bring it down. "Are you trying to claim that wasn't good for you?"

"No. You're right," she said, swinging her feet around to the floor so the blanket fell away. He frowned, realizing she was dressed in her camisole and skirt again. Why wasn't she wearing his shirt? "The sex was amazing."

"But?"

"But—" she shrugged "—it was just sex. It wasn't anything more."

"There's more between us than sex," he said, not sure why it mattered that she acknowledge that, but knowing it did.

"No, Jason." She met his eyes, giving him a long, sad

look that made him feel like he'd been kicked in the gut. "There's nothing between us."

He frowned, shoving his hands in his pockets and wishing like crazy for more than the pale shadow of moonlight so he could read her face. Because her voice was blank, and that was killing him.

"There could be," he muttered, not sure what he was going for here, but unwilling to just let it all go. He wanted to talk more. Even though anger was burning a hole in his gut, his regret was even stronger. He'd made his share, more than his share, of mistakes in their relationship. But she'd let him think she'd cheated on him. He wanted, needed, to know why.

For the first time in his life, Jason wanted to sit down and talk things through. To work at it until they'd fixed all their problems. Even if they couldn't have a future together, he still wanted them to be...okay.

"No. You were right. I need life to be a certain way, to live up to my dreams. But we'll never fit that dream. We are just too different. I'm a romantic." He started to protest, but she shook her head and put out a hand to stop his words.

"I'm a romantic dreamer," she repeated quietly, heartbreakingly. "And you're like your father."

The emotional kick to the gut came fast and ugly. Jason blinked away the furious pain, but couldn't think of a response.

"But hey," she said, giving a watery laugh that he knew was supposed to sound cocky instead of miserable. "At least we had a good time saying goodbye, right?"

Good time? That was it?

He felt so...used.

Which was a damn sight better than the miserable feeling of his heart crumbling in his chest.

13

SITTING ON THE FLOOR at the far end of the mall, Jason rested the back of his head against the wall and stared through blurry eyes at the ceiling. Early morning sunshine streamed through the windows and skylights, filling the space with pale pink light.

Larissa's words echoed through his head. Her scent wrapped around him, still lingering on both his skin and the shirt she'd left on the counter like a one hundred percent pure cotton Dear John letter.

What the hell had happened? A day ago, he'd just finished a great trip, negotiated a killer deal on a huge dick-in-a-box and was plane hopping his way home, heart whole and worry free, his only concern snagging his shoe-in spot here in the mall.

And now? Now his head hurt almost as much as his heart. He felt like shit, doubts pounded through his mind like tiny, destructive jackhammers and he no longer gave a rat's ass about the future he'd devoted most of his life to creating.

Without moving his head, he shot a glare down the length of the mall toward Larissa's cozy little nest on the bench. He wanted to blame her. He wanted to say it was all her fault that he was having all these doubts. He'd have been perfectly happy if he'd never seen her again. Well, maybe not happy, but content.

And now?

Now all he wanted was to figure out how to keep her in his life. How to fix things, the right way this time, so they could have a future together.

Jason was finally starting to realize what she used to mean when she'd said there were some dreams worth devoting a lifetime to. That there were things that meant so much, you wanted them to be a part of every single day. Before, he'd always thought his freedom was that dream.

He'd been willing to adjust that freedom—a little—for Larissa. He'd thought about cutting back on his trips. He'd had a few fantasies about maybe moving in with her, spending those weeks he was in town living at her place. Sleeping in her bed.

He'd been such a total ass.

Jason dropped his head into his hands and sighed. He'd blown it. Larissa was right. He was like his father. A jerk who couldn't put anyone's happiness above his own. Except when it came to sex. There, he'd been more than willing to let her go first. First, second and third.

But given Larissa's belief in a happy-ever-after over, what did she call it? Gratuitous sex? Yeah, a few screaming orgasms probably hadn't scored him nearly enough points to balance out the many ways he'd failed her.

But, hey. This was fine. Sure, he'd caused another round of misery and pain. But really, nobody could point any fingers, right? This time they hadn't made any promises.

And last time, he'd been duped.

Jason blinked his sleep-deprived eyes, trying to bring his knees into focus. Frowning, he lifted his head and stared blindly toward the other end of the mall.

Last time, Larissa had duped him. She'd let him think

she'd cheated on him. She'd set him up, watched him take the bait and let him fail. Fists clenched, Jason replayed their conversation, filtering through the guilt and pain and focusing on Larissa's words.

She'd known he had misunderstood the situation. Misunderstood, hell, Conner had straight up told him he and Larissa had been out for a special evening, what else was he supposed to think? But she'd known that not only had nothing happened between her and Conner, but that there was a huge difference between her spending the weekend on a romantic yachting cruise with another man and her going on a boating weekend with a group of friends.

She'd known all of that. But still, she'd expected him to believe that nothing had happened between her and a guy who was her perfect storybook hero. A guy who was always around. Who was rich and successful and could do all that fancy hero stuff that she liked to read about. A guy who, as they all knew, had a secret thing for her.

What else was he supposed to believe when faced with all of that, combined with her silence when he'd asked—okay, maybe accused—her of going out with him? It'd been like the culmination of all of Jason's secret fears. That he wasn't good enough for her, that he wasn't the kind of guy she really wanted to spend her life with. Hell, he'd even wondered if he'd done all that traveling because he was afraid of what he'd find out about himself if he stayed in one place.

Because of her, he'd had a million and one self-doubts. So he'd fought back by traveling more, by proving to them both that he was exciting and fun. And she'd fought back by letting him think she was more interested in someone else than in him.

And he was supposed to have complete faith? What good was faith? Skills and talent and bravery. Those things counted. Faith? Faith was as much a fairy tale as those damned romance novels Larissa read.

Screw faith. She'd lied to him. Maybe not in so many words, but a lie of omission was still a lie.

There. Now it wasn't his fault. Jaw clenched, Jason stared at his fists, balled on the top of his upraised knees. Nope. Not his fault.

Which didn't do a damned thing to make him feel better.

Because it didn't matter whose fault it was. He'd hurt Larissa. Again. And that's why he was hurting. Not over anything she'd done.

God, he was a freaking idiot.

He slowly rose, his aching body protesting as he stretched to his full height and tried to peer down the long mall.

Would she listen if he apologized?

Would it make any difference?

He took three steps, then stopped.

What was he doing? There was no point in trying to charm her into forgiving him if he was just going to wave goodbye and head off on yet another adventure. They were better off letting this thing, whatever it was between them, go. Even if it was ending ugly.

Hey, this way he might be able to put her off his radar once and for all and start looking at other women. Maybe.

Nodding, sure he was making the right decision, Jason was halfway down the mall toward Larissa when he heard a sound.

Buzzing. Electrical buzzing.

The lights flickered dimly in the wall sconces.

Air trickled through the vents. Warm and sluggish at first, then slowly filling the room with cool relief.

"Yes!" Jason did a fist pump in the air and patted his pockets for the keys to the front door. Nothing.

Buttoning his shirt as he went, he strode barefoot into the store to see if the keys Conner had left were anywhere to be seen.

Still nothing.

He'd have to ask Larissa. He grimaced, taking the time to put his socks and shoes on to prepare for the confrontation.

And the pending goodbye.

Slower now, Jason made his way down the mall. Larissa's curls fell around a face soft and beautiful in sleep. Lush lashes curved against her pale cheeks and she had her head resting on her folded hands.

Jason stood there, his hands fisted in his pockets and stared.

How was he supposed to say goodbye?

And how could he not?

LARISSA SIGHED, Jason's spicy scent filling her senses as she breathed deeply the cool air. She snuggled deeper into the blanket and tried to reclaim her sweet dream, the image of her and Jason holding hands filling her mind.

Something kept pulling her out, though.

Slowly, reluctantly, she dragged her eyes open. Jason was right there, his face next to hers with that lock of hair hanging across his forehead to tempt her fingers.

"Hi," she said, sure she was still dreaming. She reached out to sweep the back of her fingers over his scruffy cheek. The prickle of hair brought her crashing back to reality.

This wasn't a dream.

When was she going to accept that fact, dammit?

"Hi back," Jason said quietly.

She slowly blinked the fog out of her eyes, then frowned. Jason's face was too close. She pulled back a little, noting that he'd crouched down in front of her and was staring.

She wet her lips, wishing desperately for a toothbrush.

"What?" she said in a husky tone.

"Do you have the keys to the front door?"

She blinked again, trying to marshal her thoughts into some semblance of clarity. "Keys?"

"The power's on."

He sounded disappointed.

Larissa's frown deepened. She blinked a couple times, trying to see if that regret was echoed on his face. But Jason was too well-versed in the art of the poker face. He just stared back at her with those gorgeous blue eyes.

"The power? We can leave?" she asked.

"I just need the keys."

Larissa sat up, swinging her still blanketed feet to the floor. Jason didn't budge. Despite the cooler air now circulating, heat flashed through her body. Her nipples budded beneath the soft silk of her camisole and her heart beat faster. Even now, as angry as she was at him, he made her crazy with desire.

Her gaze traced his face. Even with lines of exhaustion etched on his tan skin, he was gorgeous. His hair was mussed, a beard shadowing his strong jaw. And his lips. Full and enticing, they were just so close. Close enough to touch. To taste.

She almost whimpered with the need for one more kiss.

"Larissa?"

She blinked, shifting her gaze from his lips to meet his puzzled blue eyes.

"The keys?"

Right. He could finally escape.

Angry at herself, and at him, she tried to shove all those lusty feelings away. Then he held out his hand to help her up, his fingers warm and strong as he offered her support.

And the lusty feelings went all lovey-dovey. Larissa knew better. She knew his romantic gestures weren't enough to overcome all the issues, but dammit, she wanted them to be.

As soon as she was on her feet, she pulled her hand from his and made a show of brushing at the wrinkles on her ruined skirt.

Out of the corner of her eye, she saw him look toward the door and the freedom beyond. That's right, he needed the keys to escape.

"I think I threw them in my briefcase," she said, her words clipped.

"You're angry?" he asked, giving her a hooded look.

"Only with myself."

"Because?"

"Because I never learn," she muttered, turning her back on him under the pretext of folding the blanket. She kept folding until she heard his footsteps depart. She stared through tear-blurred eyes at the tiny, fat square blanket she'd ended up with, and sighed.

By the time Jason was back a couple minutes later, the keys jingling in his hand, she had control of herself again. Her face blank, she watched him put the key in the lock and turn it. She waited for the security bars to rise.

Nothing. She hurried over and opened the panel on the wall next to the door. There were a series of buttons, but she didn't know the code. She felt Jason's warm body behind her, then heard him swear.

"I guess we're still stuck for a while," he said, sounding more resigned than angry.

Larissa turned around, her breath catching when she saw how close he was. Tilting her head up to look into his face, she arched her brow.

"You're crowding me," she told him. Knowing she was

tempting fate, she pressed both palms against his chest to try and push him back. He didn't budge. But oh, baby, his chest felt wonderful. Hard and warm, her fingers tingled as they curled into the soft cotton of his shirt.

"I know," he replied, reaching up to brush her tangled curls off her cheek, then sliding his finger along her jaw. "I can't seem to help myself."

"You're going to have to. We've already established that last night was a mistake."

"Did we?"

She swallowed, having to get past the lump in her throat before she could reply.

"Didn't we?"

"I thought we established that we'd made mistakes in how we'd handled things between us in the past. Not that things between us were a bad thing."

Eyes huge, Larissa studied his face, trying to figure out if he meant that he didn't think it'd been a mistake to open that door between them again. Did this mean he wanted more? That he thought they had a future?

She was afraid to ask—even herself.

Before she could figure out how to extricate herself from this conversation and the probable heartbreak that would go with it, there was a sound at the far end of the mall.

"Well, good morning."

Larissa jumped back from Jason so fast, she banged the back of her head on the wall behind her. Wincing, she rubbed the forming lump as she looked past his shoulder.

"Conner?" she whispered.

Jason's jaw clenched and he closed his eyes as if praying for patience—or mentally cussing up a blue streak. Then he gave a deep sigh and turned around, too.

"Conner," he greeted, stepping forward to shake their friend's hand. "Here to release us?"

"Man, I'm so sorry. You've been here all night, haven't you?" He gave them both a long look, his gaze lingering for a second on Larissa's bare shoulders. She quickly wrapped the blanket around her, grateful she'd put her skirt back on. "I just got a call from security that the motion sensors detected movement and realized what must've happened."

"What's up with the power?" Jason asked.

"The entire eastern seaboard is out. Something about the power grid being overtaxed due to the heat wave. I'm so sorry. If you'd called, I'd have tried to figure out how to get you out."

"No cell," Jason said. Conner nodded. Larissa just stood there. She didn't know what to do. Jason knew there hadn't been anything between her and Conner, so why did he sound so irritated?

"So how are the two of you this morning? An entire night together, I'll bet you patched everything up, right?" he asked, sounding like a little boy asking for confirmation of Santa's visit.

"No," Larissa and Jason said in unison.

Conner gave them both a long, intense frown, then shook his head sadly. If Larissa had ever known her father, she figured that's how he would have shown his disappointment.

"Oh. Well." He gave a long hum, like he was mentally regrouping, then raised his brows. "Well, what do you say we all go out for breakfast? Do some talking. Or I can order in."

He was acting all nervous and weird, like some big business deal was riding on his getting the two of them in agreement.

What in the hell was he up to? Larissa's eyes widened. Was he giving the space to someone else?

"What's going on?" Larissa demanded.

Conner grimaced. Then, seeing the impatient look on

both their faces, he finally admitted, "I'd hoped, given a little time together, the two of you would have worked things out."

"Worked things out?" Jason's voice was low. Calm, even. But Larissa heard the furious undercurrent. She stepped between the two men, knowing she wasn't much of a deterrent but hoping they both cared enough about her to hesitate before mowing each other down.

"What are you talking about?" she insisted. Then she thought back to the look on his face the previous day. Mischievous calculation, with a little bit of glee. Her eyes widened. He hadn't... Had he? "Conner?"

"You locked us in here on purpose?" Jason asked, biting off the words.

"Nope. That was fate stepping in to play her part." He looked around the store, taking in the gutted candle and empty jar on the floor, and grinned. "Looks like she did a good job."

Jason growled.

Larissa pressed her hand to his chest to keep him from moving. She was surprised to feel him take a deep breath and calm down at her touch. Blinking quickly to move past the shock that she might actually have some influence on him, she gave Conner a long, furious look.

"I'm not sure if I've got this right," she said in her calmest, sweetest tone. She hoped it disguised her desire to kick him where it hurt. "You arranged to bring Jason and I back together?"

He nodded.

"The meeting, the presentation, that we just happened to end up here at the same time... They were all part of some elaborate scheme?"

He nodded again.

She gave a low growl and her foot twitched. This time

it was Jason who put his hand on her shoulder, calming *her* down.

"Why?" Jason asked, sounding so mellow they might have been talking about the weather.

"Partially because I felt bad about my part in your breakup," Conner admitted, looking sheepish. "I shouldn't have let you think that something had happened between me and Larissa."

"Correcting any assumptions about our relationship was up to Larissa, not you."

Jason's words made her wince. He was right. Instead of telling him the truth when she should have, she'd used his accusation as an excuse to justify her own doubts. She'd seen his lack of trust as a way to get out before he realized he'd made a mistake.

Larissa pressed her lips together to keep from crying as she realized she was as bad as she'd always accused Jason of being. First chance to escape and she'd taken it. And she'd used Conner in the process. All because she was a chicken who was so afraid to fail at romance that she'd throw away her chance at having a real relationship. A relationship that meant ups and downs, highs and lows. Yes, there would be romance and great sex, but there'd be fights and disappointments, too.

She'd spent so much of her life reading romance novels and sighing enviously when the couple declared their love, then closing the book at the end, that she didn't know what to do—what to expect—after the *I Love You* part.

"Well, whoever it was up to, I felt bad. I mean, you two had a good thing going. You were clearly meant to be together and it sucked that things ended the way they did," Conner explained, now talking a little faster as he stepped out of his comfy CEO role and backslid into acting like a geeky teenager trying to make his buddies happy. "Even if you didn't go forward together, I thought maybe if you could heal the past, you might be able to go forward separately."

Larissa just stared, not knowing what to say. Jason crossed his arms over his chest. She figured they were all better off not knowing what he wanted to say.

"I wanted to try and put things right," Conner muttered.

"You waited all this time to *put things right?*" she asked incredulously.

He nodded.

"Couldn't you have strapped on a diaper and a pair of wings instead?" she muttered.

"I don't have the legs for the cupid look," he said with a grin. When nobody returned it, he shrugged. "Look, I didn't lock you two in. I didn't even realize you were here until security called to let me know that people were locked inside and I realized it must be one or both of you."

A sudden thought smacked her upside the head. Larissa stepped forward, her hands fisting on her hips.

"Was the offer of a storefront a lie? A part of your weird scheme?" The feeling of betrayal was huge. Was this how Jason had felt when he'd thought she cheated on him? And wasn't it ironic that Conner was the center of both their betrayals?

She wanted to pound on something. The bench, the walls, Conner himself.

But down a few layers, beneath her anger and hurt, was a huge sense of relief. Larissa hadn't realized until just this second how glad she'd be to not have her store here. How much she really wanted to stay in the Victorian. With or without the rest of her dream, the Jason and true love forever part of it, she still really wanted the simple joy of owning her own bookstore.

A part of her, the part that'd taken all those business

classes and reworked that damned business plan a million times, was silently screaming "no." No way, she couldn't give up such an incredible opportunity. This was just loser thinking. Her, worrying that she was going to lose out to Jason. Or guilt, since it was so hard to take away a business opportunity from someone she knew really needed it.

"Of course not," Conner said, apparently having taken it upon himself to cause stress and confusion in every aspect of Larissa's life. "The store is available, just like I said. But instead of the committee deciding, I'm leaving it up to the two of you."

"That's crazy," Larissa said, not looking at Jason. After everything she'd admitted already, everything she'd shared, there was no way she was going to tell him that she was having second thoughts. But she definitely didn't want to try to talk him into giving up the store. Especially in light of the fact that she suddenly didn't want it. "How are we supposed to make a decision like that?"

"I don't know. Maybe talk to each other?"

Larissa was about to snap that they'd already tried that. Then she shut her mouth. Because, really, they hadn't. They'd gone down on each other. They'd drove each other crazy. And they'd yelled at each other.

But talk? Not so much.

"We'll figure it out," Jason said, again in that quiet, mellow tone. Larissa half-turned to get a good look at his face, wondering why he wasn't more intense. He met her eyes, giving her a long look that sent her stomach tumbling over itself. So many emotions were there in the blue depths of his gaze.

Confusion was clear. So was desire. She saw a little bit of anger and something else. Something powerful and scary that made her heart race and hope climb way too high for her comfort.

"How are we supposed to figure it out?" she asked, wetting her suddenly dry lips and trying to calm her pounding pulse. She was asking about more than just the store, but wasn't sure if Jason realized that.

"We just need a little time," Jason told her.

Was he seeing into her heart and giving her the answers she most wanted to hear? Or was he obliviously hitting the ones that would only add to her pain later?

"Great," Conner said, his overly jovial tone cutting through the tension. "Then I'll let you two get to it."

He gave them a double thumbs up at odds with his CEO haircut and three-piece suit and skirted around them to head for the front doors.

Larissa and Jason stood silently while he keyed a code into the box on the wall and the bolts slid free of their secure position. Then he twisted the key in the lock. Larissa stepped aside a little so she didn't get mowed down in case Jason decided to rush the door.

"Give me a second to gather my stuff," she said when nobody moved.

"Actually..."

She stopped, her bare feet sliding on the floor as she turned to hear what Conner was going to say. He had a weird look on his face. Similar to the look he'd had yesterday afternoon, just like the look he'd had when he'd confessed to playing matchmaker a few minutes ago.

"Conner..." she warned, hurrying toward him.

"I think you two need to work a few things out," he said as he opened the door.

Before she could reach him, though, he stepped through the doors and quickly slid the key in to lock them from the outside.

"What the hell?"

She ran toward the doors and shook the handle, yelling

over her shoulder to Jason, "Stop him. He's locking us in here again and leaving."

And the sonofabitch did. Larissa cursed, beating her fist on the glass as Conner pocketed the keys and gave her a jaunty little finger wave. Then he glanced at his watch and held up two fingers. She responded by holding up one.

He just laughed and walked away.

Larissa hit the door a couple more times. Then, furious and knowing she'd regret it but unable to stop herself, she kicked the brass plated door with her bare foot. She gave a little scream as pain shot all the way up to her shoulder.

Seething, she spun around. Jason was leaning on the far wall, his arms crossed over his chest. He looked like he was waiting for a freaking bus.

"Why didn't you stop him?" she accused, her fists digging into her hips while she tried to catch her breath.

Jason wasn't winded. Of course, she didn't think he'd moved at all, so that had to factor in. He just stood there against the wall, looking all casual. Had he lost his mind?

"Because I didn't want to."

Oh, yeah. He'd definitely lost his mind.

Knowing she was on her way to looking like the bride of Frankenstein and not caring, Larissa gave her curls a frustrated tug, repeating with each pull, "You. Didn't. Want. To?"

"Nope," he said with a shake of his head. When she stomped over to him, he didn't move, except to arch his brow.

"Why didn't you want to stop him from locking us back in the same miserable state we've just spent the last twelve hours in?" she asked, her voice rising with each word.

"I didn't want to," he said, slowly uncrossing his arms and reaching out to take her hands. "Because I want to fix things with you."

14

JASON WASN'T SURE HOW to fix things. He didn't even know exactly what he wanted fixed or in what way. He just knew he didn't want to leave things the way they were.

From the tight look on Larissa's face, maybe she'd have preferred leaving things at their earlier goodbye. He grimaced. Yeah, this pitch was guaranteed to go well.

But what was he pitching for? Now that he stood here, committed to making one last plea, his brain was blank.

"What do you want, Jason? Do you want it all tied up in a tidy bow?" she challenged, the frustration in her voice clear on her face as well. She threw up one hand, narrowly missing his face. "Maybe we can be friends? Or what was it you suggested earlier? Your version of bootie call buddies?"

"Well, you always said I had a fine bootie," he said lightly, more to buy time than because he thought smart-ass comments would earn him a smile.

He was right. He got an eye roll instead. But the tension seemed to drain from Larissa's shoulders and she gave him an indecipherable look before shrugging.

"Look, the only thing we need to fix is this store situation. The rest—" She gave a wave of her hand, whether to dismiss the past or shoo away the present, he wasn't sure. "We said all there is to say about that last night."

"Actually..." He took a deep breath and paused, looking at Larissa. She was gorgeous. Her curls were now a fuzzy halo around her head. The skillfully applied makeup of the previous day was gone, leaving her pale and hollow-eyed. Tension and hurt lingered in her huge dark eyes, and she was wrapped once again in that body-disguising blanket.

Gorgeous.

"Actually," he said again, "I'm not happy with the way we settled things. Not before, and not now."

Her sigh was shaky, nerves playing across her face. She shook her head and gave him a pleading look. "Let's not do this, please? We said things, I said things, that I regret. I shouldn't have compared you to your father. I'm sorry. I really am. But beyond that, I just want to let it go. We need to get out of here and get on with our lives."

It was his turn to shake his head.

"It's not that easy," he told her. Risking everything, he reached out to take her hands in his. He felt her pulse speed through her slender fingers as she tried to tug away, but he held tight. He needed the contact. And if she got mad and tried to take a swing, this should minimize the damage.

"Look," he said quietly, staring into the dark depths of her eyes. "I don't want to let things go. I especially don't want to let you go."

"I beg your pardon?" She pressed her lips together, blinking fast as if trying not to cry. Then she shook her head. "I don't think this is funny, Jason."

"I'm not trying to be funny. I figure Conner did us a favor, bringing us back together like this. And since having an interfering friend create a second chance like this is probably a once-in-a-lifetime thing, we shouldn't waste it."

She gave him a suspicious look. "Seriously, is this another pitch to get me to have sex with you?"

Jason grinned, not so much at her words but at the way she blushed when she said them. They'd spent almost eight hours doing each other every which way, and talking about it still made her cheeks turn pink. God, he loved her.

The realization hit him like a swinging tree branch. Reeling, he sucked in a breath and vowed that this time, he was going to make it work. This time he wasn't going to run away. Not from Larissa, not from commitment, and definitely not from his feelings.

"Not a pitch," he assured her, trying to recapture his smile. "But do me a favor and keep sex between us front and center in your mind."

"Why?"

"Because we're incredible. We're hot and wild and make each other feel things that nobody else can," he insisted. Thrilled that she didn't deny his words, he continued, "We're great together. I've climbed mountains, kayaked oceans and dropped out of planes and none of that comes even close to the thrill I get when I'm making love with you."

Her eyes huge, she took a shaky breath and stared. She reached out, her palm barely grazing his cheek before she pulled back and balled her hand into a fist at her side. Then, her brow knit tight, she shook her head.

"I can't, and won't, deny that the sex is incredible. I feel things with you, do things with you, that I've never imagined with anyone else."

Even though he knew damned well it was inappropriate given the seriousness of their conversation, Jason grinned. Instead of getting mad, Larissa just rolled her eyes. Then she got that serious look again.

"But sex, even mind-blowingly awesome sex, isn't enough," she said quietly.

"It's a start."

"No. When it's all we have between us, it's an end."

He clenched his jaw against the rising panic. He'd never tried to talk someone into a relationship before and the stakes were so high. Dammit, he wished he had time to practice or something.

"No. We have more. We can have as much more as you want," he promised rashly.

"You're just saying that because you want the store," she accused, tears lurking behind the anger in her voice.

Because he wasn't expecting it, this time when she tugged her hands away, she pulled free. Then she took a huge step back, as if putting a big exclamation point at the end of her declaration that she wanted to get away from him.

"You think I'd say all those things, lay myself bare like that, just to get some freaking store?" Fury danced in little black spots before his eyes. Jason couldn't remember ever being this pissed.

How could she make him feel so much love, so much pain and so damned much anger, all at the same time? It shouldn't be possible to feel all of those things at once.

It was too hard. This emotional crap. Romance? Screw this, it demanded too much. He just didn't know if he had that much to give.

And he was asking for more? To sign on to this craziness for the long term? Why was he bothering? Jason started pacing, from one side store to the next then back again, and shoved his hand through his hair. He was crazy. He should have left things alone. He should have stopped Conner from taking off and locking them in again.

He glanced at Larissa, noting how sexy and sweet she looked standing there, all rumpled and mussed. The blanket had slipped off one bare, silky shoulder so he could see the swell of one breast.

He knew she'd be the first to insist that she wasn't looking her best. But he wanted her like crazy. Just looking at her got him hard. Which was saying a lot given that his dick had gotten more loving tonight than it'd had in the last six months combined.

Still, he should have kept his damned pants on.

His hurt must have got through to her like his anger hadn't. Larissa pulled a face, taking step toward him. Not touching, God forbid, but close enough to get in his way.

"I'm not accusing you of lying," she insisted. "I'm just saying that maybe you're so focused on getting the store that you are willing to do anything to make that happen."

"You being anything?"

That took care of the conciliatory light in her eyes. "Are you trying to say you don't want the store?"

"Let's just leave the store out of this for a minute," he demanded, beyond frustrated that he had to explain himself. And that he was doing such an abysmal job of it. No wonder they'd split up before—they clearly had lousy communication skills. "This isn't about the store or either one of our businesses. This is about us. About our future."

"No. There is no us." She shook her head. "And we don't have a future, remember."

"You don't think we should be together?" he asked, working to keep the hurt out of his voice. What the hell had he been thinking? He'd had it right before, to keep most of his heart tucked away safe and hidden instead of putting himself out there and believing they could have a real relationship.

"I don't think we *can* be together," she said with a sniff, the tears in her eyes finally pooling over and starting to run down her cheeks.

"Fine." His heart ached, but he'd be damned if he was

going to beg. Jason started to turn away, then gave a frustrated growl and stopped.

He couldn't just give up. Instead, he gave her a long, intense inspection. Pain and regret were clear on her face. But as he looked closer, he saw resignation. She expected him to walk away. She knew if she pushed, he'd just toss up his hands and go. And he'd damn near proved her right.

"Look, I know we blew it before," he paused, waiting to see if she still thought the blowing was all his doing. When she just sighed, her shoulders sagging a little, he continued, "But I'm not giving up this time."

He reached for her hands again, pulling her closer.

"You're not ready to trust me, that's fine. Eventually you will. I'm sticking around this time," he decided.

As he said the words, it was like a light went off in his heart. It didn't matter if she believed him, or if she was ready. He was willing to do whatever it took to make things work between them. He was sticking it out. He was through running. It might be tomorrow or it might be a year from now. Sooner or later, she'd realize they would make it.

"Sticking around?" Skepticism coated her words.

"Yeah. I can't cut back my trips since I've got financial responsibilities I can't shirk, but no more personal trips unless you want to go with me. Maybe places like Barbados or Greece? Those are romantic, right?"

She stared. Her lips opened but no words came out.

"I'm still bunking at my parents' house, but Peter and Meghan are going to live there after they get married. I'll get an apartment instead of taking their spare room. Or maybe I'll even put a down payment on a house," he mused. Now that he was fixating on this settling down thing, it was feeling like its own adventure. One he planned to spend with Larissa.

"You're seriously thinking about buying a house?" Her

tone said she thought the only thing he was serious about was bullshitting her.

"Yeah," he decided. He remembered something she'd said one night years ago, curled up in his arms after they'd made love. "Maybe one of those Victorian houses like Murphy's store? You dig those, right? Didn't you say that's the kind of place you'd like to buy someday? Once the bookstore is gone, you'll be missing that old-house vibe. So until you believe I'm serious, you can come hang at my place and get your old-house thrills."

She pulled away. Again. He was starting to think she should be wearing a cord, she was in and out of his arms like a yo-yo.

Three feet away, she started pacing. Every few steps she shot him a confused look. Jason just waited.

"And if I say I want to keep the store?" she finally asked.

He grimaced. He wanted to tell her he'd step aside. He wanted to promise her anything. But this wasn't just about his wants.

"Maybe we can go get some coffee, real food and talk about it? If you can help me figure out a way to keep things going so I can still cover my mom's care until Peter starts bringing in enough to really help out, then I'll step aside."

The waiting, and the stepping aside to let her decide, were about the hardest things Jason had ever done. God, why hadn't he just handed over the store? Why hadn't he promised her anything, everything, to get her to agree to get back together with him? Knowing he'd just blown all his romance points, Jason mentally cringed, waiting for her to tell him to get screwed.

Instead, she gave a long, shuddering breath and closed her eyes for a second. When she opened them, she looked so peaceful and happy he knew this was the kiss-off.

"You can have the store," she said.

"What?" he exclaimed, sure he'd heard her wrong. "Why?"

"Because..." She hesitated, then shrugged and said quietly, "Because I love you."

LARISSA WAITED FOR THE ROOF to cave in. Or for Jason's eyes to bug out like a cartoon character's right before he left a body-shaped hole in the wall when he ran away.

But he didn't run. He just grinned like he'd just been handed a check for a million dollars. By a naked woman. Dangling the keys to a Lamborghini on her equally naked finger.

"Look, I definitely want you to keep loving me," he said, his grin widening again as he said the words. "But I don't want you making any sacrifices for me. For us."

He made a c'mere wiggle with his fingers, obviously preferring that this conversation take place in his arms.

Larissa stepped backward instead. She preferred this conversation take place with all her brain cells intact.

"What about a compromise?" she offered, hoping she was making the right decision here. She had this big huge dream at her fingertips yet she was thinking about tossing it aside for a more comfortable, non-fancy dream. How was Jason going to think she was amazing and special if she settled?

How could she compete with his exciting life if she was, well, not exciting?

His grin turned into a frown when she wouldn't let him hug her. "What kind of compromise?"

"You take the store, but help me make my romance column a little sexier," she said through a tight throat as her stomach churned with nerves. Was that enough? She knew it would be for her, but what about him? "I'm realizing that romance is definitely better with a little heat."

"That will be my pleasure," he promised. "But what about

your business? I thought this mall was perfect for your plans. Are you sure you're okay with giving it up?"

"I'm sure. If I realized one thing being trapped in here, it was that I don't quite fit. I'd never be comfortable, never feel like I could be myself in this place." She waited to see if he was going to lecture her, but he just gave the fancy store signs a sneer.

"Besides," she continued, "the real benefit that makes this location pay off is the promotion. And that's something you could use much more than I could."

"I thought you wanted your store here? Didn't you say this was the perfect place to showcase Isn't It Romantic's message?"

She stared down the length of the mall, noting the fancy store names and the feeling they invoked. Definitely not a feeling of welcome, or of love. Even if she was sure she'd get a little hot and excited whenever she saw them again, given how wild the lovemaking had gotten between her and Jason.

"This place is too superficial for romance." Finally sure, and ready, she stepped forward and laid her palm against Jason's chest, so warm and hard beneath his shirt. "Isn't It Romantic wouldn't fit. I let my self-doubts and insecurities fog my judgment."

"But what are you going to do?" he asked as he lay his own hand over hers while wrapping his other one around her waist and pulling her closer.

"I'm going to buy out Mr. Murphy and turn the bookstore into my dream store." Just saying the words sent a thrill of rightness through her. It fit her, just like Jason did. "I've always wanted the store. And like you said, I love the Victorian. I'll shift it from books to my romance niche and it'll be perfect."

"I thought you were worried about the location?"

She grimaced. Since when was Jason the harbinger of reality? "I am, a little. But I'll figure something out."

"How about we setup a little display in the store here? Feature the adventurous side of romance?"

"That's perfect," she said with a relieved smile. "Are you sure Peter won't mind? He'll be taking the job of running your place here, right?"

"No. Actually, that job will be both of ours. If Peter wants to make this work, he's going to have to take turns."

"Take turns?" Larissa reached up, her fingers reveling in the soft, silky feel of his hair as she brushed the lock off his forehead. "You mean take turns going off and having adventures?"

Jason caught her hand and brought her fingers to his mouth, brushing his lips over them before pressing a damp kiss to her palm. Larissa shivered as desire heated low in her belly. For a brief second, she wished the power—especially the power running the video cameras—was out again so they could have a little privacy to explore the sensual heat warming her girly parts.

"No. Take turns staying home with the women we love."

Larissa's mind, so busy entertaining the image of dragging him into the store's bathroom with all its privacy for some fast and hot sex, went blank.

"You love me?" she asked, both exhilarated and terrified. "Really, this time?"

"I love you," he confirmed, pressing her hand to his chest. His eyes held hers captive as he leaned down, saying just before he took her mouth, "Really, this time."

Their lips slid together in a soft, sweet promise that brought more tears to Larissa's eyes. Then, as if realizing sentiment was going to ruin their hot moment, Jason deepened the kiss. His tongue begged entrance, then proceeded to drive her crazy. Twining, dancing, entrancing, he held her mouth captive as he curved his fingers into her hair and lifted her mouth to more perfectly fit against his.

"Maybe we should send Conner a thank-you gift," she teased as they ended the kiss, her fingers twining through the hair at the nape of his neck. "You know, to show our appreciation for his trapping us together here."

Jason laughed, then glanced down the length of the mall and got a wicked look in his eyes.

"I've got just the thing."

She followed his gaze, seeing the bench they'd had their lousy meal on. She frowned, then spied the long box tucked underneath it.

"You'd give him your dick?" she said with a laugh.

"Not my dick," he corrected after a quick wince. He gripped her hips and pulled her closer to make sure she knew his was still there, hard and happy. "But I'll give him the koteka. We've already enjoyed its special powers so it's only fair to pass it on. And I think he'd get a kick out of it."

"You don't want to save that for your museum?" she asked, twining her arms around his neck and nuzzling his throat.

"The only big person I want seeing my big woody is you," he teased, his arms banding tight around her like he didn't ever want to let go. Then his tone turned serious and he said, "But this is about more than sex, okay? I'm not looking for that bootie call. I'm looking for a real relationship. One where we trust each other and depend on each other and all that grown up romance stuff."

Laughing, she nodded. Before she could say anything, he continued, "I don't want to date. Or to live together. I don't even want to get engaged. I want to move right past go and get married."

Married?

Holy shit. Larissa could see how serious he was. There was no hesitation in his eyes, no worry or doubt. Instead she saw only love and confidence.

As joy and excitement fought for top emotional billing, Larissa leaned back, wondering how she'd gotten so lucky. But fear still lingered.

"You're sure?" she asked quietly. "I mean, this time I have expectations. Real ones. A lifetime of them."

His smile was slow, sweet and positive. He nodded, then wrapping his hands tighter around her waist to lift her to her tiptoes, he brushed a soft kiss over her lips.

"I'm sure enough for a lifetime," he promised. "I believe in us, Larissa. I believe that I'm the man to make you happy. And I believe you're the woman I want to spend my forever with."

She gave a tremulous smile and, finally believing it was for real, nodded. "Then yes. I want to marry you. I want to spend my life with you. Build our careers and hold each other's hands as we face whatever comes our way."

He laid his forehead against hers and closed his eyes, giving a huge sigh of relief. Then he opened his eyes, brushed another soft kiss over her lips and arched his brow.

"You're sure? Because there's no backing out or easy misunderstandings this time. If we do this, it's for the long haul."

Larissa stared at his gorgeous face, the hope and love shining from his blue eyes. How could she ever have doubted that he was her perfect romance hero?

"Yes. I'm ready for the long haul," she vowed.

His laughter bounced off the walls as he swept her into his arms and started heading down the mall. Larissa wrapped her hands around his neck to hold on, laughing along with him. "Where are we going?" she asked.

"Conner said two hours. We have one left and I'm planning to make good use of it."

"More gratuitous sex?" she teased.

"More like grateful, amazing sex," he corrected, pausing in the doorway of the store to kiss her.

As his lips slid over hers, Larissa had to agree.

She was very, very grateful, and the sex between them? Definitely amazing.

* * * * *

Kept in the Dark

HEATHER MacALLISTER

Heather MacAllister lives near the Texas gulf coast where, in spite of the ten-month growing season and plenty of humidity, she can't grow plants. She's a former music teacher who married her high-school sweetheart on the 4th of July, so is it any surprise that their two sons turned out to be a couple of firecrackers? Heather has written more than forty romantic comedies, which have been translated into twenty-six languages and published in dozens of countries. She's won a Romance Writers of America Golden Heart Award, *RT Book Reviews* awards and is a three-time RITA® Award finalist. When she's not writing stories where life has its quirks, Heather collects vintage costume jewellery, loves fireworks displays, computers that behave and sons who answer their mother's e-mails. You can visit her at www.HeatherMacAllister.com.

Dear Reader,

I hope you're enjoying this collection with Tawny Weber and Samantha Hunter.

My contribution to this trilogy, *Kept in the Dark*, is the story of trust and second chances between a former cat burglar and her ex-lover—the security expert who sent her to prison. Talk about conflict!

Although my heroine says she doesn't believe in second chances, there are lots of people who do—including those who run animal shelters. These volunteers see to it that lost and abandoned pets get a second chance for a happily ever after. Check out the Blaze Authors' Pet Project at www.BlazeAuthors.com/blog where we highlight different animal shelters. Who knows? Maybe you'll find a new best friend like the wily Jo Jo, who scampers through *Kept in the Dark*.

Best wishes,

Heather MacAllister

www.HeatherMacAllister.com

To Marilyn, Carla, and Barb and many more breakfasts at Denny's.

1

Brooklyn, New York
Six years ago

"Don't be a fool, Kaia."

Kaia Bennet's father gestured dramatically, his hand crashing into her roommate's study lamp. As he steadied it, Kaia dumped the dirty clothes from her backpack into a mesh hamper sitting on her closet floor. She'd planned to change her T-shirt before class, but not while her parents were in the room.

"I'm not." She inhaled, secretly smiling when she caught Blake's scent mingled with hers. "I'm a student. Just like everyone else."

"You are *not* just like everyone else." He made a sound and muttered, "I thought you would have outgrown this phase by now."

"It's not a phase. It's what normal kids my age do."

One of her bras slid off the mound of dirty clothes to the floor of her tiny dorm room closet. She kicked it out of sight and bent to open the bottom dresser drawer. The drawer wouldn't open all the way unless she moved the bed, but her father was standing on the other side of it, being parental.

Her mother had positioned herself in the doorway where she could keep a lookout.

Typical. What wasn't typical was her parents making a trip into the city to see her.

"How can you live like this?" her father asked, looking around the cramped space.

"She can't. That's why she hasn't been back in three days," her mother snapped.

Her father looked pained. He was very good at looking pained.

Kaia stood upright clutching a sports bra; it was the only clean underwear she'd found in the drawer. "Have you been spying on me?"

"No," her father denied at the same time her mother said, "Yes."

"Louisa, it's not spying to be concerned about our daughter's welfare."

Her mother ignored him. "You haven't checked in with Roy Dean for your messages."

"He goes by Royce now," Kaia reminded them knowing her friend would always be Roy Dean to her parents.

She stuffed the sports bra into her backpack along with her last clean pair of jeans. Actually most of her clothes were in the mesh hamper. Mentally shrugging, Kaia pulled the drawstring on it closed and prepared to take it all with her. She could do her laundry at Blake's. "You know, most parents just call or text their kids when they want to talk with them. They don't message through a go-between."

Most kids didn't have jewel thieves for parents, either.

"We prefer to stay off the grid."

Tell me something I don't know. Kaia met her father's dark gaze squarely. "I don't have any reason to stay off the grid." It was impossible once she'd enrolled at Brooklyn College, anyway. "And I never will again." She added that last bit in case they were here to try to talk her into doing a job with them.

They were getting older, although her mother's hair was still as black as Kaia's without the need for hair dye. But after her mother's long ago fall, Kaia had been the one to climb over roofs, scale buildings and slither through air ducts.

Until she was old enough to say no and move out.

As she returned her laptop and other class materials to her backpack, she was aware of the long look her parents exchanged.

"You fixed for money okay?" her father asked.

"I'm fine." More than fine.

"We heard about the job," her mother said, and quickly glanced up and down the hallway.

"Yeah. It seems I have a knack for selling jewelry. Who knew?"

"We're not talking about your minimum-wage job at the mall." Her father reached across the bed and tapped the tiny lump at her throat.

Rats. She'd hoped they wouldn't notice the necklace beneath her T-shirt.

"Roy Dean mentioned a diamond," he said.

"Royce," she emphasized, "talks too much." Before her father could ask, Kaia tugged on the gold chain so he could see the stone.

He glanced at it and in that brief look, Kaia knew he'd assessed the grade, carat weight and color. Way too puny for him.

"Interesting flaw enhanced by the marquise cut. Like

a cat's eye. A cat's eye for a cat burglar. I see why it appealed to you." He dropped the pendant and moved to the doorway, relieving her mother, who limped over to have a look at the stone, herself.

Kaia rolled her eyes, both at their paranoia and the exaggerated limp.

"I saw that," her father said without looking at her.

Her mother stared at the necklace and then at Kaia. "You didn't get that at your little rinky dink mall jewelry store."

"It was a gift."

"Not from your boyfriend," her mother said sharply.

Kaia shouldn't have been surprised that they knew about Blake. "No."

"Casper Nazario?" asked her father from the doorway.

Kaia gasped. Now they *had* surprised her. "I—"

"Does he know you have it?" her mother interrupted.

"Of course. He *gave* it to me."

Kaia's mother looked toward the doorway and her parents changed places again.

"Payment? For the job?" Her father appeared genuinely concerned.

What was he thinking? "Yes! I mean, no, he paid me money for the job. This was something else. A bonus because he was happy and relieved that I'd pulled it off."

Kaia remembered how the silver-haired man had seemed...giddy was about the only way to describe it. Word got out that he'd wanted someone who could put various objects back inside his friends' homes without them finding out. He'd made up some story about why— Kaia had forgotten because it didn't matter. Royce heard about it, mentioned her name, and ultimately, that job, and the money she'd earned, had bought her sophomore year of college.

She remembered seeing the diamond winking at her from an open box when Casper had unlocked his wall safe to get her cash. She'd admired it and he'd handed it to her. "It's yours. A cat's eye for a cat burglar."

That was what her father had just said.

A prickle of unease flashed through her, especially when her father shook his head and said, "Oh, Kaia" in the same tone of voice he used when she'd made a mistake.

"What?"

"Men such as Casper Nazario do not give away anything."

"He did this time." But now she wondered if it was his to give.

"You have the papers for it?"

"No—"

"Kaia, you can't trust a man like that."

"According to you, I can't trust anybody."

"That's right."

"I am so sick of this!" She zipped up her bulging backpack. "I just want to be normal and have a nice, normal life with friends and an actual job I can tell people about."

Her father gave her a pitying look.

"Tell her, Manny," said her mother from the doorway.

"Tell me what?"

Her father rested both hands on her shoulders and sighed. "Kaia, Kaia, Kaia."

"Papa, Papa, Papa." The words lacked rhythm because he'd insisted she call him P*apa* with the accent on the second syllable.

"Get on with it, Manny," urged her mother.

"Kaia, this person you've been associating with, this Blake McCauley..."

Her heart froze. "What about him?"

"He's an officer of the law." Her father looked as though he'd just told her there was no Santa Claus.

Relief made her laugh. "I know." She shrugged away from her father's hands. "He told me."

"He *told* you? You *knew?*" her parents asked at the same time.

"Yes." She hoisted the backpack over her shoulders. "And guess what? Cops aren't so bad after all. In fact," she paused for dramatic effect as she'd seen her father do so many times before, "we love each other."

Kaia picked up the laundry bag, enjoying her parents' horrified expressions. "He'd like to meet you," she added.

"I'll just bet he would!" her father exploded.

"I'm going to warn Phillip." Kaia's mother disappeared.

"Uncle Phil is here, too?" What was this—an intervention?

"Who do you think is watching the street?" Her father pointed out the door. "Have you forgotten *everything* we've taught you?"

"Nobody needs to watch the street, Papa. All I told Blake is that you own a jewelry repair business." And maybe a little more.

"You told him the *truth?*"

"Obviously not all of it."

Her father was pacing now. The room was so tiny, he reversed direction every four steps. "Here's what we're going to do. Pack up everything you can carry. You won't be back. The situation is bad, but not unsalvageable, if we move quickly. Fortunately, we have plans in place—"

"Papa, stop. You don't have to disappear."

"I do when my daughter tells me she's in love with a policeman." He paused in front of the desk. "Do you need any of this stuff?"

She shook her head. "It's my roommate's. Here's the deal—when you're not doing anything illegal, you don't have to avoid the police. What a concept, right?"

"I don't like it." He moved to the window and pushed aside the blinds. All he was going to see was the building next door.

"What don't you like? Going legit?"

"Your situation. I don't trust him."

"You don't even know him."

Her father let the blinds fall back into place. "I don't trust you when you're with him."

Kaia knew that, but hearing him say so still hurt. "You don't trust anybody."

"And neither should you. Time to go." He reached for her laundry bag.

"No."

Something in her voice got her father's attention. Maybe it was because she hadn't shouted or struggled or pleaded. Maybe it was because she was acting like an adult who'd chosen a different life path. Maybe because he finally believed she was finished with the family business.

He straightened. They gazed at each other for a few moments, during which Kaia noticed him slip his hand into a pocket but pretended she didn't. He touched her arm, leaned in and kissed her on the forehead.

Like he ever kissed her on the forehead. She checked the pockets of her jacket. "What did you plant?"

"A number."

To a disposable cell, she knew. "I won't change my mind."

Wearing a half-smile, he gently cupped her cheek. "You can't trust him, Kaia."

"I love him."

Dropping his hand, her father headed for the door. "You can't trust love, either."

"I NEED MORE TIME." Blake McCauley sat in his car on the backside delivery area in the Brooklyn mall parking lot.

"You've had plenty of time," his captain said. "Got a meeting with the parents set?"

"No, but I'm close. Kaia's talking to them."

"And what did they say?"

"Nothing, yet. They're out of town."

"Right. She's playing you, McCauley."

Blake gazed through his windshield into the middle distance, picturing Kaia with her smoky good looks and thick black hair. And those dark eyes that drew him in and saw through him at the same time. They'd been sleeping together for weeks and for weeks there had not been one false note. Blake knew her. And ironically, since he was undercover, she knew him better than any other woman he'd ever been with.

The only thing out of tune was the story he'd been given about her. The Kaia he'd come to know and the Kaia they said she was didn't match. Not unless she was the best liar he'd ever met in his work as a police detective. And that was saying something, since working undercover had made him a pretty good liar, himself.

"She's not playing me," he said. "She didn't do it."

"She's wearing the diamond?"

Blake smiled to himself. "Yeah." Most of the time that was *all* she wore.

There was silence followed by a heavy sigh. "Start thinking with your other head, McCauley."

Blake wiped the smile off his face and sat up straighter. "I am, sir. If she stole it, why didn't she disappear when she found out I'm a cop?"

"Oh, gee, because maybe then you wouldn't suspect her? Because then she'd have a chance to warn her parents? Because then you'd argue that a member of one of the slipperiest family of jewel thieves around couldn't possibly have stolen a diamond?"

"She said it was a gift." Blake knew the words sounded weak.

"Funny. He doesn't remember it that way."

Blake shifted uncomfortably. He knew what his captain was saying was logical, but Blake's gut told him Kaia was innocent. His brain told him it wasn't his job to establish her guilt or innocence. Blake usually went with his gut.

"Look, son, you're too close to this one. We've all had that one case where our emotions got all tangled up." Blake heard a dry chuckle. "You were overdue."

"It's not that."

"She's real pretty. Of course it's that."

Blake ignored him. "I'm about to break this case. Eventually she's going to say something that will lead us to her parents." Because if anybody was guilty of stealing, they were. "Kaia never said who gave her the necklace. Maybe they did."

"We can place her at the scene."

"You can place a lot of people at the scene."

"They aren't wearing a diamond that looks like a cat's eye."

Blake closed his eyes. He was pushing it and the captain had been surprisingly lenient. Blake figured he'd used up all his superior's good will and the man's next words confirmed it.

"It's the end of the month. Time to wrap this up, McCauley."

Blake's stomach felt worse than when he'd eaten a bad burrito on a stakeout.

"Lemme do this alone," he asked. "I don't need backup."

"McCauley!" The captain spoke sharply, Blake's name a verbal slap in the face. "She's an expert at getting into and out of places that are impossible for normal human beings. You *can't* handle this by yourself."

Blake clenched his teeth. "And you just expect her to walk outside when I'm surrounded by patrol cars?"

"McCauley, I didn't suspend you when you blew your cover with her, but if you don't shut up and do your job, I'll suspend you now."

"Yes, sir." Blake didn't point out that Kaia discovering he was a cop had worked to their advantage in gaining her trust.

"We're standing by for your signal."

At that moment, Blake saw Kaia push through the beige employee exit doors by the loading docks. She was a few minutes earlier than usual, so she must not have had to close up tonight.

And it meant his backup hadn't had a chance to arrive yet. Blake glanced in the side and rearview mirrors before looking toward Kaia again. She saw him and flashed a big, excited smile. Calm and happiness seeped through him.

In that very brief moment of time, he felt that life was

perfect and all he wanted was to see her smile every day and night for the rest of his life.

He watched her walk toward him in slow motion, like a sappy commercial. He held his phone to his cheek and hesitated.

She was early. No backup was here yet. She was an escape expert.

He could warn her. He could pick her up as usual, drive right out of the parking lot and let her go. Or disappear with her. She'd know how to disappear. They could start over somewhere. Together.

"McCauley?"

"She's here," he said, because he couldn't put it off. He snapped the phone closed and got out of his car to meet her.

She was lugging a bag behind her.

"What's all this?"

"Laundry!" She laughed, dropped the bag, and launched herself at him, wrapping her arms and legs around him and kissing him with a hungry urgency.

And Blake clutched her, kissing the words, "I love you," into her mouth. Because he did. Because he could see everything clearly when he kissed her. Together, they'd go see the captain and Blake would convince the man that they'd been investigating the wrong person. He'd have to find a way to explain everything to her... but she felt so good in his arms...

He was barely aware of a thrumming, and then the sound of tires. Lights flashed outside his closed eyes.

Doors slammed and Kaia flinched, breaking their kiss.

Patrol cars surrounded them. One last door slammed and Blake looked into the eyes of his captain.

They'd already been on site, watching, during the

whole phone conversation. The captain hadn't trusted Blake. With good reason.

"Blake?" Kaia's voice sounded panicked. "What's going on?"

Blake glanced around at the men. His colleagues. His captain. They all knew what he'd been about to do. He could see the pity and contempt in their eyes.

Contempt.

And suddenly, he felt that contempt for himself. He'd not only been about to blow his career, he'd been about to *break* the law.

"Blake?" Kaia touched his arm.

Blake looked into her dark eyes and knew the moment she saw the truth.

The captain stepped forward. "I'll take it from here, McCauley."

"No. My case, my collar." Blake took Kaia's wrist and turned her around. "You have the right to remain silent—"

But she didn't. "Blake!"

And Blake knew the sound of his name filled with anguished betrayal would haunt him the rest of his life.

2

Washington, D.C.
Present day

WHEN KAIA BENNET walked into the Guardian Security Services conference room on Friday morning and saw Casper Nazario's lawyer sitting with her boss, she pivoted in an abrupt about-face and bolted for the ladies' room. She locked the door and was standing on a toilet seat while pushing out a ceiling panel when Tyrone LaSalle opened the door.

"Seriously?" she asked as he pocketed the lock pick. "Doesn't the fact that this is the women's restroom count for anything?"

He shook his head. "Don't do it, Kaia."

"I haven't had a chance to do anything yet." She moved the panel out of the way and looked down on the beefy, six-foot four wall of muscle. Light reflected off his shaved head. "I should never have taught you to pick locks."

"You do know that Wendell installed security

grates in our duct system after you retrieved the Bailey documents last year?" he asked.

Kaia knew. Her boss had been both fascinated and horrified at the ease with which Kaia had exploited that particular vulnerability in buildings, especially supposedly secure government buildings in Washington, D.C. He'd secured the service portals to the ventilation system at Guardian, but not the air ducts themselves. He hadn't thought it necessary because the ducts weren't designed to support the weight of a typical repairman—that was why Kaia didn't allow herself to carry more than one hundred ten pounds on her five-foot four-inch, not-typical-repairman frame. She chose not to share that info with her boss.

"Of course you knew," Tyrone answered his own question. "That means you're headed somewhere else."

The rooftop, but Kaia wasn't going to tell him that.

"Or maybe you were gonna hide out in here until everybody left, except we all saw you come in..." he mused.

In a practiced move, Kaia wiped all expression from her face, something she should have done when Tyrone first opened the door.

"Rooftop?" he guessed correctly. "And then what? Have you got rappelling equipment stashed up there?"

Yes, but more important, a prepaid cell phone programmed with the number of a helicopter pilot who owed her a favor. She flexed her arm muscles and assessed the rectangular hole left by the ceiling panel.

"Don't do it, Kaia," Tyrone repeated. "Do not run. I'll beat you to the roof."

Doubtful, but he'd certainly get there before the helicopter arrived. The question was how long would it take him to break through the rooftop door after she barricaded it?

It might be fun to time him.

Her gaze skimmed the custom black suit he wore, specially tailored to accommodate overdeveloped arms and shoulder holsters. It was the same black suit all employees of Guardian Security wore, including Kaia. She hated the slick wool-blend material. Not good for climbing.

Tyler eased forward a step, his casual movement telling her he'd decided to grab her legs instead of racing up the stairs to the roof.

"Wrong choice." She shook her head. "My feet would be out of reach before you got through the stall door."

"I could shoot through the panels."

"Too noisy. And you could kill me."

"What if I don't care?"

Kaia put the ceiling panel back in place. "There is that." She hopped off the toilet and opened the stall. "Except dead cat burglars don't tell tales."

"I've noticed live ones don't, either." Tyrone leaned against the outer door to the restroom as someone tried to come in. "It's occupied," he called over his shoulder.

"The whole thing?" protested an outraged voice.

"You knew I was going to run, otherwise you wouldn't have been here so fast," Kaia said.

Tyrone cracked a smile, his dark eyes warming momentarily. "Casper Nazario's lawyer makes *me* want to run."

"He shouldn't." Kaia mock punched Tyrone's sleeve and the unyielding arm beneath it. "If I had a choice between you and ten lawyers like him, I'd still pick you."

"He's a better lawyer than I am," Tyrone said.

"He's a more experienced lawyer than you are. Slipperier. Like his boss," she added darkly.

"I'm too big to be slippery."

"And I like that about you. Tell your wife if she doesn't treat you right, you've got options."

Tyrone grunted in embarrassment and shifted his weight. Kaia made him nervous, a fact she liked to emphasize every so often just to keep him off balance.

The only time Kaia, herself, had ever been off balance, she'd had over two years in prison to regain it.

More knocking came from the door behind Tyrone. "Hurry up!"

"Use the men's," Tyrone called. "We're gonna be a while."

"It's okay. I'm over it," Kaia assured him. "Running was just a reflex. It's good to exercise my reflexes every so often. You know, to keep in practice."

"Hunh."

Tyrone reached for the door. Kaia stopped him from opening it. "I can't." She shook her head. "Whatever Casper Nazario wants, I can't do it."

"You have to. Those are the terms of your probation." Which Tyrone knew because he'd negotiated them. And he'd continued negotiating, chipping away at the length each time some government agency needed her specialized talent, off the records.

Casper Nazario was hardly with the government. "You *know* that Casper lied about giving me the Cat's Eye diamond and that's why I ended up in prison."

"It was a he-said, she-said situation."

"Only what he said wasn't true and what I said was. And he knows it." Kaia wondered if Tyrone believed her and hated that it mattered to her. It shouldn't. "I'm not going anywhere near that man or any of his minions."

"Not alone, you're not."

Every bit of self-preservation Kaia possessed was screaming "Trap!" at her. "You can't trust him."

"I know." Tyrone met her eyes with the same steady gaze she'd held for over ten silent minutes as they'd faced each other across a table in the prison's conference room during their first meeting. "But you can trust me."

It wasn't about trustworthiness. It was about dealing with an arrogant slimeball. "Why did he ask for me?" she whispered.

"Let's go find out." Tyrone raised his eyebrows at her and Kaia nodded reluctantly. "I got your back," he murmured as he opened the door.

Yeah, but what about the rest of her?

In the doorway, a young man smiled pleasantly. "Hiya, Kaia."

She hated that. Presley seemed to think he was the only one who ever thought of rhyming her name that way.

"Do you need an escort?" he asked Tyrone.

"Bite me," Kaia said, knowing he would if the situation warranted it.

Tyrone sent the kid away with a slight shake of his head and gestured for her to precede him. Kaia ignored the annoyed glares from two female coworkers as she brushed past Tyrone and walked out the door. "You know I could still get away, if I wanted."

"I don't doubt it," Tyrone said.

"Hmm, I think you do." Kaia threw a grin over her shoulder and abruptly stopped walking, causing him to stumble against her.

"Hey!" He gripped her arms both for balance and to

keep her from running away. Naturally, she'd counted on that.

Sighing heavily, Tyrone looked down. "You took my security badge." Smirking, he said, "You'll need more than that."

Kaia held up his wallet.

He blinked and his smirk turned rueful. "Not bad," he admitted as she handed it back. "What was the rest of your plan?"

Kaia nodded at the exit to the stairwell a few feet in front of them.

"Except I'd pick the lock again and I'm gettin' gooood," Tyrone bragged.

"With what? This?" Kaia held up his lock pick.

He patted his breast coat pocket in surprise, but quickly recovered. "No. This." And he removed a second pick from another pocket.

Smiling widely, Kaia relaxed for the first time since she'd seen Casper's lawyer. Tyrone was on his game today. "I'm so proud." She tossed Tyrone the pick she'd lifted in the restroom.

As he caught the pick, Tyrone said, "You taught me never to trust anyone without a backup plan."

"And you'd better have a good one if you expect me to talk to Casper's lawyer."

For all her talk, she'd known she'd end up returning to the meeting. But that didn't mean she would agree to do the job, she vowed as she walked through the door. The only bright spot, and that was because everything else about the situation was dim by comparison, was that Casper must be desperate to seek her out. What had his kleptomaniac wife stolen this time?

Kaia sat in a comfy club chair. They were using the so-called domestic room, decorated like someone's casually chic living space. Such surroundings soothed families, especially women who were hiring bodyguards or couriers.

The legal weasel who sat on the chintz sofa across from her looked out of place.

She remembered him from her trial—same weasely eyes, hair coiffed like a television evangelist, and a little pointed goatee. He was dying the goatee a dark brown now, but left his temples and sideburns gray. Odd. And not in a good way.

His gaze flicked over the men in the room. "We require Miss Bennet's services for a delicate matter I will detail to her in private."

"No," said Wendell and Tyrone simultaneously.

Kaia's, "No," sounded a beat later because she'd prefaced it with, "Hell."

"As Ms. Bennet's counsel, Tyrone will stay," her boss said smoothly, and left the room, quietly closing the door behind him.

It was quite a concession on Wendell's part. Something big must be up.

Tyrone settled back in a leather wing chair he liked to use. It was the power chair, being a few inches higher than the sofa cushion where the weasel sat. The difference wasn't noticeable until both parties sat down. Tyrone's chair didn't give much, but anyone who sat on the sofa sank deeply and ended up with his knees higher than usual. This also resulted in an awkward power-diluting struggle to get up from the sofa at the end of the meeting. Tyrone would be standing first, in the perfect position to extend a hand to help.

It was all gamesmanship, and Kaia was for anything that diminished Alvin Rathers, aka the weasel.

He wasn't happy about Tyrone being there, but

he started talking anyway, making up a story about Casper's wife, Tina, "forgetting" to return a couple of bracelets lent to her by a jewelry designer whose chunky designs were much favored by the ladies who lunch.

Tina was a kleptomaniac, pure and simple. Kaia had figured that out right off. It was a surprise that Tina was still getting away with it all these years later.

Kaia barely listened as the weasel explained that Casper wanted the bracelets returned to the designer without anyone, especially Tina, knowing. Because, heaven forbid the man should confront his wife and get her into therapy.

Yeah, yeah. Same song, second verse.

Just like six years ago, when Casper had hired Kaia to return jewelry Tina had lifted during a summer stay in the Hamptons. In a switch for her, Kaia had broken *into* homes and left glittering baubles for their owners to find like some kind of Tiffany's Easter Bunny.

And then he'd lied and she'd gone to prison.

Did he think she'd forgotten?

"Why doesn't he just pay for the bracelets?" Kaia interrupted, earning a frown from Tyrone.

"They are not for sale," the weasel said.

Everything's for sale, Kaia thought cynically. Casper must have balked at the price. "Then—" She broke off when she felt the unsubtle pressure of Tyrone's big foot against hers.

"In any event, Mrs. Nazario has stated that she already returned the bracelets, and, indeed, they are not in the jewel safe." Alvin Rathers shifted, struggling against sinking further into the sofa. "However, Mr. Nazario has remembered that Mrs. Nazario installed a safe or safes for her personal use, ones to which Mr. Nazario does not have access."

He didn't even know how many? Kaia perked up. Okay, now *this* was great. Anything that caused Casper to suffer was great.

"It is possible that Mrs. Nazario placed the bracelets in them for safekeeping and has forgotten."

Kaia was especially proud of her restraint in letting this whopper pass unchallenged.

The weasel withdrew a legal-looking paper from his briefcase. "Mr. Nazario wishes to hire Miss Bennet to locate and open the safe and/or safes and examine the contents for these two bracelets." He placed a photograph on the coffee table and slid it toward her.

Kaia saw two wide cuffs set with a lot of turquoise chunks and some designs that looked vaguely American Indian. Strikingly beautiful, sure, but she'd been expecting diamonds at least.

"If Miss Bennet identifies said bracelets, she will—"

"Identifies to the best of her ability as a non expert," inserted Tyrone, who was studying the printed agreement.

Alvin smiled. "I'll concede the point, although a case can be made as to her expertise."

"Actually, not," Kaia said, just to keep things moving along. "I don't know anything about turquoise. That is why I'm not the person for this job. Sorry." She stood.

Tyrone spoke, "Let's acknowledge that we're all aware that prior to her employment with Guardian, Mr. Nazario retained Kaia's services—"

He made her sound like a hooker.

"—and they had a disagreement over terms."

Disagreement? She gave Tyrone a hard look. "He gave me the Cat's Eye pendant and then claimed I stole it rather than admit the truth to his wife. I went to *prison*."

"There was no record of your agree—" the weasel began.

"There will be this time," Tyrone said.

"There won't be a 'this time.' Look." Kaia held up her hand. "The thought of Casper Nazario makes me so angry my hand shakes. I can't crack a safe with shaking hands."

"Will telling you that Mr. Nazario will be paying double the fee, of which you'll receive fifty percent, help you get over the shakes?" Tyrone asked.

Kaia's hand stilled. "Yes." She sat back down. She wanted to tell herself that it wasn't just because of the money; there had to be more to this than a couple of turquoise cuffs and she was curious to discover what was really going on. But it *was* about the money.

The weasel managed to sneer without moving his lips. "Excellent decision, since I imagine the fee will be quite high due to the constraints."

"What constraints?" Kaia asked suspiciously.

"We require the utmost discretion in an extremely delicate situation." The weasel began removing folders and papers from his briefcase. "Mrs. Nazario is to remain unaware of any attempt to locate and, if located, retrieve the bracelets."

"Like she's not going to notice when they disappear?" Talk about denial.

"If so, she will not suspect Mr. Nazario, who will be in London when you search tonight."

"*Tonight* tonight? In the Hamptons?"

"No. At the Alexandria home."

Just across the river in Virginia, but still. She'd never been in that house. Trying not to be flattered that he thought so highly of her skills, Kaia shook her head at Tyrone. "I need time to study the floor plan and the security system, not to mention assemble any equipment I need. I don't even know what kind of safe—or safes—I'll be dealing with. This is a two-part job. First, I need to locate them and then come back with my equipment."

"Impossible. Tonight presents a unique opportunity and we must take advantage. You'll have access to the house." Alvin unfolded a copy of blueprints that covered the table. "Mrs. Nazario is hosting a trunk show for Royce, the designer to whom the bracelets belong."

Royce? Unreal. She hadn't had contact with Royce in years. She hadn't had contact with anyone from her former life in years.

"I've arranged for you to act as his assistant tonight."

"You want me to steal the bracelets during a party?" In spite of herself, Kaia felt her pulse quicken.

The weasel winced. "Not steal—"

Kaia waved her hand. "Words to that effect."

Some of that old feeling started pumping through her. The anticipation, the rush, the challenge and excitement. The possibility. The outrageousness of it all. Stealing jewelry from the hostess during a party. And not just any party, a *jewelry* party with extra security. If she pulled it off, it would be a high like she hadn't experienced since...since before. Since being part of her family's long, intricately planned thefts where the risk was great, but so was the payoff.

She supposed her parents and uncle were still running their cons out there. Somewhere. Without her. Because she was on the side of the law now. To be honest—ha—there wasn't a whole lot of difference on this side, except that she had to give the stuff up and her thefts were sanctioned. Tyrone saw to her legal protection and her boss assumed responsibility for her during her probation. It wasn't all out of the goodness of his heart; Kaia had made a lot of money for Guardian. And it sure beat going back to prison.

"So the designer knows what's up?" she asked, wondering if Royce had mentioned that they knew each other. Or had known each other. She wasn't admitting anything if he hadn't. That info was on a need-to-know basis and no one needed to know.

"Yes. He understands the need for discretion."

I'll bet he does. "I don't suppose we're providing security tonight."

"No," Tyrone said, neutrally. "Nor did we install the specialized features on the premises. The Nazarios are great patrons of the arts and frequently host exhibitions in conjunction with fundraisers in their home."

"You're talking museum-quality security, aren't you?" Kaia asked. "Lasers. Gates. Pressure pads. All custom. And no time to practice?" There was a difference between a challenge and an impossibility.

"I don't know the details," Tyrone said and shifted his gaze to the lawyer.

From his briefcase, Alvin had withdrawn a matte gold, silver and black folder obviously containing the system schematics. He hesitated, wearing an expression of pained conflict.

"She's bonded," Tyrone reminded him. And possibly, Kaia, too.

Just looking at the cover told Kaia that the system was first-rate. It probably cost ten bucks just to print the folder.

Carefully, the weasel set it in the middle of the coffee table. "Security was recently upgraded," he said as Kaia reached for the folder.

Joy. There was most likely some new twist she didn't

know about. "Can we consider bringing the party rent-a-cops in on this?" She lifted the edge. "I mean, come on."

"Absolutely not," Alvin said.

Kaia stared at the first page of the complex setup. What a challenge. She would have loved to have beaten this system, but without the time to properly prepare, she didn't have a chance. "If—no, when—I trip an alarm, it's going to cause a lot more attention than telling the security detail to give me access. Isn't there some sort of professional courtesy thing among security peeps?"

"As in 'look the other way while we rob your client'?" Tyrone asked. "Mmm...not that I recall."

Kaia grinned up at him. The gleam in his eyes told her he'd like nothing better than to beat the other company. She flipped through more papers. "So who got tonight's gig?"

Just as her fingers paused on a cover letter outlining the number of personnel who would be on site and the screening process for the staff and guests she heard, "Blake McCauley at TransSecure."

Kaia froze.

"TransSecure designed the system for the house, as well. That's their folder you're looking at."

Blake McCauley. Nothing in Tyrone's voice suggested the name meant anything to him other than as a competitor. She stared at the paper with the silver, black, and gold logo, and Blake McCauley's signature at the bottom, and hoped they would think she was reading the letter and not fighting to regain her balance. Yeah. She'd just been congratulating herself for never being caught off-balance except once. Blake was the once.

Blake McCauley. It had to be the same guy, because

that was just the way her day was going. Though when she'd known him, he'd been a police detective.

And her lover.

Unwanted memories flickered through her mind. His touch, mostly. Her family weren't touchers or huggers, unless they were picking someone's pocket. But from the moment she and Blake had been caught in a sudden downpour and he'd wrapped his strong arm around her shoulders, drawing her close enough to share his umbrella, she'd craved his touch. When she was in his arms, the terrible loneliness vanished. Until Blake, she hadn't realized she was lonely. She'd thought she was self-sufficient.

She'd been staring at the paper so long, her eyes started to sting. She blinked and the words slid into focus. Years ago, the need for Blake's touch had blinded her to caution and everything else. Even worse, she'd known and hadn't cared. She hadn't just been off balance; she'd completely fallen. No, Blake McCauley had been far more than just a fling. He'd been the love of her life.

Right up until he handcuffed her and sent her off to prison.

3

"I MADE IT VERY CLEAR to Mrs. Nazario that there were to be no changes to the guest list." As he spoke into the headset, Blake watched his people check-in tonight's catering staff and attach a discreet button to their uniform collar. The button was an RFID transmitter so their whereabouts could be monitored. Anyone who decided to go wandering around the house would set off an alert.

"Some lady's grandson is in town and she wants to bring him," a young voice explained.

Summer interns. Ya gotta love 'em. "Tell her no, Justin."

"But Mrs. Nazario already told her it would be okay."

Blake exhaled heavily. He'd never understand why people hired security and then did their best to sabotage it. He had very specific requirements when he agreed to a job and as a result, there had not been a single, unresolved negative incident in the five and a half years he'd been transporting and guarding valuables. A perfect record in an industry where reputation and trust were hard to earn and easy to lose, that was why he'd decided to spend this morning on site instead of letting his supervisor take care of the setup for tonight's party alone.

"I'll handle Mrs. Nazario. You vet the grandkid."

"But it's Friday!" Justin protested. "I only work a half-day on Fridays."

"How would you like to have every Friday off?"

"Wow, really?"

"Sure," Blake told him cheerfully. "And while you're at it, take Mondays through Thursdays, too."

"But...that would mean I'd work weekends."

Blake said nothing. Justin was Luke's sister's kid, a college freshman, and Luke was Blake's best supervisor. This was a favor, he reminded himself. He could stand it until...let's see; it was the end of June...when did college start up again, anyway?

As most people did, Justin filled the silence with blathering. "I mean, my weekends are... Oh. I get it. You weren't really—"

Blake inhaled.

"I'll get the info ASAP," Justin blurted out before Blake could speak.

"You do that."

Blake's hand was halfway to his earpiece when Justin yelled, "Wait—there's something else!"

"What?"

"Or...or maybe not. I don't know."

"Justin."

"Well, the designer guy is there setting up, you know? And he brought an assistant with him."

"Yes?" Blake glanced impatiently at his watch. Checking in the kitchen staff was taking too long and now Luke appeared to be having a confrontation with a delivery truck driver. Blake needed to see what that was all about.

"Except there isn't an assistant listed, you know, on the list."

Justin suddenly had all Blake's attention.

"I mean, it makes sense that he'd have one, but—"

"I'll look into it." Blake started to disconnect, then added, "Good catch." It wasn't often he found something to praise the kid for.

As he walked across the pebbled drive toward Luke and the delivery truck, Blake thumbed the keypad of a handheld computer and brought up the master list of everyone who would be present tonight.

The designer was listed as Royce—no last name. Or possibly no first name. Certainly no assistant, unless he or she was listed as a guest.

Blake touched the screen and a layout of the house appeared. He pressed the party room and an instant later, the voice of his man located there sounded in his earpiece.

"Josef."

"Do you have eyes on Royce?"

"Yes."

"Is there an assistant with him?"

"Yes, along with a mess of decorators."

"They'll be leaving. Find out if the assistant will be at the party. Anyone who stays gets tagged, including the designer."

"Copy that."

Blake stared at the room layout. There were too many exits and a whole lot of glass. He tapped the screen again.

"Josef, secure the jewelry until the room is clear."

"You got a spare man?" Josef asked.

"I'm on my way."

But just as he disconnected, the driver of the delivery van lost his cool. Luke didn't, which infuriated the man even more.

His arms waved out the window. "I've got three more setups scheduled!"

Blake ambled over, deliberately low-key. Luke was on the phone.

"What's up?"

The man erupted again as Luke met Blake's eyes and took a step away.

"I'm supposed to install an awning over the driveway! There's gonna be rain and wind tonight. There's a cool front south of here that's moving up the coast and it's causing all kinds of problems."

Involuntarily, Blake glanced skyward. "We weren't informed about an awning installation."

"I'm informing you! I'm informing you I got two other installs after this. I gotta get goin'!"

"I understand. We're verifying the job order now."

As Blake spoke, Luke caught his eye and shook his head. "Mrs. Nazario is at the spa and can't be disturbed."

Great. "Who's in charge?"

Luke cracked a smile. "You are."

"Yeah, I figured. Okay, search the van and let the man get to work." Blake scanned the area and pointed to a security camera with a view of the front entrance. "The awning will block that camera."

Luke nodded. "I'll move it."

"No," Blake said slowly with another glance at the sky. "If it does rain, then the valets will hang out under the awning making it easy for someone to slip past. Add another camera beneath the awning."

"Gotcha." Luke tapped at his phone and walked to the rear of the van where the driver waited impatiently.

Originally, Blake had only planned to be here for a few hours before heading back to his D.C. office, but he'd since decided to stay. The Nazarios had sunk a big chunk of change into a security system upgrade, which he'd designed. There had been a rash of thefts in the area and he wanted to verify that all was working correctly. Not that he thought there would be an attempt on the Nazario party tonight. In his lifetime, first as a police detective and now as a security specialist, Blake had only met one thief with the skills and audacity to hit the house tonight.

Kaia Bennet.

A memory of her face, pale with straight, dark hair, flashed in his mind as it often did when he worked a complicated job. What would she see? How would she elude the security? He caught himself trying to think the way she would think and analyze the obstacles the way she would because, even after all this time, Blake knew that he designed every system with her in mind. She was the best he'd ever encountered—as a thief *and* a lover.

Even after six years, he remembered the feel of her in his arms, her scent, her taste, and how her body fit perfectly next to his. He missed sleeping with her. Not just the sex, but actually sleeping. Something about the sound of her breathing and the weight of her body in his bed gave him the most restful nights of his life.

He thought of her smile lighting up her face when she saw him and the way it made him feel, or the way he'd felt before the night he realized it had all been a lie. She was a thief and a good one from a family of thieves.

But his time with her had felt real—more real than any relationship since. Except he hadn't had a relationship since Kaia. He'd had encounters. Empty encounters.

He was usually pretty good about remembering the thief part and forgetting the lover part. Not today. Not this week. Her last job before going to prison had been stealing a diamond pendant from the Nazarios.

His last case before quitting the force had been recovering that diamond pendant for the Nazarios.

And that's all he was going to think about that. It was done. The past.

As he headed to the large room where the party would be held, he gave a last visual sweep of the side and front entryway, noting the blind spots that would be caused by the awning. Yeah, it was a good decision to be here tonight. What with the weather, the jewelry, and all the extra people, coupled with a hostess who was playing loosey goosey with his security procedures, Luke could use the help.

Just in case.

KAIA STOOD IN THE middle of the party room and took in the huge Alexandria home. Clearly, Casper could afford to keep covering his wife's habit. Or maybe he'd simply stopped, because Kaia sure wouldn't be here if his wife had.

"Stop staring at me like that," she murmured to Royce, her gaze systematically locating all the glass-break sensors and security cameras.

"You don't look any worse after your stay in the clink."

"You sound like a movie gangster."

"I'm not up on prison slang."

Kaia glanced over her shoulder and resumed her systematic cataloging to verify that there hadn't been any changes from the schematics the weasel had given her. "Neither am I. I've been out nearly three years."

"Time off for good behavior?"

"Something like that."

She felt Royce move closer. "Are we sticking with the we've-never-met-before plan?"

"Except for those who think I'm your assistant."

"So very complicated. Why don't you become my assistant for real? You could."

"No."

Royce chuckled. There was a touch of a British accent to his voice. Fake, of course. The more expensive the jewelry, the heavier his accent.

"Oh, I think you could." He stepped away. "Kaia, look."

When she turned, he held up two rings, then closed his fingers over them. "Which one?"

It was an old game, a party trick. Her father had liked to show off his little girl's precocious ability. Kaia didn't want to play, but rather than make Royce curious about why she didn't, she answered, "The one in your left hand. It's an eleven carat pear-cut aquamarine surrounded by diamonds. The ring in your right hand is blue topaz, surrounded by white topaz, or maybe zircon, if you got a good deal."

Royce raised his eyebrows. "You haven't lost your touch."

Kaia reached for the two rings. "Neither have you." Making a costume jewelry copy of the original piece was Royce's shtick. What the clients did with it was up to them.

"So what are you doing in the security biz, Kaia? I

can understand you going legit, but not that way. Don't get me wrong, I'm grateful for your help tonight, but you have a gift. With an eye like yours, you could make a fortune as a gem buyer."

Oh, yeah. Kaia knew, but didn't feel like sharing the terms of her probation. She handed the rings back to Royce. "I need to polish my good-girl image first."

"You *have* a good-girl image?"

"See?" They both laughed and began unfolding the legs of the little round pedestals Royce would drape in black velvet and use to display his pieces.

"Sooo," Kaia began after checking that they were out of earshot of the decorators, "what's with the bracelets? Why didn't you just let Casper buy them for his wife?"

"They aren't for sale." And how interesting that he spoke without a trace of a British accent in his voice.

"Yeah, I heard that. What's the story?"

Royce pulled a table leg into position with an audible click. "We couldn't come to terms."

Kaia responded with a click of her own. "Okay, so what's the truth?"

"The cuffs are mourning jewelry." He glanced at her. "Jewelry incorporating hair of the deceased—"

"Yes, I know." And, ew.

"The value is more in the sentiment than for the stones so I wasn't sure you were aware of that particular genre," Royce explained.

"Fair enough."

"Except in this case, I reworked native American silver and turquoise, so there is quite a lot of historical value. You've seen the pictures?"

She nodded.

"The markings are a family history." He stopped working with the tables and held her gaze. "My family."

"Ohhh."

Drawing a breath, Royce concentrated on the tables. "I was entrusted with consolidating the separate pieces into the cuffs."

"So how the *hell* did Tina Nazario get your family history? And *why* the hell are you having anything to do with her!"

"Keep your voice down!" Royce shot a look around the room, but the decorators and florists were lost in their own worlds. "I can't afford to alienate Tina Nazario."

"With friends like that..."

Royce exhaled heavily. "Come on, Kaia. You know how it works."

"Oh, yeah."

"I wouldn't just lose Tina as a client, I'd lose her entire social set. And look." He gestured around. "See what she's doing for me?"

"Her way of paying for the bracelets? Which you still haven't explained how she got."

"I lent them to an exhibit of Native American jewelry with the proviso that they wouldn't be removed from the case. And then the photographers arrived and wanted to photograph Tina wearing the cuffs in the Wonder Woman pose—you know, arms crossed, ready to fend off bullets."

"Actually, I don't know, but I get the idea."

"Oh, I forgot. While some kids were watching TV after school, you had to go to cat burglar classes."

Kaia leveled a look at him. "For that you should be grateful."

"I apologize." Royce inclined his head. "I am grateful—or I will be."

"So you let them take the pictures and Tina waltzed away with the cuffs?"

"I watched. I never took my eyes off them and then a reporter wanted to ask a few questions and people wanted to see the bracelets up close. I lost sight of Tina in the crowd, and next thing I knew, she was gone."

"And when you asked for them back?"

"After my calls were finally returned, I was allowed to come here and fetch the cuffs. At that point, I was presented with two contemporary silver and turquoise bracelets. They weren't even my design." Royce looked so disgusted that Kaia had to smother a smile. "And Tina was out of the country."

"Nice." Kaia wouldn't insult him by asking if it were possible that Tina had simply been confused. It was funny—she and Tina had a lot in common what with both of them being thieves. Except for the fact that Tina was the trophy wife of the man Kaia hated most in the world, they might have been friends.

"She's borrowed before and Mr. Nazario has always paid my invoice," Royce said.

Kaia nodded. "But this time is different. I'm suddenly highly motivated to use my evil talents for the forces of good." Funny how when Tina took something, it was called *borrowing,* but when Kaia took something it was called stealing.

"I'll be in your debt." The way Royce said it, Kaia knew the sentiment carried real weight.

"Let's hope so. This is top-notch security and I'll be winging it."

It was a good story and Kaia knew Royce believed that was all there was to it. However, Casper was forking over some major bucks and had sought out Kaia, so she knew it wasn't because he cared about Royce's family history.

Casper cared about reputation and social standing, the true precious gems of his world. He was powerful enough and wealthy enough to put a reasonable spin on the loss of a couple of turquoise bracelets belonging to a moderately well-known jewelry designer.

There was something else going on here. She was not the only person in the world capable of a job like this. Casper had insisted on Kaia—the woman he'd lied about—specifically. Why would he think he could trust her after sending her to prison?

If Kaia managed to get into Tina's secret safe—which sounded like the title to a porno movie—she was going to take a look around.

She lined up the tables and shook out the velvet cloths. "These are wrinkled. Did you bring a steamer?"

"Yes. Oh, don't cluster," Royce directed, British accent back in place. "Sprinkle them lightly throughout the room."

Kaia gave him a you've-gotta-be-kidding-me look as he waved his arms around.

Whatever. Grabbing the steamer, she dutifully sidestepped one of the florists who was fussing with a centerpiece and carried the table and cloth to the far end of the room.

And while she was there, she stuck her head through the doorway. According to the floor plan, the neighboring room was a study. Now whether it was Casper's or his wife's, she didn't know, but studies were always good places for safes.

Dark wood, heavy desk. Too masculine for Tina, so it must be Casper's. Still, there were French doors on the other side of the room. Knowing where the exits were always came in handy. Holding the steamer in one hand and the plug in the other, as though looking for an electrical outlet, Kaia stepped into the study and crossed quickly to the doors. She scanned the frames and looked across the side yard to the front drive. Workers were installing an awning while a security guy attached a camera to an extension rod. Swell. Blake had everything covered. Clearly, he remembered all the little tips she'd given him thinking it would help keep him safe in his work. To her, clever ways to elude security had been pillow talk, something that excited her. To him, it had been valuable insight into a thief's mind. And incriminating evidence against her.

Oh, and let's not forget that Blake had obviously parlayed what he'd learned into an elite company designed to thwart, well, people like her.

Kaia drew a deep breath against a microscopic, but unwanted, flicker of pride.

Behind her, the door clicked softly closed.

Fixing a smile as she turned around, Kaia said, "I was looking for an outlet for the steam—er."

Casper Nazario stood in front of the door. A little grayer and no doubt a lot wealthier. She should have expected they would end up coming face-to-face because, you know, this really was turning out to be one of those this-is-your-life days.

"Hello, Kaia."

At least it wasn't *Hiya, Kaia*. "Liar, liar, pants on fire. You're not in London."

He gave a wintry smile. "I'm so glad prison didn't dull your intellect."

"It's my skills you hope weren't dulled. I suppose you're going to tell me why I'm really here?"

Casper crossed to the desk. Sitting, he unlocked the bottom drawer.

Kaia rolled her eyes. As if a four-year-old with a paper clip couldn't open a desk drawer.

"I know what you're thinking," Casper said.

Unlikely.

"But most people don't have your skills."

He was close enough. Horrors. She was becoming predictable.

He tossed a slim brochure onto the desktop. "I lock it to keep out the amateur snoopers." He opened up the laptop and plugged in a flash drive. "Go ahead." He gestured to the flyer.

It meant that Kaia would have to relocate closer to Casper and farther away from the French doors, but she might as well suck it up and see what he wanted.

A photograph of an ornately jeweled snuffbox immediately caught her attention. Fabergé, or done in that style. Setting the steamer off to one side, Kaia picked up the flyer, that turned out to be an invitation to a dinner at the Lithuanian embassy that had been held a couple of weeks ago.

"She didn't."

Casper gave her a grim look.

She gave him one right back. "Tell me Tina did not steal this."

"I don't know."

"But you suspect."

"But I suspect." At least Casper wasn't pretending any longer.

He turned the laptop around so the screen faced her.

"You know, I like how we can just cut through all the BS and be honest with each other and admit that your wife is a thief."

The muscle bulged in Casper's jaw as he clenched his teeth. Okay, enough baiting of the client. Kaia studied the article on the screen about the gift of the snuffbox from an American company to symbolize the opening of trade something or other that Kaia ignored because it wasn't important. She paged through, looking at the publicity pictures as the box was presented and then at a red-faced chef with an icing tube bent over dozens of other little boxes that looked just like it.

"We attended the dinner," Casper said. "The favors were replicas of the snuffbox made in chocolate."

"And she switched hers for the real thing?" Kaia guessed.

"Apparently. No one noticed for a couple of days."

"You are kidding." She was incredibly impressed with Tina *and* the chef.

Shaking his head, Casper withdrew a white container with a colorful seal on top from the drawer. "They're exquisite. See for yourself." He lifted the lid and the sides folded down. "I put mine in the refrigerator thinking I'd give it to our granddaughter."

Kaia caught her breath. She'd heard of edible gold leaf, but had never seen it up close. And how had the pastry chef made the "jewels" shine? Some kind of sugar? Kaia bent to study it and could see the chocolate lid glistening with moisture from condensation after being in the refrigerator. "Go ahead and put it back in the fridge before it gets ruined."

Casper folded the sides and replaced the lid. "If you don't find the real box, *I'll* be ruined."

Goody, Kaia thought.

Carefully, Casper replaced the chocolate replica in the drawer. "Officials from the Department of State are quietly interviewing all the guests who were present at the dinner that night. It's only a matter of time."

Time before someone—or several someones—said, "Hey, if you're missing something, ask Tina Nazario." Wink wink.

"So that's it." Now everything made sense. "The bracelets were an excuse for you to hire me. You really want me to find the snuffbox?"

"And the bracelets."

Kaia pushed away from the desk. "I was hired to find only the bracelets."

"I am aware of that. I will pay—"

"Not a chance." Snagging the steamer, she started walking out of the room. "If you want to expand the scope of the job, you can talk to Guardian."

"I can't do that."

"Ditto."

"Name your price," he barked.

Kaia could make a dramatic exit, or she could actually name a price. She stopped and turned, but stayed halfway across the room. She was still dressed in the black Guardian suit uniform with all the Guardian-issued equipment, including a cell phone. She pulled it out of her pocket and held it up. "You don't say another word unless my lawyer is on speaker."

Casper automatically made a sound of protest and then slumped, nodding his head.

Oh, man, was he desperate. Kaia thumbed a number. "Tyrone? We've got a situation. I'm putting you on speaker."

There was rustling in the background. "I'm recording," Tyrone said. "Who is present?"

"Me."

Kaia nodded to Casper who said heavily, "Casper Nazario."

She imagined Tyrone making faces, not that Tyrone would ever be so unprofessional. But Kaia liked to imagine it. "Mr. Nazario would like to amend the terms of his agreement with Guardian."

"Continue," Tyrone said.

Kaia waited for Casper to call in Alvin the weasel. He didn't. Holy moley. That meant she was in a most excellent bargaining position.

"While Kaia is retrieving the bracelets, I want her to catalog the contents of the safe," Casper stated.

"And/or safes," Tyrone said.

"Agreed. If she finds a certain snuffbox, I wish her to bring it to me."

"In London?" Tyrone asked, drily.

"At a time and place to be determined."

"We'll determine that now," Tyrone said. "Along with a description of the object."

Kaia really did like Tyrone.

Casper clearly did not. In fact, Kaia noticed quite a similarity between his tight, wrinkled lips and the weasel's. "At the Perking Lot, a coffee shop located within one mile of this address."

"I will not allow my client to leave the premises with any object she does not own."

Casper looked as though he was going to blow a gasket. If he did, it would make her day.

"We'll meet at the pool house at the conclusion of the party."

"I will also be present," Tyrone stated. "Kaia, you do not leave the main house without calling me first. When I arrive, I will notify you and then, and only then, will you proceed to the pool house."

Blake's people would never allow that. "If I can't get to the pool house without attracting notice, what do I do?"

Casper smiled faintly. "Leave the snuffbox in the drawer."

"Specify," Tyrone instructed.

"He's talking about his desk drawer and he keeps it locked."

"Unacceptable," Tyrone said.

"This is absurd!" Casper slapped his hands on the desk and pushed his chair back. "She'll leave it where I tell her to leave it!"

Silence.

"She will leave the object where *I* tell her to."

Atta boy, Tyrone.

Casper's gaze flicked to her. *Yeah, that's right. This time, you're not the only one with high-powered legal backing.*

"Kaia?" Tyrone prompted.

"In the vase on the third shelf, southwest corner of the room."

"In the event that Kaia is unable to take the object to the pool house at the conclusion of the party, she will leave said object in a vase on the third shelf, southwest corner of the room in which you are now present."

"Agreed," Casper snapped.

"I'll need a description of the snuffbox."

"He gave me a picture," Kaia said.

"Fax me a copy?"

Casper exhaled. "Yes, fine."

"And now, remuneration," Tyrone said.

Even though he knew she had the upper hand, Casper met her gaze with contempt.

Contempt. How. Dare. He. Anger bubbled within

her and Kaia ruthlessly contained it. "I want my name cleared. And I want the Cat's Eye. That's my price."

Casper gave a crack of laughter. He was really pushing it for a man on the verge of ruin.

"You're right. Forget it," Kaia said. "Sorry to bother you, Tyrone."

"Wait." And Casper actually chuckled. "One or the other, Kaia. Not both." And there was the contempt again.

He'd just asked her to put a price on her good name. Except, she'd never had a good name. As someone once said—perhaps Casper, himself—if she wasn't guilty of the crime for which she'd been sent to prison, she was guilty of others. True. But having her record expunged and not being subject to the restrictions of her probation would make life a lot more pleasant. And profitable.

"Clear my name," she said, sweetly. "Because, as you know, the Cat's Eye already belongs to me. You'll just be returning it."

Casper was a dangerously powerful man and Kaia was pushing him. If they didn't come to terms, she had no doubt she would meet with an "unfortunate accident" since she now knew about the snuffbox. Tyrone also knew about the snuffbox, which meant he and his family would be at risk, as well. Attorney-client privilege and Kaia being bonded wouldn't matter to Casper.

Failure wasn't an option here. Neither was refusing him, but that didn't mean Kaia was going to back down. Casper would expect it of her.

"No one knows," he said at last. "No one finds out or our agreement is null and void. Agreed?"

"Agreed," Kaia said.

4

BLAKE WALKED INTO THE main party room, stopped, and exhaled. Multiple exits. A wall of windows. Yes, he'd known all this, but the massive bouquets in six-foot urns, the cascading vines of lighting, and the dozen tables covered in black cloths were all new. The lights, okay, he got it, make those jewels sparkle—but how easy would it be to hide jewelry in the flower arrangements and retrieve it later? The jewelry had to sit on something, but the black, floor-length table cloths not only interrupted the line of sight, they provided a hiding place beneath.

Again, people hired security, and then ignored all his advice.

Blake headed toward a man with overly styled hair ending in a ponytail. Yeah, he looked like a Royce. He extended his hand. "Blake McCauley, head of security."

"Royce." The designer shook his hand with a grip that wasn't as effeminate as Blake had expected.

He gazed at the open case of jewelry that gleamed expensively, and noted the sister cases standing to one side. "I'm going to have to ask you to hold off on putting out the jewelry until the temporary staff has exited the premises." Blake accompanied this with a pleasant expression intended to convey that he wasn't asking anything, he was telling.

Royce assessed the room and consulted a fancy watch on a chain. "That won't leave me enough time to construct the displays before the guests arrive."

"There're too many people here for me to guarantee souvenirs won't walk out with them." As he spoke, both men had to step out of the way of a florist blindly carrying a huge arrangement toward the stairs. Pollen from one of flowers left a yellow trail on Blake's sleeve.

Instead of the argument that Blake expected, Royce capitulated and deftly returned the half dozen or so sparkling baubles to the case.

Blake brushed at his sleeve. "I appreciate your cooperation. Do you have an inventory sheet for me?" As he spoke, Blake scanned the room, eyes ever watchful.

Royce removed a printed list from a black folder, and handed a flash drive to him. "Here are the pieces and photographs. The drive contains the detailed specs on the stones as well as any laser IDs. Let's hope you don't need it. And I ask that you don't copy the drive or refer to it unless circumstances warrant it." And there was Blake's own pleasant this-is-not-a-request smile aimed right back at him.

Okay. Some day, if he had time, Blake might amuse himself by delving into Royce's background. A pity that it was unlikely he would ever have time. "Mind if I verify the list against the contents of the cases?"

"Yes," Royce said. "I do mind."

Tough. "You understand there can't be any claims of theft unless TransSecure certifies a piece was brought to the party."

Royce held his gaze a moment, and then shrugged and opened the first of the cases. "This will take some time."

"Perhaps your assistant can help. I was told you brought one with you." Blake made a show of looking around. "But such a person is not on my list."

"She is now," Royce said easily.

"And where is this assistant?"

"Assisting."

"If you want her to remain this evening, I'll need a name."

"Why ever does it matter?"

"Background check."

Royce chuckled. "That's hardly necessary."

He was hiding something. "How well do you know this assistant?"

"All her life. My niece, Samantha Whitefeather. Home from college, needed a summer job. She's family." Royce smiled. "You know how that goes."

Blake made a note. "Actually, I do."

Royce pointed to the open case. "Case C. Ready?"

At Blake's nod, he said, "Number forty-three, Tahitian pearl choker—the eighteen inch, not the fifteen inch."

Blake put a tick by the necklace Royce indicated.

"Aquamarine ring, sixteen carats."

Aquamarine was a bluish stone. There were four rings with blue stones. Blake studied the case. Sixteen carats was big, right?

Royce pointed to the ring. If Blake had packed the cases, he would have lined up the list and the jewelry in the same order.

"Aquamarine, fourteen carats with ten diamonds."

Blake ticked it off.

"Aquamarine..."

He was already impatient. Josef was supposed to be in here watching the room—where was he? For that matter, where was Royce's assistant? She could make the whole tedious process go faster.

"Pavé chocolate and yellow diamond leopard bracelet..." Blake marked it.

"The other," Royce corrected. "That's the cheetah."

For the love of—"Hang on." Blake pressed his earpiece. "Josef? Where are you?"

Across the room, Josef turned and held up his hand. Blake gestured for him to come there. "My associate will finish up," he told Royce. "I'll see what I can do to hurry the decorators along and give you some more time."

CASPER HAD ACTUALLY caved. Kaia was feeling pretty darn good as she made her way back to Royce and the hired muscle standing with him.

Sure, she totally expected Casper to try to pull something, but Tyrone had faxed him a contract addendum and wouldn't let Kaia say one word until Casper signed it and faxed it back.

Kaia almost wished Casper *would* try something. Yeah, bring it on. There was only one, tiny, hardly-any-big-deal thing standing between her and the freedom to do what she wanted—she actually had to find the snuffbox and she had to do it without anyone besides her, Tyrone, and Casper knowing about it. Shouldn't be a problem. Kaia wasn't exactly planning to announce her activities to the world.

If she got caught, things would get tricky, but not impossible, at least not for her. Casper wouldn't dare press charges because the get-out-of-jail-free pass Tyrone had made him sign was proof that he suspected his wife had stolen the box. But if Kaia got caught, she could kiss the Cat's Eye diamond pendant goodbye.

She didn't plan to get caught.

Who ever did?

"Glad you could join us," Royce said after he and the muscle initialed a list and the guy took off.

"I was looking for an outlet and then I steamed the cloths." Kaia knew Royce wasn't really griping about her being gone for so long. It was all for show and anyone who might overhear.

"And did you find everything okay?"

"Casper keeps chocolate locked in his desk drawer," Kaia said.

"Shh!" Royce darted a look around.

"Nobody's paying any attention to us. And you didn't think finding the bracelets was going to be that simple, did you?"

"Somebody might be paying attention. The place could be bugged. I get the feeling that nothing much gets past these guys." He handed her a container with velvet display stands and cubes and cylinders of various heights. "The head guy made me give him my assistant's name for a background check."

Kaia went on alert. "And did you?"

"I gave him Sam's. I hope she's been a good girl."

Kaia relaxed marginally. She'd been too smugly complacent after besting Casper. She should never get complacent. Ever. "Thanks."

"Don't mention it. Really. Don't mention it."

"Sam I am?"

Royce gave a crack of laughter that caused a little hairy dog on the landing above them to start yipping. "I don't think we need to go that far."

As Kaia watched, a woman swooped up the dog and carried it off. "That reminds me, I'm going to have to find an excuse to go upstairs and look around." Two decorators wound floral garland between the slats of the banister. One was on a ladder and the other, who'd returned from wherever she'd stashed the dog, knelt on the landing.

"I've learned that we're all going to be tagged tonight," Royce said.

"RFID?"

"I have *no* idea what you're talking about."

"Radio Frequency IDs. Little transmitters—stores use them for inventory control, passports have them embedded, the toll road tags use them," Kaia explained. "They're everywhere. You should look into getting some for your jewelry. Then when pieces walk off, you'll know where they are."

"Oh, hon, that sounds expensive and I don't have that kind of money." And how ironic that Royce was hovering over cases filled with thousands of dollars worth of jewelry.

But Kaia believed him. "And you never will if you keep giving out free samples." She gathered a stack of display stands and headed to another set of tables.

Royce made a face at her. Laughing, Kaia chose the table closest to the stairs, slipped behind a floral arrangement that cost who knew how much, and set her stands on the lower steps. Glancing around, she glided up the stairs, managing to avoid being seen by the decorators only to hear yipping and growling down at her feet.

Kaia growled back.

There was silence as dark brown eyes peered at Kaia through silky strands of blond hair that looked as though they'd been given expensive highlights. A pink tongue licked out.

"What are you doing up here?" The two decorator women regarded her suspiciously.

Kaia hardly felt it was their place to question her. "I'm supposed to tell you that Mrs. Nazario doesn't like the floral garland. She's decided to go with greenery only."

Their expressions didn't change. "Really," said the one on the ladder.

Tough crowd.

"No, not really," Kaia said sarcastically. "I'm looking for the bathroom."

"Look downstairs." They went back to fastening the garland. "I'm the only one who has permission to be upstairs," the woman who knelt added. The dog barked as if in agreement.

As Kaia glared at it, the dog stole a piece of ribbon and ran off, the spool unwinding behind it.

"Jo Jo!" The kneeling woman struggled to get up, muttering, "Stupid dog."

"I'll get her." Kaia, no fan of dogs—were any cat burglars?—headed down the hallway after Jo Jo.

Jo Jo very obligingly trotted into the master bedroom and Kaia trotted right after her.

"Hey! You shouldn't go in there!" she said and stomped her foot, scaring the dog into scurrying under the bed.

Thus, she was on hands and knees, talking baby-talk to the dog when the other woman arrived, huffing and puffing. "Jo Jo, come on out, sweetie."

The dog watched her carefully while chewing the ribbon.

"I don't know who you are, but—"

Kaia looked over her shoulder. "I'm Royce's assistant and pardon me for trying to do you a favor." She scooted backward and stood. "But hey. You're welcome to crawl under the bed after the dog." They both knew that there was no way the woman was going to fit beneath the bed.

The decorator glared at the bed with loathing. "Jo Jo's supposed to be in the hall bathroom, but she kept scratching and making such a fuss, we let her out."

Kaia smiled her best trust-me smile. "I'll get her and put her in there for you."

There was an insultingly long pause.

Her trust-me smile had never worked very well with other women.

"Just don't let her swallow any of that ribbon," the decorator said with ill grace. "She likes to eat stuff she shouldn't."

Kaia kept smiling as the sounds of Jo Jo gnawing on ribbon came from under the bed. "I'll have better luck with little Jo Jo alone."

The woman glared at her, obviously not trusting Kaia. Okay, so Miss Capri Pants was a good judge of character. They had a little stare down and it wasn't until a truly disgusting choking sound came from Jo Jo that the decorator reluctantly left the room. Kaia scooted beneath the bed. "All right, you mangy mutt, drop it!"

Startled, the dog did just that. Kaia pulled the ribbon away and then maneuvered completely under the bed with a speed that stunned Jo Jo. Kaia grabbed her and was back on her feet fast enough to allow for a quick look around the bedroom before Capri Pants became suspicious. From the plans the weasel had shown her, Kaia knew there was a wall safe behind a flat-screen TV in the bedroom, but didn't waste her time checking it out. Taking a chance, she opened the door to a closet full of suits, shut that door, and opened the next one, that was a fantasy closet that could have doubled as a guest room.

Tina's, obviously. With Jo Jo snuffling at her ear, Kaia searched the floor, finally discovering the tell-tale seam of carpet she was looking for beneath a chest. A floor safe. Had to be. But she was out of time.

She backed out, grabbed the ribbon and avoided Jo Jo's tongue. The stupid dog seemed to think Kaia was her new best friend.

Kaia was not.

She would have liked to check out the other rooms, but the decorators were already suspicious, so she carried Jo Jo down the hall. "Where's the bathroom?"

Capri Pants gave her a head nod. "On your left."

There was something else on Kaia's left—the metallic edge of a security gate recessed into the wall. A latch was on the opposite wall, a few feet before the landing overlooking the party room. Someone had tried to disguise the edge of the gate with a trellis-type stencil. Someone had not done a very good job. Probably the grumpy decorator.

This was a new wrinkle in an already-serious security system. Kaia knew that when an alarm was tripped, this gate and any other gates that had been installed, would seal off the hallway, either keeping out an intruder or trapping one until the police and security company arrived.

The gate was not on the plans the weasel had shown her. Of course not. But there was nothing to be gained by keeping the information from her, so Kaia's guess was that Alvin didn't know about it. Maybe Casper didn't, either. Kaia could see traces of Sheetrock crumbs on the edge of the carpet next to the baseboard. Either the system had been recently installed, like within the last week, or Mrs. Nazario had lazy cleaning staff.

Kaia was going to bet that the gates were new.

So where were the rest located? And how would she get around them if she tripped the alarm? Speaking of which, where were the alarms? There were certainly new ones, probably laser-powered. What fun.

Kaia took the tail-thumping Jo Jo into the bathroom, and then flushed the toilet for effect as she stood on it and ran her fingers around the window. Jo Jo gave a sharp bark of protest at being set down.

The window was a hexagon shape that looked out onto a steep dormer and a whole lot of pebbled concrete below. The window was small, so small it didn't have any sensors attached to it. Only a very slim, very athletic person would be to be able to climb out of this window.

Someone like Kaia.

Unfortunately, the bathroom was on one side of the gate and the bedroom was on the other. That meant there was something to protect in the bedroom. Kaia wasn't discounting the other rooms in that wing, either. In her experience, the master bedroom was the most common place for a safe, with a study coming second. Frankly, if Kaia were installing a safe, she'd bury it in the back yard, but that was just her. Actually, if she really had something to hide, she'd put it at the bottom of a swimming pool and disguise it as part of the maintenance filtering system.

All righty, then. Jo Jo yipped and whined. Absently, Kaia climbed off the toilet and picked up the dog, patting her before she realized what she was doing. Jo Jo licked her wrist. When she went for Kaia's ear, Kaia set her on the floor.

"Jo Jo, I should walk away from this one. Far, far away. Unfortunately, my movements are restricted. Now, girl to girl, I'll admit there was a time when that wouldn't have meant anything, but you know something? I really, really want to pull this off. You see, there was this guy. Isn't it always about a guy? Anyway, he did me wrong and I want revenge. So I'm going to stick around. See you tonight." Kaia headed for the door. "It's too bad Blake will never know that I beat his system."

"CAM 1."

"Check."

"Cam 2."

"Check."

Through his earpiece, Blake listened as Luke did the camera checks with their man in the van parked just inside the front gate at the end of the drive.

He had almost made the mistake of taking over, which would have undermined Luke's authority not only on this job, but on future jobs. Blake had already seen the looks from the crew, but he couldn't very well make a general announcement that the Nazarios were his first big client and he was here because he owed them, without implying that he didn't fully trust Luke.

The irony was that the Nazarios thought they were repaying *him*. Blake had just been doing his job—the one he used to have.

Actually...Blake leaned against the stone half-wall surrounding the kitchen herb garden and watched as the serving staff arrived and was checked in.

Actually, he'd come very close to *not* doing his job

back then. He'd been distracted by Kaia Bennet. He had nearly let her get away with a diamond pendant.

He was not proud of that. He was not proud that she'd tempted him into violating his integrity. Even now, when he thought about it—more often than he'd like to—Blake felt queasy. He'd come to his senses just in time and yet, he still second-guessed himself. Maybe it was her eyes. Or maybe it was the shock in her expression and the way the blood had left her cheeks leaving them a greenish white before going gray.

But was the shock because she hadn't fooled him?

Or because she hadn't been trying?

She was good. Really good, he reminded himself as he had countless times over the years. Trained by her family since birth. He'd made the right call. He knew he had.

It had just taken him too long.

But maybe he hadn't made the right call. And that's what had driven him away from the police force. Blake McCauley could no longer trust his instincts.

He'd started TransSecure and shortly after Kaia Bennet's trial and conviction, Alvin Rathers, the Nazarios' lawyer, had contacted him about security for a charity art exhibit. The Nazarios had passed Blake's name around their social set and that was all it took to make him the go-to guy when someone needed valuables transported.

He smiled to himself. It hadn't taken long for wealthy widows to dust off their diamonds to justify hiring a good-looking bodyguard for the evening. Sometimes Blake felt he was more of an escort service than a security company. But nobody got hurt, which was the point.

Sure he trusted Luke. Absolutely. But he felt better

being on site for the Nazarios tonight. Maybe because jewelry was involved—he didn't know. But his instincts—the ones that he still didn't quite trust—told him to be here.

"THERE JUST ISN'T any place to put your little pin." Kaia smiled up at TransSecure's hired muscle. There were two body types in the security biz—those who looked like the hired muscle they were and those who didn't. Each had their advantages. This type—no neck and overly developed shoulders—was meant to be visible and intimidating.

He'd be a lot more intimidating if he weren't blushing as he stared down at her neckline. "I, uh..."

"Anyway, I work with Royce. It'll be okay." Kaia made as if to move past him.

"Ma'am."

She sighed inwardly. It had been worth a try to avoid wearing the RFID tag. TransSecure had some poor guy stuck in a van watching a bunch of dots on a monitor as they all moved around. It also meant when Kaia's little dot went upstairs, he'd see it. And if she took it off and left it somewhere, the lack of movement would be noticed.

Inconvenient, but she'd think of something. She held out her hand. "May I at least put it some place where it doesn't show?" She smiled her best trust-me smile.

The guard smiled back. "As long as we can receive the signal."

See? Her smiles always worked better with men than with women. Watching him watch her, Kaia slowly slid her fingers beneath the bandeau neckline of her dress and punched the pin through her bra. "How's that?"

"Ma'am?" He looked dazed.

She lowered her voice. "Are you getting my signal?"

He stared at her mouth.

"Hmm?" she prompted.

"What? Oh." Blushing even more, he waved a handheld reader next to her chest and nodded. "Everything looks great. I mean—I'm getting the signal."

"Loud and strong?"

"Uh-huh."

"Good to know." Kaia smiled again, and drifted into the party room. Maybe later she'd drift back and chat with the guy about "all the security" in the house and what Royce could install to "make her feel safer" working in his showroom.

She did look good. It had been a very long time since she'd worn this dress and she never thought she'd wear it again. No ordinary evening gown, the dress could be worn any number of ways and was flowy enough to conceal the tools strapped to her legs. The metallic roping around the bodice and belt was actually real rope, should she need one, and there were pockets within pockets where small objects, like, oh, a snuffbox, could disappear. She wore leggings underneath, just in case she needed to go climbing, say through a small hexagon-shaped window in an upstairs bathroom.

Kaia normally didn't do strapless, but Royce had insisted that she be prepared to model some of his necklaces. He was acting as though he'd forgotten why she was really here. Meaning getting his bracelets back and not the other real reason—finding the snuffbox for Casper. It was complicated.

For just a moment, as she surveyed the party area, Kaia imagined her parents and uncle already working the room, being the perfect guests—as long as you ignored the stealing part.

But they weren't here. They weren't going to be here. Tonight, Kaia was on her own.

THUNDER RUMBLED IN the distance and the wind picked up.

It was dark for seven-thirty on a summer night. A Friday night. A casual meet-for-drinks-after-work date night. If you were dating. Which Blake wasn't. Dating meant planning, meant a relationship, meant commitment. Ever since Kaia, Blake had been going through a let's-not-complicate-things phase.

He sat on the decorative stones by the kitchen and watched the activity. From this vantage point, he could see through the windows where the chefs plated trays of hors d'oeurves and barked at assistants. He watched as the decorators drove off—but not before Luke had the van and personnel inspected. He sat there long enough to see that his men had changed into their dress suit uniforms, and watched the valets receive their instructions and jump to attention as the first of the guests drove up to the awning.

Time to join the party.

As he stepped from beneath the sheltered kitchen area, Blake felt the sudden coolness that heralded a storm. Twenty-four hours ago, it hadn't been on the weather radar. Now it was moving up the coast, fast and furious, but should clear out by the time the guests left.

He could hear the fabric of the dark green awning flapping and started to press his earpiece, but changed his mind. If he used the com system, all his men would hear. He punched in Luke's cell number.

"Yeah, boss?"

"The wind is kicking up. We probably ought to walk around and check wiring and connections, especially on the temporary installs."

"Already on it."

"Good." He should have known. "If you need me, I'll be observing the main room."

Blake positioned himself outside at the center of the windows showing a panoramic view of the long room. Bright lights. Lots of sparkle. A jazz quintet. Black and white clad waitstaff carrying silver trays passed through the crowd. A bartender tossed a shaker into the air and caught it to the amusement of a small group waiting for drinks. Everybody was moving, smiling, looking normal.

The addition of the large floral displays and eleven tall black columns displaying Royce's jewelry crowded the room. Yes, Blake had made a good decision to be here tonight. There was too much going on for a normal crew to keep track of.

Blake scanned the room again, marking reference points, noting the eleven display columns. Except when he counted this time, there were only ten.

He was rusty, he thought, swearing softly when he counted again and came up with eleven.

And then one of the pedestals moved and Blake saw that it wasn't a black-covered column, but a woman in a black strapless gown. A woman with beautiful, creamy shoulders. Lush dark hair twisted up in back. Strong profile. Elegant fingers deftly undoing the clasp on the necklace she wore. Red lips smiling as she held it out for another woman to admire. Gracefully side-stepping to fasten it around her neck. Raising her head to give him his first unobstructed view of her face.

He stopped breathing, not because she was a stunning beauty, although to him she was, but because after years of dreaming about her, he was staring into the face of Kaia Bennet.

5

BEFORE THE PARTY got under way, Kaia pulled out her cell phone and keyed in Tyrone's home number. She called his landline because she wasn't trying to reach Tyrone, who was on alert for her tonight; she was trying to reach his wife. Clearing her throat, she prepared to be casually friendly. And cheery. Or at least pleasant.

"Hi, Yolanda!" she gushed. Too much, too much. Way more than pleasant. Even way more than cheery. She sounded like a pathetically eager geek calling the most popular girl in school.

"Hey, girlfriend."

And that was the way to do casually friendly, even though Kaia wasn't exactly a girlfriend. But she was certainly trying.

Her court-ordered counseling sessions had led to the discovery that Kaia did not have any women friends. Technically, she didn't have *any* friends, but she was afraid of what the counselor would make her do if he found out. Practicing on Tyrone's wife was painful enough. Yolanda was nice and all that, but Kaia wasn't the meet-for-lunch-and-shop type. She was the break-into-your-house-when-you-aren't-home type.

"I wanted to thank you for letting Ty get my back tonight. I know it's your date night."

"Not a prob," Yolanda said, and Kaia could hear the TV in the background. "'Cause you know what I want."

Relaxing, Kaia grinned for real and walked toward Royce. "All I can do is steer Ty in the right direction, but it's going to be an expensive direction."

"Girl, it's our fifth wedding anniversary! For what that man makes me put up with, it had *better* be an expensive direction!"

Kaia laughed, also for real. Maybe this was how women friends talked to each other all the time. Maybe Yolanda hadn't figured out that Kaia had been ordered to find a woman friend outside of work. Maybe Ty didn't mind his wife getting chummy with an ex-con.

As Kaia reached Royce, he stepped back and she got the full effect of the animal-inspired bracelet display he'd been fussing with. She actually gasped. She, who had seen some serious jewels in her day, gasped.

"What? What?" sounded in her ear.

"Leopard," breathed Kaia. "And tiger, and zebra, oh my." The bracelets were so fine. And they looked it. They glittered with the authoritative sparkle the way only real stones could.

"Keep talking."

"I'll do better than that." Quickly, Kaia snapped a photo of the display and sent it to Yolanda. "Incoming. Check it out."

"Hey." Royce raised an eyebrow. "Did you clear photography with security?"

Kaia held the phone away with her thumb over the mouthpiece. "Hey, nothing. I'm making a sale for you."

Squealing sounded from the phone as the picture came through. "See?" she said. "That's my attorney's wife. Their anniversary is coming up and she likes your stuff."

"I hope he's a well-paid lawyer."

Kaia mentally appraised the pieces. Small diamonds, black, white, yellow and brown. Not the best quality, but they didn't have to be. The design and workmanship more than made up for it. In particular, there was a green and black snake meant to coil from elbow to shoulder that Kaia wouldn't mind owning, even if she had to pay for it. "What kind of prices are we talking?"

When Royce told her, Kaia's eyebrows raised. "That's quite the markup."

"While you were in the clink, I got popular."

"Stop it." Kaia gave him a deadly serious look. "Not funny."

Royce held up both hands, palms out.

"Kaia!" Judging by the tone of Yolanda's voice, she'd been trying to get Kaia's attention for a while.

Without looking away from Royce, Kaia spoke into the phone. "I'm here."

"I love the leopard! I *want* the leopard! I *need* the leopard!"

Royce could hear her. "It's cheetah," he murmured, looking heavenward and shaking his head.

"Which one?" Kaia asked.

Yolanda told her and Kaia pointed to the bracelet on the bottom of the artful stack.

"My mistake," Royce said. "It is leopard."

"How much?" she mouthed.

"Thirty-five," he mouthed back.

And he didn't mean hundred. "Seriously?" she mouthed again. Aloud she said to Yolanda, "Let me see what I can do. These are a little pricey." She ended the call. "What are you on?" she asked Royce. "Haven't you heard that we're in a recession?"

"I'm an artist. It's not only about the stones. It's the name and the exclusivity. I never repeat a design. Variations, sure, but each piece is unique, the workmanship impeccable, and the gold solid."

"Oh, please. Spare me the spiel. And the gold would be 22k, not solid."

"That's understood." Royce glanced up at the lights and made several minute adjustments to the bracelets and darned if they didn't sparkle that much more. "I thought the ad copy sounded great. I've found it very effective."

"Bully for you. I want a leopard bracelet and I'm not paying thirty-five."

He arched a brow. Kaia was pretty sure it was plucked. When had Royce become the sort of man who plucked his eyebrows?

"I didn't think you were paying at all," he said.

She smiled.

"For you, thirty."

"Come on, Royce. They're good people."

"How rare." He made a last pass over the display with a jeweler's cloth.

Kaia waited and then said, "You know, I don't blame you for giving my name to Casper's people—then or now."

"I never thought you did." He glanced at her. "Interesting that you should mention it while we're haggling."

Kaia made a tsking sound. "'Haggling is such a common word'." They'd both heard her father say it more than once.

"That it is." Royce stared at the stack of bracelets

and then lifted the top ones and removed the leopard bangle. After examining it, he reached for a folder and opened a monogrammed case filled with colored artist's pencils. "I might be able to make some adjustments and still maintain the integrity of a Royce original." He began sketching.

A Royce original. Kaia turned so he wouldn't see her roll her eyes. She'd known him back when he had two names and worked for her dad making copies of estate jewelry. And some of the copies were actually legit.

Kaia scanned the room, noting the unconscious straightening of the waitstaff and lights shining through the windows as cars arrived at the valet stand. Showtime.

The first guests had spilled into the room when Royce tore out a sheet of paper, held it at arm's length, squinted, and then handed it to Kaia. "Fourteen karat instead of twenty-two, with just enough sparkle to distract from the generous use of enamel. Thirty-five. Hundred."

One tenth the price. Kaia studied the sketch. "You know, Royce, this is so good, it's actually worth the price."

Royce plucked the sketch from Kaia's fingers. "What's her name?"

"Yolanda."

He wrote, "For Yolanda" and signed the sketch with a stylized "R."

Kaia took out her phone and sent a photo of the design to Yolanda. "Now, what about doing something similar with the snake for me?" she started to ask when someone called to him.

"Royce!"

He raised a hand to wave across the room. Kaia

followed his gaze and saw the beautifully groomed trophy wife of Casper Nazario, aka Tina the Klepto.

Quite an age difference between Casper and his wife. Kaia would bet that if Tina were twenty-five years older and had lost her looks, Casper wouldn't be so tolerant of her little idiosyncrasy.

"Duty calls." Royce straightened the bolo tie at his neck.

"I'll let you know what Yolanda thinks," Kaia said.

"Oh, she'll love it," he replied confidently, and spread his arms. "Tina!"

Of course, Yolanda loved it, beyond thrilled to have a Royce original designed especially for her. "He did that? Just now? After you told him about me?" she asked over and over.

"Yes." Kaia laughed. "But I've gotta go. The party's started."

Now all Kaia had to do was convince Tyrone to buy the bracelet. Because that's what a friend would do.

She ignored the unrepentant little voice inside that whined that a true friend would steal it.

Kaia put on the first of the pieces Royce wanted her to model. The heavy necklace was so not her style. A diamond pendant was her style, specifically, a smallish yellow diamond with a black flaw that made it look like a cat's eye. And if all went her way this evening, she'd have it back.

Kaia stood silently behind the main jewelry display, observing the people, getting a feel for the rhythm of the gathering.

Since this was a trunk show, the guests would be trying on the pieces that interested them. Beneath each table was a notebook for orders and sales. Royce had given her a quick overview of his system, but she was more into acquisitions, than sales.

Her eyes were drawn to the knot of people surrounding the hostess. Tina wore a half a dozen bracelets on each arm, a ring on every finger and multiple necklaces, including one she wore as a headband. What piece would she steal as her commission tonight? If she only took one.

Bad Kaia. Tina Nazario didn't steal. She borrowed.

But whatever her faults, Tina sure knew how to throw a party. People poured in, the music was catchy, and the bartender had created colorful "jewel" drinks—diamond, sapphire, emerald, and ruby, all served with a festive rock sugar swizzle stick. If she weren't working, Kaia would have liked to taste them. Unfortunately, drinking on the job slowed her reflexes and she'd need them sharp tonight.

Was she allowed to eat the party food? Kaia wondered as a waiter carrying a silver serving platter passed by. On it quivered gelatin jewels in keeping with the theme. Maybe too much theme.

Time to circulate. Just for grins, Kaia added the snake bracelet to her upper arm, earning her a frown from Royce. She put it back. One piece at a time, he'd said. Fine.

Just as she'd attached the bracelet around the display cylinder, a woman approached.

"What a gorgeous necklace!"

Her cue. "It's one hundred thirty-two carats of matched aquamarine." She hoped Royce hadn't fudged the carat weight in the catalog. "Would you like to try it on?"

As she spoke, lights flickered and flashed, drawing

her attention to the windows. There was lightning in addition to the car headlights.

"Oh, it's that storm! The flooding and wind damage down south has been all over the news," the woman said. "They say it should move through pretty fast."

Kaia hoped so. Weather always stirred up a crowd and tonight, she didn't want anybody stirred up.

She took off the heavy necklace and sidestepped around the shorter woman, bending to fasten it around her neck.

She opened her mouth to assure the woman that it looked beautiful on her but was surprised into a genuine compliment. "Oh, the blue exactly matches your eyes! And it's such a pretty color. Royce has been using aquamarine a lot this season."

She had meant to imply that it was fashionable, but the woman looked disappointed. "Well, I wouldn't want to have what everyone else is having." She frowned and touched the necklace as though getting ready to remove it.

"No, I meant that he acquired several parcels of superior quality stones that have inspired him."

The woman looked doubtful, so Kaia caught Royce's eye and beckoned him over. He practically shot across the room, so Kaia knew either the woman or the necklace was worth serious bucks. Probably both.

"Royce, you just have to see how these stones match her eyes," Kaia said, and stepped back to let Royce do his thing.

He picked up his cue. "You're the only one I've ever seen with true aquamarine eyes. Such a unique look."

Thunder rumbled as lightning flickered and a gust of wind rattled the glass panes. Kaia gazed out to the front drive where red-coated valets jogged back from parking on the street that ran in front of the house. There was a line of cars now. Just how many people had Tina invited?

A crowd would work to Kaia's advantage. There was no way Tina could expect all the guests to use the powder room downstairs. An excellent excuse to go upstairs later, Kaia thought just as several lightning strikes lit up the outdoors.

She saw a figure standing outside looking in at the party as wind swirled the bushes and the valets scurried behind him. Probably one of the security guards. The next crack of lightning was followed by a boom of thunder that caused a few gasps, including Kaia's.

The figure was brightly illuminated for only a second this time, but it was enough to see his face clearly. Blake McCauley.

That was Blake standing out there watching the party. Watching her.

Kaia waited to feel shock or anger or bitterness—something. She'd had more of a reaction just seeing his name this morning. But maybe all the emotional hits she'd taken today had numbed her. Numb was good. She didn't need to battle any emotions this evening.

Ignoring Royce and the woman, Kaia walked over to the windows and tried to see past the reflection of the bright room into the darkness outside. If Blake was out there, he'd already seen her, so there was no point in pretending otherwise. When lightning next flashed into the shadows, the figure was gone, like a ghost—a ghost from her past, if she felt like being dramatic.

Kaia wanted to convince herself that it had been her imagination, that she'd been thinking of Blake, so she'd imagined that she'd seen him, but she was too practical. His company was on duty tonight, so it wouldn't be unreasonable for him to be here, too. And also, hadn't it just been that kind of a day? It was like old home week for her life.

So, Blake was here. And, clearly, he'd seen her and recognized her.

How should she play this? Kaia drew a deep breath, centering herself, remembering the job, which had to come first, and walked back to Royce, who was scribbling in the invoice book. The woman had gone.

"See? You're better at sales than you think," he said and snapped the book closed. "Wear the cabochon rubies next," he ordered. "And refresh your lipstick."

Had he forgotten she didn't actually work for him?

"Go, go, go." He made little shooing motions with his fingers.

Fine. Whatever. Kaia found the necklace Royce wanted her to wear and put it on. Looking at her reflection in one of a cluster of silver picture frames, she refreshed her lipstick.

Behind her, she saw a dark, distorted figure reflected in each of the shiny frames grouped on the bureau.

Blake, she thought as the figure loomed larger. Had to be. Dark and distorted described him perfectly.

ACROSS THE ROOM, Blake swallowed, his mouth dry.

Kaia.

He never thought he'd see her again, at least in person. To be honest, he'd never wanted to see her again, not with her last anguished cry of his name ringing in his ears. And now here she was in the Nazarios' house? She was clearly out for revenge. Too bad for her he'd decided to stay on site for this job.

She wouldn't be expecting him to be here, either. Blake could handle her quietly without disturbing the party guests. He wasn't a police detective any longer, and as long as she hadn't taken anything, he could let her go. *Would* let her go.

But the closer he walked toward her, the closer he wanted to be. Memories bombarded him. Blake had forgotten the strength of his attraction to Kaia. No, not forgotten. He thought he was past it. But, if possible, over time it had become more intense and more baffling. What was this hold she had over him? He did stupid, stupid things when he was around her. And he didn't care. She was like an addiction he had to fight.

Kaia Bennet wasn't a typically pretty woman. Pretty was too soft a word to describe how she looked. She was seductively attractive, alluring more than overtly sexy. Usually, time burnished memories, but in Kaia's case, his memories hadn't done her justice.

Potent. That was the word to describe Kaia Bennet. And dangerous. When he was around her, she filled his thoughts. Truthfully, he thought about her even when she wasn't around.

He couldn't believe she was here tonight. In the open. Not disguising herself as waitstaff or a parking valet. No, she was here, handling the jewels in front of everyone. Didn't they know who she was? This was the fox in the henhouse cliché come to life.

From outside, he'd studied Kaia long enough to realize that she was acting as Royce's assistant. That was bold, even for her. That meant that either the designer had lied to Blake, or Kaia had lied to the designer. Maybe both. She was the guy's niece? No way. These two were partners, probably running some scam. Too bad for Kaia that Blake had decided to be here this evening.

He drew a deep breath. His instincts, his gut, had

told him to be here tonight. It was back—the itch in his mind, the sense that something was off. It had taken six long years for him to trust that feeling again.

He pressed his earpiece. "Luke, you copy?"

"Yeah, go." Static sounded in the background as wind blew into Luke's microphone. That meant he was still outside.

"I need everything you can get on Kaia Bennet and Royce…whatever his other name is. The designer. See if they have a connection."

"K-I—"

"K-A-I-A. Bennet, one T," he spelled impatiently. Didn't the whole world know about Kaia Bennet and the Bennet family? Didn't Luke know about Blake's connection to her? Had he forgotten?

Blake's name had been in all the news stories when he'd testified. He just assumed everyone remembered. Maybe he flattered himself.

"There isn't a Kaia Bennet on the guest list," Luke said.

"There wouldn't be!" Blake snapped. "She's only one of the most legendary cat burglars of the past decade—at least she was before she went to prison. Where she should still be. Why was she paroled so early? Tell Justin to get me that info."

"Yes, sir!" Luke's exaggerated tone let Blake know he was overdoing it. Tough. He would neither acknowledge ruffling Luke's feelings nor apologize. This woman had slipped through his most stringent security procedures and he was damn well going to find out how. And why.

Across the room, Kaia fastened another necklace around her neck. Bloodred stones glistened against white skin.

Desire for her tugged at him. She was so compellingly

beautiful. How could any man in the room look at any other woman? The other women needed jewels to enhance their beauty, but Kaia didn't. Which was ironic, when he thought about it.

He surveyed her for countless minutes, making all kinds of excuses for doing so, fighting an attraction that was just as acute as the first time he'd seen her. If he were the sort of man who believed in spells, he'd claim she'd cast one on him.

If he were the sort of man who believed in love, he'd admit he'd been in love with her. Her appeal wasn't solely in the way she looked. It would have been easier for Blake if it had been. He'd expected an experienced, world-weary criminal, but she'd been skittish and almost shy. Certainly more inexperienced than he'd expected, but she made up for it with endearing enthusiasm.

In short, she hadn't been at all what he'd expected and before he'd known it, he was thinking crazy thoughts about the two of them. Crazy thoughts about being in love.

Blake shifted uncomfortably. It had been a long time since his and Kaia's story had ended, but his lust hadn't cooled. Maybe their unhappy ending had something to do with it.

He stopped fighting his fascination with her and let the emotions wash over him. *Acknowledge. Feel completely. Set aside.*

But hadn't he already felt them completely? Hadn't he set them aside?

Abruptly, Blake headed for the bar. Waving off the bartender, he helped himself to a glass of club soda and squeezed two lime and one lemon wedge into it. He gulped the first mouthful, hoping the bubbly tartness would clear his head.

She had to have cast a spell or the modern variation—drugs. Or maybe her family put something in the air, piped in some narcotic that made them irresistible into the ventilation system of their targets. Blake swallowed another mouthful and let the fizz linger on his tongue.

Kaia turned her back to him and primped in the reflection of a silver frame, drawing her red lips together and reminding him of the way they'd felt and looked as she'd drawn him—

He tossed back the rest of his drink and bit down on a lime. And then he walked over to confront Kaia Bennet.

He stopped a few feet away, uncertain as to the best approach. As he considered his options, the designer swooped between them.

"Mrs. Sanderson wants to see the rubies. Quick, take them off."

"I just put them on." Kaia turned around, an irritated look on her face quickly masked.

She'd always been good with masks.

As she raised her hands to her neck, she also raised her eyes and looked past Royce's shoulder directly at Blake.

His heart tripped a beat the moment their gazes locked. His was searching, he knew it was, and hers was as hard as black diamonds.

As she handed Royce the necklace, the designer turned to see what had captured her attention. Rather than stand there like a dummy, Blake stepped forward.

"This must be your assistant." He spoke first to gain

control of the situation and also to see if Royce would lie to him.

"Yes. Mr. McCauley, is it?"

"Blake." One name was the fashion, right?

Royce gestured. "My assistant, Samantha—" He turned toward Kaia as he spoke.

Blake didn't see her move or change expression, but somehow she tipped Royce off.

"—couldn't be here tonight, so Kaia stepped in," he finished.

"We've met," Kaia said.

They stared at each other and Blake sensed Royce looking from him to Kaia and back.

"Excellent," the designer said. "I'll be taking this to Mrs. Sanderson now." And he slipped away.

Normally, Blake would have watched him leave, but normally he wasn't face to face with Kaia's dark gaze.

Her expression revealed nothing of her thoughts and he only hoped his expression hid the chaotic feelings he battled inside.

She should be the one battling chaotic feelings. She was the one who'd broken the law and he was the one who'd upheld it. He'd been right and she'd been wrong. So why was he torn up about it and how could she continue to look icy cool?

One of them was going to have to break the silence. Blake figured he'd do it. "Does Royce know who you are?"

6

THEY'D COME face-to-face for the first time since her trial and that's what he chose to say?

"And who am I?" She was interested in Blake's answer. Who *did* he think she was? Because clearly, he'd never truly known her. Then again, she'd never truly known him.

"You're a woman who went to prison for jewel theft."

"A woman *you* sent to prison for jewel theft. It doesn't make me a thief."

"I call 'em like I see 'em."

"You need new glasses."

He stared at her for so long, she thought he might be considering her words.

"So what are you doing here, Kaia?" he asked, and she knew he hadn't considered anything.

It wasn't as though she'd been deluding herself that their relationship had meant anything to him. But for him to demonstrate so clearly that no part of it had been real—not his kisses, his touch, or any of the times he'd told her he'd loved her—hurt. A lot.

He'd been undercover. Doing a job. And she'd been

taken in completely. One look into his topaz-brown eyes and she'd been hooked. She was someone else with him, able to try on a different life. A normal life. And then came the moment when she'd told him about her family and what her childhood had been like and he hadn't run screaming into the night. Well, he wouldn't have, would he? He'd already known all about her. "I'm glad you told me," he'd said. "Because now it's your past and you're going to have a whole different future."

That was the truth. And it was also the first time they'd made love. Except, they hadn't made love; they'd had sex. That's what she needed to remember.

Kaia stared into his eyes and wondered how he'd been able to fake it for weeks without her suspecting. His eyes still looked hot and intense, that Kaia, in her inexperience, had interpreted as love, when it had been nothing more than empty desire. He'd had to play a role but that didn't mean he couldn't enjoy it.

Her parents had warned her. She'd been raised not to trust anyone. And when she'd ignored them, they'd abandoned her.

Kaia could tell a fake stone from the real thing with a glance from several feet away, but she couldn't tell empty words from true love. In fact, "You can't trust love," was the last thing her father said to her.

Even now, Blake's eyes told her nothing, but the rest of him telegraphed hostility.

And impatience. She hadn't answered his question. "What do you think I'm doing here?"

"Let's see...a private party, cases of jewels, and a member of a legendary family of cat burglars. What would you think?"

She smiled. "That it's too obvious."

Blake gestured with his chin. "Does Royce know you're a Bennet?"

"Yes."

"Does he know what the Bennets are?"

What, not *who*. "Don't most jewelers?"

"They should." Blake's nod encompassed the room. "And so should everyone here."

"I tell them my name if I'm asked. Just the way you tell them yours."

Blake made a cynical sound. "But nobody asks."

"Nope." She made the *P* pop.

"So you're hiding in plain sight."

"I'm working, not hiding." Kaia walked toward another display, this one featuring chunky, raw emeralds. The necklace was large and heavy, a statement piece that made the typical polished emeralds look prissy. Kaia liked emeralds because their flaws made them interesting and real. Too many clouded the beauty of the stone. Not enough, and the stone looked fake. Too good to be true.

Like her relationship with Blake. She'd been dazzled by the sparkle and setting, but it had been nothing more than a flawless fake.

"What kind of a scam are you and Royce running?" He'd followed her.

She clamped down on any emotional reaction to his accusation. No need to feel hurt. This time around, she knew what he thought of her. "What makes you think we're running a scam?"

"He lied."

"About what?" Kaia removed the necklace from the display and held it to her neck.

"His assistant."

"Sam? She *is* his assistant. She's just not the assistant

who's here tonight." Kaia turned her back and looked over her shoulder. Long ago, in another lifetime, he'd been turned on at the sight of her looking at him over her bare back. Tonight her back wasn't bare, but there was enough skin showing to give him a little reminder. "Fasten this for me, please?"

A beat or two went by before she felt Blake's fingers brush against her neck. Warmth buzzed through her. Kaia closed her eyes at the unexpected tingles. She'd been numb. In control. And now there were tingles.

After all Blake had done to her, she would have thought she'd be immune to his touch, especially one meant to be impersonal. As though his touch could ever be impersonal. Caressing, exciting, and betraying, yes. Impersonal, no.

"Where is she?"

Did his voice sound rough, or was that Kaia's imagination? Was it possible he was still attracted to her? This could be interesting. "Who?"

"Samantha Whitefeather, sophomore majoring in political science at Vanderbilt, GPA 3.1." Blake's breath caressed the back of her neck and the little hairs there rose in response.

Kaia squeezed her eyes shut. "On a hot date?"

"Don't you know?"

"I didn't get to see her date. He might not have been my type."

Blake was taking an incredibly long time with the necklace's lobster clasp. "Why didn't Royce give me your name when I asked?"

"I'm a last-minute sub." The way his fingers brushed her nape drove her crazy. She longed to turn and press herself to him the way she used to when they were desperate to get close to each other.

For a second there, she almost did. Wow. She hadn't seen that coming, at least not with such a punch.

She hated that she was still attracted to him. Hated that when she inhaled, she could tell he used the same soap.

"When you arrived this evening, Josef checked in a Samantha Whitefeather."

Kaia got a grip on her emotions. *Concentrate.*

Josef, the blushing kid, was in all kinds of trouble. She could hear it in Blake's voice. Once, she wouldn't have cared, especially about someone she didn't even know, but she'd grown soft working in the security biz. It was all this being around people. It made her feel things. It made her *care*. Caring made a person lose her edge.

And that's what she was going to tell the counselor the next time she saw him.

"I told your man I was Royce's assistant, and since I followed Royce in and Josef heard us discussing the displays together, *and* I'm wearing a tag, he made the reasonable assumption that I was Samantha."

"TransSecure staff doesn't make assumptions."

He hadn't asked to see her tag, which was just as well, because she might have shown him where she'd hidden it. The thought raised gooseflesh across her shoulders and chest.

Stop it! This is the man who seduced you for the sole purpose of arresting you. Tonight, you have a chance to outwit him, make a pot full of cash, and get the Cat's Eye back. Don't blow it because you've got an itch and you like the way he scratches.

Blake's fingers finally, *finally* stopped their ticklish movements and dropped away.

Kaia released the necklace she'd clutched against

her chest and felt the weight hold. She turned to look Blake in the eyes. "Did you directly ask Royce if Sam would be here, or did you *assume* that when he gave you his assistant's name, she would be the one working the party tonight?"

She saw the truth in his eyes and allowed herself to show the barest of victory smiles. "So the staff can't make assumptions, but the owner can?"

Ooo. That didn't go over well.

"Royce knew what I was asking. He deliberately misled me."

"You don't know that."

"He hid your identity. Why do you suppose he did that?"

They glared at each other as the window panes rattled and rain drummed on the fabric awning outside the front entrance.

"Maybe he wanted to avoid having me grilled when I should be doing my job." Kaia glanced around at the room. The guests seemed more interested in the weather outside than the jewels inside as they clustered in little groups facing the windows. "Maybe he wanted to avoid making a scene when his assistant is singled out by security for more than idle chit-chat at a gathering of wealthy clients and potential clients. Maybe he knows how hard it is for an ex-con to get a job."

Blake blinked, his only reaction.

"Maybe he believes in second chances," Kaia finished quietly.

"Do you?"

"No." She turned her back once more and walked away, mostly to prove that she could.

She felt off-balance again. It had been an off-balance

kind of day. Until today, she hadn't had much experience in feeling that way.

Kaia didn't want the practice.

She kept walking until she was at the far end of the room by the study door—now closed—where she'd met Casper earlier today. It was cooler and quieter at this end. Not as many people. Tina had set up a discreet conversation grouping in case someone was contemplating a serious acquisition and wanted to discuss terms with Royce. It wouldn't do for anyone in the social elite to be overheard engaged in anything as gauche as haggling even though it was done all the time. But discounts for one might not be discounts for all.

Drawing deep breaths, Kaia stood for a moment and fiddled with a display while she centered herself, focusing on the job. Then she went through her relaxation routine, visualizing the steps of the plan.

Her encounter with Blake had rattled her. She used to imagine all kinds of scenarios for their first encounter. Usually, it was some version of Blake realizing that he'd Made a Horrible Mistake.

After her arrest, she'd called the number her father had planted in her pocket that day in her dorm. "You know you can't trust anybody and you trusted a cop? What did you expect?" her parents had asked. And they'd been right. She couldn't even trust them.

What was the matter with her? It happened. She'd moved on, but her heart hadn't gotten the memo. So to harden it, Kaia spent the next several moments reliving some of the more unpleasant memories of her incarceration. Then she replayed the moment Blake had stepped out of her embrace, spun her around, and cuffed her.

Okay. Okay, enough. Now, the job. Visualize the method. The problem was the method's details were sketchy. Kaia had memorized the floor plans of the house, but as she'd discovered this afternoon, there had been changes, that she'd duly reported to Tyrone, who'd duly reported to the weasel.

It would have been nice to get an apology.

As if it would make a difference. Wasn't wanting one just more proof that she was losing her edge?

Forget the apology. What she really needed was a set of current blueprints.

Smiling vacantly, Kaia moved from group to group and described the emerald necklace while keeping an eye on Tina Nazario and simultaneously ignoring Blake. At that moment, Tina was speaking to the jazz band. Immediately, they pepped up the music, probably to distract from the weather. Next, Tina sent waiters with the jewel drinks out into the crowd.

The woman was smart. She was the sort who would install multiple safes. And she wouldn't install them all in the master bedroom.

Carrying Jo Jo, Tina moved through the room, mixing up groups, holding out an arm so women could admire the collection of bangles she wore.

It could be said that Tina was the reason Kaia had ended up in jail, but Kaia wasn't going to say it or think it. It was simply more wasted emotion. Tina was her mark tonight. Kaia needed to think like Tina to guess where she might have installed the safes.

Tina had a touch of the theatrical in her personality. The decor, her clothes, the way she piled on the jewels, a look that worked for her, her gestures, the over-the-top food and drink—this wasn't a woman who'd be content with a garden-variety floor safe in the closet. This was a woman who would install one as a decoy.

The way bracelets were coming off and on her arms,

Kaia wished Blake had tagged them instead of the guests. Keeping track of them was like trying to find the prize in a shell game. Actually, Kaia was pretty good at shell games, but Blake's security problems were not hers. She smiled to herself. She *was* one of his security problems.

She heard the scritch scratch of tiny dog nails before a joyous yipping sounded at her feet.

"Hey, Jo Jo," she said to the little ball of fur. "I see you got sprung."

Jo Jo danced around and licked her toes.

"Wow. Look at you, all gussied up." Kaia picked up the wiggling animal, holding her out of tongue's reach. Jo Jo's silky blonde hair was clipped at the top of her head with a diamond bow pin. She wore a string of diamonds on a wide black velvet ribbon as a dog collar.

"That's some serious bling, Jo Jo. Probably worth more than I make in a year. Well, maybe not this year, if your daddy comes through."

Kaia wondered if Casper was skulking about somewhere or if he had taken off to London for real. Not that it mattered.

"Jo Jo, where are you, sweetums?" Kaia heard.

Jo Jo wiggled insanely, and Kaia set her on the floor where her feet churned until she got some traction and took off.

"There she is!" Tina Nazario had a throaty, sexy voice in addition to everything else. No wonder Casper was besotted.

Tina scooped up the dog and allowed it to lick her face. Blech.

"That necklace is to die for!" squealed a woman to Kaia's left.

No kidding, she thought as everyone in the vicinity looked at her.

"These are rough-cut emeralds..." As Kaia described the necklace to the group of three women, she sensed another set of eyes on her, too. Just beyond Tina's shoulder, Blake silently watched her play jewelry salesman, his suspicious stare almost a tangible thing. She was surprised no one had remarked about the way he looked at her.

He presented a real problem unless she could find a way to either distract him or reassure him she was exactly who she claimed to be. Except she wasn't. How ironic that this time she was the one who was undercover.

Jo Jo gave a couple of squeaky yips and wiggled her way out of Tina's arms. "Jo Jo!"

The little dog made a beeline for Kaia. "Hello, Jo Jo!" Pretending delight, Kaia picked her up again.

Tina approached. "I see Jo Jo has a new friend."

Kaia scrunched her nose at Jo Jo, who tried to lick it. "We met this afternoon when I was helping Royce set up. I'm his assistant," she added, to reinforce her cover for Blake's benefit.

Tina scrutinized her way too closely for Kaia's comfort. "Jo Jo usually doesn't like strangers."

"Jo Jo has good taste," Blake said, walking toward them. He wore an admiring look that they both knew was fake, although Kaia had to admit that it was a pretty good fake.

He was a good actor. But she already knew that.

Tina clearly didn't like the competition. "Do you see the woman sitting on the end of the couch over there?" Tina gestured vaguely. "That emerald necklace is just her style." She reached for Jo Jo and Kaia gladly handed the dog over before escaping to the far side of the room.

BLAKE WATCHED HER go, torn between believing her and acknowledging that she was probably lying, an all too familiar conflict where Kaia was concerned.

She handled the jewelry like a pro—which she was, he reminded himself.

But why did he have to keep reminding himself? Why couldn't he trust his feelings?

Why did he still want to sweep her away and start over somewhere new, just the two of them?

Before Kaia, Blake had never had any trouble telling the good guys from the bad guys. Kaia had been convicted. She was a bad guy. Only—how could he have not sensed that badness in her? Sure, he knew all about psychopaths, but that didn't apply to her. She'd been so open about her life. She hadn't told him everything about her parents, but she'd shared way more than he'd expected. She had a job. She'd been going to college.

What he'd been told about her didn't fit. How could he have fallen for someone who exemplified the opposite of everything he believed in?

His captain had assured him he'd been taken in by an expert, but Blake was never one-hundred-percent sure. Not even fifty-percent sure.

He had no idea what the truth was about her now. The Bennets had disappeared off the face of the earth, obviously using different identities. Or maybe they were here tonight. Who knew?

Clearly, Tina had no idea who Kaia was and so far, his former lover was behaving herself. But she had to be thinking about going to jail for stealing from the

Nazarios. She wouldn't be human if she didn't want a little revenge.

Something he should remember concerning himself.

Blake continued to study her, hoping for a clue to the truth. As he watched, Tina's dog streaked across the room. Kaia bent and picked her up again and the dog licked her ear. Dogs had a sense about a person, didn't they?

Great. He was looking to an animated dish mop for character references.

KAIA ALLOWED AN ecstatic Jo Jo to lick her chin so she could chance a quick look at Blake. He still stared straight at her, as though they were the only people in the room.

She shivered, and excused herself from the group, leaving the emerald necklace behind.

At least he hadn't thrown her out or made a scene. That was something. Except she wasn't going to be able to do either of her jobs tonight if he kept staring at her as though he expected her to grab a bunch of jewelry and bolt from the room at any moment.

"Time for some more bling, Jo Jo." The dog went for her ear.

"Stop it."

Jo Jo settled against her. "I know you get a lot of attention," Kaia said. "So what's up with the clingy behavior? It's not like we got off to the best start."

She slowly moved toward a display, scratching Jo Jo's ears beneath the diamond bow. Sneaking a look in Blake's direction, she saw him talking to one of his men.

Finally, a distraction.

Turning her back to the room, Kaia quickly reached

into her bodice and unpinned the RFID disk from her bra. "Want some more bling, Jo Jo?" She pinned the device to the dog's velvet collar and set her down. Jo Jo scrambled off.

One problem solved.

Kaia pretended to make a minute adjustment to the display before following Jo Jo. Until she sneaked upstairs, she needed to stay close to her tag. Blake probably had her highlighted on the monitoring system.

Speaking of... She raised her eyes to his and found him back to staring at her once again. This time, she didn't look away. Earlier, his touch had awakened prickles of awareness in her. Was it all one way? Did he still feel anything for her? She knew he had once—there were some things a man just couldn't fake.

Blake stood there, a handsome hunk who saw the world in black and white, good and bad, right and wrong.

Kaia was more...colorful.

From across the room, she could tell from the set of his broad shoulders that Blake's body was tense. Without looking away from her—Kaia didn't think he even blinked—he held a hand to his ear. His lips moved.

They'd always moved really, really well, surprisingly full and tender for a man so hard everywhere else.

He tapped the earpiece he wore and lowered his hand. The entire time, he'd stared at her.

A tiny movement at his side caught her attention. Blake was moving his index finger between his thumb and middle finger, cracking the knuckle, Kaia knew. It was a habit he'd developed after breaking his finger and he did it when he was stressed.

As they stared at each other, Blake's dark gaze skimmed over her with unmistakable desire.

He shouldn't be looking at her like that and he knew it. Obviously, he thought she'd let it go unchallenged. Kaia started walking toward him. He was wrong.

7

TROUBLE IN A BLACK dress was headed his way.

Blake probably deserved it for staring at her.

As Kaia came straight toward him, he forced himself to remain motionless, feet slightly spread in the power position, even as his heart rate increased. She drew closer, her gaze fixed on his, and Blake watched the black dress mold to a body he remembered in detail. He'd been contemplating those details all night.

Kaia had the smoothest skin of any woman he'd known. She didn't get out much, after all, since most of her work occurred at night. But he'd loved to run his hands over it, liking that she'd purred like the cat burglar she was.

Purred like the cat burglar she was. Listen to him. That was just bad, as corny as anything he'd ever heard in any chick flick. Also bad was standing here waiting for her to come up to him instead of taking control of the situation.

The situation approached the edge of his personal space and kept right on going. Blake stepped back before he could stop himself. How was she able to do this to him?

Kaia's lips curved as she registered his slip. "Do I make you nervous?" she murmured, her voice throaty.

"No."

She stepped forward until they were nearly touching. One deep breath on somebody's part and they would be. He stopped breathing.

She leaned next to his ear. "Liar." Her tongue flicked his earlobe.

Blake inhaled sharply, his skin going hot and cold from just that tiny point of contact.

"You've been watching me," she whispered.

"I'd watch any thief around this much jewelry."

"Hmm." She looked up at him, so close; he couldn't focus on her face. "But I'm just a lowly jeweler's assistant."

"You've never been a lowly anything."

"Oh, yes." She moved back and deliberately looked him up and down. "I have."

He swallowed against a mouth gone suddenly dry. Her gaze moved to his throat.

He'd lost control of the encounter, not that he'd ever had it. The entire evening he'd been focused on her exclusively. Even now, he had no idea where Tina Nazario was, where Royce was, or which guests were trying on jewelry. Someone could swallow a ring. Hide a bracelet in a napkin whisked away by an unwitting catering staff. Any of these bunches of flowers could have a necklace lying in the bottom of the urn. Blake wouldn't know. He was depending on Luke one hundred percent because he'd been useless tonight, and all because of this woman.

He knew she was up to something, yet he still wanted

to draw her into his arms and crush her against his chest as he devoured her mouth.

Her mouth. Unwillingly, his gaze dropped. He'd spent hours kissing that mouth. He'd always left her skin pink from his beard no matter how soon it had been since he'd shaved.

They stood motionless. What now?

Rain blew against the windows, rattling the glass, probably setting off one of the alarms. One of his men could check into it.

"Look! The awning's going to blow over!" someone shouted.

Concerned noises rippled through the crowd, but neither he nor Kaia looked away from each other as the guests became caught up in the drama going on outside. He should be grateful for the weather because otherwise, he and Kaia standing close like this would attract all kinds of attention.

No matter what, he was not going to move away first.

And then Kaia did something really stupid. She pouted those red lips of hers in a slow, soft, tiny kiss.

Blood pounded in his head as he fought the urge to touch her. Kaia raised a finger to her lips, brushed slowly back and forth, and then hovered her finger over his mouth. He could feel the warmth, could feel the nerves in his lips respond even though she didn't touch him.

But he wanted her to. Desperately. He was mesmerized enough to forget where he was and who he was with. Lightning flashed, followed by a boom of thunder. Blake was wound so tightly, he flinched.

Kaia saw and laughed, infuriating him.

Then her head jerked. She looked down at her arm and he saw his fingers wrapped around it. Blake didn't even remember grabbing her. Instead of releasing her the way he should have, he pulled her behind one of the huge floral arrangements at the base of the stairs. The room lights dimmed and flickered, like his good sense.

He stared at her, at the taunting expression on her face. *I'm not going to let her get to me,* he thought while he moved his hands to her shoulders. And then he hauled her to his chest and kissed her, because she did get to him.

Pure electricity sizzled through him, recharging parts of him he'd thought were dead—the parts that were alive only when he was with Kaia.

No. He wrenched his mouth away almost immediately and stared at her, breathing heavily, hating her and hating himself.

"That wasn't much of a kiss," she scoffed.

She was right.

"This will be." He kissed her again, parting her lips, feeling a dangerous relief as their mouths fused together.

This was all kinds of wrong, but he needed to do it. He'd acknowledge the chemistry and get it out of the way so they could both move on. Prove to himself that his feelings were nothing more than an echo of a dead relationship. She'd been playing him then, just the way she was playing him now.

But she felt so good in his arms. So right. Why? He knew what she was; why did she fascinate him so? Why couldn't he forget her? How could he be attracted to someone who was against everything he stood for?

She tasted the same, but richer, more womanly. Desire heated his blood and burned away all sense of reason. He was right back to being that undercover investigator who'd allowed his emotions to become involved. He was listening to his heart and not his mind.

Blake stroked his hands from her shoulders to her elbows and back again. Her arms were hanging at her sides and not wrapped around him the way they should be. It slowly dawned on him that he was in this alone. She wasn't kissing him back. He pulled her lower lip into his mouth and sucked gently; something she used to love.

Nothing.

She'd manipulated him into revealing his desire while letting him know she felt nothing.

He supposed he deserved it, and yet he still wanted her. He gentled the kiss prior to pulling away and releasing her because it showed that he hadn't lost *all* control.

"Did you like that?" Her voice was a husky whisper. "Did it make you feel like a big, strong man?"

There was contempt in her voice and the set of her mouth, but Kaia's eyes were black and opaque.

"That wasn't what it was about."

"You're right. It was about showing me who's got the power. Who's stronger. Who's in charge."

She gave him a half-smile and pointed at his chest. "And you know what?" She smoothed her hand down his tie, past the end, skimmed his belt buckle and tugged down his zipper. Then she slipped her hand inside and grabbed his balls. "It's not you."

She'd shocked him.

Blake had a surreal moment. "Ka—"

She squeezed.

He couldn't stop the gasp. No man would have been able to. "Hey, now." He tried to move away, but she tightened her grip, not hard enough to cause damage, but she definitely had his attention.

Her expression never changed.

Blake was unnerved and there wasn't much that unnerved him. This wasn't the Kaia he knew. Had he ever truly known her?

The pressure from her hand increased slowly. But relentlessly.

My God, what's she going to do?

He inhaled through clenched teeth. "Let go," he commanded with all the authority he could muster. It wasn't much.

"No." Black eyes. Blank face. Firm grip. *What are you going to do about it?* went unsaid.

And what was he going to do? What could he do? She'd positioned herself perfectly. He had no leverage and no way to reach for his gun. Push her away? No. Blake broke into a cold sweat. *Clearly,* he was facing a very angry woman who was letting him know just how angry she was in a way that left no doubt.

They stood like that for an eternity. Eventually, they'd be discovered, and he'd be embarrassed, but the loss of his pride was currently number three on his list of priorities. Numbers one and two were in Kaia's hand. "This isn't funny," he said.

"I'm not laughing."

"It's not sexy."

"It's not about sex. It's about power. Isn't that what you were just showing me?"

No. He'd been responding to an overwhelming attraction. To her. He thought it had been mutual and the mistake was costing him dearly. Now wasn't the time to explain or argue or demand. Now was the time to grovel. Blake had never been a good groveler. "I'm sorry."

She looked into his eyes. "For what?"

"Kissing you."

"Not yet you're not." And she squeezed ever so slightly.

It was enough. "Kaia!" He gritted his teeth. "Let go *now*."

Her lips tilted upward. "When I'm ready."

Blake fought to keep his breathing even. "I apologized. You've made your point."

"Oh, I know. Now it's about making sure you won't forget my point."

No way would he ever forget this moment. They were standing, partially hidden from the room, but someone was bound to wander by soon. If that happened, Blake knew with absolute certainty that Kaia wouldn't flinch—or let him go.

Sweat trickled from his armpits and down his spine as Blake imagined scenarios from having his own men rescue him to being caught by Tina, his most important client. "So is this payback?"

Smiling, Kaia raised her chin until her mouth was close to his and her breath caressed his lips. And damn it, he felt himself growing hard. "This doesn't *begin* to pay you back."

Okay, he got it. He really got it. He'd humiliated her; now she was humiliating him. Enough. "Release me, or you'll regret this."

"Go ahead. Call your people." She tugged. "Tell them I've got their boss by the balls."

He'd never live it down. He swallowed. "What do you want?"

At that moment, screams sounded as the awning blew apart and pieces crashed against the windows. Blake automatically tried to turn, but could only move his head. Kaia didn't even twitch.

"Kaia, I need to help out in there! Tell me what you want so we can end this."

Her gaze never wavered. "I've got a new life." She released him. "Stay out of it."

Blake stepped back. Thank God. He tried not to react as relief flooded through him, but his hands fumbled with the zipper as he closed his fly. "Stay on the straight and narrow and I will."

Without responding, she walked past him to the stairs.

"Where are you going?" he asked.

Her lip curled. "To wash my hands."

A little parting punch to the gut.

Even though he should be with Luke helping to keep things calm while they checked outside for damage, Blake watched her climb the stairs, his emotions in a turmoil that defied description.

Nothing like this had ever happened to him before. She'd totally blindsided him.

And he didn't hate her. God help him, he was more attracted to her than ever. How messed up was that?

Totally. It was safe to say that Kaia Bennet hated him with the white-hot heat of a thousand suns.

But at least she felt something.

As she climbed the stairs under Blake's angry gaze, Kaia was glad she wore a long dress because it hid her shaking knees.

If Blake had seen them he would have thought she was afraid, but she knew from past experience that an abundance of adrenaline let loose all at once caused the shakes. She'd kept her emotions in check and now all that pent-up energy had to go somewhere. Right now, she was headed to the upstairs bathroom where she'd revel in the euphoria of besting Blake, and do a few calisthenics to work the quivering out of her muscles.

Now *that* was the kind of reunion to have with The Man Who Done Her Wrong. The thing about a bold move was that you had to commit fully or it wouldn't work. And once you started, you had to see it all the way through, which she had. *Take that, Blake McCauley.*

Blake had struggled to keep her from seeing how shocked he was. Truthfully, she'd shocked herself. She was not impulsive by nature and when she'd been walking across the room, she hadn't planned to grab him by the balls. Then again, she hadn't planned to let him kiss her, either.

And that's what keeps life interesting.

She hated it when people said that.

Kaia couldn't risk looking to see if Blake still stood at the bottom of the stairs, but she figured he'd leave her alone for a little while.

She passed by the open landing overlooking the party room and entered the enclosed part of the hallway. At this point, she was out of Blake's view unless he'd followed her up the stairs. Highly unlikely.

Surprisingly, no one was upstairs. Kaia listened at the guest bath door and then cautiously pushed it open enough to see that it was empty.

This was a bonus. Now was her best chance to search for the bracelets. She glanced back and didn't see Blake following her up the stairs, so she flipped on the bathroom light and closed the door. Hitching up her dress, she silently ran down the hall to the master bedroom closet.

The clock was ticking. At some point, Blake would notice her absence and either come looking for her or check her tag's location on the monitor. She wished he hadn't seen her go upstairs, but she couldn't have everything.

Inside the bedroom door, Kaia fastened her skirt into the waistband and withdrew a pair of sheer latex gloves from a hidden pocket. She'd already been in the bedroom today, but it would be difficult to explain her fingerprints on a safe. "I was chasing Jo Jo" would only go so far as an excuse.

The first order of business was not to look for the safe, but to plan her exit strategy.

From the floor plans, she knew that the master bedroom bath connected to a room the Nazarios had turned into a home gym and sauna.

Using a tiny LED flashlight, Kaia moved through the bathroom and noted a twin of the high, hexagon shaped window in the guest bath. That was one exit possibility, she thought, and opened the door to the gym.

Nice. Almost as nice as the one she'd had growing up. But hers had been equipped with specialty balance and strength training machines. Until she'd left home, Kaia had spent part of every day of her life in that room.

But now was not the time for sentiment. Was there ever a good time? Sentiment was wasted emotion.

Kaia crossed to the sauna, pulled open the door and discovered a nice, large window facing out over the back of the house. Beautiful landscape lighting. If it weren't storming, the view would be spectacular. The window was a bump-out with a bench in front of it, and doubly insulated, but more important, there weren't sensors on it. Kaia pressed against the glass and from what she could see, there was nothing but a sheer drop to the ground. And she'd need to break both the inner and outer windows and most likely have to use the free weights to do it. Tough, but not undoable.

Once outside, she'd have to climb up to the roof, but it wasn't as if she'd never been on a roof before. And it was doubtful anyone would think to look in the sauna until she was long gone. Or in this case, back at the party, innocent expression firmly in place.

Okay, then. On to Tina's closet. Back in the bedroom, Kaia checked to see if the hall was empty before quietly positioning the door halfway closed and wedging a piece of crumpled plastic beneath the bottom. If anyone pushed the door open, the plastic would crackle and alert her. When they checked to see what was catching on the door, she could sneak away.

Though she would prefer not to do so, Kaia closed the closet door behind her and flipped on the light.

Tina's clothes were organized by color. There was a motorized rack that rotated out of season clothes, a wall of shoes, drawers galore, racks, a three-way mirror, a little bench, a clothes steamer, and something that looked like a glass sauna, but turned out to be a climate-controlled closet for Tina's furs. There was even a flat-screen TV. What, Tina couldn't listen to the one in the bedroom? Kaia thought just before she saw the camera. Kaia was allergic to cameras. Her heart blipped until she noticed that it was pointed in a strange direction for a security camera.

Kaia picked up the remote and taking a chance, clicked it. The TV screen blinked on and she saw herself. Pressing another button started a slide show of Tina wearing outfits with the occasion and date displayed on the bottom of the screen.

Holy cow. This was one organized woman.

Was it possible she'd kept a similar record of her

souvenirs? Kaia pressed buttons, hoping to see them or discover a different file, but saw nothing helpful and acquired a serious case of shoe envy.

She turned off the TV. Earlier, when she'd had Jo Jo, Kaia had noticed a strip of carpet in a slightly different shade of taupe. It was beneath a small chest that looked like an old-fashioned pirate's treasure chest. Yeah, that Tina sure had a sense of humor. Kaia lifted the lid on the chest and discovered packages of tissue paper, cedar blocks, bags and assorted closety type supplies. Fortunately, it was all light-weight stuff. A good sign, since Tina would be moving it frequently.

Kaia pushed it aside. Under the chest was a pull ring in the floor. Bingo. She lifted the square of carpet and flooring and there was the safe. Or one of them. This was too easy.

Fortunately, it was a garden-variety floor safe with a standard dial lock package. Floor safes were usually installed in concrete on the ground floor, so Kaia knew there had to be reinforcement under the floor to keep someone from merely cutting the whole safe out. Definitely, a custom job and she guessed not one of Blake's.

She wondered how angry he was and whether she'd gone too far. But for years, she'd mentally replayed their time together and wondered how he could fake emotions for so long. And why. Okay, he thought she was a thief—but why hurt her emotionally like that?

No. She hadn't gone too far. She hadn't gone far enough.

From beneath her leggings, Kaia withdrew a Vernier ring that fit over the dial and allowed her to see more precise measurements. The interesting thing about safes was that people spent a lot of money and attention on the safe and how it was installed and then skimped on the lock. It wasn't because of the expense, it was because the higher-rated locks were more tedious to open for the person with the combination, as well. People were lazy.

Fortunately.

Opening a safe by manipulation wasn't that hard to learn. It was a matter of becoming familiar with the imperfections in manufacturing and exploiting them to line up gates in three wheels, get the fence to drop, and retract the bolt.

Kaia spun the dial to the left and got started.

NONE OF THE VALETS had been hurt when the awning had blown apart because they'd been in the den beside the kitchen area playing poker and staying out of the rain. Blake could hardly fault them. In fact, he wouldn't mind sitting in.

The awning was a total loss and only the fabric cushioning the poles had kept the windows from shattering. The alarms were reset; Tina organized an impromptu fashion show of Royce's jewelry, and everybody calmed down.

Except Blake.

He paced. He paced into the kitchen, where the catering staff clustered around a small TV and watched weather reports of wind damage and strained power grids, and back to the main gathering where he watched women "ooh" and "ahh" over a bunch of metal and shiny rocks. And he paced some more.

Thoughts of Kaia filled his head and he couldn't concentrate on the job. What was it about her that got to him? Even now, when she clearly hated him, he couldn't let go of his feelings for her. It didn't matter to him that she wasn't the same Kaia; he wanted to know the woman she was now. Never mind the fact that he didn't trust her. He didn't trust himself.

Had she come back downstairs yet? Reluctantly, he scanned the room for her. She wasn't part of the fashion show and he didn't see her. And he hadn't seen her since she'd walked upstairs after their...encounter.

That, in a weird, twisted I-don't-ever-need-to-go-through-again way, had reassured him. She was strong, and she could take care of herself.

For someone with her background, she'd been strangely naive when they'd been together. Giving and open. He thought now of her hard, opaque eyes and unsmiling red mouth. Time and experience had hardened her. Then again, time and experience had hardened him.

He shook his head as if to shake away the memories. She'd been out of his sight too long. Blake casually strolled to where Royce spoke to a couple. "Where's Kaia?" he asked. He was interrupting and he didn't care.

Irritated, Royce said in an undertone, "I sent her off to clean jewelry."

When Blake gave him a skeptical look he added, "It gets makeup smudges and lipstick smears all over it. We must keep our sparklies sparkling!" He moved off.

Okay. Blake would buy that. So how long did it take to clean jewelry?

He watched the party for another minute, and then slipped outside the room. Tapping his earpiece, he asked his man monitoring the tags to locate Kaia.

"She's in the party room."

Blake stepped into the doorway and looked. "Where?"

"According to the ID tags, she's right there by Mrs. Nazario."

Holding her dog in her lap, Tina sat at the end of a

row of chairs that had been hurriedly pushed together for the show. The man sitting next to her was not Kaia, nor was the woman sitting next to him. Or anyone sitting anywhere.

"I am looking at Mrs. Nazario and Kaia Bennet is not in sight."

"That's where her tag is—almost right on top of Mrs. Nazario."

"The only thing—" Tina's dog licked her face and Blake froze.

"Wha—"

Blake disconnected and hurried toward Tina Nazario and her little dog, already knowing what he'd find.

"Excuse me." He pulled the dog from Tina's arms. The dog growled and snapped at him.

"What are you doing to Jo Jo?" Tina demanded.

"Looking for an ID tag." Blake ran his hands around the collar.

Just as Blake's fingers touched the disk, Jo Jo wiggled like crazy and snarled. Tina looked as though she was about to snarl at him, too. Blake set the dog down and it ran off, still wearing Kaia's tag.

"Sweetums!" Tina called after her.

He'd expected to find Kaia's tag on the dog, but he still couldn't believe she'd actually try to steal something on his watch. And he'd wanted to believe her, wanted to believe she was nothing more than a jewelry designer's assistant. Actually, he'd hoped he'd been wrong about her six years ago so he could justify his unending fascination with her.

Now that he knew she'd been lying all along, it should be easier for him to forget about her.

But first, he had to find her.

8

KAIA STARED INTO A well of jumbled jewelry and knick-knacks. The mess was so unexpected and tragic. Unexpected because of the way the rest of Tina's closet was stringently organized and tragic because the way everything had been dumped together damaged the pieces.

Kaia could imagine Tina furtively opening the safe and tossing whatever she'd stolen into the hole in the closet floor, slamming the lid on, and forgetting about it. The safe was full, too. Tina hadn't installed a secret hiding place because she was clever; she'd installed it because she needed the room.

Kaia gingerly pulled out a strand of baroque pearls, a sterling spoon, three Montblanc pens, some crystal figurines, ugly and scratched, bracelets, perfume bottles, an Hermès scarf and a ruby-red lobster claw keyring—with the keys still on it. Somebody wasn't very happy about that.

Shaking her head, Kaia peeled away layers of Tina's plunder until she spotted the blue and silver of Royce's bracelets. They seemed to be okay with only a few minor scratches that could have been the result of normal wear.

Kaia set the cuffs aside and continued sorting through Tina's stash.

This was taking too much time. The longer she stayed, the greater her chance of getting caught by Blake. At least she had Royce's bracelets. But the snuffbox wasn't in this safe.

Casper had wanted an inventory of what Tina had hidden, so Kaia quickly videoed everything with the camera on her cell phone and returned all except Royce's bracelets. She didn't worry about the order everything went back into the safe—there hadn't been any order. Did Tina ever look at the stuff after she'd stashed it? Take it out and admire it? Kaia doubted she'd realize the cuffs were gone or even remember that she'd taken them in the first place.

Kaia fastened the cuffs into one of the hidden pockets in her skirt and searched the closet for safe number two.

It had to be close by. She checked the bathroom, tapped floor tiles, searched the bedroom, and even looked in the chimney of the gas fireplace.

Nothing. Therefore, the other safe was in the closet. Had to be, cliché or not.

Kaia stood in the center of the room and pantomimed returning from an event. A fancy one with Casper in tow. His dressing area was beside this one, so Kaia imagined the two of them discussing their evening, putting on pajamas. Casper in PJs. Now there was an image she could do without, although it was preferable to imagining Casper *without* PJs.

Now Blake without PJs...Kaia drew a calming breath, willing Blake out of her mind. Focus on Tina.

Tina would have to talk, change clothes and hide the stolen goods all without alerting Casper.

If he wandered into her dressing area, the little chest could easily conceal an open safe. So what else in the closet could do the same and be conveniently accessible?

Turning in a slow circle, Kaia's gaze landed on the fur storage cabinet. It had a lock.

But not much of a lock, and seconds later, Kaia was looking at a collection of not politically correct furs as cool, dry air puffed over her skin. It was a fur refrigerator.

She couldn't resist petting a dark coat and discovered an antique silver cigarette lighter in the pocket. She checked other pockets and found most of them hiding little prizes.

Tina, Tina, Tina. Ran out of time, did you? Kaia knew she was on the right track. She tapped on the back and the sides of the cabinet, but they sounded solid. However, the bottom was raised instead of flush with the floor. Kaia knelt and pressed and pulled. The wood bottom of the closet slid toward her, revealing a safe exactly like the first one.

Maybe Tina had stumbled onto a buy one get one free sale. Either way, this safe had the same combination as the other, which was a real time-saver.

After she opened it, Kaia found it contained far fewer items, but what stood out immediately was a white container with the colorful seal of the Lithuanian embassy on top.

Kaia opened it, and the sides folded down revealing a snuffbox that looked so much like the chocolate one Casper had shown her that she actually sniffed to see if it was real.

It was.

Gorgeous, gorgeous, gorgeous. Jewel encrusted, exquisite workmanship, truly fine stones, and its provenance as a gift between countries enhanced the value.

In the palm of her hand, Kaia held an object that could cause an international incident, would surely lead to Casper's downfall, social scandal, and maybe even result in jail time for Tina. Correction, it *should* result in jail time, but Tina would never serve a day. The weasel was too good and the Nazarios were too rich.

Still. All Kaia had to do was put back one, small box and tell Casper she'd never found it. Then she'd buy some popcorn, make an anonymous tip and watch the show.

She was tempted, sooo tempted. But then she'd never get her diamond or have the fun of witnessing Casper's weasel tell whoever needed telling that Casper had made an error and Kaia was *innocent*. Well, not innocent, but at least not guilty of stealing the Cat's Eye.

Except if she put the snuffbox back, Blake would never know how much he'd wronged her.

Not that she cared what he thought any more.

After this was all over, would Casper fire TransSecure because Kaia had been able to circumvent their system without Blake knowing?

Not that she cared what happened to Blake anymore.

Or she could take Royce's bracelets *and* the pendant, assuming she found it, put the snuffbox back and watch what happened.

Kaia sat on the floor of Tina Nazario's closet and held her future in her hand. Options. She had options.

What she didn't have was time.

She stared at the snuffbox.

Okay, fine. Casper would get his box because she

wanted her name cleared. And she wanted the Cat's Eye pendant. But really, this was about her name. Go figure.

Kaia set the box aside while she recorded the contents of the safe in the fur cabinet. She never would have anticipated how important clearing her name had become. She thought she didn't care. She knew, or thought she knew, that Tyrone believed her. Her boss was iffy because her past guilt or innocence wasn't important to him, only her future honesty. But Kaia wanted to be able to look him, and Tyrone, and everyone who worked with her at Guardian right in the eye and…

And what? Know she'd been gullible enough to be taken in by an undercover cop? Respect her because she was innocent? Innocence wouldn't get her any respect, not with that bunch. Or maybe this wasn't about guilt or innocence so much as getting caught. If Kaia had been guilty of actually stealing the pendant, she wouldn't have been caught. *That's* why she wanted them to know she hadn't stolen the pendant. It was a skill thing.

Whew. For a minute there, she thought she'd gone soft. Thought she actually *cared*. It wasn't as though the folks at Guardian were her family or anything. She had a family. She just hadn't seen them for six years.

Kaia finished recording the contents of the fur safe, closed it up with the empty white box, and was going through all the pockets when she heard whining.

Jo Jo?

Jo Jo who was wearing Kaia's RFID tag and was now upstairs. With Kaia. This was not good. Knowing Blake, he was probably sitting in front of some monitor watching her tag. Instead of thinking Kaia was back downstairs, he would have watched her dot on the screen separate from the rest of the dots and run up the stairs and into the master bedroom.

Quickly securing the snuffbox in a pocket, she crept from the closet and listened. Jo Jo saw her and yipped.

"Shh!" Of course, that only made Jo Jo whine louder, which Kaia would have known if she'd been a dog person, which she wasn't, and this was why. And yet, dogs and cats loved her.

"Go back, Jo Jo!" She snarled at the dog, hoping it would run away, but Jo Jo gave the most pitiful whimper Kaia had ever heard. Sighing, she knelt and petted the animal, feeling the little body quiver.

Kaia had a hard heart, but she wasn't inhuman. "Aw, you're scared," she whispered on a sigh and picked up the dog. "Too many people downstairs?"

Jo Jo licked the palm of her hand. "You're not getting any sympathy from me," Kaia said. "I'm not a dog person." Or an animal person. Actually, not really a people person, either.

With Jo Jo cradled on her hip, she finished frisking the coats and closed the cabinet.

Kaia was glancing around the closet to make sure she hadn't left traces of her presence when Jo Jo's body buzzed with a low growl. A second later, Kaia heard her crumpled plastic alarm crackle as someone pushed open the door.

Dropping to the ground, she shoved Jo Jo beneath some long formal gowns while urging, "Jo Jo, sweetie, please come out." Kaia hoped the dog would ignore her. Luckily, Jo Jo continued to growl. "What's got you so scared? Is it the thunder and lightning? Jo Jo doesn't like the storm?" Kaia wished whoever it was would hurry up and find her in the closet. Jo Jo wasn't exactly the world's greatest conversationalist.

The air shifted and Kaia sensed someone behind her in the closet doorway. Keeping up the pretense, she crawled forward a few inches. "Come on, Jo Jo." She reached into the dresses. "Let Kaia take you back downstairs to your mommy. You don't have to be afraid."

"Or maybe she does," said a deep male voice. Blake, as she'd expected.

"Blake!" Kaia thought her gasp sounded convincing. Not over done, but clearly audible.

He threw a glance around the closet before settling it on her. "Have you been threatening the dog now?"

She sat back on her heels. "I don't threaten anything unless it deserves to be threatened."

"Like me?" He gave her a half-smile.

"Exactly like you."

He gazed at her and as far as she could tell, he wasn't angry. Maybe curious and a little wary. Maybe ready for a truce. A truce would be good. A truce would be *great*.

"Now about this dog," he began.

Jo Jo yipped and raced out from beneath the gowns straight toward Blake. Growling, she attacked his shoe.

"Hey!" When he reached for her, she yelped and, bless her furry little heart, ran out of the closet and hid under the bed.

Way to go, Jo Jo. Kaia couldn't have planned it better.

"Oh, wonderful." She got to her feet. "Do you know how long it took me to get her out from under there this afternoon?" She marched up to Blake, glared, and continued on to the bed. "I do not have time to keep coming up here after this dog!" She got down on all fours. "Jo Jo!"

Growling sounded from beneath the bed. Excellent.

Kaia sighed for Blake's benefit and bent to look under the bed. "Jo Jo, come here, sweetie," she crooned.

"You actually expect me to believe you were in the closet to get the dog?" came Blake's voice from above her.

Kaia looked up at him. "I expect you to help me get her out from under the bed," she spoke with exaggerated sweetness. "Try moving to the other side and maybe you'll scare her toward me."

"I'm sure she'll be fine where she is." He held out a hand to help her to her feet. "And if Tina should want to find her, it'll be easy, since the dog is wearing your tag."

And here we go. "That was the idea." Kaia took his hand and got to her feet. "Jo Jo likes to run off with things and hide while she chews on them. Finding her can be a real time sink. You ought to sell Tina a tag system so she can keep track of Jo Jo." She couldn't tell if he was buying this or not. Probably not.

"It's not your job to keep track of Jo Jo," Blake pointed out.

"I know, but earlier, she nabbed an earring—she likes ears. Can you imagine if she'd run off with it? That's when I tagged her. Because, really, Blake, tagging Royce and me was overkill."

He was wearing what she called his "stern authority" mask. No matter what he was feeling or thinking, the idea was to appear confident and in control. Kaia knew him well enough to know the mask meant he was reconsidering the situation and that's what she wanted.

"Tagging a known thief is not overkill," he said.

That was a short truce. "I work for the man! You think I can't find a better opportunity to steal from him than at a party? And what do you expect *him* to do? Steal from himself?" Shaking her head, she made as if to leave the room.

Blake grabbed her arm. Okay, she really hadn't expected to get away that easily.

"He could claim something was stolen here to get the insurance money."

"And risk losing Tina as a client?" She jerked her arm out of his grasp. "Not likely."

"You could be planting something. Revenge on the Nazarios. Or you could just be plain stealing, hoping to get away with it this time." He ticked off his fingers. "You've got motivation and opportunity."

"Oh, please! Do you think I'm stupid? Oh, wait." She flung up her hands. "Of course, you do. After all, I was stupid with you."

It would have been nice if he'd jumped in with a denial, but that would have been insulting. Nice, but insulting.

She kept talking. "It would take someone a lot stupider than I am to try anything tonight with you constantly stalking me."

Blake had positioned himself so he was between her and the door. "That is how I know you weren't up here looking for the dog. She was downstairs. With me."

"So *you're* the one who scared her. Poor thing." Kaia knew she was going to have to give him a better reason for being in the bedroom or he'd never leave her alone. The truth, or a version of it was always good. "Yeah, she came up here and found me when I was getting these." As she spoke, Kaia reached through her pocket to the inner pouch with the cuffs and drew them out. "Royce sent me upstairs to get them. They're his design and he wanted to show them off. Tina modeled them for an exhibit of Native American jewelry a few weeks ago."

Blake looked skeptical.

"There are pictures. You can search for them on Google."

"Good idea." Taking out his phone, he activated the screen and tapped.

Kaia hadn't expected him to actually do it, at least not right then. He'd been upstairs with her an awfully long time. Shouldn't he be getting back to the party?

"What are the bracelets doing in your pocket?" he asked as he studied the screen.

"Fingerprints. I'll have to buff them now." She rubbed one cuff on her skirt, conscious of the weight of the snuffbox against her calf. She really, really hoped she wouldn't have to tell him about her deal with Casper. She might be forced to reveal her relationship with Guardian to get Blake to back off, but not yet. She still had a chance to bluff her way out of this.

Once upon a time, she'd told Blake about this dress and other clothing like it. Any minute now, he'd remember and—

"What else have you got in your pockets?" He'd remembered.

"A lot. I don't carry a purse." That he knew already.

He glanced up. "Show me."

She indicated his phone. "Didn't you see the picture of Tina and Royce?" She held up one of the cuffs. "Notice the match?"

"Yes." He turned off the phone's screen. "Show me, anyway."

This was not the situation Kaia wanted to be in.

What were the chances of convincing Blake that the snuffbox was a really fancy breath mint holder?

Nil. For now, all she could do was stall and hope

somebody called him on his earpiece or, wonder of wonders, he believed her.

An interruption was more likely. Carefully, she placed the cuffs on the bedspread, near enough to the edge that she might be able to knock one to the floor, if she needed the distraction, but not so close that Blake would think she'd done it on purpose.

Next, she reached into a side pocket, going for the easy stuff first. "Money clip, lipstick, keys, tissues." She pulled the pocket inside out to show it was empty.

"Keep going."

She tossed the items onto the bed and reached into another pocket. "Jeweler's loupe, latex gloves—"

"I don't know another woman who would carry latex gloves to a party."

"It's not a party for me. I'm working."

"That's what I'm afraid of."

Was that a touch of humor? Kaia didn't want humor. She wanted Blake stern and unreasonable and using that deliberately neutral voice she hated. Hate. That's what she wanted to feel, if she had to feel anything. And she didn't—shouldn't.

"The gloves keep fingerprints off the jewelry." For jewelry, they should be cotton, but she was counting on Blake not catching that. Luckily, she actually had a small polishing cloth with her, that she pulled out to show him before dropping it onto the bed with the other stuff.

He nodded to the pocket. "What else have you got in there?"

"Keys." The fob on the ring was a tool set in the shape of a key, but she wasn't going to point that out. Next, she pulled out a small pen, that was actually a mini blowtorch, one more thing she hoped he wouldn't notice. And her other pen was a flashlight. She didn't have a real pen.

"Let me see that." He held out his hand and she dropped the light into his palm.

"Nice," he said, after examining it. Leaning forward, he carefully placed it onto the bed.

Jo Jo growled.

Smothering a smile, Kaia held up her phone. "My cell."

"I'll take that." Blake reached for it.

Kaia snatched it away. "Not without a court order."

He raised his eyebrows. "Oh, I think—"

"Not without a court order." She put the phone away. "I have confidential client data on this phone." Not Royce's clients, but the principle was the same. "You're not a cop anymore, Blake. Should you confiscate my phone, it would be a gross overreach of your authority. I guarantee you would be sued and you would lose." She let that sink in. "Even if you were still a cop, any information you found on my phone would be inadmissible in court."

He blinked, finally showing emotion in his carefully blank face. "True. You've been studying."

"I had time." She'd never spoken to him like that before and could tell it surprised him. *Yeah, Blake, I'm not the same little girl who deferred to everything you said or did.* "And I'm only showing you what's in my pockets so you'll leave me alone."

She pulled out her Vernier ring and tossed it onto the bed. "Yes, I used it when I opened safes, but now it's a ring sizer." She gazed at him steadily, hoping he didn't know anything about sizing rings.

Blake stared at the items on the bed. In the silence,

Jo Jo growled louder, probably reacting to Kaia's raised voice.

"You've got an explanation for everything." He drew his hands to his hips and regarded her through slightly narrowed eyes. "I guess that's what makes you so good."

Kaia maintained eye contact. "Or I could be telling the truth."

"Maybe."

At least she'd planted doubt in his mind. *Reasonable doubt.* Wasn't that what it was called? Something her inexperienced court-appointed attorney hadn't been able to achieve.

"But I'm not convinced," he said.

"You never were."

A couple of beats went by before he slowly shook his head.

Kaia wanted to scream in frustration. It didn't help that technically, this time Blake was right.

"Is that all you're carrying?" he asked.

All she intended to show him. "There are a few bits and pieces for emergency repairs in the bottom of the pocket." She held it open for him to look, but he remained several steps away.

"And?" He just would not give up.

"And nothing."

In the background, the jazz band amped up the music. She and Blake had been away from the party a long time, but if she pointed it out, he'd get suspicious. Like he wasn't already suspicious?

Still, why hadn't he hustled her downstairs or called for one of his security guards? Or *called* Royce. Or Tina.

Did anyone know he was upstairs?

Interesting. She'd assumed his intense gaze was

because he was trying to decide whether or not to believe her, but maybe it was something else. Maybe he was intrigued that she'd stood up to him.

Maybe she hadn't obliterated his desire for her.

Warmth rushed through her. No. She did not feel desire for him. She *would* not feel desire for him. She was in control of her emotions and she'd decide when and where and with whom she'd feel desire. Now was not the time, the place, and certainly not the person.

Beneath the music she heard a tiny sound. A pop. Blake was cracking his finger. He wasn't as detached as he wanted her to believe.

Was it possible he was still attracted to her? Still? If so, it was a weakness she could use against him, maybe play the distract-with-sex card. So what if it was obvious? That didn't mean it wouldn't be effective.

She softened her posture to a less belligerent one. "Are we done here?" She gave him a tiny smile and lowered her voice. "Or are you going to frisk me?"

Blake never blinked, but his gaze grew dark. "No. I'd like to reserve the right to father children at some point in the future."

Kaia gave a throaty laugh. "I just wanted your attention."

"Oh, you got it and then some." His voice deepened. "I know you were evening the score, Kaia. So consider us square now."

A rush of anger made her fingers tremble. Not even close. She knew men put a high value on the family jewels but Blake was totally clueless. Totally. "You wouldn't say that if you'd ever been in prison."

They held each other's gazes, his searching, hers determinedly opaque.

"Fair enough," he said at last. "So you're suggesting that if I let you walk out of here now we'll be even?"

They would never be even. "You act like you'd be doing me a favor."

"Looking the other way to theft is a very big favor in my world."

"That is why you'd never offer to let me walk if you truly thought I was stealing," she said. "Admit it."

Long moments went by. "No," he said.

"'No' you won't admit it, or 'no' you wouldn't offer?"

"Are you asking me to let you go?" he countered.

Would he? With a flash of insight, Kaia knew that if Blake were the kind of man who would do such a thing, she wouldn't have once loved him.

"You don't have any reason not to let me go." She held her arms wide. "Go ahead. Check for yourself." She was taking a huge chance. What if he did start to search her?

Then...then she'd kiss him. That was her plan. All of it. Simple, but it had its good points.

His gaze traveled over her and Kaia waited, heart pounding, actually hoping that he would touch her so she'd have an excuse to end up in his arms.

Blake's expression told her he hoped the same thing.

"I'm safer standing where I am." His voice was rough. His finger cracked.

If she hadn't heard the tiny sound, Kaia might have gathered her things, made a remark about Royce waiting for the cuffs, and escaped from the room.

But she had heard it. For whatever reason, he still wanted her. And she...was about to be very stupid. Again. "Then I'll frisk myself."

Blake's gaze was transfixed on Kaia's hands as they began a slow descent down her sides.

Dangerous, dangerous decision, but one that made her feel more alive than she had in years. Her blood hummed. She felt confident and in control. And reckless, because who knew where this would lead?

Blake had always enjoyed her body, that is why he'd been so convincing in the role of attentive boyfriend. And she'd enjoyed his, and that was why she'd been blind to the rest of it. They could still enjoy each other, as long as she remembered that was all it was.

Kaia propped one leg on the bed and smiled to herself as her hands felt the subtle bumps of picks and other tiny tools still strapped beneath the leggings hidden by her dress. Bumps that Blake would also feel if he'd called her bluff. But Blake didn't look as if he was doing much thinking. His eyes followed her movements as though she was a puppet master controlling them.

Kaia raised the other leg, watching him watch her. If he wasn't affected, he would have stopped her, right? Or frisked her himself. She lowered her leg to the floor.

Slowly, sensuously, she turned and looked at Blake over her shoulder, her signature move to get him turned on. Other than breathing, he was completely still; not even cracking his finger anymore. His chest rose and fell faster than normal.

Excellent.

Watching him, Kaia ran her hands over her hips, nice and slow and thought she heard a whimper.

Actually, she did hear a whimper, but it was Jo Jo and not Blake.

He didn't seem to notice.

Turning to face him, she slowly moved her hands over her breasts, pulling the fabric tight.

Blake stared, unblinking. Kaia threw in a tiny

breathy moan, but immediately wished she hadn't. She didn't want to oversell it.

He swallowed, watching her hands skim her stomach and lower, and then down her thighs. She turned her palms upward. "You see? Nothing to hide." Except the snuffbox near her calf.

There was a hitch in the breath he drew. "Maybe you didn't have time to take anything."

"Now you're insulting me."

"Kaia." He exhaled her name as he stared at her mouth. "I can never think straight when I'm around you."

She took a step toward him. "Then don't think."

"That's when I get into trouble." He gave her a wry smile.

"So what are you thinking now?" *Kiss me. You know you want to.*

Once he kissed her, she knew she had him. She'd make him forget where they were, make him forget his responsibilities and risk discovery. She'd manipulate him the way he'd manipulated her.

She couldn't hurt him the way she'd been hurt because a person had to care to be hurt and Blake didn't care.

But she did. Still.

But she'd be okay as long as she remained in control, that meant they needed to move this along while she could still pull it off. Maybe she should kiss him, except it was important for him to make the first move. She gazed at his broad shoulders and wide jaw and the short hair she'd teased him into growing an inch longer. Why was it was important that he make the first move, again?

Somebody needed to move.

Blake eased forward. Kaia swayed.

The bass and drums from the band directly below them reverberated through the floor with the same rhythm as her heartbeat.

Blake stared at her mouth and she knew he was locked in the same battle she was: desire versus common sense. She tilted her chin up in the slightest of invitations. *No more. He has to want you more than you want him.*

His jaw worked. She saw him swallow. His eyelids lowered. "Kaia…"

Kaia beamed "kiss me" thoughts at him. *Kissmekissmekissme.*

Stepping forward, Blake skimmed his hand along her jaw.

At his touch, Kaia shivered and closed her eyes. She couldn't help it. The combination of memories and anticipation nearly overwhelmed her. When Blake didn't go ahead and kiss her, she opened her eyes to find him gazing at her as though searching for something. He used to do that, she remembered and momentarily forgot all the bad stuff that had happened between them. She smiled, because his eyes would always light up when she smiled.

This time, they not only lit up, he smiled back and lowered his head. And then, when their mouths were just a breath away, he grimaced and pulled back.

Touching the transmitter in his ear, he said, "Yeah, go ahead."

What? No! Not now when she nearly had him.

But what were you going to do with him? a little voice asked.

Kaia sighed inwardly. Pretty much anything he wanted.

She wasn't experienced enough, hardened enough to remain completely unfeeling. Seduce him sure, but she'd get hurt all over again. Even as she was running her hands over her dress, she was remembering the feel of his palms on her skin and thinking, *maybe they could start over and forget the past...*

Forget the past? She should have her head examined. Oh, wait. She was. When her therapist had told her to find friends, this wasn't what he meant.

The interruption had saved her. Not getting tangled up with Blake again was for the best, she told herself. *Finish the job you were hired to do and go on with your life. Leave the past in the past.*

Blake was still looking at her, but he wasn't seeing her. Casually, Kaia returned the objects to her pockets since it didn't appear there was going to be any shedding of clothes in the near future.

"I do. She's up here with me."

Someone was looking for her? Surely Royce couldn't be stupid enough to draw attention to her absence, could he?

"Yeah. Hiding under the bed."

They were talking about Jo Jo.

"Tell Mrs. Nazario that I'll bring the dog down. By the way, Luke? You're in charge until I tell you otherwise." Blake tapped the earpiece. "Tina freaked out because she couldn't find Jo Jo."

When Blake said her name, the dog growled.

"Told you." Couldn't Tina have freaked out earlier? While it bolstered her story, the interruption had absolutely killed the mood. That was good, Kaia repeated to herself, and put the gloves and polishing cloth in her pocket.

Blake drew a deep breath and she felt the atmosphere

change. "Will you help me get her out from under there?" He was back to being the consummate professional, neutral tone and expression in place.

She could do professional. "Sure." Did that mean he believed her? Was she going to be able to waltz out of here with both the snuffbox and the cuffs? Best not to ask. Just assume. "Go around to the other side and grab for her so she'll scoot toward me."

"That could work." Blake got down on his hands and knees as did Kaia. "Come here, Jo Jo," he said. The dog snarled.

Kaia could learn something from Jo Jo.

She looked under the bed and saw Jo Jo backing against the wall. "She's going the wrong way."

"Jo Jo!"

"Don't yell at her! Talk baby talk like Tina does."

Blake's face appeared next to the floor, his expression disgusted. "I do not talk baby talk."

"Call her sweetums."

"No."

"Wow." Kaia looked from Jo Jo to Blake. "You never seemed like the kind of guy who'd let pride get in the way of doing his job."

Blake glared first at her, then at Jo Jo. He inhaled. "Come here, Jo Jo. *Sweetums,*" he said through gritted teeth.

Kaia giggled, tried to stop, but couldn't. "Jo..." It was all she could manage without bursting into laughter. She collapsed onto her back and laughed. It wasn't *that* funny, but she couldn't seem to stop.

"I've never heard you laugh like that before."

There hadn't been much to laugh about in a long time. Kaia turned her head and saw Blake watching her.

"You sounded scary. I wouldn't come out from under the bed, either."

"I notice she's not running to you."

Kaia patted the carpet next to her. "Come here, Jo Jo," she said, still chuckling.

"Yeah, Jo Jo. Go to Kaia." Blake reached under the bed.

Jo Jo yelped and with a surprisingly deep growl, ran at Blake, catching him off guard.

Kaia could hear the teeth snap all the way on the other side of the bed.

"Ow! She bit me and—hey!"

Kaia saw him raise his hand to his ear before Jo Jo came scrambling at her. Kaia wasn't prepared.

Jo Jo ran out from under the bed, across Kaia's stomach and out the door, which set off a fresh bout of laughter.

"Get her!" Blake yelled. "The damn dog's got my earpiece!"

Kaia found this funny, too. Laughing, she got to her feet and started for the hall after Jo Jo.

And then everything went black.

9

BLAKE WAS OUT THE door just after Kaia and at first, he thought the hall light had gone out.

"Jo Jo!" Kaia called and kept running, disappearing into the blackness.

A second later, the eerie silence registered. The power was off. *The gates.* They were up ahead but he was disoriented and didn't know how far. "Kaia, stop!"

He sprinted forward faster than he'd ever moved in his life. *"Kaia!"*

Arms outstretched, his fingers found her and grabbed hold. Yanking her to his chest, he dragged her backward as a whirring sounded and the metal security gate slammed into place.

All around them thuds and clanking sounded as the shutters closed and locked over the outside windows.

He could hear gasps and the beginning of concerned babble from the party guests in the room below.

What he didn't hear was the yelping of an annoying little dog crushed by the gate.

Heart pounding, he exhaled in relief, but he kept Kaia

clasped against his chest and tried not to visualize her pinned by the gate. She was so tiny. But not fragile.

He bent his forehead to her head. It landed in a springy knot of hair. He inhaled, but remembered that she avoided using scented products, except for the brief time she'd lived with him.

He should release her, but she wasn't pulling away, so he didn't. "That was close," he murmured into the back of her head.

"Don't you have those things on a delay?" Her voice was a little shaky and he could feel her heart beating against his arms.

"Five seconds."

"I'm glad Jo Jo had more than a five-second head start."

"Yeah. Now let's hope she doesn't choke on my earpiece."

She gave a short laugh. "Come on, Blake, say that like you mean it."

Her heart rate had slowed. His hadn't.

Back there, back in the bedroom before Luke interrupted them, Blake had been going to do something very, very dumb. He'd been going to kiss Kaia and he hadn't been going to stop until the nagging, burning, itching, craving, hungry desire he *still* felt was slaked. He'd even convinced himself she felt the same way.

She was clouding his judgment now the same way she had six years ago. If Luke's call hadn't interrupted them, who knows how far things would have gone? The way he felt about her they might have ended up naked in Tina and Casper's bed.

Inappropriate didn't begin to describe it.

But Luke's call had broken the spell and Blake was grateful. And then the lights had gone out. Blake's reaction to Kaia's near miss with the gate forced him to admit that his feelings for her went much deeper than they should. Right or wrong, they were true. So now what?

"Everyone please remain where you are," he heard Luke say to the party guests downstairs.

He tightened his arms. "You heard the man."

Kaia shushed him, but stayed where she was.

"The electricity has gone out," Luke was saying. There was some shushing from the guests. "What you heard were the security shutters closing. They're programmed to shut when the power is cut to the house. Until the power comes back on and we reset them, I ask that you all remain in this room. Other security measures are now active in the house and would cause a hazard if they were tripped."

"Do tell," Kaia murmured.

"That would spoil the surprise," Blake murmured back.

"Lasers and gas, right?" She groaned. "I *hate* lasers and gas."

"Good to know."

"Seriously, Blake, you know somebody is going to sneak away to the bathroom or Jo Jo will cross one and that gas leaves you with a hideous headache."

"Speaking from experience?"

He felt her tense. "Part of my training."

He thought about what it must have been like for her to grow up, trained from birth to steal. What kind of parents would do that to their child? "No. No gas," he told her.

She relaxed a little. "Luke's bluffing?"

"Sort of." His men would be operating by a different protocol, so it wasn't all a bluff.

"Good one."

"We're working on getting some light in here." Luke's voice rose above the crowd noise. "For your personal safety and the safety of those around you, please remain seated."

"Is it my imagination, or does he sound like a flight attendant?" Kaia asked.

"It's familiar. People respond to familiar."

"I've got loads of candles," they heard Tina say.

"Ma'am—"

There was a yelp.

"Jo Jo," he and Kaia said at the same time.

"There's Mommy's sweetums!"

Sweetums. In the dark, he felt Kaia's silent laughter and found himself smiling, too.

"I can't get a cell signal!" someone called.

An eerie blue glow became visible in the open landing on the other side of the gate as a dozen or so guests checked their cell phones. Kaia had hers out, too.

"Look." There was a "no connection" message.

"That's not good," Blake said. "If the cell towers aren't functioning, it means the outage isn't just local. Either their battery backup has failed, or they're reserving bandwidth for emergency communications."

Kaia left her cell phone screen lit and faced it forward. "You know what else isn't good?"

"Hmm?" Kaia was in his arms again and she wasn't trying to maim him. It was all good.

"We're not on the right side of the gate."

"I know."

They were standing a few feet from it because when he'd yelled for her to stop, miraculously, she had. If not…she *might* have made it through, but it would have been so close his heart was still pounding at the thought.

"You don't seem all that concerned."

"You could have been hurt." He could hear the emotion in his voice and knew she could hear it, too. He didn't care.

"But I wasn't." She patted his arm and he reluctantly let her slip away. "What are the Nazarios doing with a setup like this, anyway?"

"They host benefits and sometimes there are pieces of art here for a few days." He slowly inhaled and exhaled, striving to match her "business as usual" tone. Because for now, that was the way it had to be. "Insurance companies are limiting exposure and won't allow works to be taken to venues they consider to be at risk. If the Nazarios wanted to continue being the generous patrons of the arts that they are—"

Kaia snorted.

"That's not an attractive sound, in case no one has ever told you."

"So they upgraded. I don't need to hear how wonderful they are." She walked to the gate and examined the latches by the light of her cell phone. She tapped along the wall vertically and horizontally. "Excellent reinforcements."

"Thank you."

"Hurry up and open it." She stepped back.

Blake had wondered when they were going to get around to that. He'd been hoping the power would return before now. "I can't."

"What do you mean, you can't?" Kaia waved her arm at the latches, her phone making a glowing arc. "How are you going to reset it?"

"The office will reset the alarm code remotely when the power is restored."

"Oh, come on. You can't tell me that every time

there's a power glitch, the Nazarios are trapped in their house."

Blake avoided looking directly at the phone in her hand so his eyes would have a chance to adjust to the dark. "If the full system is turned on, then yes, they and anyone else will be trapped inside and anyone outside will not be able to get in."

"Bummer." She turned back to the locks, studying them more closely. "But I guess that's the idea."

"Right. It also means we're stuck here together." He joined her at the gate. Now that she was no longer in his arms, he felt the full impact of their situation. A high-profile job, a house full of people, his best men on duty, and Blake, himself, was AWOL. Helpless. "This is my worst nightmare," he said under his breath.

She heard. "That kind of enthusiasm could give a girl a complex."

"So could grabbing a guy by his balls."

"I thought you were over that."

"You told me not to forget, not that there's any chance," he snapped, increasingly frustrated at being unable to join his team below.

"I didn't expect you to keep bringing it up."

"No? How do your victims usually act?"

"They're very polite. Much politer than you." She started walking back toward the bedroom wing, taking the light with her.

"Where are you going?"

"In search of better company," she called over her shoulder.

He was being a jerk. "Kaia—wait. I'm angry and frustrated and I'm taking it out on you. The power failure is not your fault. Is it?" he asked, trying for a little humor.

"I'm flattered you think so highly of my capabilities." She slowly returned. "But no. And it's not your fault, either."

"Doesn't matter. Not only are the Nazarios my biggest clients, I have other clients in the crowd downstairs. And now they get to see me in action. Or inaction, as it happens." He laced his fingers through the gate's diamond patterned grid and stared through it toward the hall's open area.

Shadows flickered, punctuated by flashlight beams. He could hear Luke directing the men to bring chairs into the room. There was chatter, but not panic. So far.

"Sounds to me as though Luke is doing okay by himself," Kaia said.

"It's not Luke's company."

Kaia turned around and leaned against the gate while looking down at her phone. "Still no signal." She turned off the screen and darkness swallowed them. "You don't have an override code? A panic key?"

"No." Blake gave the gate an impotent shake. "I don't recommend them. If all thieves knew there were panic keys, they could force owners to override their own systems."

He stared toward her, wishing he could read her expression. Was he telling her something she already knew?

"You're staring at me," she said.

"How do you know?"

"I can feel you."

He laughed.

"You're wondering if we ever forced a mark to use a panic key."

"Yes," he admitted after a beat.

"No." She turned and faced the gate. "There's no

skill involved in that. We were burglars, not robbers." Her tone said that robbers were the scum of the earth.

He found that oddly reassuring. Why, he had no idea. In the end, it was theft either way.

"So aren't you going to let your men know we're up here?" she asked. "The balcony isn't that far away. If we both yelled, they could hear us easy."

And how great would it look that Blake had been trapped by his own security system? He shook his head. "No." Maybe the power outage wouldn't last long and no one would have to know they'd been trapped. "They've got enough to do keeping the guests from panicking."

A yellowish glint shone in her eyes, a reflection of the wobbling yellow candlelight that had joined the blue cell phone glow from downstairs. She moved away.

"*Now* where are you going?"

"Over here."

He strained to see and made out her arms and shoulders sliding down the wall. "What are you doing?"

"I'm sitting for my personal safety and the safety of those around me. Come on, Blake. Just chill, okay?"

He remained where he was. "I should be down there." And he would have been, if he hadn't been so focused on Kaia.

"So should I. Royce must be *freaking*."

"We'll do an inventory before we allow anyone to leave."

"*That'll* be real popular."

"Yeah." Blake exhaled. "I'm not looking forward to implying Tina's staff and guests can't be trusted."

"You've tagged everybody, Blake. I think that ship has sailed."

"Maybe so. But it was for their safety, too. Kidnapping. Hostages. You know."

"Uh, no. I don't know. Wow. You're either paranoid or very thorough."

"Both." He stared at the flickering light. It was brighter now, enough to make out the walls and the railing on the landing. "I hope Royce has already started packing the jewelry away."

"Are you kidding?" Kaia asked. "He's got a captive audience and the romance of candlelight. He's in seller's heaven."

"Where's the music?" Tina's loud voice carried easily from below. "Let's have some music!"

"No amps," someone replied. Probably one of the musicians.

"You don't need amps!" Tina called out. "Just play louder!"

"Can't see," another complained.

"Oh, for pity's sake. Half the time you've got your eyes shut anyway because you're making stuff up as you go along!"

That drew a couple of chuckles. The bass player started plunking and some anemic jazz followed.

"People, this is like one, great, big ole slumber party!" Tina shouted. "Whoo! Keep those drinks a' comin'!"

"Oh, great." Blake stalked over and sat next to Kaia. "Alcohol and candles. Wonderful combination."

He saw her look at the ceiling. "It would be reeeaaallly bad if the sprinklers were set off, wouldn't it?"

Blake groaned.

"Millions of dollars in artwork ruined."

"Kaia…"

"Just saying."

Blake stared at her uneasily, trying to read her

expression. Not that he could ever read it, even in bright light, if she didn't want him to.

"You just can't trust me, can you?" she asked.

Blake was silent.

"Did I say anything you weren't thinking?"

"It was the way you said it."

"Because I wouldn't be sad for Casper and his wife? I'd be sad for the loss of the art. I'd even be sad for the insurance company. Somebody downstairs would be guaranteed to slip and fall and I'd be sad about that. But Casper and Tina?" She made a derisive sound. "They don't deserve what they've got."

"Is that how you justified stealing from them?"

The air seemed to freeze as Kaia slowly turned her head and faced him. "I stole nothing."

She was facing the landing and he could make out her expression, thanks to the candles and her pale skin. But it was the tone in her voice that caught him. "I'm supposed to believe Casper Nazario gave you that diamond necklace."

"Why do you believe he didn't?"

"Because—" Blake broke off.

"Because that's what he said," Kaia echoed his thoughts. "And the word of a rich, powerful man with a smart lawyer is worth more than a nineteen-year-old college girl with a public defender."

"But—"

"You knew me, Blake. You didn't know him and yet you believed him instead of me."

She was right. "I was given the case."

"To investigate? Or had you already made up your mind?"

His mind had been made up for him. And he hadn't

been investigating; he'd been supposed to get close to her so they could get to family.

As he stared at her in the dim light, her expression softened and he was facing the young woman he'd known. "I never lied to you," she said.

In that moment, everything that had made Blake a talented police detective told him she was telling the truth. He felt it in his gut.

He thought his instincts had let him down with Kaia, but that had been because he'd been told she was lying, that she'd stolen a diamond pendant. She'd worn the thing around her neck and told him it was a gift, which was so unbelievable, she'd almost convinced him it was true. It *felt* true. So when he caught himself doubting his superiors, he figured she was the most dangerously, clever liar he'd ever come across.

But she hadn't been lying. His instincts *hadn't* let him down. The whole premise of the case had been wrong.

At the realization, something within him settled and calmed. It was as though he'd been trying to see through a snowstorm and it was now the morning after with the sun shining and the air clear and still.

But he was going to have to deal with the snow.

One of the lieutenants he'd worked with on the force had a saying, "When the puzzle pieces don't fit, try a different puzzle."

Blake had blamed faulty judgment, beat himself up over getting emotionally involved with a criminal and had quit police work because he'd thought he'd gone soft. The case against Kaia had never felt *right* to him, the pieces hadn't fit, and he'd never been able to put it out of his mind. If she was telling the truth, then Casper had lied and Blake was looking at a different puzzle.

Kaia was innocent. He made himself think it, even

though it meant he'd made the mistake every officer wants to avoid.

He studied her, mentally working out the new puzzle. "You had the diamond."

"Casper *gave* it to me."

It's what she'd said all along. "Why?"

"You read my statement," she said with weary resignation.

"Tell me anyway. I need to hear you say the words." They'd never discussed the details; he'd only read them.

"Will it make a difference?"

He started to demand, to raise his voice, but what came out of his mouth was a whispered, "Please. For me."

It surprised both of them.

"Okay." Looping her arms around her raised knees, she leaned against the wall. "I did some work for Casper." She stared straight ahead instead of at Blake, but he didn't need to see her expression. He'd be able to hear the truth in her voice.

"You're all worried about me being around jewelry when you should be worried about Tina." Kaia glanced at him. "She's a kleptomaniac. She's the one with the problem." She turned away. "And Casper knows."

Interesting. Blake mentally filed the info. "How did you get involved with him?"

"Royce. He used to work for my dad."

"I thought—"

"Designing and repairing jewelry! Jeez! He's totally legit, or he has been for years, so don't go there."

Blake held up a hand. "Not going there."

"Casper's weasel of a lawyer was sniffing around because Tina's souvenir gathering was getting out of control. Their friends were getting suspicious, so Casper got the bright idea of putting the missing things back so they'd be found and there'd be a lot of 'Oh, how did that get there?' and 'I've been looking for that!' and my personal fav 'the maid must have knocked it off the shelf.'"

"So you're saying Casper hired you to break into houses and put back the items Tina had stolen." And she hadn't seen a problem with that?

"Yes." She nodded. "Four houses and one office. I put some guy's grandfather's service medal into a briefcase."

"And Casper paid you with the diamond?"

"No, in cash—that's how I got the money for school. Where we met." She bit off the words. "Giving me the diamond was an impulse. He'd seen me looking at it and he was so relieved that I'd returned everything without anyone knowing, that he gave it to me. 'A cat's eye for a cat burglar' he'd said."

"It was a generous impulse," Blake said, deliberately neutral. The thing was worth thousands and the Casper he knew was not impulsive.

"I figured it was like a tip, you know?"

"That's quite a tip."

"Not when you consider what was at stake for him. And I knew he'd need me again so I figured that was part of it, too. Kind of like a retainer. In fact—" Blake saw her shift. "...these cuffs?" She held up one of the silver and turquoise bracelets. The silver caught the ambient light and glowed. "Tina walked off with them after that exhibit I told you about. Casper usually pays the invoices when she 'borrows' from designers and stores, but these aren't for sale." She turned the cuff over in her hands. "Something to do with Royce's family history, so he wants them back. Whatever. Casper went looking for them and lo and behold, discovered that Tina's installed new hiding places. He hired me to retrieve these and tell him what else I found."

"You mean, after he sent you to prison, he had the nerve to contact you? And you agreed? Are you insane?"

Her mouth twisted. "He met my price."

"And what was that?"

"A lot of money. There aren't many job opportunities for an ex-con with my skills." She put the cuff on her wrist and twisted it, admiring the silver in the dim light. "And I wanted to get these back for Royce."

Blake could accept that, although if it were him, he'd use this opportunity for revenge. "Why didn't Casper just get the bracelets himself?"

"He doesn't have the combination to Tina's safes—I found two, but there might be more. And here's the kicker—he doesn't want Tina to know he's aware of her problem."

No way. And yet Blake could believe it. "That's..."

"Sick?" Kaia supplied.

"I was going for unrealistic."

"But sick works."

It sure did. "Casper has to know that Tina knows he's ignoring her kleptomania."

"Duh. I'm thinking that's why she got her own safes."

That Blake hadn't installed. "You say Tina's been stealing for years?"

"Apparently."

Wonderful. His most important client was a compulsive thief. "Eventually she'll get caught. Why doesn't Casper deal with it and get her some help?"

Kaia gave a derisive laugh. "You've seen Tina and you've seen Casper. Why do you think?"

An image of the voluptuous Tina and her much older husband appeared in Blake's mind. "He's been covering for her all these years because he's afraid she'll leave him if he confronts her?"

"That would be my guess."

And there was the missing gold-plated puzzle piece: Casper's motivation. Unreal. How could a powerful and ruthless businessman have such an obvious weakness?

Kaia was watching him, reading his expression. Blake suspected she could see in the dark a lot better than he could.

"What I don't understand is why he reported the diamond stolen," he said. "You could have blackmailed Tina."

"He knew nobody would believe me. You didn't. The police didn't. As far as they were concerned, I was confessing to multiple burglaries."

Casper had been ruthlessly clever. He'd duped the police and he'd duped Blake. He'd set up Kaia—maybe that had been his plan from the start. "After what he did to you, how could any amount of money be enough to work for the man again?"

"I had no choice." Kaia blew out a breath. "Terms of my probation. This time, though, the weasel knows, my lawyer knows, Royce knows, Casper knows—and now you know. Tina doesn't know, but she claims she already returned the cuffs, so if you tell her I've got them, what's she going to say? You ought to see the junk she's stolen. She's probably forgotten all about these."

Blake was reeling. Casper had said nothing to him, yet had authorized what was essentially an attempted theft on Blake's watch. Or an actual theft, since Kaia had the cuffs. *What are you up to, old man?*

"Why didn't you tell me this when we were in the

bedroom?" he demanded. "One call, and I could have verified your story."

"Confidentiality clause. That I've just broken." She shifted and he guessed she was putting the cuffs away. "If you say anything, I'll claim the blackout as extenuating circumstances."

Blake was convinced that not only was this story legit; Kaia had been telling the truth all along. Casper had lied and sent her to prison. *Casper had lied to Blake.* Anger welled within him. He was going to make this right. Somehow. "I won't say anything to anyone. I swear I won't."

He felt her gaze on him, could see the gleam in her unblinking eyes. "You believe me?"

Blake swallowed hard against a knot of anger and regret. "Yes." His voice was rough.

He reached for her, wrapping his arms around her. He needed to hold Kaia, but her body was stiff. Blake didn't blame her. Right now, he hated himself, too.

"Part of me believed you before, but I told myself I'd lost my objectivity instead of trusting my instincts. I'm sorry." He rubbed his hand across her unyielding back. "So very sorry."

She didn't move away, but she didn't relax, either.

His fingers caught the edges of her shoulder blades and skimmed the muscles above them. They weren't as developed as they'd been, but her upper body still had a gymnast's shape. She was exercising, but she wasn't training and he remembered that when they'd met, she'd been trying for a gymnastic scholarship.

She'd lost that opportunity, too.

He wanted to make it up to her. He wanted to make up everything to her.

"You lied to me," she said. "Our whole relationship was a lie."

Blake squeezed his eyes shut. Yeah, first they had to get past some stuff. "It was my job."

She pushed out of his arms. "And you did it *really* well." What he could see of her expression was blank, but the rapid rise and fall of her shoulders as she breathed gave away her agitation.

"You must hate me."

"I should!" She waited several beats. "I *want* to." With a disgusted sound, she turned away. "But I don't. I can't."

Relief made him release the breath he hadn't known he was holding. "Good. Because our relationship may have started out that way, but there was a lot of truth to it."

She turned her head warily. "What part?"

Blake took her hand. Her fingers were curled into a fist. Gently, he loosened them. "This part." He pressed her palm against his chest, above his heart.

She stared at her hand. "I can feel your heart racing."

"It's this way every time I'm with you," he told her. "When I touch you. When you touch me. When I *think* about touching you. And only you."

Seconds went by.

"Arresting you tore me up. I studied the paperwork, tried to get them to reexamine the case until I was put on indefinite leave. But your background and the other burglaries...I'm sorry."

"Blake," she whispered, finally.

And it seemed like the most natural thing in the world for her to lean forward and for Blake to bring his mouth to hers.

He wanted the kiss to be a tender apology, sweet and

giving. Soft. Gentle. All about showing Kaia he'd had genuine feelings for her. *Still* had genuine feelings for her.

He'd hurt her and he'd hurt himself and he wanted her to know that. He wasn't going to ask for her to kiss him back, but wasn't going to object if she did.

Above all, he would not lose control. He'd remain aware of her body language and at the first tensing, the first tug backward, he'd release her. He had no right to expect her to forgive him, especially when he hadn't yet forgiven himself.

But with the first touch of her mouth, desire raged in spite of all his good intentions. It was as though knowing the truth had removed what little restraint he'd had. He wanted to part her lips and tangle his tongue with hers. And he wanted her to kiss him back with the passion she'd shown six years ago.

But how could she?

So much had happened. So much betrayal and hurt. Not hating him was a long way from wanting him. Loving him.

If he wanted another chance with Kaia, he'd need patience, lots of patience. And he'd give her time, all she needed. And space. But not too much space.

Blake held himself with an iron control as he softly kissed her, daring to touch her lower lip with the tip of his tongue only once because the wave of longing he felt made him clench his fingers against her back.

Kaia's hand was still pressed against his chest. She slipped it from between them and Blake prepared to pull away. But instead of withdrawing, Kaia slid her hand around his neck to the back of his head and urged him closer.

Her mouth opened beneath his.

She was kissing him back.

After everything that had happened, *she was kissing him back*.

His tongue met hers and Blake went a little dizzy. Maybe a lot dizzy. His pulse pounded and desire flooded his senses. He couldn't think straight when she was in his arms. He didn't *want* to think straight. He wanted to let go and just feel. The truth was that this was the first time he'd felt right since that horrible night in the mall parking lot.

Blake hauled her into his lap so her legs draped over his thighs, desperate to have as much of his body in contact with as much of hers as he could. His elbow banged against the gate, momentarily reminding him of where they were, but he didn't care.

That was the power she had over him.

She could have asked him to do anything for her and he would have agreed. The feeling was devastatingly familiar.

This time, instead of panicking, he kissed her harder. He kissed her until his lips went numb, also a familiar feeling.

Wrenching his mouth from hers, he pressed kisses along her throat, gently sucking at the steady pulse in her neck.

"Blake!" Kaia pushed his mouth away. "I'm supposed to be modeling necklaces!"

"Sorry," he muttered, not sorry. "I wasn't thinking."

"And I like that about you," she said, her voice breathy. "You were always totally in the moment, completely with me."

He raised his head. "Why would I want to be anywhere else?"

Kaia smiled and his lips tingled.

She wiggled in his lap and his lips weren't all that tingled. "I want to be completely with you some more," he added.

She lifted her chin. "Then kiss me again."

And this time, I won't let you go, Blake vowed as he lowered his mouth. He wanted to say it aloud, but it was too soon for her. So for now, he'd cherish her and give her such pleasure that she wouldn't *want* to leave.

10

Kiss me again. What was she thinking? Where was this headed? She should never have kissed him back because now she didn't want to stop.

Kaia hadn't let any man get close to her since Blake. She didn't trust men. She didn't trust herself. With good reason, if the way she felt now was any indication. She remembered this gnawing craving to be close, as though nothing less than climbing into his skin would be enough.

Good and bad memories of him warred within her. She would not, *not* weaken, not give in. Wanting to know if any part of what they'd had together had been real was dumb and self-indulgent. His kisses were distracting her from her purpose for being here tonight. She had a lot at stake and she wasn't going to throw away a better future for momentary pleasure.

Truth or lies didn't matter any more. The past couldn't change.

Sure, Blake had said all the right things—well some of them, anyway. And she'd told him as much of the truth now as she dared, which was everything except about the snuffbox.

Lies were still between them, only this time, they were hers. How ironic.

"No other woman makes me feel the way you do," he murmured against her mouth. "That's why I quit the force."

"You quit because of me?" She was stunned.

"When you go undercover, you've got to be able to trust your gut and mine was all twisted. You got to me then and you're getting to me now."

Kaia was helplessly aware of her frozen emotions thawing and about to flood her sense of self-preservation. She wanted to believe him; of course she wanted to believe him. What woman wouldn't want to think she had that kind of power over a man?

Her heart thudded wildly as the little voice inside her insisted he could be lying now. He could be telling her what he thought she wanted to hear. And he'd be right—it was exactly what she wanted to hear. She hated that. Now, this very moment, he could be kissing her with lying lips and caressing her with lying hands.

She was wrong, all wrong. The truth did matter. It shouldn't, but it did.

Kaia drew back to clear her head. "You're admitting that I get to you? Aren't you afraid I'll use it against you?" She was crazy to point that out.

"Absolutely." He gave her a crooked smile that charmed its way into her heart.

But her heart was smarter this time around. Wasn't it? "So now what?"

He leaned down until his mouth was positioned a breath away from hers. "Now you kiss me."

She swayed toward him in spite of herself. "Why?"

"Because you want to." His fingers spanned her shoulders and his thumb ran beneath her collarbone. "And I want you to."

Kaia shivered. "Why?" she asked again, mostly to stall for time. Her original idea had been to seduce *him*, to let him think he could manipulate her the way he had before, not to actually *let* him manipulate her.

Not such a great idea after all.

Especially since she wasn't sure who was doing the manipulating. Was he telling the truth? Or was he lying the way he had before?

Kaia had a headache. And aches in other places.

"You can tell a lot from a kiss," Blake murmured.

Kaia certainly hoped so. "Especially if you kiss a lot."

Blake touched his forehead to hers. "Wanna test your theory?" He stole a butterfly kiss.

Kaia laughed, suddenly feeling happy for no good reason. And then she kissed him, also for no good reason, fitting her lips to his as though time hadn't passed and he hadn't betrayed her.

Warmth, a sense of relief, and a lot of other complicated emotions she didn't want to uncomplicate just then flowed through her. When Blake cradled her next to his body, it just felt right. As simple and as complex as that.

This, this was what a kiss was supposed to feel like. No anger. A soft promise of later passion. As though they had all the time in the world. As though they were the only two people in the world.

It was…nice. Kaia hadn't experienced nice a whole lot in her life. At the moment, nice had more power over her than passion and that was dangerous. She drew back.

"That wasn't much of a kiss," he echoed her earlier taunt.

"This will be," she quoted his reply. *Because passion will be safer than tenderness.*

Then her mouth was on his and she was kissing Blake, really, seriously kissing him after six long, long years, and all her hate and resentment was melting away when she wanted to keep it wrapped around her for protection.

She pitied women who did dumb things because of the way a man made them feel. Now she pitied herself as longing swept through her and she knew she was going to do something stupid before the night was over. Clearly, passion wasn't any safer than nice.

But speaking of nice... Blake's mouth was hot and sweet and addictive. In seconds Kaia was back to those days when they'd kissed for so long, her lips had gone numb. Her body continued warming and thawing as though a long winter had ended. She couldn't stop wanting him, even though she'd regret it.

She explored his mouth and invited him to explore hers, and then realized it was more about remembering the taste and scent of their mingled breaths than discovering something new.

Blake made a low sound in the back of his throat and deepened the kiss because she'd pressed herself as close as she could get to him. She could feel the heat of his body through his shirt and suit jacket. Burrowing her hands beneath the fabric was like sticking them into an oven. His shirt had gone damp and limp, like her willpower.

It was the touching that was her weakness. Kaia had been raised as a loner and her parents weren't the demonstrative types. There hadn't been a lot of hugging or loving touches. Hugging was for picking pockets.

She'd been a surprise to them, especially to her father who was in his forties when she'd been conceived. Her mother was younger by ten years. Maybe more, maybe less. She'd always been vague about her age. Kaia hadn't felt unloved, exactly, but she'd sensed she'd been a bother until her father had discovered her gymnastic talent. That coupled with her tiny hands and uncanny ability to assess jewels had made him a much more enthusiastic parent. As long as Kaia performed. Perfectly.

Kaia felt Blake's hands on her shoulders, skimming down her arms and back up again, caressing her skin. He'd liked her soft skin, she remembered. And she liked having him touch it. With her parents, any touch was light, if she felt it at all, and it meant they were lifting something from a pocket or a purse. Testing her. They'd trained her never to relax. Never let her guard down. Never trust anyone.

And so she hadn't, until Blake.

When he caressed her, it was because he found pleasure in it and wanted to give pleasure to her. And he did. He *so* did.

Kaia sighed into his mouth as his hand left her arm and circled her waist, drawing her closer to his chest. She'd never had enough of the pleasure, the closeness.

They'd spent their few precious Sunday afternoons together sitting this way with Kaia in his lap, her legs draped over his, doing her class work while Blake watched some football game on TV, the sound muted in consideration for her.

They kissed during commercials.

And sometimes more.

She'd had no idea there were so many long commercials during football games.

Kaia withdrew her hand from beneath his jacket and traced his jaw with her fingertips, circling his ear. The sharp edge of his fresh haircut prickled softly the way she remembered. He felt the same and with her eyes closed, she could imagine that it was the same.

Except it wasn't. "Blake—"

She forgot what she was going to ask because his hand left her waist and slowly skimmed upward. She tensed in anticipation, biting her lower lip, wondering if he would stop, equally hoping he would and hoping he wouldn't, until his hand closed over her breast.

She inhaled at the sharp pleasure, wishing it didn't feel *quite* so good.

"Blake," she breathed and this time, she wasn't thinking of anything else as she tilted her head back.

He kissed her jaw, the side of her neck, and her throat. "Your skin is still so soft, so smooth."

"And your beard is still rough."

He raised his head. "I used to shave three times a day because I couldn't stand seeing the red marks I left."

"Didn't work."

"No. I couldn't stay away from you." He kneaded her breast, his thumb maddeningly skimming the edge of her neckline. "I can't stay away from you now."

"I'm not going anywhere," she heard herself tell him, even though she should get to her feet, run down the hall, grab a set of free weights, smash the sauna window and make her escape.

But then she'd have to stop his fingers from toying with her neckline...slipping beneath

She drew a shuddering breath and wiggled against the bulge in his lap. He wanted her. She wanted him.

It was decision time. Either she was going to end this now—gently, but firmly. In a classy way and not a pathetic, whiny, clingy way.

Or she was not.

And if she was not, then she wasn't going to stick her toe into the water; she was going to jump in and make a big splash, hollering the whole time.

Blake nuzzled the side of her neck, her collarbone, and traced his tongue in the hollow there as his thumb dipped beneath her neckline to the strapless bra she wore. Involuntarily, her back arched so much she was nearly bent in two.

Time to jump and make a big splash. Kaia pushed away Blake's hands, but that was only so she could peel down her dress and bra.

Calling a halt, classy or otherwise, was no longer an option.

He murmured something. She didn't know or care what.

"Touch me," she whispered, hoping it didn't sound as if she was begging.

And he did, murmuring, "So beautiful," with his mouth against her breast.

Kaia laughed a little wildly. "You can't see anything."

Blake ran his hands over her bare skin. "I can feel and I can remember."

Kaia's breath hitched as she felt and remembered, too. Because really, that was what this was about. A last time together to remember the good and erase what came after. Kaia wanted to re-create the intense emotional and physical connection with Blake that she'd never had with anyone else. Or if it was broken, then she wanted to know that, too.

The world they'd created now could only live in the

dark. Once the lights came back on, they'd return to their real lives.

Kaia had always preferred the dark. She placed a hand on either side of his face and kissed him lightly before winding her arms around his neck.

Blake cupped her breasts. Drawing one tip into his mouth, he rubbed his thumb across the other, sending a hot zing straight to her middle.

She gasped as her muscles jerked. She was so used to training and exercising to maintain perfect control over her body that when it reacted without any effort on her part, she was caught unaware. For some reason, she'd thought she'd be able to control whether or not she felt anything with Blake this time. But her body remembered and was participating whether she wanted to or not.

Of course she *wanted* to, but the more she enjoyed herself, the harder it would be to walk away later. This had better be worth it.

Blake must have been able to read her mind. His tongue swirled over her with *just* the right speed and *just* the right pressure. Kaia quivered and flexed and bit her lip as a low moan escaped. The back of his neck felt like iron and she realized he was supporting all her weight the way she was hanging off him. She shifted one hand to his shoulder and burrowed the other beneath his jacket as it covered her like a tent.

She was surrounded by his scent and inhaled deeply. She'd remember this combination of soap and man forever.

Blake's breath was hot and when he moved from one breast to the other, Kaia barely felt the coolness on her damp skin.

No power, she recalled. No air conditioning. No way to open the windows. A room full of people. Heat rises.

Beneath the suit jacket, she was becoming uncomfortably warm. Blake must be burning up. She ran her hand over his back. His shirt was seriously damp. "It's so hot!"

"Oh, yeah," he mumbled around her breast.

She chuckled. "I meant temperature."

"Is it?"

Kaia worked the jacket off his shoulders. Blake raised his head long enough to shrug out of it.

"Uhm, maybe the gun and holster, too?" she asked.

"Were you always this picky?" His teeth gleamed and she knew he was grinning.

"I have standards," she said, as she loosened his tie.

"Hmm." Blake dropped the gun and ran his hands up her thighs.

Kaia stilled instantly as his palms bumped over the cuffs in her hidden pockets and the tools beneath her leggings. She'd been so caught up in memories and feelings, she'd forgotten. *Forgotten.* If he'd started running his hands at her calf instead of her thigh, he would have discovered the snuffbox, not that he would have known what it was. But it might have stopped him. He might have asked. And she'd have had to tell him.

How could she have lost her mind like that?

But she always lost her good sense around Blake. She ditched reality and entered her own little world with him. It had got her into trouble then and was about to get her into trouble now.

He was laughing lightly, but her heart pounded. "You travel with a lot of baggage."

Baggage she didn't want to show him if she didn't

have to. She tried to sound sexy. "Well, you know me and pockets."

"I do." He leaned back and shadows flickered behind him. "Are you going to finish taking off my tie? Or…" He moved suggestively in time to the jazzy beat in the background. Taking over the task, he slowly loosened his tie, drew it from around his neck and then twirled it over his head, making Kaia laugh before he tossed it toward the discarded suit jacket.

Then, still moving in time to the music, he started unbuttoning his shirt. "Feel free to join in."

Kaia gestured to her naked torso. The top part of her dress was scrunched at her waist. "I have a head start."

He suddenly stopped unbuttoning his shirt and pulled it over his head in a single motion. "Now I've caught up."

"So you have." Obviously, Blake wasn't thinking about Kaia's pockets or what might be in them and she wanted to keep it that way. She splayed both hands on his chest, tracing his muscles and skimming over his ribs. He was more muscular than before and he'd been no couch potato then. "Bulking up?"

"Not as much as when I first started out on my own. People like their security escorts with big shoulders."

Kaia nodded, thinking of Tyrone and his big shoulders, that made her think of Blake's men and *their* big shoulders and that they might come looking for him at any moment.

Kaia glanced down the hallway. Due to the dim light, they would see anyone who came up the stairs before being seen—if they were paying attention.

That was highly unlikely since Blake chose that moment to take her hands and loop them around his neck before distracting her with a thorough kiss.

Kaia immediately lost herself in his kiss. It had been so long since she'd been able to completely lose herself in a kiss. Not since Blake. Loneliness had driven her to make the attempt, but she'd always remained detached, wary, and watching. Being with another man had never felt right. But then being with Blake had felt right and that turned out to be wrong.

She was going to stop thinking now, which was a good decision because Blake's deep, drugging kisses made it impossible.

Kaia ran her hands over the taut skin of his back, reacquainting herself with the play of hard muscles and the indentation beneath one of his ribs where he'd caught the edge of a table in a fight. She moved her mouth away and pressed their naked torsos together, craving the feel of skin on skin. She enjoyed being surrounded by a man's body, this man's anyway.

"You always were a burrower," Blake murmured against her ear.

"I like being touched," she confessed.

"And I like touching you." His hand was lightly moving up and down in the small of her back. "I like the feel of your skin." He moved his hand up her arm. "I like how strong you are." Skimming her shoulder, he fanned his fingers over the side of her neck. "I like feeling how fast your pulse is beating and knowing that you look so cool on the outside, but you're wild for me on the inside."

"Not cool on the outside." Kaia pulled back reluctantly as she felt a drop of sweat trickle in the valley between her breasts.

Blake took advantage. "And I *love* touching you here." He cupped her breast and rubbed his thumb across her nipple.

Kaia caught her lip between her teeth as she felt a warm tug deep in her stomach. Yes, she was pretty much all thawed out now.

Blake's mouth took over from his hand and he licked and swirled and sucked while Kaia wiggled and squirmed and clutched at his iron-hard shoulders.

She needed more, she *wanted* more, but Blake persisted in his maddeningly slow attentions.

At one point, a frustrated Kaia actually balled her fist and smacked him on that iron-hard shoulder. It had no effect whatsoever. He was holding himself back, she realized. That's why his arms were hard and the cords in his neck stood out and there was the slightest quiver of straining muscles. He wasn't allowing himself to feel the passion that wracked her body, probably out of a misguided sense of nobility. She didn't want nobility; she wanted him incoherent with desire and kissing her hard wherever his mouth landed and not thinking about it so much. "Blake!" She meant to be demanding, but it sounded too much like a sob.

He blew across her breasts, raising gooseflesh. "Better?"

"Yes, but no." Kaia drew a trembling breath. "I want you with me."

She leaned forward and licked Blake's neck, kissing her way to the spot just above his heart. She stopped there and traced a heart shape with her tongue.

She hadn't intended to. It was something she used to do, telling him she loved him without saying the words. She'd never told him that's what it meant or that it was a heart.

She'd loved the person he was pretending to be, not the real person.

"Oh, Kaia. I've missed you. I've missed this."

He bent his knees that caused her to roll against his naked chest and it felt so good, she wanted to weep. Then he started playing with her breasts again and it felt even better. It felt real.

She lifted her mouth to his, nipping at his lip as she wiggled back and forth over the hard length in his pants, finding just the right spot. Finding the right spot used to be easier, back when they sat on the couch, but she'd been wearing less clothing then.

"Let me." Blake's hand skimmed beneath her dress.

As soon as his fingers touched the edge of her leggings, Kaia jumped as though she'd been burned.

"Kaia?" Blake withdrew his hand. "I thought..." The breath whistled through his teeth. "I'm making some serious assumptions when I have no right to."

"No!" She touched his arm as he leaned back. "It's just..." *It's just that I didn't tell you about my little side job, the one that affects my future, and possibly world peace.*

As good as they were together physically, if the electricity hadn't gone out and they hadn't been trapped, Blake would never have listened to her version of what happened six years ago. At the moment, he seemed to believe her and to trust her, but when the lights came back on, would he still?

She couldn't take the chance that he wouldn't. She was going to have to keep him from discovering the snuffbox and exactly what she was wearing beneath her dress.

"You didn't misread the signals," she told him. "But...while we can't get completely carried away..." She gave him a sexy smile and put her hand on his thigh. "There are still a lot of things we can do."

Blake stared at her for a moment. *"Oh."* He exhaled and relaxed. "You're worried about a condom."

Well, no, but she should have been. Anyway, it was the perfect excuse. "I've got a lot of stuff in my pockets, but not one of those. But I don't think you'll mind too much." She reached for his zipper.

This time, Blake flinched, which she should have expected.

"I wasn't—"

"I know. That was just reflex. Anyway, I'm prepared." He started pawing through his jacket.

What? "You are?"

There was a click followed by a beam of bluish light. "Yeah. I'm a regular Boy Scout."

The flashlight showed the face of a man on a mission. Kaia used to stare at him when he slept and now noted subtle changes. His face had matured; his cheekbones were more pronounced and his jaw was fuller. The shadows emphasized a line or two at the corners of his eyes that probably weren't visible in normal lighting. There was nothing that said "boy" about him.

"Boy Scout. That's not exactly the way I think of you," she said.

He laughed softly. "I'm talking about the 'be prepared' part."

"I got that." He had a condom? Talk about mixed emotions. On one hand, yippee, but on the other, getting out of her leggings without him noticing all the stuff she had secreted beneath her dress was going to be problematic, not to mention a mood killer.

On yet another hand, there was a lot to be said for being highly motivated. And it *was* dark. The dim light created interesting shadows on his sculpted torso and Kaia decided that she was very highly motivated.

Blake unzipped a flat pouch about the size of a paperback. "Standard TransSecure issue. All my men carry them. You wouldn't believe what security escorts and bodyguards get asked for, especially when a limo is involved."

He shined the flashlight on the open pouch and Kaia saw tape, safety pins, a tiny mending kit with scissors, bandages, aspirin, hand sanitizer, wipes, tissues, transit way tokens, a comb, mirror, lip balm, breath mints, antacids, and, yes, condoms. Multiple brands. Flavored and unflavored.

"Wow." She could be motivated for a very long time with that stash.

"I would have said something earlier, but I didn't think we were there yet. Come on." He nudged her off his lap. "Let's go find a bedroom and get naked."

"Wait." Kaia thought quickly. Darkness was her friend. Although he was currently distracted, once the lights came back on, Blake would notice things Kaia didn't want him noticing, like her thick leggings. Right now, if he'd even noticed, he probably assumed they were some type of underwear, and she wanted to keep it that way.

"I don't want to wait." Blake's voice sounded thick and single-minded.

"Neither do I," Kaia said. "That's my point." She got on all fours and crawled toward him. "We don't need a bedroom."

His eyes widened. "You mean...here?"

She nodded.

"Now?"

"Umm hmm."

She could see the glint in his eyes and watched it

shift as he glanced down the hall. "Someone might come up the stairs."

"I know." He'd be thinking about being caught and about the sex and he wouldn't have the brain cells left to think about anything else. "It kind of turns me on."

"*Does* it." His voice took on an entirely different tone and Kaia discovered that it *did* kind of turn her on.

She stood on her knees and extended her right leg into the shadows. Blake looked down the hallway once more, his head tilted as he listened to the crowd noise and music, assessing and analyzing. Calculating the odds of someone searching for them.

Not focused on her. Yet.

Kaia reached beneath her dress and peeled off one legging and an elastic band filled with bits of metal picks and wires that was stuck to her thigh. She hid the soft ripping sound in the rustle of fabric and straddled his legs, arranging the folds of her dress to cushion the contents of her hidden pockets.

Blake looked up at her. "Are we really going to do this?"

"Yes." She could hardly believe it herself. Blindly, she grabbed a packet from the pouch and tossed it to him. "Yes, we are." And once more, she reached for his zipper.

His hand clamped around her wrist. "Not so fast."

Kaia felt as if her heart jumped to her throat. Did he suspect something? Had she been too aggressive? They'd never done anything like this before and she was no exhibitionist. In fact, she'd spent her life trying to blend in.

But Blake turned her wrist until her palm was face up and kissed it. His hair brushed against her nipples and she twitched.

He smiled up at her as he released her hand. "If we're going to do this, we're going to enjoy ourselves." Slowly, he moved his hand under her hitched-up skirt and skimmed it up her bare leg.

Her heart pounded and she went all liquid inside. As his hand crept along the soft flesh of her inner thigh, she felt her nerves tighten in anticipation. She was ready for this. She was ready for pretty much anything.

Kaia clutched at his shoulders, tugging him toward her, but he held himself away and instead of moving faster, his hand slowed, the pressure somewhere between a tickle and a caress. She rocked toward him and he immediately stopped.

"Hold still."

Was he kidding? "I...don't want to."

"I know." And he waited.

Why? She could hardly stand it. Suddenly, she lunged for him, hoping he'd stop playing and give in to raw desire, but he leaned out of reach. "Don't. Move."

Don't move? *Don't move?* Was he kidding? She pressed his hand against her thigh and tugged upward, but he resisted. And then he slid in the wrong direction.

Okay, *fine*. Making a frustrated sound, Kaia clamped her legs on either side of his, but her muscles betrayed her with a tremble. "I can't!"

She felt his smile. "Good."

"Blake!" she wailed.

He inched upward.

Kaia moved before she could stop herself and again, he stopped. "Why are you doing this?" she moaned.

"The slower the burn, the hotter the fire, and the bigger the explosion."

"Unless the fuse goes out."

"I'll light it again." But he moved faster, his fingers lightly stroking from side to side.

Kaia felt her skin prickle from the inside out. She felt both hot and cold at the same time. Her muscles trembled with the effort not to move and she was grateful that Blake didn't hold it against her.

The only thing she wanted held against her was his hand, higher and harder.

Her fingers clenched and unclenched as the tension built. She knew what was going to happen—he'd reach the juncture of her thighs and then he'd stop to torture her some more. Kaia didn't know if she could stand it. In fact, she might have to light her own fuse.

Well, now, there was an idea. Why not? She had a couple of free hands and a couple of free nipples. She cupped her breasts and squeezed.

"Hey." Blake's hand stopped, but now Kaia didn't care.

She plucked at her nipples and rubbed against his thighs.

"You're breaking the no-moving rule."

Kaia threw back her head and moaned.

"But I like it," Blake said.

Kaia shivered. Her desire intensified, concentrating in a tiny knot of need. She moved faster, but it wasn't enough; she couldn't get the right angle because her legs were too far apart.

And then unexpectedly, blessedly, Blake's hand cupped her with just the right pressure in just the right spot.

For an instant, everything stopped. Time, sensation, sound. And then warm pleasure bloomed through her like petals unfurling. Kaia let the relief float through her. Nice. Blooming was nice. Not an explosion, but very, very nice.

"You've been a naughty girl," Blake murmured. "Spoiling your appetite like that."

"Hmm." Kaia stretched her arms over her head. The tension seeped out of her muscles leaving her limp and relaxed. "Well." She patted the side of his leg. "I guess I'll be going now."

Pretending to stand, she collapsed in laughter when Blake grabbed her hips and kept her firmly in place. "You guessed wrong."

She gestured to his lap. "But you're not dressed for the party."

Keeping one hand on her hip, Blake tore open the condom packet with his teeth.

Once more, Kaia reached for his zipper and once more Blake stopped her. "Your zipper privileges have been suspended. Don't move and keep your hands where I can see them."

She snorted and then clamped her hands over her mouth to stifle the laughter.

"Again, not an attractive sound. You're lucky the rest of you makes up for it."

"And you're lucky that I *will* make up for it," she said when he was ready.

Kaia raised herself on her knees, leaned forward and kissed him, aware of his hands gripping her hips. But he didn't take control, didn't try to hurry things along even though he was clearly more than ready for her.

Kaia didn't mean to spend so long kissing him, enjoying the hot sweetness, and she certainly didn't expect to feel her own desire start building again.

She heard a moan—it could have been his or it could have been hers. Grabbing the gate with one hand, she supported herself on his shoulder with the other and slowly lowered, taking him in inch by inch, wanting to make him wait the way he'd made her wait.

His hands spasmed on her hips and with a guttural, "Kaia!" he moved her up and down, setting an increasingly faster, harder pace.

And she was right there with him, feeling the pressure building again until, with a final, deep thrust, Blake groaned her name and shuddered. She rocked once more and felt a hot rush of exploding sensation.

Gulping for air, she collapsed against his sweaty torso, her own skin also slick. Her hand hurt where she'd gripped the metal lattice.

Her heart hurt because she knew she would never find a connection like this with anyone else.

"Kaia?" Blake stroked her back.

Lovely, but it was so very warm. She pulled back and fanned her face. "Okay. Long fuse, big explosion. Got it."

Blake captured one of her hands and pressed a kiss to her palm, as he'd done before. "This was about more than a big explosion."

Kaia stilled, unsure whether she wanted him to continue or not. Once he said whatever he was going to say, it couldn't be unsaid. "Or, in my case, a couple of explosions."

He shook his head. "I'm serious."

Kaia's heart had just started to slow down and now it kicked back up again. "Blake," she began. She didn't know what she was going to say, but she wanted to give him time to think and get past the immediate post-sex glow before he made promises he'd regret.

"Kaia, I can't erase—"

"Folks," Luke's voice interrupted. "I've been informed that the entire East Coast is blacked out due to a power grid failure. We're going to be here for a while."

_11_

A BLACKOUT.

Alarmed chatter drowned out Luke's next few sentences. Blake cocked his head, straining to hear, hoping Luke's announcement hadn't caused hysteria. All it took was one person to lose it and the crowd would feed on the panic. The next few seconds were crucial. Luke would have to maintain control. And he shouldn't have to do it by himself.

Blake punched the gate in frustration, which accomplished nothing except making his knuckles hurt.

"The whole East Coast?" Kaia repeated.

His attention swung back to her. He'd been about to tell her that he couldn't erase the past and ask for her to give them another chance. He still needed to say it, and more, but he'd have to wait until later.

"Yes." He brushed a few stray hairs from her damp cheek and leaned forward to kiss her, but she was already shifting off his legs.

"That means it'll be hours before the power comes back on."

They stared at each other. If ever there was a cue

for one of them to give a cheesy smile and say, "However will we pass the time?" this was it. But he could only think that it also meant hours with all those people downstairs and Blake caught behind the gate. Hours with his professional reputation on the line and nothing he could do about it. He couldn't even communicate with Luke. He felt like punching the gate again when he should be holding Kaia and savoring what they'd just shared. She'd always liked the cuddling part, he remembered.

He reached for her to try and make up for his abrupt mood change, but heard rustling as Kaia rearranged her dress. "Kaia, come he—"

"You said Luke was your best guy?" she interrupted. Her back was to him as she stuck her leg through whatever underwear thing she was wearing.

"Yeah." He hesitated, feeling like a jerk. Grabbing his shirt, he drew it over his head and jammed his arms through the cuffs. "But I'm sure he's still wondering where the hell I am." Luke would notice that Kaia was also missing and make assumptions. He knew of their past. No way would he send somebody looking for them.

"You told him he was in charge."

Blake remembered. "But the circumstances have changed." Understatement. "I'm looking really bad, here."

"Honestly, I think you look pretty good." Kaia got lightly to her feet.

"You know what I mean."

"I do." Kaia leaned against the wall, watching as he finished dressing.

She was fast. His eyes had adjusted to the dark

enough for him to marvel at how cool and serene she looked when minutes earlier, she'd been anything but.

"What would you be doing if you were downstairs?" she asked.

Blake got to his feet. "Working on getting us out of here."

"By doing what?"

"I don't know—trying to start the generator. Something." Truthfully, there wasn't much he could do, since that was the way he'd designed the system.

"If there's a generator, why isn't it running?"

"It's programmed to require manual activation if the security system deploys."

"I know you've got men stationed outside," Kaia said. "Why haven't they started it?"

Blake exhaled as he strapped on his holster. "It needs a code, too."

"Wow," she said. "You put a lot of thought into this."

That made him feel kind of good. He gave a last shake to the gate and admired the installation. "I guess that's the bright spot. At least I know I've designed a foolproof system."

A couple of beats went by. "There are always ways around a system."

And she'd taught him those methods. "Not this system. No one can get in or out until we want them getting in or out."

Kaia laughed. "I can."

Her words hung in the silence between them.

Did she think he'd forgotten all the little tricks and techniques she'd revealed to him? "Well, sure, if you blow holes in the walls."

"Oh, please." She grimaced. "I've got more finesse than that."

Now she'd piqued his curiosity. "You, ah, took a look around?"

She lifted a shoulder. "A little."

"And you seriously think you can get out?"

"And back in."

In the background, Blake heard a shrill voice going on about medicine and Luke's calm reply. He couldn't make out the words, because Luke wasn't trying to be heard above the crowd, but he knew the drill. Luke would be reassuring the woman that they were doing everything they could and so on and so on.

From here on out, the situation would only deteriorate. "Okay." Blake knew Kaia wasn't going to offer; he was going to have to ask. "Show me. Please," he tacked on.

Without a word, Kaia took off down the hall toward the bedrooms, leaving Blake to trot after her. He'd turned on his flashlight, but she didn't appear to need one.

She led him to the sauna in the home gym. "This is one of two possibilities. It depends on whether you want to re-enter the house or not."

Blake was disappointed. He pointed to the interior window facing outside the house. "That's not ordinary glass."

"I know." She walked inside the sauna and gestured for him to join her. "I'd use weights to smash it—but only if I were in a hurry and didn't care if anyone heard."

"And then what?" He looked out into the blackness. "That's a sheer drop to concrete."

"I didn't say getting out would be easy. I'd either go up and find a better place to climb down, or I'd rappel down."

Right. He waved his flashlight at her. "And you just so happen to have rappelling equipment on you."

She simply looked at him.

I've got a lot in my pockets... A whole bunch of ugly emotions started swirling within him: distrust, betrayal, wariness, and doubt. Blake exhaled heavily and blew them away. This time, he was going with his basic gut feelings. "Okay, I'm a Boy Scout. You're a Girl Scout. What's the second way?"

"The bathroom." She started walking toward it.

"What? The little window?" He'd measured it and the one just like it in the hall bath. "Nobody can get through that window."

"You'd be surprised."

Blake had a feeling he would be.

"Besides, I could put jewelry in a canister and shoot it outside and pick it up later."

He followed her into the master bathroom. "But you'd still be caught inside. And then we'd know to search and locate the canister."

"Not if I had an accomplice waiting."

Blake could visualize just such a scenario. He got the queasy bad-burrito-on-a-stakeout feeling in his stomach. "But you'd still be caught."

"I know." She pushed a vanity bench beneath the window. "That's why it's obviously not my first choice." Kaia hitched up her skirt and climbed onto the bench.

Blake momentarily flashed to her hitching up her skirt and climbing onto *him*. Incredible. He could hardly believe it had happened or that he was ready for it to happen again.

He looked up at her and knew he was ready for a lot to happen again. Whether Kaia could get out of here or not, he was going to convince her to give them a second chance together.

No, a first chance. Wipe the slate clean and start with who they were now. No pretending. No lying. The past would always be a part of their history, but it wouldn't define them.

Kaia was standing on her toes as she shined a concentrated beam around the windowsill. Her mini flashlight was better than his. He'd have to ask her where she got it.

"The window has been painted shut," she announced as she dug into one of her voluminous pockets—the ones that made him nervous. She withdrew something, he heard a snick, and guessed she'd unfolded a pocketknife which she was now running around the edge of the window.

She was very quiet and very efficient. Blake had never seen her in action before. He knew what she'd been and had listened when she'd told him snippets from her life, but he'd never actually visualized the details.

He felt a puff of welcome breeze and saw that she'd opened the window without him hearing. He should pay attention.

She pushed the window outward to the nine and three quarters of an inch clearance he'd previously measured.

"As I said, nobody is getting through there. And I'd go so far as to challenge you to get the right angle to shoot a canister anywhere but straight down," he said.

"You'd challenge me, would you?" Kaia was bent over, doing something.

Blake shined his flashlight at her in time to see her straighten. He heard a "psst" and a scraping sound. "Compressed air?"

"No."

She didn't elaborate. That was okay. He'd find out later.

After a wrenching creak, the entire window was in Kaia's hands. "Hold this for me, will you?"

Stunned, Blake automatically took the glass from her and set it on the bathroom counter. When he turned back, Kaia was leaning halfway out the opening.

"What is that—eighteen...twenty inches? You still can't get through that."

She didn't say anything.

"I've got quite a view here."

She wiggled her rump and he laughed and lightly smacked it. He couldn't resist.

"Hey, I am not into that," he heard.

"Just checking. Are you stuck?"

She popped back down. "I've been through smaller. I was just figuring out which way I was going after I got out."

As Kaia spoke, she tugged up the top of her dress, poking her arms through holes he hadn't known were there, covering her shoulders and chest and skimming fabric down her arms. The material had unfolded like an accordion.

Next, she pulled off the silver and black belt and tested its strength.

The queasy, bad burrito feeling returned.

"Calm down," she said. "Remember that I was hired to get Royce's cuffs back."

"How did you know what I was thinking?" he asked, rather than deny it.

"Your breathing changed and you cracked your knuckle."

He immediately unclenched his fist.

She straightened and pulled some more, tucked some more, and even though Blake shone his light on her, he couldn't figure out how the evening dress she'd been wearing had turned into a long-sleeved shirt, tights and a backpack.

"How...how did you do that?"

"Practice." She glanced up at him and kicked off her shoes. Ripping out the lining, she ended up wearing what appeared to be ballet flats. "Better for climbing," she explained. The shoes disappeared into the backpack.

Only her hands and face were exposed. The rest of her was covered in form-fitting black. She looked like, well, a cat burglar. And she'd transformed into one with a breathtaking efficiency he wasn't going to think about.

"I'm impressed," Blake admitted.

"Yeah, and you're worried, too." She exhaled heavily and looked him right in the eyes. "I guess you'll never completely trust me, will you?"

He hesitated. It wasn't intentional, but she noticed.

"I—"

"Don't." She placed a finger over his lips, then kissed him, lightly and quickly.

It felt like a goodbye.

Stepping onto the vanity bench, she waggled her fingers. "See ya."

If Blake hadn't seen what happened next, he would never have believed it.

Kaia raised her leg and poked it through the window. Then she stretched her arms over her head an impossibly long way and her shoulders seemed to disappear. There were a couple of twists, a pop—did she dislocate her shoulder socket?—and she was straddling the ledge. Balancing herself, she maneuvered the backpack through the opening, shifted her hips and head and finally, Blake watched her remaining leg snake upward and she was gone.

He'd watched her and he still didn't believe it. Blake stepped onto the little vanity bench and looked out.

"Boo," Kaia said, her head hanging inches away.

"Kaia, my God, the drainpipe isn't meant to hold your weight!"

"It's not." She dropped and he barely heard the padded thud as she landed on the dormer to the left.

"Relax." Her whisper drifted up to him.

Blake's mouth was open so he must have gasped. He swallowed. "Don't fall," he managed to say.

"Don't plan to."

Blake glanced around the roof and sky. At least it wasn't raining anymore. In fact, the moon was trying to peek out of the thinning clouds. But the tiles were still shiny and had to be slippery.

Kaia looped her makeshift rope and tossed it upward a couple of times before it caught on something.

Blake didn't like how dangerous and iffy it looked. "Hey," he called softly. "You don't have to prove anything more. I'm convinced you could get away."

"Don't worry. This is nothing." She looked upward a moment and added, "Well, maybe something. As far as difficulty, this is only a three or four out of ten. Maybe as much as a five because of the rain." She tested her weight against the rope and when it held, she started climbing. "At least I don't have to jump across open spaces or walk a tightrope. I really hate that."

She was going to give him a heart attack with that kind of talk.

Just then, the moon poked through the clouds, and Blake got a clear view of Kaia easily climbing to the roof above them. At least she made it look easy, as only the most skilled can. Once on the ridge line, her figure in the tight outfit was silhouetted against the sky as she unhooked the rope.

She'd been so quick and so silent, in complete control of her body.

Blake knew that body. He'd recently been incredibly intimate with that body and yet he'd had no idea what it was capable of.

He watched, fascinated, as Kaia make her way across the rooftop, her movements gracefully sinuous. It was the hottest thing he'd ever seen and desire flared within him. He didn't even try to tamp it down. He would never forget the sight of Kaia in the moonlight, scampering over the gleaming tiles, as silent as a shadow until she disappeared over the other side and out of sight.

Wow. Blake stared after her, still admiring the way she'd efficiently gone through an opening he'd dismissed as not worth putting sensors on.

He wasn't going to make that mistake again.

Blake mentally redesigned some of his clients' installations as he breathed in the humid night air and enjoyed the breeze. He'd have to ask Kaia for hints about the transportation side of his business, too. For pay, of course. She deserved it. She could make big bucks as a security consultant. Maybe he should hire her permanently. He tested the idea, liking it more and more. Seeing her every day would reinforce their personal relationship.

Blake closed his eyes, the breeze on his face, and recalled the utter surprise of making love to Kaia with the possibility of discovery. He could get addicted to the extra punch that brought to sex. Kaia...

Had not come back. The desire that had flamed to life again went out. Blake opened his eyes, waiting for her head to pop back into sight. He replayed their conversation and couldn't recall Kaia telling him where she was going. Well, obviously she was going to try and get back into the house. But then what? They hadn't discussed a plan because Blake hadn't believed she could really escape. But she had.

He stared at the spot where she'd disappeared over the top of the roof, straining to hear. Would she find Luke and tell him what had happened? Blake should have given her a message...but if Luke saw her in that getup, would he listen to her?

And what exactly would she say?

Then again, why assume she'd seek out Luke?

Or Royce, for that matter. Suppose she was planning to keep the cuffs? Or maybe she made the whole story up and he'd just been conned by a thief.

Blake slowly stepped off the bench and sat on it, slumping against the wall.

Had he just made an incredibly stupid, stupid mistake?

What reason did Kaia have to return for him? Did he honestly think he was such a hot lover that it would make up for sending her to prison?

I guess you'll never completely trust me, will you?

And the quick goodbye kiss. He felt sick—worse than any food poisoning. He wanted to trust her. He wanted to make up for not believing her before, but did that mean he should believe her now?

IT WAS A LOT HARDER to break in than it was to break out. From the other side of the roof, Kaia took a moment to gaze at the darkened landscape. Car headlights bounced slowly along the road and she could see pinpoints of light through windows or from someone walking outside with a flashlight. The night was quiet without the hum from the air conditioning units. She did hear the motor from a van in the drive below. It was unmarked, so it must belong to Blake's crew. The crumpled valet awning blocked the front pathway to the house and she didn't see anyone standing around.

Turning back to the window, Kaia removed it from the frame and carefully lowered it as far as she could inside before letting go. There was a thud and a rattle, but since she'd removed the wooden sill with it, the glass apparently survived. This window was easier to get in and out of since the architect had thoughtfully provided a handy decorative protrusion to stand on.

Seconds later, Kaia was inside the hall bathroom. Fortunately, it was vacant. She opened the door to the hallway and made a dramatic, "Ta da!" type entrance, but Blake wasn't waiting by the gate.

Maybe he hadn't expected her to be so quick. She waited for a couple of minutes before walking in the opposite direction to the open part of the hall that overlooked the party room.

Now that she was back inside, she noticed how warm it was getting in the house. She peeked over the landing's banister to the room below and saw people sitting in chairs, surrounded by candlelight, chatting away, while others had staked out the couches and looked to be sleeping. A few of the younger crowd were on the floor. She didn't see Royce, but she couldn't see the band or the bar area from this angle.

No one was looking up, but Kaia didn't want to attract attention. Keeping to the shadows, she moved down the hallway toward the stairs until she could see the far end of the room where Casper's office was located.

Life would be so much easier if she could just nip downstairs, get into the office, and unload the snuffbox. Then she wouldn't have to worry about Blake or anyone else discovering that she had it.

As she watched, trying to decide whether she should risk it or not, a stealthy movement caught her attention. If anyone knew stealth, it was Kaia.

People trying not to attract attention by sneaking around were more noticeable than if they moved as though they had a right to be where they were.

If anyone had a right to be wherever she wanted in this house, it was Tina Nazario, and that's who was sneaking over to her husband's office door.

She was carrying a candle, which she set on one of the jewelry display pedestals. Kaia hoped wax didn't drip on the velvet—kind of a strange thought to be having at this moment, but there it was.

Tina glanced over her shoulder to see if she was being watched, and Kaia shook her head. What an amateur move. And judging by the stash upstairs, Tina was no amateur.

She bent over the doorknob.

She's picking the lock. How interesting.

Tina took long enough to get inside for Kaia to know that while she wasn't an expert, she'd certainly picked a lock or two in her time.

"Kaia!" Blake was at the gate.

Drawing her finger to her lips in the universal sign to be quiet, she gestured for him to wait. They didn't have to wait long. Half-a-minute later, Tina quickly slipped out of the office and closed the door behind her.

That could not be good, Kaia thought as she ran lightly toward Blake. "Where have you been?"

"You're okay," he said on an exhale. Even in the dim light, she could see that his face was pale.

She blinked. "Were you *worried* about me?"

He extended a finger through the grating and brushed her cheek. "I thought..." He cleared his throat. "When you didn't come back..."

"You thought I'd fall down and go boom?"

He gave a surprised laugh. "Well, yeah."

"The idea was to show you I could get around your system, Blake. That means getting out *and* getting back in." She gestured to the gate. "You will note that we are now on opposite sides of the gate."

"I'm..."

"Clearly stunned. I'm not sure if that's a compliment or an insult."

His mouth twisted in a rueful grimace. "If it had given you more trouble, it would be better for my ego."

"I'm just really, really good. Does that help?"

"Not so much. Hey." He leaned forward against the gate. "I don't want anything to be between us ever again."

She leaned forward, too. "So whatcha gonna do about it?"

"I'll think of something." He bent down and she stood on tiptoe and they kissed through the grating.

Kaia raised her hand and met his there. They linked fingers and pressed against each other, mouths clinging through the gate.

They probably looked ridiculous, but Kaia didn't care. As soon as he saw that she was on the other side, he could have started barking orders at her, giving her instructions about what he wanted her to do. Instead, he was kissing her, letting her know that she was more important than his responsibilities or his reputation, or anything else.

She melted into the kiss a little more and felt the weight of the snuffbox at her waist both literally and figuratively. Once she was out from under that, once she'd completed her job for Casper, then the future was a blank slate and there *would* be nothing between them.

She squeezed Blake's fingers and they broke apart. "You're amazing," he said.

She smiled. "So far."

"Have you talked to Luke?"

"I haven't been downstairs. But I did see Tina skulking around. She went into Casper's office."

"Kaia, she lives here. She can go anywhere she wants."

"So why is she sneaking around and picking locks?"

Kaia could tell by Blake's expression that she didn't need to spell it out.

"This could become incredibly awkward." He stared past her toward the stairs. "I need you to tell Luke to keep an eye on her and where I am. And I'll need an earpiece."

"You can tell him yourself."

Blake reared back. "I thought we were together in this."

"Jeez, Blake! You can tell him yourself, because I'm going to come and get you."

"Nooo." He shook his head. "No way can I get through that window."

Kaia grinned at him. "Trust me."

12

"You're enjoying this, aren't you?" Blake held Kaia's hands in a death grip.

"Little bit." Facing him, she backed her way up the roof.

Yeah. She was climbing backward.

The curved clay tiles were slippery, especially for Blake who was wearing regular shoes. Kaia had tried to convince him to try the climb barefoot, but he felt he'd be good to go with the rubber soles. That might have been a mistake.

Then again, he'd never believed he'd actually get through the window. But by Kaia removing the wooden frame and showing him how to position his body—and a whole lot of pushing and tugging on her part—Blake had worked his shoulders through the opening. After that, it was a piece of cake to get the rest of him through.

They'd had to cannibalize some of the gym equipment for wire to rig extra support for Blake's weight—and he'd really objected to that—but here they were, on the roof, climbing toward the ridge line on their way to the other bathroom window.

Kaia backed up and Blake inched toward her, his foot slipping before it found a good hold. He grabbed her hands even tighter.

"I've got you. Trust me." She was so calm and seemingly unconcerned.

"Trust isn't the issue. Me out-weighing you by a hundred pounds is the issue."

"It's all about leverage."

Blake slipped a bit again. "I should have listened to you and taken off my shoes."

"Maybe not. I didn't realize you had rubber soles."

"That's in case we have to chase somebody." He looked over his shoulder. "I don't think it helps for climbing on wet tile."

"Don't look down," she instructed.

"I don't have a problem with heights." Yet he wasn't exactly *enjoying* looking down.

"I've heard that before."

As they approached the ridge line, Blake could see what was on the other side and he wasn't looking forward to it. At least on this side of the house they had grass to break their fall. On the front, there was only the driveway.

"Don't think about it." She was reading his mind.

"Then give me something else to think about."

"Okay. Answer a question for me." She pointed to where she wanted him to place his foot. "Why did you have to go undercover?"

Blake stopped staring at his feet and met her eyes. "That came out of nowhere."

"I've been wondering. You knew I had the Cat's Eye diamond. I never hid it. Why go the fake boyfriend route? And for so long? Weeks. You let me…" She swallowed. *"Why?"*

The clouds had mostly cleared and a partial moon gleamed down. Kaia's face showed more emotion than he'd ever seen. Hurt and betrayal and a tortured bewilderment.

He hated that he was responsible for those emotions and he hated that if it was part of his job, he'd probably do it again. Thank God it wasn't his job anymore.

Blake knew his answer would anger her and this wasn't the time for Kaia to get emotional. He chose his words carefully. "We wanted to know if you'd acted alone."

A few seconds went by before she understood. "My parents." She gazed off to the side. "You were using me to get to my parents and uncle."

"And anyone in their circle."

"You didn't." She looked back at him. "How disappointing for you."

"I got chewed out, yeah."

She made a face. "So did I." She started backing up again.

That was it? No explosion? "Is there going to be yelling now?" Blake asked, very aware that they were on a rooftop and his footing was none too secure.

"From me? No. I asked. You answered. Now I know." Her face had gone blank again.

That was too easy. He should explain more. "I dragged it out so I could be with you longer. I should have pressured you harder to meet your family. But I didn't. I told myself you'd get suspicious. But it was just an excuse to stay with you."

"Now *that* makes me mad."

Great. "I thought it would make you feel better!"

"Hmm." She gazed off as though considering.

"Prolonging a lie for your own selfish reasons... No. I don't feel better."

Neither did Blake. "Why don't you just shove me off the roof now then and get it over with?"

"I'm rehabilitating you. Hold on there." She pointed to a reinforced opening around a vent. "I want to check for loose tiles."

She left him clinging to the side of the roof as she checked the ridge line. "I did bring up you meeting my parents. They told me you were a cop and I told them you'd already told me. They said I couldn't trust you and it came down to choosing either them or you. I chose you and moved in." She looked off into the distance. "I wonder whatever happened to that last bag of dirty laundry?"

Blake hadn't realized she'd moved in. He'd just thought she was sleeping over. A lot. Was he going to tell her that? Hell, no. "I didn't realize I'd come between you and your parents. I'm sorry." And he was, but not for the way she probably assumed. If they'd managed to arrest the whole bunch, Kaia might not have served any time at all.

"Don't be. At least not for that." She momentarily disappeared over the ridge line and her voice drifted back to him. "Things hadn't been that great between us since I figured out what they did."

"But...how could you not have known?"

She reappeared and gestured for him to climb toward her. "Keep to your left. There are some wonky areas."

He started climbing while she watched. "When I was little, it was mostly games and party tricks. A portion of my parents' business was making copies of jewelry pieces for insurance purposes."

For when clients didn't want to risk wearing the real thing, Blake knew.

"Part of my dad's sales pitch to have a duplicate made was proving how vulnerable a client's safe was. He'd take me along on his calls and nobody paid attention to me, a little kid. I'd do my thing, and then my dad would parade me and whatever I'd recovered, and get the commission. 'Look at that. Your safe is so flimsy, a child can break into it.'"

Blake glanced up to where she crouched, waiting for him. "You heard that a lot."

"Oh, yeah. The day he couldn't ignore the fact that I had breasts was the saddest day in his life."

"I promise never to ignore your breasts," Blake told her.

She made a strange sound and gestured with her foot. "Pay attention to your climbing."

He grinned and looked down again. "So what was their scam—giving clients back two copies?"

"Probably. Or returning the original missing some stones. But I didn't know that. And when I got older and asked more questions, my parents always had an answer that made sense."

Blake reached the ridge line and sat, straddling it. Kaia started to move, but he stopped her. "Wait. Tell me the rest. When did you figure it out?"

She sat next to him. "They sent me to a ritzy boarding school so they'd have an in with the other parents. Up till then, I'd been home-schooled. I was just so happy to finally get to go some place and be around people my own age. To have friends." She turned away. "I don't like talking about it."

"I don't like your parents a whole lot." Blake swung

his other leg over the top of the roof. "They manipulated you. You were just a kid."

"Not all the time." She stood and looked down at him. "I got invited to go on a ski trip with a friend and her family. First time, ever. Only time, ever. They robbed the house while we were gone. I know they did. They never admitted it, but when we got back, her parents discovered the break-in. I recognized the technique. Dad was getting old and clumsy."

Some day, Blake hoped he'd meet her parents so he could tell them exactly what he thought of them. "Kaia, that wasn't your fault."

She handed him the end of a rope she'd tied around her waist. "I knew they'd try something. I shouldn't have gone. And afterward, when I wouldn't accept any other invitations, they yanked me out of the school. Speaking of yanking—try not to. Use the rope to keep your balance."

"Forget it." He tossed the rope back at her. "If I slip I'd take you with me."

"Then don't slip."

"Kaia—"

"Blake." She put the rope in his hand. "I'd slow you enough to give you a chance to get your footing."

He decided to quit arguing, but he had no intention of using the rope.

Blake stood and surveyed the scene below. It was strangely dark with little pockets of light here and there. In the distance, streets full of vehicles were either gridlocked or moved sluggishly without the traffic signals.

"Follow me," Kaia said. "Put your feet exactly where I put mine."

"Wait." When she turned back he found it surprisingly hard to ask his question. "Did you do any jobs after that—after the ski trip?"

They stared at each other. "What do you think?" she snapped, and took off across the roof top.

Blake struggled to keep up. "I think you were forced into it."

Without warning, she stopped and whirled around. If he'd tried a move like that, he would have ended up on the ground.

"Don't make excuses for me. Don't make me into something I'm not. Something more palatable to your sense of right and wrong. I didn't have much of a choice, but I had one. I could have turned my parents into the police, gone to a foster home until I was eighteen. But I didn't."

"Who would have? Kaia, they're your parents!"

"So? We can't afford family loyalty. I haven't seen or spoken to them since I called them after I was arrested. I wouldn't know how to get in touch with them even if I wanted to. So don't get any ideas."

Blake was horrified. He couldn't begin to comprehend a family dynamic like the one Kaia had. "That's not why I asked."

"It doesn't matter. The point is that I knew what I was doing. I agreed to go on jobs if they'd give me college money. But once I enrolled, I was done with them. That's why I thought Casper's job was a godsend. It bought me another year. But Blake, don't pretty it up in your mind. For two years, I knew exactly what I was doing." She drew a breath. "I wasn't guilty of the crime I went to prison for, but I was guilty of others. I've paid. Now, I can move on."

She met his gaze defiantly, clearly expecting him to be repulsed when he felt exactly the opposite.

"You think that's going to scare me away?" he asked.

"Does it?"

"No."

"Because you feel sorry for me?"

"Because you're taking responsibility for your actions." Her integrity pinged his buttons more than anything else right now. Blake wasn't falling off the roof, he was falling in love. Had fallen in love. "That's hot."

Her eyes narrowed. "Are you joking? I just told you that I'm no Girl Scout—"

"And I don't care. I mean, I *care,* but it's not a deal breaker." The conversation was too intense to be held in such a dangerous place.

"A...deal breaker?" Kaia was looking at him as though he'd grown two heads. "Do we have a deal?"

"Yes." He took a step, wobbled and regained his balance. "Our deal is you get me off this roof and I'll let you have your wicked way with me."

"I've already had my wicked way with you."

"You've only got one way?"

A surprised burst of laughter escaped from her. "I have many ways."

"Good. You can pick. Deal?"

"What if I say no?"

"Then, I'll pick."

"I meant, what if I leave you on the roof?"

"You won't." Blake placed the end of the rope into her palm and closed her fingers over it. "I trust you."

Kaia looked at her hand. "What's that supposed to be...some kind of symbolism?"

"Well...yeah." And he thought it was pretty good, too.

"Being stupid equals trust?"

"No." She was so prickly. "I just...wanted you to

know that I...trust you." He opened his arms. "I accept you for who you are. All of you."

"Blake." She gave him back the rope. "I appreciate that you're feeling all touchy feely because of my 'poor little me' story, but just hang on to the rope, okay?"

So much for grand gestures. "Okay."

When he thought about it, as he followed Kaia across steep angles of slippery tile, he figured she was the one trusting him to let go and not drag her down if he found himself heading for the ground. He watched where she put her feet, didn't argue when she pointed to handholds and accepted that she was the expert and he was a big guy on a slippery slope. It was a different experience for Blake not to be the authority in a situation, but no less adrenaline-charged. He figured this was one of those character-building situations. That didn't mean he liked it. Still, he tried not to let his ego get in the way, even though he caught Kaia taking a safer, but longer route.

"We could go over that way." He pointed to the decorative part of the house's elevation. "I'm a pretty good jumper."

"You'd slide into the drainage valley and probably crash through to the attic."

"I—"

"Blake." She gave him a don't-argue-with-me look.

He surrendered. "Fine."

"There're plenty of places you can show off when we get to the front of the house."

"I said 'fine.'"

She could have left him with *some* ego. That's when he saw the three dormers and knew right away that he was going to end up trusting his life to a decorative flourish the builders probably slapped together in fifteen minutes.

"We're going for the middle one."

"Those look like dollhouse roofs." And they didn't look as though they'd support him, let alone both of them. His heartbeat kicked up a notch.

Kaia held onto the edge of the roof and let herself down until she stood on the dormer, her head about two feet below where Blake perched.

"I've already removed the sill, so there should be enough room for you to get in. Watch me. When you do it, I'll be right here and can guide you inside. Tie your end of the rope through your belt loops."

Blake did not like this.

She disappeared inside. What was there to watch? One instant she was standing there and the next, she was gone. Blake studied the drop and the miniature roof. Where, exactly, was he supposed to put his feet?

He looked down at the concrete pebbled drive below.

"Don't look down," he heard.

"How do you know I'm looking down?"

She stuck her head out. "'Cause you're not in front of the window."

If he dropped and his feet slipped, he'd be straddling the thing like a horse. Ouch.

"Hey. You can do it. Trust me." Her smile showed all her teeth.

"Sure I can do it," he said. "Though maybe not successfully."

He studied the drop, below the drop, and Kaia's head for several moments.

"Hey," she said again.

"What?"

Her head disappeared and a naked leg replaced it. "We had a deal. It's wicked way time."

Well, when she put it like that...Blake eased over the

edge of the roof, grateful for all the pull-ups he'd done in the gym, and lowered himself carefully to the little dormer. Squatting, he peered underneath through the window.

Barelegged, illuminated by a flashlight propped next to the mirror, Kaia sat on the bathroom counter and crooked her finger.

All righty then.

Odd how Blake was no longer concerned with the drop or the hard driveway below. His feet naturally found a hold and he miraculously remembered the way Kaia had shown him how to position his body to get through the window. He didn't even need her to hop off the counter and help him. He was motivated. Highly motivated.

"You're going to hurt yourself," she cautioned as he forced his shoulders through the opening.

"Nah. It's okay." What was a little pain compared to the pleasure waiting on the counter?

He paused halfway through, but Kaia spread her legs apart a few inches. Blake was socked with a combination of dizziness and lust and the next thing he knew, he was dropping head first through the window of the Nazarios' guest bathroom.

Rolling, he got to his feet. "That," he said, "is an excellent look for you."

She leaned back against the mirror and gave him a half-smile.

The danger was over but the adrenaline still coursed through Blake's body. One more crook of Kaia's finger and he was standing between her legs, his mouth fused to hers.

"I can't believe we did that," he murmured. "You, alone, over the roof was incredible, but to take me with you was miraculous." He kissed her again. "I can't believe it." He was repeating himself.

"You're talking too much," she whispered and reached for his zipper. This time, he let her clever fingers inside to stroke his hard length. His muscles quivered. Everything quivered. His brain shut down.

"You really liked that," she said.

"I really like you."

"I can tell."

She had no idea. Blake kissed her as though his life depended on it because he suspected that it did. He didn't care about anything else but Kaia at this moment. He wanted her as he'd never wanted anything in his life.

He wanted her *in* his life. He wanted her smiling and making him feel as though the world was perfect. And he was going to do anything it took to put that smile on her face.

Caressing her hair and holding her cheeks, he used his kisses to tell her how he felt without words.

When she wrapped her legs around his waist, he thrust into her, clutching her to his chest as he stared at their reflection in the mirror behind her. He barely recognized himself or the rapt expression that would have concerned him had he been with anyone else but Kaia.

She threw back her head and moaned, clamping her lips together to swallow the sound. The combination of danger, adrenaline, the erotic shadows, and Kaia, herself, brought him to an almost instant climax, one he was helpless to hold back. He thrust deeply and exploded, the force causing him to see bright colors kalaidescoping behind his eyelids. He couldn't move. He couldn't think and was barely aware of Kaia rocking hard against him as she gripped his shoulders.

He gulped air as he heard her low moans, glad she'd been with him because he was completely spent. They clung together, shaking, or maybe Blake was the one who was shaking. It didn't matter. He opened his eyes to meet his reflection and silently vowed that nothing and no one would ever hurt the woman in his arms again.

"Danger makes a great aphrodisiac," she whispered.

"Yeah," he agreed eloquently. And then, "I love you."

He felt her go quiet before she looked up at him. "That's the adrenaline talking."

"Doesn't mean it isn't true."

She studied him silently.

Blake understood and didn't blame her. "You don't have to say it back," he told her. "It won't change how I feel."

"Tell me again when this is all over. Tell me when you're back to your life and I'm back to mine. Tell me when you've had a chance to think."

He didn't need to think. He knew. Blake kissed the top of her head. "Deal."

13

"READY?"

Kaia, her dress back to looking like a dress, nodded. She and Blake had their plan and were going to part ways at the bottom of the stairs. Kaia would find Royce and Blake would track down Luke and see if anyone had noticed Tina's activities.

Kaia descended first, keeping to the shadows as much as possible. Seconds later, Blake did the same.

When Blake had told her he loved her, she'd almost, *almost* told him about the snuffbox. For him to really mean it, and for her to believe he loved her, he needed to know everything.

But something had held her back. They needed cooler heads—cooler bodies. A cooler time.

Kaia glided toward Royce, who was sitting in the conversation pit at the end of the room near Casper's office. The table was covered with candles and Royce held a penlight over some papers as a gray-haired man signed them. The woman next to him—Kaia presumed it was his wife—was admiring a chunky ring on her hand.

Kaia stayed in the shadows until the couple left, and then approached Royce as he put away the paperwork.

"Hey," she said softly. "Got turquoise?"

His head snapped up and his eyes brightened. "Did you...?"

Nodding, Kaia bent down and placed the cuffs on the table in front of him.

Royce stared at them, his lips pressed tightly together. Kaia was a little surprised at the emotion she saw him holding back. She'd known they were important to him, but she hadn't *known*. It made her feel as though she'd done something good for once and she liked it. She should be thanking *him*.

He cleared his throat. "If there is ever—"

"Do you know where my parents are?" she asked suddenly.

Royce looked up, startled, and then leaned back. "No." He eyed her carefully.

"But you could find them."

He hesitated and then shrugged. "I could possibly get a message to them. Do you have such a message?"

"Other than go to hell? No."

"Kaia." Royce gave her a long look as though he was disappointed in her.

Was he serious? "They let me go to prison. I couldn't even afford a lawyer!"

"Refresh my memory...how much of your sentence did you serve?"

What did that have to do with it? "Less than a fourth."

"And why was that?"

"Because the government needed me to do them a favor."

"Oh, right." He nodded. "And how is it that out of all

the specialized government personnel and all the talent in all the prisons that *you* were chosen?"

Was Royce implying that her parents had had something to do with it?

"And, how convenient that Wendell Yost of Guardian was not only willing to sponsor your parole, but to provide you with a top-notch lawyer?"

Kaia assumed it was because she was making a lot of money for Wendell.

Royce tapped a finger against his mouth. "And correct me if I'm wrong, but you continue to have these little jobs come your way, do you not?"

"Yes," Kaia said, slowly.

"You were also quite lucky to find a furnished apartment. Overseas owners wanted to have it occupied... an extremely reasonable rent if you signed a two-year lease... It just seemed to fall into place for you."

"Ty-Tyrone found it."

"Who found it for Tyrone?"

"Did you?" she asked, already knowing the answer. Royce shook his head.

Her parents. Kaia blinked. "I thought—"

"As you were meant to."

So her parents hadn't totally abandoned her. It would take time for Kaia to get past the years of hating them. And it was unlikely they'd ever have a family reunion, complete with picnic and potato salad, but it helped to know they weren't totally devoid of feelings.

"So do you have a message for them?" Royce asked.

"Tell them I'm okay."

"They know you're okay."

She gazed across the room to where she saw Blake talking to Luke. "Tell them I'm...happy." She smiled. "Very happy." And realized it was the truth.

Royce cleared his throat. "There is another matter."

"*Another* matter? You sure have a lot of matters."

Royce reached into his pocket. "I found this." He slid a mangled earpiece across the table.

"Blake's. The dog ran off with it," she told him.

"Yeah, well, I didn't know whether to give it to the big guy or not," Royce said.

"Where is Jo Jo?"

"Tina put her in a room off the kitchen. But the dog isn't our problem. Our hostess's sticky fingers are the problem."

Kaia exhaled. "What's missing?"

"A Tahitian pearl earring."

"Just one?"

"The other was in someone's ear."

"Oh."

"I saw her take it, but I don't know if she's still got it. She's been going in and out of here." Royce indicated the office.

"I saw her once, myself," Kaia said. She watched Blake for a couple of moments. He was involved with Luke and some other men. Now was the time to unload the snuffbox. "I'm going to take a look."

"Want me to run interference?" Royce asked.

"Light interference. Don't blow your cover."

"I'm not undercover!"

"Blake's already suspicious because of me."

"I'm the injured party here," she heard Royce grumble as she melted into the shadows and approached the office door. It was unlocked, thanks to Tina, and Kaia slipped inside. She actually felt a few internal butterflies as she clicked on her flashlight and realized how close she was to her goal. Before anything else, Kaia crossed to the vase where she was supposed to leave the snuffbox and felt inside. To her surprise, her fingers closed over a familiar lump and she withdrew the Cat's Eye pendant.

For a moment, she held it in the beam of light and admired the glitter.

It was hers. Twice she'd earned it, but it wasn't as valuable as what else Casper had promised. Carefully, Kaia put the snuffbox in the vase and then slipped the pendant back, as well.

If Casper was setting a trap, she wasn't taking the bait. She was going to make him hand her the pendant, preferably with Tyrone looking on.

Now that she'd delivered the snuffbox, she could deal with Tina. When Kaia had seen her come in here, Tina hadn't spent much time, so it was unlikely she'd hidden anything in a safe. Kaia glanced around the room and then, with a shrug, tried the pencil drawer in Casper's desk. It slid open and Kaia actually gasped. Gleaming in the beam of her flashlight was the leopard—cheetah—bracelet that Tyrone's wife had admired.

No way. What was with Tina and bracelets? And earrings, too, apparently.

Kaia slipped the bracelet into her pocket and checked out the rest of the room. She found a watch in an empty ice bucket on the credenza, a pair of eyeglasses behind a book, and a pen in the plant by the shuttered French doors.

If the things had been on Casper's desk, Kaia wouldn't have thought anything of it, but hidden as they were, she knew Tina had taken them from her guests. Maybe not tonight's guests, but guests some time.

Collecting the objects, she left the office and headed straight for Blake. He smiled when he saw her, but she shook her head and gestured for him to join her away from the people.

"What's up?" Still smiling, his gaze moved over her face sending a little warming feeling through her.

"For starters, here." She gave him the chewed-on earpiece. "Royce found it."

Blake examined the plastic. "And he chose to give it to you. Interesting."

"Not as interesting as what I found in Casper's office." She showed him.

"Kaia," he began with fake pleasantness, "why did you take it upon yourself to search Casper's office?"

Kaia didn't have time for a turf war. "I work for Guardian Security."

Blake looked utterly taken aback, as though that was the last thing in the world he'd expected her to say.

"Okay," he said slowly. "But why are you here tonight?"

"The cuffs." Officially. "Casper didn't want anyone to know about Tina. Speaking of, a Tahitian pearl earring is still missing. Royce saw her take it."

"Oh, man." Blake looked over her shoulder. Kaia figured he was watching Tina.

"She's probably lifted other stuff we don't know about," he said.

"Probably."

"Luke says that officials estimate power will be back on line in the morning." He rubbed his jaw and exhaled. "When people gather their things to get ready to leave, it'll be a mess."

"Yes."

Blake looked at her.

"Yes," Kaia said.

"I didn't say anything."

"You were going to ask if I'd try to get the earring off Tina."

"I was thinking about it," he admitted.

"I'm on it. It's likely that she still has it on her."

"I appreciate it. And have Royce pack up, will you? We should start inventorying."

Kaia nodded. Blake looked tired. She touched his arm. "Don't worry. It'll all work out."

BLAKE WATCHED KAIA thread her way across the room. He was going to have a chat with Casper when this was all over. He didn't even have to bring up Kaia; the behavior of Tina was bad enough. He thought of the reports of theft that spotted the area and suspected it was Tina's doing. The sad thing was that she'd been great for Blake's business.

He figured he'd lose the Nazarios as clients over this, maybe all the clients they'd sent his way, but knowing what the man had done to Kaia, he wasn't sorry. Together, they could build the business again.

Kaia approached Tina, stopped, leaned forward and said something to her, lightly touched the woman's shoulder, and then moved away. Blake figured she was setting up her attempt. He wondered when she'd actually lift the earring when Kaia reached the other side of the room, turned, and held up her hand.

She already had it? No way. He'd been watching, had known she was going to make the attempt, and had still missed it. She was scary good. He blew her a kiss, glad she was on his side.

KAIA SHARED TINA-WATCHING duties with Blake for the rest of the night.

Around eight o'clock in the morning, there were a

series of clicks and the house hummed back to life. Light illuminated a roomful of sleepy guests who sat up and looked around. The players in an all-night poker game kept dealing.

Blake's office sent whatever codes or signals needed to be sent and suddenly, the shades retracted and in the distance, Kaia heard gates sliding back into the walls. Sunlight flooded the room and the real work began. As the rest of the crowd awoke and blinked against the sunlight, the catering staff circulated with cups of coffee.

Blake and his team, along with Kaia and Royce began a delicate dance of shepherding everyone out the door while making sure they were entitled to any jewelry going out the door with them.

Tina had finally fallen asleep, off in the back room with Jo Jo, allowing for a thorough search of the party area. Other than a cufflink and a jeweled button, which could have been legitimately lost, they couldn't find anything else. Royce balanced his sales receipts and signed off on the inventory of remaining jewels. He and Kaia began dismantling the displays.

Blake and his team monitored the guests and retrieved their RFID tags as the valets quickly brought the cars around.

Fatigue suddenly hit Kaia and she sank onto the cushy chairs near Casper's office. She was tempted to stretch out, but was afraid she would fall asleep and miss Casper or his weasel. They had unfinished business that she hoped they could conclude before Blake wanted to leave.

She sat, head back, eyes closed, but opened them when she heard the office door. She expected to see Casper, but it was Tina sneaking out. She didn't notice Kaia sitting there.

I thought you were asleep.

Something about the way Tina walked gave Kaia a funny feeling.

She's got the snuffbox.

Kaia didn't know how she knew, but she did. She ran into the office and straight to the vase. The Cat's Eye was there, but the snuffbox wasn't.

"I hope this means good news," said a male voice and Casper entered by the French doors. "In anticipation of your success, I left your reward in the vase."

"You missed your wife by about three minutes," Kaia told him.

"Ah, that was intentional," Casper said. "Since she believes I'm in London and is leaving shortly to join me there. It's required some creative scheduling on my part, but worth it, I hope. The box, please."

"You'd better send someone to intercept your wife, because I put the snuffbox here, as we agreed, but I suspect she came in and took it again."

Casper's face changed immediately into something very unpleasant. "How could you have let that happen!"

"Your wife is a kleptomaniac! Your security people and I have spent the entire night retrieving things she stole from the guests!"

"You told others?" His face was turning such a dark red, Kaia wondered if he would have a stroke.

"You're missing the point. I didn't have to tell anyone. They saw her."

"No." He shook his head. "I don't believe you. You're trying to embarrass me, to get back at me. It didn't work before and it won't work now."

The man had gone a little insane. Kaia couldn't even get angry with him. "Tina has got a real problem and you need to get her some help."

"I will not be talked to in that manner by the likes of you!"

"The likes of me? You mean a thief, like your wife?" Casper's face was nearly purple.

Kaia didn't want him croaking before he could clear her name. She softened her voice. "You can't keep covering for her. Too many people know."

"We had an agreement!" He strode across the room.

"And I fulfilled my part of it. I put it in the vase." Kaia refused to let him make her angry. "If you want the snuffbox back, you'll have to ask your wife for it."

Ignoring her, Casper grabbed the vase and upended it. The pendant dropped to the desk. "There is no snuffbox."

"Because your wife took it," she repeated.

"I have only your word that she did." And he left no doubt of his opinion of Kaia's trustworthiness.

"Fine." Kaia started for the door. "I'll go get it from her."

"No!"

"I'll be discreet," she said sarcastically.

"Stop!"

There was a tap on the door and Blake opened it. If he was surprised to see Casper, he didn't indicate it. "Excuse me, Kaia, is this part of Royce's collection?" In his hand was the snuffbox.

She didn't know how or why he had it, only that he did. She met his eyes. "Thank you," she said under her breath. Louder, she answered, "No, it's not. It must belong here." She turned and gently placed it on Casper's desk.

He stared at it, breathing deeply. When he didn't say anything, Kaia picked it up and placed it in the vase. "I have fulfilled our agreement."

Quietly, Casper withdrew the snuffbox. "Unfortunately, you failed to keep anyone else from knowing about the snuffbox." He looked past her shoulder and she knew Blake was still in the room.

Her mouth went dry. "There were extenuating circumstances. A blackout."

Casper sat at his desk. Unlocking the drawer where he'd kept the chocolate replica, he placed the box and the pendant inside and took out the faxed agreement Tyrone had him sign. "There is nothing in this contract about 'extenuating circumstances.'" He met her eyes with a dismissive gaze. "A good lawyer would have thought of that." He ripped the paper in two.

Kaia stood there, frozen. He was doing it again. He was going to cheat and lie and get away with it again.

"I'll ask you to leave now." Casper locked the drawer. "Mr. McCauley, was there something in particular you needed to speak to me about?"

Numbly, Kaia pushed past Blake and fumbled for her cell phone. Tyrone would help her. He *had* to help her.

She was outside the office punching in the number when Blake spoke, loud and clear. "My men are making some repairs to the upstairs windows."

"Was there storm damage?" Casper asked.

"Just some minor adjustments for security purposes. The system will be down for about twenty minutes. I'll remain on-site until we've finished testing and it's back online."

Blake was giving her carte blanche to the house. Without knowing what was going on between her and Casper, he trusted her.

Wow. He really did love her. Grinning so wide her lips hurt, Kaia stayed out of sight as Blake and Casper left the office. And then she got to work.

BLAKE WATCHED AS KAIA scarfed down a delicious three-egg omelet with ham and cheese and other fatty goodness. He knew it was delicious, because an identical one sat on the plate in front of him.

They were in a breakfast place about a mile from Casper's house. They hadn't discussed what had happened after Kaia left Casper's office and Blake hadn't asked. But he really hoped she'd tell him.

He'd overheard her talking with Casper and figured out that she'd had some sort of side deal with him. When Tina's name came up, Blake suspected she'd lifted one more thing. Rather than confront her directly, he shamelessly used a snarling Jo Jo. "I can take that for you," he'd offered and took the box from her as he thrust the dog into her arms. Distracted by Jo Jo, Tina hadn't noticed when Blake pocketed the jeweled box instead of setting it on a table.

He didn't know what the thing was, but he knew Kaia needed it. Afterward, he heard enough to realize Casper was reneging on another deal.

"You haven't asked what I did," she said. Eyeing him over her orange juice, she took a long drink.

"I wanted you to tell me."

"I wanted to tell you. And I was going to, but afterward in my moment of triumph, not after getting taken by Casper again."

"You had a side deal with him. I've guessed that much."

Kaia nodded as the server refilled their coffee. "The snuffbox belongs to the Lithuanian embassy and Tina stole it during a dinner. Our government is investigating the guests. Casper was afraid Tina had it and even if she didn't, he was afraid her kleptomania would come out." She took a sip of coffee. "The deal was that if I recovered it without anyone knowing, he would clear my name."

"Kaia!"

She nodded. "He'd also give me back the Cat's Eye, but the real biggie was recanting his accusations."

"He'd be admitting to perjury." And Blake didn't see that happening.

"Alvin, the weasel—his lawyer—would have worked out something."

Blake rubbed at the condensation on his orange juice glass. "Kaia, I don't think so. You were set up from the beginning."

Shaking her head, she set her coffee mug back on the table. "I have a great lawyer."

"I mean, before." Blake had been thinking about it. "There had been a rash of thefts, but the Nazarios hadn't been hit until you. If anyone had any suspicions of Tina, they went away once you were arrested—and admitted to being in their houses. Think about it—there were five or however many opportunities for you to be caught. And when you weren't, Casper set you up and made Tina and him look like victims, too."

"Oh, my God." She stared at him. "You're right and I never saw it. He was trying to set me up last night, too. He left the pendant in the vase where I'd find it. But it was part of the deal. I have it in writing."

"Witnessed?"

She nodded. "Tyrone, my lawyer, was on the phone. He negotiated the agreement."

"And Casper's lawyer?"

"Wasn't there." She grimaced and squeezed her eyes shut. "Casper could claim extortion or something, right?"

"Probably." Blake was done with Casper. Once he

severed ties, he still had friends on the force. If he had to, he'd drop a few hints about Tina. "So let's see it."

She opened her eyes. "What?"

"The infamous Cat's Eye diamond."

"I don't have it." She picked up her fork and continued eating her omelet.

"I—I gave you twenty minutes! I figured that was more than enough time!"

"And I love you for that." She smiled. "'Course I love you without that, too."

"Yeah?" A grin spread across his face. She seemed okay and if she was okay, he was okay. "Kaia, I want you to know that your record doesn't affect my feelings for you. I'm sorry you went to prison and I'm sorry for my part in it. Someday, Casper will trip up. I have to believe that."

She activated her cell-phone screen. "It's been about forty-five minutes. I figure he'll be tripping soon."

"What do you mean?"

"You didn't ask me what I did with the twenty minutes you gave me." She took a biscuit and slathered butter on it.

"You're killing me here. What did you do?"

She looked pleased with herself. "Since our agreement was 'null and void', I put the snuffbox back."

"Back where?"

"In Tina's safe where I found it. If Casper wants the snuffbox, he'll have to ask her for it." She took a bite of the biscuit.

"Wait—hasn't Tina already left for London?"

Kaia nodded. "Oh, yes. Private helicopter. Lot of noise. And when we left, I believe the weasel was en route to pick up the snuffbox prior to his meeting with embassy officials."

Blake laughed. "That's brilliant! Now I get why you wanted to stop here for breakfast." Blake speared a mouthful of omelet. He'd better eat. They were going to be returning to Casper's soon.

"I was hungry! This is good. I don't normally eat butter or bread. Yum!" She was so calm.

"What do you think he'll do?" Blake was the one with the nerves.

"Call and threaten me." And right then, her phone buzzed. She looked at it on the table. "Shall I put it on speaker?"

"By all means." He held up a finger for her to wait, took out his phone and started recording.

She pressed the screen. "Kaia Bennet."

"Where is it?" erupted Casper's voice.

"Where is what?"

"You know exactly what I'm talking about."

"I'm not a mind reader."

A couple of beats went by and Blake figured Casper knew he was going on the record, but wasn't in a position to make demands.

"Where did you put the snuffbox?" Casper enunciated clearly.

Be careful, Blake mouthed at her.

"Once you voided our agreement, everything reverted to its prior state," Kaia said.

Not bad, Blake thought.

"Ms. Bennet," sounded another voice Blake recognized as Casper's lawyer. "We would like to negotiate another agreement with you."

"You have my lawyer's number," Kaia told him. "He's expecting your call." She disconnected.

"What do you think will happen?" Blake asked her.

"I think we'll have to finish our breakfast quickly

so we can head back to Casper's. I'm in a very good negotiating position, thanks to you."

Blake shook his head. "You did this all by yourself. I just gave you the opportunity."

"Let's talk about that. You trusted me to do the right thing. Even better, you trusted me to figure out the right thing." She grinned. "You can tell me you love me now."

He started to do just that, but something prompted him to say instead, "I trust you."

Kaia's expression changed from happy to luminous. "Blake," she whispered, her eyes bright.

Were those tears? He reached for her hand across the table. "I need you to trust me, too. I want to start fresh with you and I need you to trust me not to mess it up this time. Can you?"

When she stayed silent, he added, "I love you. I never stopped."

She covered their clasped hands with her other one. "You hurt me a lot."

"I know."

Drawing a deep breath, she said, "I forgive you, I do, but I can't forget what that felt like. Not yet."

"I understand." He hadn't forgotten what it felt like, either. "Maybe we're not supposed to forget. Maybe remembering will remind us to be honest with each other."

"And not to take each other for granted," she said.

"Yeah. I like that. This is going to work, isn't it?"

"Absolutely," Blake said, beyond grateful that he was getting a second chance from a woman who didn't believe in second chances.

They smiled at each other and slowly unclasped their hands.

"And one more thing," Blake said as Kaia reached for her coffee.

"What?"

He held up his bare wrist. "Give me back my watch."

* * * * *

Book of the Month

We love this book because...

Against the stunning backdrop of Argentina's vineyards, Nic and Madalena's passionate, intense, and evocative story of a forbidden young passion reignited unfolds…and this time they'll finish what they started.

On sale 3rd August

Visit us Online

Find out more at
www.millsandboon.co.uk/BOTM

0712/BOTM

Special Offers

Every month we put together collections and longer reads written by your favourite authors.

Here are some of next month's highlights— and don't miss our fabulous discount online!

On sale 3rd August

On sale 3rd August

On sale 3rd August

Save 20% on all Special Releases

Find out more at
www.millsandboon.co.uk/specialreleases

Visit us Online

0712/ST/MB381

Can sparkling summer flings ever turn into forevers?

Tamsin's ready to spend her summer relaxing, until Alejandro—the man who nearly destroyed her reputation—comes back into her life. Now his world of champagne and scandal awaits her once again…

Sarah's summers are about spending time with her little girl. She never has a chance to think about herself. Until an encounter with a film director turns her life upside down and thrusts her into the exciting world of glitz, glamour and gossip pages.

www.millsandboon.co.uk

Mills & Boon® Online

Discover more romance at
www.millsandboon.co.uk

- 🌹 **FREE** online reads
- 🌹 **Books** up to one month before shops
- 🌹 **Browse our books** before you buy

...and much more!

For exclusive competitions and instant updates:

 Like us on **facebook.com/romancehq**

 Follow us on **twitter.com/millsandboonuk**

 Join us on **community.millsandboon.co.uk**

Visit us Online — Sign up for our FREE eNewsletter at **www.millsandboon.co.uk**